SOPHIE'S HAWK

spirit of the raptor

FLAT PLAINS OF NORTH DAKOTA
NEAR FORT ABERCROMBIE

SOPHIE'S HAWK

spirit of the raptor

ARVID LLOYD WILLIAMS

BONNIE SHALLBETTER

EVERGREEN PUBLISHING
MINNEAPOLIS

SOPHIE'S HAWK

spirit of the raptor

Second in a Series

Evergreen Publishing
15539 Shadow Creek Road
Minneapolis, MN 55311
www.evergreenpublish.com

ISBN 0-9633480-8-6

Printed in the United States of America.

COVER: REPRESENTATION OF BIG WOODS
IN OTTER TAIL COUNTY, MINNESOTA

DEDICATION

ARVID LLOYD WILLIAMS

*This work is dedicated to my father, Kenneth John Williams,
to my grandfather, John Williams, and to my great-grandfather,
John (Curly Jack) Williams (1839-1909).*

*Special thanks to my friend Charlotte Theret for her help
with the French language in this book. If you see any
mistakes, talk to her—I don't want to hear about it.*

*And a special thank you to my daughter Sue Sullivan for her hard work
and her expert help with the editing and proofing of this work.*

BONNIE SHALLBETTER

*I would like to dedicate this book to my husband, Steve,
and my two boys, Erik and Matt. I thank them for allowing me the time
to delve into my writing and research, something I have always wished to do.*

*This dedication would not be complete, however, if I did not
thank my parents, who were always there to encourage
whatever path our hearts led us. Thank you for believing in me,
one of the greatest gifts one can give…Dreams can come true.*

*Also, sincere thanks to my dear friends who have
been there to listen and share in my happiness.*

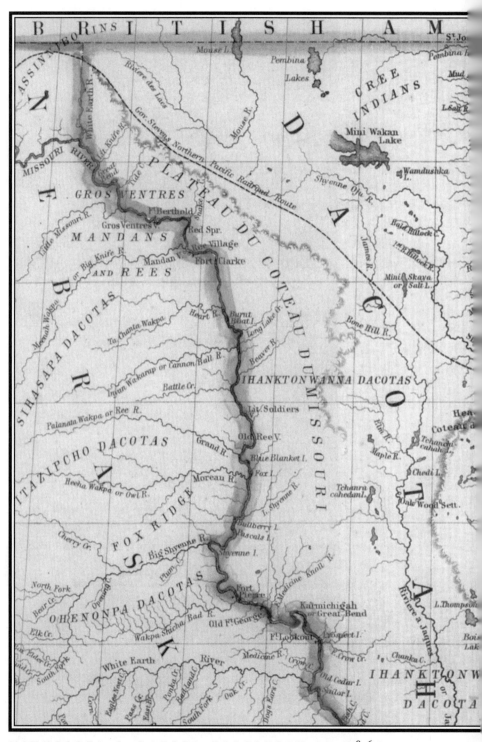

MINNESOTA & DAKOTA TERRITORY IN 1863
(Minnesota Historical Society)

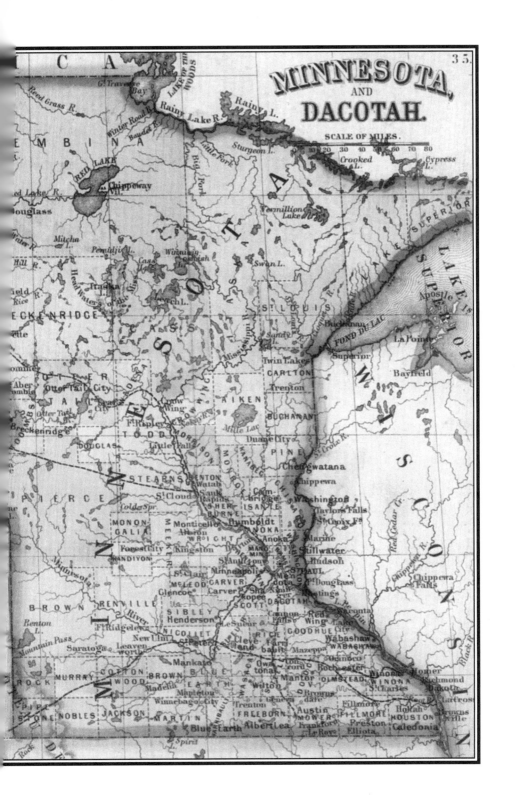

MINNESOTA,
AND
DACOTAH.

SCALE OF MILES.

TABLE OF CONTENTS

MAP

FOREWORD

On the back porch of a small log cabin on the bank of Hawk Creek, journalist Return I. Holcombe from the Saint Paul Pioneer newspaper and his secretary, Abigail Biegler, waited on soft chairs for the old Indian fighter to wake from his nap. Two cups of cold coffee sat on the small table between them. Their fountain pens scratched relentlessly across their note pads and they talked softly to one another as they compared notes.

Across the creek the trees were dropping their leaves into the stream and laying a thick colorful blanket on the ground. Squirrels scampered among the dry leaves gathering food for the coming winter. A crow called from the far side of the trees and another answered from a distant perch.

Hawk Owen opened his eyes and slowly focused on the man and woman sitting before him. They waited with pens in hand for him to continue his account of the Sioux Uprising in the Minnesota Valley in eighteen sixty-two.

Lorraine kissed him on the forehead. "Would you like a cup of coffee, Dad?" she said softly.

"Yes, that'd be good. Thank you." He scratched at the scar on the side of his neck.

"Mister Owen, may we ask your age?"

"Those crows have been waking me up every mornin' for close to ninety years," he said, gazing into the woods.

The old man slowly raised himself from his rocking chair, took up his cane and walked to the edge of the porch. He leaned on the railing and stared out at Hawk Creek. The crystal clear water shimmered and danced over the rocks and gravel in its bed. Near the edge of the stream and just below the cabin was a patch in the water where the gravel and rocks had been cleared away and fine sand laid in its place.

His eyes followed a red maple leaf being carried along on the surface of the stream. He pondered the journey of that leaf from his home on Hawk Creek to the Minnesota River, then down to Saint Paul where it would be taken into the stream of the Mississippi. It would reach the warm waters of the Gulf of Mexico by the time ice covered the lakes of Minnesota.

At the edge of the woods stood a granite marker, polished on one side and inscribed with words illegible to the reporters thirty yards away. A chair sat close to the marker and newly planted wildflowers grew on the fresh grave. The old man stared out at the creek as his mind wandered back to days gone by. He turned his head toward the grave marker. His body quivered as a sob came from his heart.

"God-dammit," he said in a soft trembling voice, "You said you'd never leave me." Tears rolled down his cheek, and as he turned he wiped them away with the sleeve of his sweater.

"Here's your coffee, Dad," Lorraine said, as she set the cup on the small table next to his chair.

"Damn," he muttered, as a pain wracked his leg and made him lean more heavily on his cane.

"Do you need help, Mister Owen?"

"No, damn it all. I don't need any help."

"Dad is suffering another attack of rheumatism in his left hip," Lorraine said. "It's from a wound he got while looking for a friend who'd been captured by the Indians."

"Mister Owen, would you mind telling us about that?"

Hawk walked painfully to his chair, then turned around and slowly sat down. He let the rocker roll back as Lorraine slid a footstool close and helped him raise his legs onto it. He reached for his pipe and filled it with tobacco. Lorraine struck a match on the side of the paper box and held it to the pipe. He puffed until a cloud of blue smoke came from the side of his mouth. He leaned his head back, closed his eyes, and blew a stream of sweet-smelling smoke into the air.

"I'm going to tell you about Sunkist and Posey. They were as much a part of this story as Sophie and me."

"The sun has kissed your face and made it red like the sumac in the fall. I will call you 'Kissed by the Sun'."

I

THE SIOUX HAD BEEN DEFEATED in the Minnesota Valley and were escaping to the prairies of Dakota. Small bands of renegades still roamed the area and continued to attack settlements, farms and travelers.

The weather was beginning to show signs of fall. The leaves displayed bright yellows and oranges that blended with the deep reds of the oaks and the bright reds of the maples. The aspens added a shimmer of gold. Patches of sumac dotted the hillsides with their blankets of crimson. Cornfields planted by the Indians were dry and brown and left to the weeds. Potato fields, pumpkin patches, and vegetable gardens had all gone to waste.

Sunkist and Posey left Fort Ridgely and set off to the north to find a place to spend the coming winter. Posey rode next to Sunkist and one pack mule followed behind. Along the road they passed burned-out houses and farms. Half hidden in the brown grass and blanket of fallen leaves was the skeleton of a man—or woman—killed by the Sioux. The bones, bleached white by the sun and scattered by wolves, were a grim reminder of the horrors of the past months. Beyond the horizon smoke curled skyward telling of another attack, or perhaps another heartbroken settler saying good-bye to a dream. They moved quietly, remembering the battles they had survived and the friends they'd left behind.

They traveled north along the rim of the valley, holding close to the protection of the heavy woods along the streams. Night fell and the air became cool. Steam rose from their horses as Posey led them into a thicket to make camp for the night.

As Sunkist cleaned their guns and tended to the livestock, Posey built a lean-to of white ash saplings tied with cord made from the inner bark of basswood trees. She covered it with a canvas tarp that was once white, but was now tattered and gray with age. They were comfortable with their silence, each knowing what was expected of them and both knowing what the other was thinking. Sleep came easily to the partners as they settled in under a bundle of elk robes and woolen blankets.

Morning came cold and clear and they awoke before the sun lightened the eastern sky. They saddled their horses, loaded the mule, and set off to find their winter home.

As they rode, Sunkist's mind went back to his childhood and to the trade store his father owned. His mother had died of pneumonia when he was an infant and his father talked often about her flaming red hair and green eyes. Christian Whistler never got over his wife's death. Every night was spent at Pig's Eye's tavern where he would wallow in his own misery, then stagger home inebriated on the rot-gut whiskey the nasty old voyageur sold.

The young Sunkist stayed in the store and learned the art of gun repair. He became well-known for his expertise in the trade. By testing each gun he repaired, he became the best shooter in the growing settlements around Fort Snelling. When he had free time he went out to the Sioux village called Kaposia, and ran with the Indian boys. He knew Little Crow and his brothers as children. He played wrestling games with them and learned to use a bow. He ran foot races with them, but because of his unusually large frame he generally crossed the finish line last. He learned from them about trapping for furs and hunting meat and living off the land.

His name was James. He wouldn't tolerate being called Jim. At sixteen years of age he was well-known around the settlements. Men of all ages respected his five foot-nine frame, his solidly built body, his barrel chest and thick powerful arms. His fists were hard and fast as lightning.

He sat one night with his father in their home in the back of the store. Pa worked on his ledgers by the light from a candle lantern and James ran a cleaning patch in and out of the bore of his fifty-four caliber southern mountain rifle. The only light in the small room came from the two candles and the fire in the hearth.

Pa looked up at him. "James—where's yer mother?"

"Pa, I ain't got no mother." He had repeated that scene with his father many times.

Pa looked at James with vacant eyes, then went back to his ledger. He shuffled through the papers pulling one out from the other then rearranging them over and over. James could see how frustrated his father became when his papers

SOPHIE'S HAWK

didn't do what they were supposed to. He jerked a paper from under the pile, crumpled it into a ball and threw it into the fireplace. It flared up, sending sparks up the chimney. James wanted to help his father sort the papers but he didn't have the education it required. He could read a little and do simple mathematics but the business papers were too much for him.

"James," his father said, "ye aught not be goin' out to that Indian camp so much. Yer gonna git yourself in trouble out there with them bucks."

"Pa, I ain't afraid of them Injuns," he said. He held his rifle to his ear and listened closely to the sharp clicks of the lock as he slowly pulled back the hammer. "Besides, most of 'em are friends of mine."

"Yeah, well, I been seein' them squaws, how they look at you, and them bucks don't take kindly to white men gittin' sweet on their women. Best you be damn careful who you be chasin' around there."

"I ain't lookin' fer no girl to be seein'. I got no use fer a girl, enna ways." He looked at his father, "Pa, I wish you wouldn't call 'em that name."

"How old are you now, boy?"

"Sixteen—be seventeen in December."

"Then yer old enough to be chasin' girls." He paused and looked down at his papers. "Listen, son—girls are nice to have around most of the time—but sometimes a man just don't want 'em around." He turned in his chair and held his pen up at James. "But ye see, son, they can't understand that. If ye don't want 'em around, they think you don't love 'em anymore." He turned back and shuffled the papers frantically. "A man's got to have his freedom, son. He's got to be free to do what he wants without having to explain why."

"But Pa, if you like being with a woman, why can't she come with you when you go someplace?"

"When you find yerself a woman who wants to do the things you like doing, grab her, son—and don't let go. Ye got the best of all worlds goin' fer ye."

"Kinda figgered it that way, Pa. Most of them Indian girls like goin' out in the woods and trappin' and all like that."

"Ye got yer eye on one of 'em?"

"Naw. But there's this one called Barley Corn who keeps hangin' around. I think she's sweet on me."

"How old is she?"

"Don't rightly know, Pa—but she's comin' around a woman, I think."

Pa looked up at James. "And how would you know that?"

"Aw, Pa, a man can tell."

"Ye mean she's gettin' titties and a round backside?" Pa asked with a sly grin.

"Well, yeah, gettin' kinda round all over and gettin' the bumps and curves ye see on full-growed women."

"Sounds like she's prob'ly still a girl. Best ye stay away from 'er fer a while."

"I ain't lookin' to git hitched up, Pa. I told ye that."

"James, I'm goin' down to the tavern. You git yerself some sleep, we got a lot of work to do in the mornin'."

"Okay, Pa. When you comin' home?" He knew the answer to the question but it seemed he had to say something.

"Don't know, maybe late."

"See you in the mornin'."

James finished cleaning his rifle and threw a log in the fireplace. He blew out the candle and crawled into his bed without removing his clothes. It was early winter and the cabin got cold in the night. The fireplace only warmed the area directly in front of it and the heat never reached his bed. The corn-shuck mattress rustled as he slid under the blankets. He was asleep as soon as his head hit the pillow.

Late into the night he heard his father crash through the cabin door. He'd heard that sound too many times before and had learned to ignore it. He rolled over to face the wall and pulled the blankets up over his head to try to drown out the sounds of his father puking up his whiskey.

When morning came, James threw the covers off and swung his legs over the side of the bed and pulled his moccasins on. He saw his pa lying in the middle of the floor, which he had also seen too many times before. The door stood open and ice-cold air blew in. He stepped over his pa to close the door and touched him lightly with his toe.

"Git up, Pa."

He shuffled to the fireplace and tossed a couple of sticks into the embers, then squatted and fanned the embers until the yellow flames danced around the wood. He looked back over his shoulder at his father still lying motionless on the floor.

"Git up, Pa—we got things to do."

Pa didn't move.

He walked over and looked down at his pa. James saw then that his father, Christian Whistler, was dead. His eyes were open and his head lay in a puddle of frozen vomit and blood. He stood and looked down at the body.

"Figgered this would happen sooner or later."

He laid the body flat, straightened the half-frozen legs and folded the arms across the chest. He threw a blanket over his father and went to sit on a chair by the table. He put his elbows on his knees, cradled his face in his hands and stared at his father's body. The only sound in the room was the crackling of the fire and the steady ticking of the pendulum clock on his father's desk.

For the last few years James had been the responsible one in the house and took the job of getting the day started by boiling coffee and making the breakfast. He'd been watching his father grow worse each week from the whiskey. His skin had turned a pale yellow, his eyes were sunken and bloodshot and the skin on his face was spider-webbed with tiny red veins. He moved more slowly than he'd used to and often sat for long periods of time staring at the walls and sucking on a jar of Pig's Eye's brew.

His pa was once heavily built and muscular when James was a boy, but now he was so thin his shoes didn't fit and he looked as though a strong gust of wind could blow him apart. His hands were still big from the days he had worked hard, but his arms were thin and weak. He'd stopped taking care of himself and wore the same clothes for weeks at a time and he carried a foul odor about him. His mind wandered and he was confused by the simplest task.

James was suddenly brought out of his thoughts by the clock chiming one time, telling him it was five-thirty in the morning.

He took a shovel and pick, went to the backyard and dug a hole through the thin layer of frozen dirt until it was about waist deep. He wrapped the body in blankets, carried it out and lowered it into the grave, then covered it with a buffalo robe and filled the hole.

Death was nothing new to James Whistler. He had seen Indian people carried off and buried and had helped with more than a few. His father was not a friend to James. He had been more of a problem in the last two years than a family member. He knew his father was killing himself with the whiskey and had told him that enough times to make him realize that he was wasting his breath. He finally gave up trying and let his father kill himself.

His father was gone now and it made no sense to James to sit around worrying about what comes next. A man has to make his way in the world without waiting for someone to tell him which fork in the road he should take. He remembered the words of his friend he called 'Doc'. Doc was the man in the community people went to when they were sick. He was not educated from any university, but he had ways to make people think they were getting well. James always laughed when Doc said, "When you come to the fork in the road, take it." James saw the humor in the statement, but he also saw the wisdom. When a man has two ways to go, he needs to take the one that suits him best. A man needs to do the things that make his life enjoyable. The things that make a man happy with life are the things he enjoys most, and walking the woods and prairies was what James enjoyed the most.

For the next two days he refused any work that was brought to him. He told the people who came into the store what had happened and they tried to console him. They didn't know that James Whistler did not need sympathy. He needed to get out of that cabin and head west to the mountains—and the trapping—and the exploring that he had heard about.

He'd heard about mountain men, wild Indians and rendezvous in the spring. He imagined eating fresh buffalo steak roasted on a ramrod over a hot fire in the middle of nowhere. He knew from watching his father how to barter with Indians for furs and hides. The Indian boys had taught him to trap, and how to make the traps from the materials in the forest rather than carrying the heavy steel traps of the white man.

He knew the abundance of food in the forests and prairies. He could very easily feed himself on lamb's quarter, wild onions, roots and the inner bark of the poplar trees. He knew that any bird that could be caught or killed is a source of nutrition. Rodents are edible and easy to catch. Grasshoppers that have been roasted in the prairie fires are a delicious meal for an empty stomach. Fish are easily caught on a string made from basswood bark or nettle, and the bones of small animals can be used to make good hooks. He knew from boyhood how to fashion a shelter of willow branches and birch bark or to lay a canvas or brush over the roots of a fallen tree for shelter from the cold winds of winter. He knew that a man in the wilderness doesn't need a big house to be comfortable. All he needs is a small place to build a fire to keep warm and cook his meat.

James knew how to tan hides to make clothing. The sinew from the animal was his thread, and the bones made needles and awls. Animals provided the materials to make weapons for their own destruction. Deer antler could be shaved down to make deadly arrowheads and strong bow strings could be made by twisting strings of tough sinew from the back of the animal. Ash, maple, birch, and oak made powerful bows, and James knew how to make them all. James Whistler was a natural-born woodsman and the mountains of the West were calling him.

He was eager to be free and on his own hook and he took time to load into packs all of the things he would need for his journey west. He loaded blankets, guns, knives, tomahawks, and a good supply of gunsmith tools. For food he packed biscuits and corn flour and the bacon that had been curing in the smokehouse.

On a bright, cold morning, he loaded his two mules and saddled his father's mare. He piled all of his father's papers and books in the middle of the cabin and set them afire. He stood back and watched as his home went up in smoke.

"Ain't gonna be needin' this old roost no more," he said under his breath.

The flames leaped high into the sky and folks from the surrounding cabins came out to watch. They knew that James Whistler would not be seen in this country again and they knew why he burned the cabin. That was the cabin his father and mother had built twenty years before and no one else was going to be allowed to live in it. It was the place he was born and lived for his sixteen years.

The Sioux had told James about the Spirits of the dead and how they remain in their homes to watch over the living. He knew his mother's spirit was in that house. Now she would be free to begin the journey to the land beyond this life.

He rode south to Kaposia, to the village of the Sioux, and to the girl who watched as he rode in. Barley Corn stood in the snow wrapped in a blue striped blanket. Her braids hung over her shoulders and the part in her hair was colored with red clay. She watched as he walked to her.

"Where will you go?" she asked.

"Out West—I hear there's beaver the size of pigs out there and I aim to catch me some."

"You will come back?"

"No, I ain't comin' back here—too many people crowdin' in around me. I gotta git out where I can breathe air that ain't no one ever breathed before—where people don't make trash to burn and stink up the air."

"We will miss you when you go." She reached up and ran her finger over his face and said, "The sun has kissed your face and made it red like the sumac in the fall. I will call you 'Kissed By The Sun' and when I hear your name I will remember you."

He took her shoulders in his hands and said, "I will think of you, Barley Corn." He bent down and kissed her awkwardly on the forehead, then turned and walked away.

"Goodbye, Sunkist…" the girl said as he walked away.

. . .

The name echoed through his mind until he realized he was hearing Posey's voice.

"Sunkist?" she said quietly.

"Yeah? *Oh, I guess I was daydreaming.*"

Posey smiled and touched his face. *"This is a good place to build our home."*

Sunkist looked up from his thoughts and gazed out over the valley. The trees were in full fall color and the bottom of the valley was brilliant.

"Yes, this is a good place."

They got down from their horses and began clearing a spot for the bark hut that Posey would build. She would build the hut alone, as is the way of the Cherokee. Sunkist would not be allowed to help with its construction.

Posey scoured the woods and began to cut saplings one inch in diameter and to the length she needed. She tied them together to make them long enough to reach over the top of the shelter. She bent them into half circles and tied them with cord made from basswood bark until she had made a frame of arches and circles. One pole was bent into a half-loop about four feet high and set for the door, then tied securely into place. By evening the framework was finished. The night was cool and dry and they slept rolled up in blankets under the stars.

When morning came, Posey was up with the light. She covered the frame with elk skins that they had packed. She stripped bark from fallen and half-rotted elm trees and laid the bark over the frame, one sheet over-lapping the one below it until it was covered to the top. She threw a canvas tarp over the top and tied it down. Buffalo robes and blankets were laid on the floor and soon their home was ready to be lived in. The shelter that Posey built was waterproof and solid enough to stand the strongest of Minnesota's winter winds.

Together they built racks for drying meat and a fire pit lined with rocks. Posey made mats from willow sticks to sit on. The backs were supported with poles driven into the ground. Sunkist had hobbled the horses and let them graze while he sorted through his possibles and cleaned his guns.

They sat side-by-side without talking. Posey plied sinew and awl to buffalo leather and deerskin to make winter moccasins for each of them. She made a pair of large moccasins from buffalo hide with the hair on the inside, and a pair of deerskin moccasins with the hair on the outside. Then she pushed the deerskin liners inside the heavy buffalo skin boots, combining two layers of insulating hair between the feet and the cold ground. The tops were made of a single layer of soft deerskin that covered the calves. They would be warm and light and the buffalo skin would be tough enough to last them through the winter.

SOPHIE'S HAWK

She dreamed of a giant man with fire for hair, riding hard on a black horse and swinging a flaming tomahawk above his head.

2

CHAPTER   TWO

POSEY SAT QUIETLY ONE MORNING and stared into the fire. Her mind took her back to the days on the reservation in Oklahoma Territory after the Cherokee removal. The Cherokee had been moved from their beloved land east of the Mississippi and forced to go to Oklahoma Territory. It was an unfamiliar land to them and they had to learn new ways to live. The American government provided them with food, but it was not nearly enough to feed the multitudes of starving Indians on the reservation. They had to hunt their own food, but game was hard to find on the reservation around Fort Gibson.

Posey's mother gave birth to Posey while on the 'Trail Where They Cried', which would be later known as 'The Trail of Tears'. She didn't want the baby girl to have to live from the meager handouts from the white man or to adopt his strange ways. She decided the child would be better off going to live in the Spirit Land. So, when the baby was born she took her to the top of a high hill and laid her on a large rock to await the call of the Great Spirit. She cried as she laid the infant on the rock, and her tears fell all around. Then she left and joined the mile-long column of Cherokee Indians moving slowly westward to a place they did not know. She stopped to look back.

"What is it, sister?" another woman asked in Cherokee.

"I can hear my baby crying. I must go back and take her with me."

"Yes, the Spirits want you to bring her with us."

The mother turned and ran back toward the rear of the column. Soldiers tried to stop her but she pushed them aside and ran past them. They laughed at her and struck her with their rifles. Then, thinking she was just another Indian gone mad, they let her go. She ran to the hill and to the rock where she had laid the tiny girl. The baby stopped crying and reached out to her mother who picked her up and wrapped her in a blanket.

All around the rock she saw flowers growing, pushing their blossoms up through the snow. There were seven leaves on each stem that reminded the mother of the seven tribes of Cherokee on the trail. The petals were white, which told of the tears of the mothers who had lost their loved ones. Each flower had a gold center, which told of the gold taken by the white men from the land of the Cherokee. The flowers would come to be known as Cherokee Roses and would continue to grow along the path of the Trail of Tears for generations to come.

She looked at the baby girl and said, *"You will be called 'Flower Among the Rocks'. Surely the Great Spirit has allowed you to stay here with me. You will not grow to depend on the white man—you will learn to live without him. I will teach you the ways of the old Tsalagi and you will know all there is to know about living in this new land."*

When they arrived in the new land, Flower's mother took her out of the reservation each day and taught her about the wild foods and medicines. She taught her about trapping wild animals for food and clothing, and how to use the weapons of the Tsalagi Indians. She told her to never use the name 'Cherokee' because that was the white man's name for them. She should always say 'Tsalagi' as the Old Ones did before the white man came.

Each day she bathed her little girl in the icy waters of the streams and rolled her in the snow to toughen her nerves and teach her to ignore pain and cold. She taught Flower Among the Rocks to eat the things the Old Ones ate.

"You must never learn the white man's tongue," she told the girl, *"because the white man's tongue lies. The Tsalagi do not know how to tell lies. The Tsalagi only tell what is true. Only when the white man came did we learn to say things that were not true. It is the way of the white man, and if you are to live among them you must learn all of their ways even if you know they are wrong. You must always listen to the words of the Old Ones when they talk to you in your dreams. The Old Ones are very wise and they will guide you if you will listen to them."*

And so the girl named 'Flower Among the Rocks' grew. She didn't grow thin like the others. She grew healthy and strong by living from the bounty given the Indians by Mother Earth. She stayed away from the camp because the dreaded white man was always there. She saw the white men walking away with the Indian girls and didn't understand why the girls would do that. Her mother had taught her about making babies and what the white men would do with her if they got the chance. Flower could not understand why a girl would want a white man to do those things to her if she did not love him.

The years went by and Flower's mother passed on to the Spirit Land and she was left alone. Her sisters and brother had died on the Trail of Tears before she was born so she never knew them.

She built herself a home in the hills below the Ouachita Mountains, away from anyone who would disturb her solitude. Men who came to the reservation heard about the solitary girl who lived like a wild animal and they were curious.

One morning, as she was separating berries, Flower felt a strange presence. Her instincts told her to go to the deep woods and hide. So she quietly slipped into the forest and hid herself among the rocks and brush. She could see her camp below and watched as three men walked in slowly. One stood in the middle of the camp and shouted something that she could not understand, then they all went away talking and laughing among themselves. The ways of the white man were strange and it was useless for her to try to understand them.

She stayed in her hideout until dark, then made her way down the slope. She moved as quietly as a deer as she came into her camp. The foul odor left by the white men sent a shiver through her. It was a scent she would never forget. She quickly gathered her meager belongings and moved farther up the mountain to a safer place.

That night, she slept against a tree where she could see the trail below. She dreamed of a giant man with fire for hair, riding hard on a black horse and swinging a flaming tomahawk above his head. In the morning she awoke and remembered the dream. *The Spirits have come to me with a message,* she thought to herself. She didn't understand the message but she would remember the dream. She packed up and again moved farther up the mountain. Many times she felt the presence of the white men and each time, she moved her camp farther away from the Indian village below.

SOPHIE'S HAWK

She stood tall and confident and in her face he saw
someone it seemed he had known in another time.

3

CHAPTER THREE

"POSEY?" Sunkist said.

"I have been remembering the days when I lived alone and did not know you. It was a good time then, but it is better to be with you."

Sunkist leaned over and took her in his arms and kissed her deeply. She had learned to enjoy this one custom of the white man and responded with a soft moan. The sun was low in the western sky and without letting go of each other they made their way into the bark hut.

As darkness fell, Sunkist laid back on the robes with his Cherokee wife snuggled into his shoulder. He thought back to how he had found her.

By that time, Sunkist had been in the mountains and plains for twenty-three winters. He'd trapped along all the major rivers and the small streams that came down from the mountains. He fought the Sioux and the Blackfoot and carried three bullets inside him from the Arikaras and Hidatsa guns, and a stone arrowhead in the meat of his left thigh. He was known from the Mississippi to California as a fighter and first class trapper and explorer.

He sat one night with his friend and trapping partner, Curly Jack, making plans for their next trip to the mountains for beaver. They would go into the Ouachita Mountains—a place not well known by most of the other trappers.

They traveled together until they reached their destination, then Sunkist went one way and Curly Jack went another.

Sunkist rode along a stream bed when suddenly he heard voices. He climbed off his horse and tied him to a clump of brush, leaving enough line for the horse to feed himself. Slowly and quietly he moved toward the voices. He heard laughing as he crawled under the brush and peered over the top of a small rise. Before him, about thirty yards away, he saw three dirty, ragged white men around a naked Indian woman they had tied to a tree. One of the men slapped the girl across the face and turned around laughing.

Sunkist stood and stepped into the clearing.

"You boys hadn't aught to be treatin' a lady that-a-way."

All three turned around quickly, surprised at the sound of the voice.

"What the hell's it to you how we do this squaw?" one of them shouted.

"This here's our woman, we found her and we'll do whatever we want with her," another man said.

"Like hell you will. You'll untie that girl er you'll be feedin' the buzzards."

The biggest of the men started toward Sunkist.

"Maybe you aught to just mind yer own damn business, old man," he said with a grin. "Best you should turn around and walk on otta here while you can."

Sunkist's rifle exploded and the man's chest collapsed as his heart flew out his back and he fell to the ground, dead. Sunkist let his rifle drop and caught it with his toe before it hit the ground. In a simultaneous movement, he pulled the two Plains pistols from his belt and pointed them at the remaining two men.

"Now—you." He pointed the barrel of one pistol at one of the men. "You go untie that girl."

"Mister, we wasn't gonna do nothin', we was just having a little fun."

"Beatin' up on a little girl ain't my idea of fun. What's fun to me is sending worthless sons-o'-bitches like you to hell."

The hammer on the flintlock pistol dropped, sending sparks into the pan and igniting the charge in the barrel. The pistol recoiled and sent a cloud of white smoke and a fifty-four caliber round ball through the air and through the heart of the man. He fell to the ground, dead.

"You wanna join yer partners here or are you gonna untie that girl?"

Wide-eyed horror filled the man's face, "Don't shoot, mister—don't shoot! It wasn't me, it was them who done this, not me!" he cried as he scrambled to cut the rope that held the girl. The girl dropped to her knees.

Sunkist walked past the terrified man toward the girl. "How long you had her tied to that tree?"

"Just a couple of days. She ain't hurt or nothin'."

"She looks to me like she's been hurt a-plenty."

The girl's eyes had been blackened and her face was bruised. She had small cuts on her legs and breasts. Sunkist walked to her and wrapped his coat around her. She shied back as he touched her and stared at him with emotionless eyes.

"I ain't gonna hurt you."

She only looked at him.

"You don't speak English," he said. Then he spoke to her in Cherokee. *"Where are your people?"*

She still didn't answer but showed some surprise that he could speak her language.

The man stood back and watched as Sunkist lifted the girl to her feet.

"Why you helpin' that squaw? You an Injun-lover?"

"This is a woman, whether she's red, white, black or green—makes no difference. How 'bout you jiss git the hell outta here while ye kin?"

"Mister, you just killed two white men over a damned squaw!" he shouted, as he pointed down at his dead friends.

Sunkist left the girl standing and began walking toward the man. "If you ain't gone by the time I git over there I'm gonna jump down yer throat and kick yer guts out."

The man pulled a knife out of his belt and bent forward waiting for Sunkist to reach him. Sunkist didn't slow his step but kept walking toward him. The man stepped back as Sunkist came closer. Suddenly, the girl came from behind, pulled the knife from Sunkist's belt and leaped on the dirty man, driving the knife into the side of his throat. He fell backward with the naked girl on top of him. Blood shot from his neck as she pulled the knife through the arteries and windpipe. She slammed the blade deep into the man's chest and stood up leaving the knife there. She looked down at him, breathing deeply and clenching her fists. She reached down and pulled the knife out and wiped it across the dead man's shirt. She walked by Sunkist and handed him the knife without looking at him.

She picked up the coat and wrapped it around herself then spoke to Sunkist in Cherokee. *"I am not a squaw."*

"Didn't say you was."

"That man called me a squaw and he died for it."

"I'll try to remember that," he said in English. *"Where are your people?"* he asked in Cherokee. *"I will take you to them."*

"I have no people," she said angrily and walked quickly and silently into the brushwood and disappeared.

Sunkist threw his arms in the air looking into the brush then turned to find the men's horses. He took the saddles off and threw them into the underbrush, then slapped the horses on the rump and sent them off in three directions.

He mounted his horse and walked slowly away from the place along a game trail, hoping to find a beaver stream. He stopped for the night in a patch of alder and set up his canvas lean-to for the night. In the morning, he threw off his robes and blankets and stumbled to the fire pit. He found it ablaze with a stone pot of venison stew sitting next to it. He leaned down and found small footprints in the dirt. *Musta been that girl,* he thought to himself and smiled.

He stayed in that camp for the next night. Before he went to his bed he placed a blanket out by the fire hoping the girl would take it. The next morning he found the blanket still there and a rack of venison ribs hanging over the fire. *Damn...* he thought, *ain't no one got that close to me in the night in many a year.*

He spent the day scouting the countryside for signs of beaver. He found only a few fallen-down lodges and broken dams in dried-up ponds.

He couldn't get the girl out of his mind as he worked around his camp, cleaning his guns and tending to his horse and mule. He smiled at the thought of her out there in the brush somewhere, probably watching him. After each chore was finished he stopped and gazed into the woods, turning this way and that, hoping to catch a glimpse of her. As the sun disappeared behind the mountains and darkness closed in on him, he strung a line around his camp and tied two tin plates to the line. If the girl came to his camp and tripped the line the plates would rattle and wake him. He then slipped under his robes and went to sleep.

He awoke just as the sun was turning the tops of the mountains gold. He went out to the fire pit and there, next to the fire, was the string and both tin plates. He looked up and smiled. *"Come on out!"* he shouted in Cherokee. *"I ain't gonna hurt you.* Hail, I doubt I could if I wanted to," he said under his breath.

Hearing no response from the girl he turned to his shelter and began to take it down. "Ain't no use hangin' around here," he muttered to himself, "ain't no beaver no how."

Sunkist was tired of hunting beaver and didn't really care that there were none in this stream. He was primed for moving on to smoother trails. He pulled his things together and loaded them onto the pack mule. He started down the mountain keeping his eyes moving, hoping to spot the girl. He could feel her close. The quick glimpse of movement in the brush or the snap of a twig told him she was around, but he couldn't get an eye on her. The sounds also told him she wanted him to know she was there or she would not have made those sounds. She had been in his camp three times without making any sound. He knew it was not an enemy he was hearing or he would have been ambushed long before this. He stopped his horse and looked deep into the woods.

"Come on out!" he shouted in Cherokee.

Suddenly, she stepped out of the brush just twenty feet ahead of him. She

SOPHIE'S HAWK

wore a deerskin dress and a belt around her waist with a butcher knife tucked into a leather sheath. She carried a bow made from the wood of the Osage orange tree strapped across her back, and a quiver of arrows slung on her belt. The dress was plain without the beading he was used to seeing on other Indian women, and it had no fringing at the seams.

He walked his horse forward and reached a hand down to her. She looked up at him, took his hand, and swung herself up behind him. He touched the horse and they walked down the mountain toward the place where he had planned to rendezvous with his partner, Curly Jack.

They said not a word to each other as they moved down the trail. He smiled as he felt her hands grip his shoulders.

When they reached the rendezvous site, the girl slid off the back of the horse and Sunkist swung a leg over and dropped to the ground. Her eyes showed no emotion as she looked up into his, and he looked at her curiously. There was something about this Indian girl that made him know that she was supposed to be with him. He remembered the girl named Barley Corn at the Sioux village, but this one was different—she was not small and timid like the Sioux girl. She stood tall and confident, and in her face he saw someone it seemed he had known in another time. He wanted to touch her, but took a short step back and studied her closely as he fought to reclaim control of his emotions.

A blue jay screeched from the treetop above them and the silence was broken. *"You comin' with me?"* he asked quietly in Cherokee.

"Where will you go?" she asked.

He smiled at the sound of her soft, low voice. *"Don't know for sure, li'l gurl. Gettin' to feel like headin' outta these mountains and hunkerin' down somewhere."*

"You are like the animals that have no home. You cannot stop and stay in one place."

"Yer prob'ly right about that—been too long doin' what I please."

"We will go where the white man cannot find us?"

"Li'l gurl, there's white men all around this country. Ye cain't hardly turn around without steppin' on one."

"It is sad," she said.

Sunkist pulled the packs from the mule and began rolling the tarp out for the lean-to shelter. The girl pushed him aside.

"I do this."

"Well hell, I can do it, you don't need to."

She stood and looked into his eyes. *"The home is the woman's place and she is the one to build it. If the man does it, it will not be a happy home."*

"Well, excuse me all to hail," he said, "guess that's why I been so unhappy lately. *What are you called?"* he asked her in Cherokee.

"I am called 'Flower Among the Rocks'." She said it in Cherokee and Sunkist couldn't pronounce the words. The language of the Cherokee was made up of sounds from the throat as well as sounds made with the tongue, and very hard for white men to master. Sunkist had a basic knowledge of the language but his tongue was not trained to make the sounds the Cherokee used in their communications. He knew the words for 'flower' and 'rocks' but the words wouldn't come out of his mouth the way they were supposed to.

"How about I call you 'Flower'?"

She looked curiously at him. He pointed at a fall flower on the ground and said, "Flower."

"Flouwa?"

"How about we try, 'Posey'?"

"Pos–sey?" she said curiously.

"Yup," he said in English. "Your name will be Posey."

"Yup," she said, mimicking his word and nodding gesture with her head, *"My name Posey,"* she said in Cherokee. *"How are you called?"*

"They call me Sunkist because of the way the sun touches my face in the summer and turns it red."

She looked at him and said, *"I go for wood."* She turned away and went to the woods.

"Hey—" he started in English, caught himself and changed to Cherokee, *"I can do that."*

"Gathering wood is woman's work," she said.

"Look, I've been watchin' out for this ole coon for better'n thirty years, I guess I can git my own firewood."

She turned at him and hissed like a cougar. *"You think I cannot do woman's work?"* she said, glaring into his eyes. *"You think I am soft like the white woman? I am Tsalagi. I can do my work."* She walked away, leaving Sunkist standing with his mouth hanging open.

Soon, she returned with an armload of wood and dropped it near the fire pit. Sunkist sat on the ground scraping a deerskin. Posey grabbed the skin and scraping knife from him.

"This is woman's work," she said.

"Well hail, if you do all the work around here what am I supposed to do?"

SOPHIE'S HAWK

"You hunt and bring meat. You fight the enemy when they come. That is all."

"Now jist a damn minute here!" he said in English.

He switched to Cherokee and said, *"I cannot sit here while you do all the work."*

"You are the man, you hunt and bring meat."

"Hunt, hunt, hunt, is that all a man has to do is hunt?" he said. *"Cain't a man do some of the work around here?"*

"You are the man—you hunt."

"Then I will go hunting tomorrow." He sat and watched Posey's expert hands work on the skin. *"Why did you come with me?"* he asked.

"You are not like the white man—you are free and do not do bad things to the Indians. You are a good hunter and fighter. That is why I am with you. The Spirits told me in a dream that you would come."

"I didn't ask you to come with me."

"You put out the blanket. Is that not the way to ask me to come with you?"

"Damn," he said in English, "never thought about that. *I just wanted you to be warm—I was not looking for a wife.*"

"Do you want me to go away?"

"No, I want you to stay. But you must let me do some of the work."

She tossed the deerskin at him and said, *"You can do this—I do not like it."*

Night came and they each rolled up in robes and went to sleep. In the morning he awoke to find Posey squatted by the fire boiling deer meat.

"You sleep late," she said.

"I s'pose you are going to tell me when I should get up in the morning, too."

"You come out of the shelter when you are ready."

"That meat done?"

"Yes. Eat."

He took the stick that the meat was on and sat cross-legged next to Posey.

"You are not going to wash before you eat?"

"Wash what?" he asked, as he took the meat in his teeth and cut it off with his butcher knife.

"Your body and your face."

"I did not think of it, but no, I am not," he said while he chewed.

"You are a white man."

"Was that an insult?"

"I do not know what that means."

"It means, did you find something about me you do not like?"

"There are many things about you I do not like."

"Well, git used to 'em—I ain't changin'."

"That is one of the things I like about you."

"Now, what does that mean?"

"You do not try to change your ways to make everyone happy. You are the man I see."

"I am going hunting. I do not understand you. You accept me as I am even though there are things about me you do not like."

"That is because I know what you will do and I do not have to wonder. I can trust you."

He stood and walked into the forest. He stayed out until almost dark, shot a small doe and carried it back to the camp. As he came close he laid the carcass on the ground and crept quietly toward the camp. He knew that to survive in a hostile land the mountain man had to be wary of danger at every turn—even as far as silently slipping into his own camp, watching for possible enemy. He crept low to the ground peering through the brush toward the camp when he heard the sound of Curly Jack's voice. He stood and walked into the camp. Curly Jack stood at the edge of the camp talking to Posey. She sat on the ground with her bow and half-drawn arrow pointed at Curly. He looked up when he saw Sunkist walk into the camp.

"What the hell is this? I walk into camp and this woman threatens me with an arrow. Who the hell is she, anyway?"

Sunkist motioned for Posey to put the bow down but she held it tight aimed at Curly Jack's belly.

"He's a friend—put the bow down," he said to Posey in her language. She lowered the weapon but kept her eyes fixed on the new white man.

Curly Jack walked into the camp.

"Where'd ye pick her up at? Looks damn dangerous to me."

"Don't think it would be wise to make her mad. I saw her jump right over me and kill a man with a knife."

"Where'd ye git her? She's kinda perdy."

"Up the mountain a couple-three miles back. Three guys had her tied to a tree. I got her otta there."

"She kilt one of 'em?"

"Yep."

"Posey," Sunkist said in Cherokee, *"this is my trapping partner,* Curly Jack.*"*

She walked to him, stood in front of him, looked him up and down, then turned away.

"She ain't much for talkin'," Sunkist explained.

"So, I see. Sunkist, I made up my mind. I'm going back to Minnesota Territory. I've had my fill of these mountains. There ain't nowhere a man can go anymore where ye ain't hearin' some tenderfoot cryin' cause ye stepped on his tender foot."

"Yeah," Sunkist said quietly. "I been thinkin' the same thing but I cain't go back to the settlements around Fort Snelling, that place got more people than bees in a hive. I hear they're callin' it Pig's Eye fer that good fer nothin' Frenchy who sold the whiskey that kilt my pa."

"Why don't ye come up to the north country? Ain't hardly no one there 'sept a few farmers and a small town. Got me a brother lives up there and a couple of nephews—Hawk and Jake. Good boys they are, too. Coupla redheads. Too bad they gotta live with that worthless brother of mine."

"Sounds like a place a man could find some loneliness."

"That ye could, my friend. Ye goin' up through Saint Louie?"

"Been to that town, too and don't care if I ever go back. Too damn many people around there, a man cain't catch his breath fer the stink."

"Which way ye figurin' on goin'? Straight up?"

"Curly, you make it sound like I shoulda made plans or somethin'. We'll jist take our time and mosey on up that-a-way. We'll git there when we git there."

"Ain't that just like you, Sunkist—you ever made a plan and stuck to it?"

"Nope. Always something gettin' in the way and a-changin' things."

Curly Jack smiled. "Ye mean like hitchin' up with a perdy little Injun gal?"

Sunkist looked over at Posey. "She is a sight to please the eye, ain't she?"

"Damn sure is, my friend. Figger on takin' her with ye?"

"Yep. I ain't lettin' go a this one. She ain't like the ones out west. She don't care fer the fancy foofrah and geegaws like they do. All she needs is fed and watered once a day and she's plenty happy."

"When do ye wanna leave?" Curly asked.

"Ain't nothin' keeping me here. We can move out first light tomorrow, if ye want."

"How about the girl? She got family?"

"Far as I know she's got no one. I found her alone and she tole me she got no people. Don't think there'll be a problem with her."

"First light it is, then."

Posey walked off without saying anything to Sunkist. The rest of that day was spent checking saddles, leather, guns, powder and lead.

Later, Posey returned riding one of the horses that Sunkist had driven off.

He looked at her and smiled, shaking his head. He was pleased with this girl and it showed.

She carried two leather sacks, one slung over each shoulder. The rest of the day she spent in the woods gathering berries, roots, and herbs. She carried a bundle of thin sticks tied tightly with rawhide lacing for making arrows. Heads for the arrows would be made from stones she found along the trail, and fletching would come from the feathers of geese and turkeys they killed for their meals.

The morning sun lit the tops of the mountains, making them appear to be on fire. Fog lay in the bottom of the valley as they moved slowly north onto the plains following the buffalo trails and keeping to the lowlands.

Three days out, Curly stopped his horse, turned to Sunkist and said, "Sunkist, I guess this is where we part company. I'm headin' over to Saint Louie and takin' a steamer up to Minnesota country."

"Yeah, I was thinkin' ye might do that. Ye seem to be in kind of a hurry to git yerself up there. Ye got you a woman waitin' fer ye?"

"Well, not exactly. Kinda like to see them two boys before they git too big for wanting to hang around with their uncle."

"And their ma, too?"

"Yeah, that too. She's pretty special." Curly sat on his horse and looked at Sunkist. He took a deep breath and said, "Can I tell you something, Sunkist? Something I gotta git off my chest…"

"You know you can tell me anything, and it ain't goin' nowhere from here."

"I know that." Curly paused.

"Well? What is it?"

"Well," Curly looked at the ground, then up at Sunkist. "Well, damn, them two boys are mine. I'm their pa. Me and Mary was in love since we were kids but her mother didn't want her to be marrying the likes of me, so she made her marry my brother, John. John was no damn good from the start. He was always sick and lazy as a bear in winter. Mary and me spent way too much time together—we got along better than she ever did with John. Every time he'd go to town on one of his drunken sprees we got together and did what a man and woman do when they're in love. It wasn't like we was just pokin' for the fun of it, we were in love and we just did what comes natural. John couldn't do for her what a man should do, so I did.

"I ain't sayin' it was right, what we did, but I ain't sayin' it was wrong, neither. It was just something that was gonna happen sooner or later. And I ain't sayin' I'm sorry for it, neither. I'd be a damn sight sorrier if it hadn't happened. I'd spend

SOPHIE'S HAWK

the rest of my life wondering what it would be like to love someone so much and regretting that I never took the chance. Can you understand that, Sunkist?"

"Yeah, I guess it's the same with Posey. I could have left her back there, but somehow I knew there was a reason she had to come with me. Like you said, I'd probably be sorrier for not bringin' her along."

"Well, now you know—Hawk and Jacob are my sons. They don't know it and I'd like to keep it that way for Mary's sake."

"Guess I can understand why you're in such a hurry to git up there."

"Reckon I'll be turning off east. Come on up when you can and we'll have some fun in the north country."

"We'll be there, jiss give us a little time to git acquainted."

"You be watchful—keep yer flint sharp and watch that red hair." With that, Curly Jack walked out of Sunkist's life.

"He is a very good friend." Posey said in Cherokee.

"They don't get better'n that man," Sunkist mumbled to himself.

Posey looked straight forward. *"You will not see him again."*

"Yeah, I know," he said quietly.

They moved north and crossed the plains of Kansas and Nebraska and into Dakota Territory.

"Posey, *you ever been to the Black Hills?"*

"I do not know of these hills."

"West of here a couple hundred miles."

"We will go there?"

"Yes, I have seen them but have never been in them. The Indians say bad Spirits live there. The hills sound like thunder and they are afraid of it. I hear the land is strange and hard to travel through."

"The Indians do not go there?"

"They go there to hunt and to do spiritual ceremonies but they do not live there."

"Then we will go. We make our home there?"

"I do not plan on it. I told Curly we'd come up and live in Minnesota Territory. But if it is a good place we will stay for a while."

"I will go where you go."

"I am glad you will be with me."

Posey stayed close to Sunkist and he enjoyed her company. They rode quietly, stopping when either of them needed or wanted a rest. They ate their meals on horseback or stopped in an especially beautiful spot to camp until they felt the urge to move on.

One day, as Posey stirred the stew pot, she abruptly stood and said to Sunkist, *"I wish to be your wife."*

"Wife!" he said. "I never thought I'd have me a wife."

"Sunkist, do you love me?"

"Well… yeah, I guess. I like having you with me, if that counts."

"Then we will be married."

"But there is no preacher here. We cannot get married."

"We do not need a white medicine man. We have the Spirits of the Old Ones. They will see that we are married."

"But you are just a girl, and I am getting old."

"How old we are does not matter. We love each other, that is what matters."

"All right, when do you want to do this?"

"Now." She went into their shelter and brought out three blankets—two green and one white. She wrapped a green one around Sunkist and one around herself. *"Come with me."*

He followed her down to a stream and they walked into it to their knees. She stood before him with the blanket over her head so that just her face showed and looked up into his eyes.

"Sunkist, I will forever be your mate and will have no other man in my lodge."

He looked at her not knowing what to do next.

"Now you say it," she said.

"Aw, hail…" he said in English. A bit embarrassed, he said in Cherokee, *"Posey, I will forever be your mate and will have no other woman in my lodge."*

She led him out of the water and took the blanket from him. She then wrapped them both in the white blanket.

> *"Now we will feel no rain, for each of us will be shelter for the other.*
> *Now we will feel no cold, for each of us will be warmth for the other.*
> *Now there is no loneliness.*
> *Now we are two persons but there is only one life before us.*
> *We go now to our dwelling to enter into the days of our life together*
> *and may our days be good, and long upon the earth."*

For the first time since he knew Posey he saw her smile. It was the most beautiful smile he had ever seen and her black eyes shined as she looked up at him. He wrapped his arms around her and kissed her on the lips. She backed away and looked at him.

He lowered his voice and said, *"It's all right, Posey, we call it 'kissing'."*

"Kissing?" she said in English.

"Yes, kissing." He leaned down and pressed his lips to hers. She slowly began to respond. Her hands slid up his back and clutched at his shoulders. She wound her fingers in his hair and pressed her lips against his and her arms circled his neck as she held her body tight against his. He held her for long moments, treasuring the sensation and the deep emotional experience that sent waves of passion through his soul as well as his body.

He pulled her tightly to him and an involuntary groan came from deep in his throat. His eyes closed to shut out the world around them. He buried his face in her hair and inhaled the sweet smell of wild sage. The embrace demanded more. They walked from the river to their camp. Posey went inside ahead of Sunkist and when he came into the tent he found her lying naked on the robes.

"Oh, my gawd…" he said quietly. With shaky hands he stripped out of his clothes and lay next to her. She wrapped her arms around him and they kissed and made love for the first time.

He stopped his horse and as he started to get down,
darkness closed in on him.

CHAPTER FOUR

T RAVELING ACROSS THE PLAINS became home to Sunkist and Posey. Each time they moved, they were simply going to see another part of it. All the comforts of home were there in abundance—food, water, shelter and the company of each other.

To the eye adapted to the confusion of city life, this country would seem monotonous. Sunkist and Posey found it interesting and wonderful. They loved seeing the low hills and the deep valley of the Missouri River—the rivers and streams that didn't seem to go anywhere and the small clumps of trees that told of water in the middle of endless grass plains. They saw herds of buffalo covering the sides of the hills and the flat prairie, and the fleet-footed antelope standing on a ridge watching them, then darting away. All of these things would go unnoticed by the city dweller's eye, but to the partners they were life at its best.

They traveled across the plains of Dakota until they could see the Black Hills on the horizon. They appeared no more than a day's ride away, but five days had passed before they came close enough to make out the trees and mountains. A herd of antelope took off as they topped the crest of the hills. They rode down the hill and across the flat bottom for four miles to the foot of the mountains on the far side. They made their camp near a small stream of clear, cold water that ran out of the mountains.

"The mountains are beautiful," Posey said. *"There are no white men here?"*

"No, and no Indians, either, as far as I know. Tomorrow we will go into the mountains and see what is there."

In the night they heard strange rumbling sounds coming from the hills.

"Is that the Spirits talking?" Posey asked.

"That's what the Indians think is the Spirits talking. I think it's thunder. Sometimes

in the mountains there are storms blowing so far away you cannot see them, but the thunder echoes through the hills and we can hear them for many miles."

"The sounds do not frighten you?"

"No, and they should not frighten you, either."

"I am not afraid."

"Tomorrow we will go and see the storms and we will know."

They settled into their robes and made love adding their own music to the tapestry of the night. Posey nestled into Sunkist's arms. He pulled the blankets up to her chin then wrapped his arms around her tightly and smoothed her hair. He listened to her breathing become slow and rhythmic as she drifted off to sleep with her head on his shoulder.

They stayed in the shelter for most of the next morning before saddling their horses and riding up a valley into the mountains. The trail was narrow and lined with rocks of many different shapes, textures, and colors. Some of the cliffs they passed were smooth and they shined in the sunlight as if some giant hand had polished them. The mountainsides were covered with pines and looked like a solid wall of trees. Small streams ran in nearly every valley they saw and more than a few great rivers rushed down the rocks to form deep pools at their bottoms.

They stopped and looked straight up at the great columns of rock that stood around them as high as the clouds. They saw large rocks set atop tall columns as if playful gods had set them there. They looked down at the base of the cliffs and saw heaps of jagged rock that had been broken free by wind, rain, frost, and snow. There, they will lay undisturbed until another billion years of time and the elements break them down further to sand, dust and clay. In another billion years, the rain will carry them to the rivers and further still, to the oceans. Of course, the couple had no awareness of these natural processes, nor did they question why or how. They stayed in the mountains several days, captured by the strangeness of the countryside.

Posey climbed down the hill to the pile of rocks and found crystals the size of her thumb and put them in her side bag. Sunkist watched as she played among the rocks. He smiled as he watched the girl. *She is, without doubt, a flower among the rocks*, he thought to himself.

Like a child in a candy store, she inspected each and every rock, big and small—pink ones, black ones, green ones, and blue ones—keeping some and tossing others, then scrambling for more.

Sunkist laughed, "Li'l gurl, *we can't carry every pretty rock we find out of these mountains."*

"I will keep the ones I feel the Spirits in and leave the rest."

"You feel Spirits in the rocks?"

"Yes, everything has a Spirit, even the trees and the stones and the water. They all have Spirits."

Suddenly, she raised her head, sniffed the air and scrambled up onto the trail.

"Come, we must go. There are Indians here."

Sunkist looked around and saw nothing, but he knew that when Posey sensed trouble, he'd better listen. Posey mounted her horse and they started down the mountain. Sunkist was feeling the presence of someone watching them—he knew they were being followed. They heard a soft rumble from somewhere in the hills. Sunkist held the horses at a walk as they continued toward the bottom of the mountains.

"They are gone," Posey said quietly. *"Whoever it was, was frightened away by the Spirit Thunder."*

They spent the night in a small ravine. In the morning, they were once again on the trail to the bottom of the mountains. They rode quietly, holding the reins on the horses tight to keep them from breaking into a run on the downward slopes.

Suddenly, the ground began to shake. Rocks tumbled past them from the cliffs above. The horses became frightened and nearly threw them to the ground. The shaking stopped as quickly as it started and the animals settled down to a cautious walk. Sunkist had a hold of the reins on Posey's horse.

"Just an earthquake," he said.

"What is that?" Posey asked.

"That is when the earth shakes and makes those sounds. My father told me of one back in eighteen-eleven when the earth shook so hard it split open, and rivers flowed backwards."

"It is not the Spirits?"

"No, it is not the Spirits, just an earthquake. I have seen them before. Some are bad and some are small like this one."

Posey got a disappointed look on her face and kicked her horse to move ahead.

"Sorry, Li'l gurl. I was hoping it would be the Spirits, too. I have never seen one."

When they came to the foot of the hills where they stayed the first night, they found a pole stuck in the ground with a deer scull set atop it and feathers fluttering in the breeze.

"Maybe we should get out of here," Sunkist said. *"I think we're on someone else's land."*

As they neared the top of the ridge, a line of mounted Indians appeared on the crest. One of them walked his horse forward and held a war lance high over his head. He yelled something in a high-pitched voice.

"Sioux," said Sunkist. *"They think we are intruding on their ground and want us to leave."*

"We are leaving. Do they not know that?"

"Looks like we're in a kind of fix here, they want us to leave but they don't want us to go over their land—which is behind them."

"What will we do?"

"We will move forward and see if they move out of our way."

Sunkist had just touched his heels to his horse when an arrow hissed through the air and struck him on the left side of his chest.

"Turn and head back for the hills!" he shouted.

They kicked their horses and ran full-gallop toward the hills with the Sioux on their tail. They rode up a narrow draw and turned their horses onto a small game trail. The Sioux broke off the chase and Sunkist and Posey rode on until Sunkist said, *"We gotta stop and get this arrow out of me."*

He stopped his horse and as he started to get down, darkness closed in on him.

He awoke lying on the ground with Posey kneeling beside him. He was covered with a blanket and his head rested on a pillow of soft moss. Posey had built a small fire next to him.

"You are wounded very badly," Posey said. *"I have taken the arrow out but you are bleeding inside."*

"Ain't gonna make it, huh?"

"You will live."

She reached into her parfleche and pulled out a bundle of moss that she carefully rolled into a small ball. She laid green sweet-grass over the fire to make it smoke heavily, then held the moss in the smoke while she softly chanted a prayer and raised it to the sky. She lowered the blanket and pushed the ball of moss into the wound, then turned Sunkist over and pushed another ball into the hole in the back of his chest. Sunkist felt the world begin to spin around and his mind told him that he was dying.

When he awoke it was bright daylight and Posey was by his side.

"You will live," she said.

Posey built a shelter of pine boughs and spruce under an over-hanging cliff. She made a bed of soft boughs and moss for Sunkist to lie on, and one for herself.

Time passed and Sunkist regained his strength and was able to move around, but his wound was too painful to allow anything more than slow walking.

Fall had set in hard and the temperatures dropped as the snow fell and covered the hills with a blanket of pure white. Storms blew over the mountains from the west. They were on the east side and the winds blew themselves out before they got to the small camp.

Posey had killed a large wolf and made a hat for Sunkist to wear. The skin of the wolf draped down his back so the tail nearly dragged on the ground. She shaped the head to fit over his, and the wolf's face, in its natural shape, extended out in front of him to shade his eyes from the bright sun. It kept him warm in the coldest times of the winter.

Several times during the winter they heard the sound of the Thunder Spirits and each time they spoke, Posey raised her hands to the sky and offered a prayer.

"You still think those are Spirits talking, don't you?"

"Yes, they are the Spirits that keep the Sioux away and they are the Spirits I called to when you were wounded. They made you live. They are friendly Spirits."

"They did keep the Sioux away, I'll give them that."

Through the winter Posey prayed to the Spirits and nursed Sunkist. She did the hunting and the cooking while Sunkist healed.

One day, they saw the stream close to their camp running with fresh snowmelt. They watched the stream run faster and faster until it was a rushing river of mud.

"We must move our camp to higher ground," Posey said.

"I was just thinking the same thing. Let's go."

They packed the little they had and moved up the mountain.

"Posey—" Sunkist said.

"We will keep moving and leave the mountains now?" Posey asked.

"We will have to move slowly and keep a good watch for the Sioux. They ain't gonna like the idea that they didn't kill me."

"They will be afraid of the Thunder Spirits and will not attack us," Posey said.

"You think that's true?"

"Yes, I know that is true. They will know that the Thunder Spirits healed you and will not dare to anger them."

"Well, if it's all the same to you, I'm going to be careful and keep an eye open."

"Yes, it is good to be careful."

They walked their horses out of the hills and into the valley below. They crossed the flats and started up the grade on the other side when suddenly, before them, a line of Indians appeared.

"Don't stop—just keep walking," Sunkist said in a low voice.

He pulled the wolfskin hat over his head, drew himself tall in the saddle, and walked directly at them. As they neared the line, the Indians parted and let them pass quietly. They were soon back on the plains of Dakota and in another month they were in Minnesota Territory.

"She has been taken captive by the Indians and
she hasn't been seen for over a month."

CHAPTER FIVE

SUNKIST AWOKE TO THE BRIGHT SUN coming through the door of their shelter.

Sunkist said to Posey, *"Let's go to town and see what's going on."*

"You will buy powder and lead for your guns?"

"Hadn't figgered on it, why?"

"The Spirits have told me we will need these things."

"The Spirits told you?"

"Yes, in a dream."

Sunkist had learned to listen when the Spirits talked to Posey. She had a way of knowing that things were going to happen but could not tell exactly what they were.

They ate a small breakfast, saddled their horses and set off for the town of Sacred Heart, leading a pack mule. They traveled over-land staying off the roads and out of sight of other people. They rode at a slow walk into town. People along the way stopped to look at the big redhead and his Cherokee wife. Some tipped their hats as they passed. One man stopped and said, "Mornin' Sunkist."

He nodded his head and returned the greeting with a deep, audible grunt.

They walked into a store and looked around at the shelves covered with wooden boxes, cotton bags and tins of fruit. On the floor were bags of flour, grain, cracked corn and barrels of molasses. On the walls hung coils of rope, harness leather and tools of all kinds. Heavy leather boots and fine shiny shoes lined the wall to the left.

"Good morning," said the man behind the counter. "What can I help you with?"

He was a thin man in his middle years. He had a handle bar mustache and wore small round spectacles that sat on the end of his nose. He moved quickly, like a squirrel packing away its winter rations. He wore a calico shirt with garters at the top of the sleeves, a bow tie at his throat, and an apron that covered him from chest to knees. On his head he wore a cotton clerk's cap made from a flour sack with part of the printing still on it.

Sunkist looked at the man, "We're needin' coffee and flour."

"Got all yer gonna need." He stepped from behind the counter and groaned loudly as he picked up a fifty-pound sack of flour. "Fifty pounds do ye?"

"Yup, and the same for the coffee."

"Can do, my friend, but I gotta tell ye, it's not ground when it comes in that large a quantity."

"What d'ye mean it ain't ground?"

"Well, it's still whole beans."

"Ye mean they even grind the beans fer folks now?"

"Well, sure. Haven't you ever bought ground coffee before?"

"Nope, I always roasted it and busted it on a rock and boiled it."

"Well, you can buy it all ground up for you now. Would you rather have it that way?"

"Nope, jist give me the whole beans, I can still grind my own."

"We have coffee mixed with chicory too, it's a little cheaper that way and it makes the coffee go farther."

"Jist give me the beans. I've had all the chicory I care for."

"Whatever suits you, my friend. Anything else?"

"Got powder and lead?"

"Yup. How much ye need?"

"Gimme two pounds of powder and coupla hundred fifty-six caliber minie balls."

A woman in a long full dress and a wide hat on her head walked into the store straight past Sunkist and Posey, without looking up. Sunkist watched her go by. "Careful ye don't look at me, lady, ye might turn ugly." The woman glanced at him.

"Whoops," he said, "too late, I see ye already looked."

She sniffed, turned her nose in the air and turned away from him.

"That's an awful lot of powder, figuring on doin' some hunting?"

"Yeah, gonna do some huntin'."

"Goin' out west I guess, huh? Out to the gold fields?" he asked as he pushed his glasses up onto his nose where they momentarily rested before sliding down again.

Sunkist watched him with amusement, then shook his head and said, "Mister, you ask too damn many questions. Jist gimme that stuff and we'll be otta here."

"Yeah, sure. Sorry, didn't mean to pry." He sat their goods on the counter and said, "That'll be twenty-two dollars and fifty cents."

Sunkist looked at Posey then at the clerk. "Um, well, we ain't got that much money with us."

"Aw, hell," said the clerk with a wave of his hand, "you can pay me when you come back to town."

"Now, why in the hail would you trust me? You ain't never seen me before and you jist might never see me agin."

"I know who you are—you're Sunkist and that's yer wife, Posey. Everyone in town knows who you are."

"We'll be back tomorrow with yer money and we'll pick up our stuff then."

"Go ahead and take it now. If I can't trust you, who can I trust?"

"Mister, in these parts it ain't wise to trust no one."

"Mister Sunkist, if I don't give these people credit, I'll go out of business tomorrow. Nobody has money around here."

"We'll be back tomorrow."

"I'll be lookin' for ye." He tipped his hat to Posey, nodded his head, pushed his glasses up and said, "Ma'am."

They walked out the door and got on their horses.

"Posey," Sunkist said, *"I don't like having people knowin' we're here."*

"We will move to another place?"

"I don't want to, but maybe it'd be a good idea."

"Will there be trouble if we stay?"

"I guess I can't see what more trouble we could have than what we've already had."

"What will we do?"

"You want to stay, don't you?"

"I will go where you go."

"Let's stay through the winter and see what happens."

A slight smile crossed her face as she looked up into his eyes. She leaned toward him in the saddle and gently kissed him on the cheek.

The next day they were up with the birds and on their way back to town. They walked into the store and handed the clerk a bag of gold.

"Gold? Mister Whistler, where did you find gold?"

"In the mountains out west. There ain't no gold in Minnesota."

"Well, you had me going for a minute, there. People have been looking for gold in Minnesota for years and haven't found any yet. I hear they're finding some up in Rainy River. They found copper up by Lake Superior, too, I hear—and I heard someone say there's iron up there, too—but they don't know if there's enough to…"

"You sure got good hearin', don'tcha?" Sunkist interrupted.

"Well, not lately. Seems like I don't hear quite as well as my missus thinks I should. She calls it selective hearing. I think she talks softly so she's got something to compl—"

Sunkist slapped his hand on the counter and pointed his finger at the sack of gold.

The clerk looked back at him and said, "Ah, yes, the gold." He opened the sack. "Mister, there's a lot more money here than you need to pay for what you bought."

"I got more, you jist take that to pay for what we'll be needin' through the winter."

"I'll have to take it down to the assayer and see how much is here."

"Do what you have to. We'll take our things and be on our way."

"You gonna just leave me here with this gold? You ain't coming with me to see how much is here?"

"Mister, you were gonna trust me with yer stuff, I guess I can trust you with mine."

"There's gotta be two hundred dollars in this bag."

"Mister, I've been around a long time and one of the things I learned is that, if a man don't trust people, he cain't be trusted. He thinks everyone's as crooked as he is. I like trustin' people. Trust is like a rock—it's either there or it ain't."

"This is kinda like you're testing me, right?"

"Guess you could see it that-a-way," Sunkist said as he picked up his goods and turned for the door.

"You'll get yer money back," the clerk shouted out the door, "you'll see."

On the boardwalk outside the store a man stepped up to Sunkist, "Mister Whistler?"

Sunkist stopped and looked at the man in a black suit with a white collar around his neck and a wide-brimmed hat on his head.

"Call me 'Sunkist'," he said to the man.

"I'm Steven Riggs. May I have a word with you?"

"You're Steven Riggs? You know Jake and Hawk Owen?"

"Yes, of course. That is partly why I'd like to talk with you."

"They ain't in trouble agin, are they?"

"No," the Reverend said with a smile. "They're not in trouble—not yet, at least."

"What d'ye mean, not yet?"

"Come with me and we'll talk."

"Let me put this stuff on the mule."

"Yes, of course."

Sunkist loaded the supplies on the mule and turned to walk with the Reverend. They went into a cafe and took a table next to the window.

The waiter came to the table and said, "Sorry, mister, we don't serve Indians in here."

"This here's muh wife."

"She's a damn squaw! We don't serve—"

He hadn't finished the sentence before Sunkist had him by the shirt and half carried him backward to the wall. His green eyes blazed inches from the man's face and he said through clenched teeth, "This here's my wife. She is Cherokee Indian. And she is not a squaw. You call 'er that agin and I'll tear yer heart out and feed it to yer customers."

The waiter was staring down at Sunkist's face. His toes were just touching the floor.

"Put me down."

"Did you hear what I jist said?"

"I heard you."

He let the man down and turned to take his chair.

The man turned and said, "Mister, I don't care who that damn squaw is, we ain't serving her in this place."

In a flash Sunkist had him by the shirt and threw him through the air against the wall. The man hit with a hard thump and opened his eyes just in time to see two huge, hard hands grab him by the belt and lift him high into the air.

"I told you not to use that word agin."

He turned with the man over his head and carried him to the door and without bothering to open it, threw the man into the street.

Reverend Riggs sat on his chair with a half-smile on his face. Sunkist walked back to his chair and sat down.

"Now, what was it you wanted to talk to me about, Reverend?"

"Sunkist, you might be interested to know that that man's brother was killed by the Indians a few months ago."

"Well, it weren't Posey who killed his brother."

"You love this woman very much, don't you?"

"Yer right about that, Reverend. Now what's this all about?"

"General Sibley has asked me to employ you and your company to find Lorraine Bernier. She has been taken captive by the Indians and she hasn't been seen for over a month."

"How the hail—uh, excuse me, Reverend. How did she get captured?"

"She took it upon herself to go to Little Crow and ask him to surrender, but before she could reach him another Indian captured her and took her away."

"Do you know who this Indian is?"

"No, they don't know that. They only know she is not with Little Crow."

"And how the—how do they know that?"

"He was sent a message, written by me, asking for her return. Apparently, Little Crow knows Lorraine and he sent a message back saying she is not with him."

"And Sibley wants us to go lookin' for her, right?"

"Yes. You will be paid for your services and you will be issued all the supplies you need. You will be in the employ of the United States Army and will be subject to orders from Sibley."

"I got no doubt the boys will take the job, but I doubt they'll want to join the army."

"You won't have to join the army. You'll be civilian scouts with honorary ranks."

"So, where do we start lookin'?"

"I'm afraid I can't help you with that. Your best bet would be to go and talk with General Sibley and see if he can help. He has scouting parties all around the country looking for renegades who didn't escape to Dakota Territory."

"I'll see if I can round up the Owen boys. I can almost promise you they'll take the job."

"Thank you, Sunkist. That is a big load off my shoulders."

"We ain't found her yet, Reverend."

"I have all the confidence that you will, and that you will bring her back alive. Would you like something to eat?" the Reverend asked.

"I ain't eatin' in a place like this. We got better food out there on that mule."

"Very well, then. I will leave you and wish you the best of fortune."

"Reverend, can you get a letter to Jake down in Courtland and tell him to meet us at Hawk Creek as soon as he can? Tell him what's goin' on."

"Why, yes. I can do that. Will you write the letter?"

"Um… well, maybe you better write it and jiss tell 'im it's from me."

"Yes, of course. I'll do that."

Sunkist and Posey rode out of Sacred Heart.

"Guess this is why the Spirits told you we need more powder."

"The Old Ones are very wise."

Sunkist went to work cleaning and tuning their rifles and checking the supplies of lead and powder. Posey put together a traveling camp with canvas, food, winter clothing, a cooking pot, and dried food. They waited several days before moving out and heading north.

Now they sat at their camp at the mouth of Hawk Creek. Sounds from up the riverbank startled Sunkist. He reached for his rifle and quickly slipped behind a fallen log. The sounds of horse's hooves on the rocks came closer and both Sunkist and Posey laid their rifles over the log aimed in the direction of the sounds. Then the sounds stopped. They watched for long moments waiting for whomever it was coming close to their camp. Flies circled their heads as they watched and waited. Slowly, Sunkist pulled back the hammer of his rifle holding the trigger back to keep the lock silent.

"Yer pointin' them guns the wrong way," they heard from behind them.

"Took ye longer'n I figgered on," Sunkist said without turning around.

"Yeah, well, I got me a partner now," Jake said. "Things go a little slower than they used to." He motioned toward the trees and a woman on horseback came out leading two mules and Jake's horse. "Sunkist, this here's Eve—she'll be coming along."

"Howdy, Eve," Sunkist said as he stood and turned. "This here's Posey, muh wife."

"I've heard a lot of good things about both of you," Eve said. "It's a pleasure to finally meet you."

"We'll see how much of a pleasure it is when we git on the trail."

"Does Hawk know we're coming?" Jake asked.

"Nope, figgered on surprising 'im."

"This will be a surprise, all right."

"You know how to find his place, Jake?"

"Yeah, it's up this crick about five miles. It's kinda hidden in the trees, but if you stay close to the river for five miles then stay on the banks, you can't miss it."

"Ye want to start right now?"

"You go ahead on," Jake said. "We have to rest these animals for a day and let 'em feed. We've been riding pretty hard."

"We'll jiss do that. We been sittin' too long and my butt's gettin' chapped."

. . .

Lorraine stood and put her hand on her father's shoulder.

"Mister Holcombe, Dad is very tired. May we continue this in the morning?" she asked the reporter.

"Yes," he said. "I think we could all use some rest."

"We have a two-room cabin in the back with a bed in the front room and a cot in the back room. You are welcome to stay there if you'd like."

"Is there a place we can go to get something to eat?"

"You will not go and get something to eat. My father and mother always fed their guests and I shall do the same."

"That's very generous, thank you."

Lorraine made a dinner of fresh venison, boiled potatoes and creamed peas. They had their dinner and the reporters retired to the cabin.

Morning found Hawk sitting in the chair next to the grave, talking softly. Lorraine came out of the cabin.

"He's been doing that since Mother passed away three weeks ago." She walked out to her father, "Dad, the reporters are waiting."

"Let 'em wait. I'll be there in a while."

A short while later, Hawk climbed the steps to the porch and sat in his chair. He lit his pipe, settled back, and continued his story.

"I ain't never seen a hawk yet that could sit on one branch for too long."

6

CHAPTER   SIX

"SOPHIE AND I RODE BACK through Fort Ridgely and headed to the camp I had on Hawk Creek. We'd fought the Sioux in the Minnesota Valley that fall and when it was over we came here to get away from it all and try to scratch a living from the rich ground around the Minnesota Valley. The small shelter I'd built for myself was overgrown with hazel brush and willow and the roof had fallen in and needed repair. Our days were filled with work but the nights were spent enjoying each other's company. We put things back in order and settled in.

"Soph, how would you like to buy some ground and try farming?"

"Do you really think you could be a farmer, Hawk?"

"I don't know, but I'd like to own my own land."

She drew in a deep breath. "It's awfully nice right here. Do you think *this* area is for sale?"

"We can go to Sacred Heart and see the claims clerk tomorrow, if you want."

"Let's do that."

The next day, we saddled up and rode to Sacred Heart and went into the claims office. The man sitting behind the desk looked up as we walked in.

"May I help you?" he asked.

"Yes. I'm Hawk Owen. We're looking to buy some land a little north of here."

"Do you have a particular piece you are looking at?"

"Yes, it's about five miles up Hawk Creek from the valley."

"Let me look," he said.

He opened a large book and thumbed through the pages.

"Yes, here. We have a tract of one hundred and forty acres in that area. Indians killed the farmer that lived there and the land is abandoned. That particular piece of ground is mostly rock and wetland, but there is enough dry, fertile land for planting crops and ranging a few cows. There's a house and a log barn on the property, but they've been somewhat destroyed. I haven't been there to see it, but they tell me both the house and barn are repairable."

"Is there woods?"

"Yes, and quite a lot. You will have to remove a few trees to make room for crops if you're planning on doing it for profit."

I looked at Sophie, "What do you think?"

"It sounds like it would be worth looking at." She put her hand on my shoulder. "But, we won't be cutting any trees."

"When can we see the land?"

"I can take you out there right now, if you'd like."

"Let's go."

The man took his coat from the hook on the wall behind him and said, "I'll get the buggy and meet you on the road."

We went out and stood in front of the building.

"Are you sure about this, Hawk?" Sophie asked.

"Sure as the snow in winter."

"It's going to mean staying put and no more chasing around the country..."

"Ain't that what we decided on after the wars?"

"Yep. But somehow I just can't see you farming," she said.

"We don't have to farm, there are other things we can do to make a living."

"Yeah? Like what?"

"Well, I don't know. Maybe a sawmill or a store—we'll think of something we can do together."

"Too bad we can't think of a way to make a living running around the country," she said.

"That would be nice."

The man came around and motioned us to follow. We rode northwest along the valley rim and crossed Hawk Creek, then turned north on the road that led past our camp. As we passed the camp, Sophie nudged me with her elbow and pointed toward it. I smiled and nodded.

Another half-mile up the road, the man stopped and said, "Well, by the map, this is it."

"This is it?" I asked.

"Yes, Mister Owen, this is your new home. What do you think?"

"We'll take it," Sophie said.

"You don't want to look around?"

"We already have and we like it."

"You have seen this place before?"

"Yes, we passed our camp a half-mile back. Where is the house and barn?"

"Come, I'll show you."

We rode on a trail that led into the trees and came to an area that had been cleared and saw the log house. The roof was burned off halfway across and the glass windows were broken out. Household items were scattered on the grass outside the front door and windows. The barn was burned almost completely but there was enough left to work with.

We walked into the house. Inside was a table and three chairs, one of them broken, and a bed that had been burned. There was a stone fireplace in one corner with a cast iron pot hanging over the ashes. The house had been ransacked and the household items were scattered all around.

"The Indians attacked this place?"

"Yes, the poor people who lived here were killed. When the Indians went through the house they threw everything they didn't want out the door and windows."

"How much do you want for it?"

"Well, considering the condition of things we have set the price at four hundred dollars."

"Wow, that's pretty steep. Let us look around." We walked out of the house and around to the back. The grass had grown high and the small garden in the corner was grown over with weeds. Sophie walked to the garden and looked around.

"Hawk, come over here."

I walked over to her. She pointed down the hill to the creek at the bottom. Hawk Creek flowed lazily in its bed, clear as fresh snowmelt, and the bottom was covered with stones and gravel. The bank on the other side was covered with sumac that was taking on its bright red fall color. Cottonwood trees a hundred feet tall and oaks, maples, poplar, pine, elm, and birch made a solid wall of trees.

"Hawk… this is perfect."

"I was hoping you'd say that." I turned to the agent. "We'll take it."

"Mister Owen, there will be a lot of work to make this place livable."

"I'm not worried about the work. We want this place," I said, looking at Sophie.

"One more thing you should know. The people who lived here were killed inside that house."

"Should that bother me?"

"Well, no, I just thought you should know that. Some people are not comfortable with that."

"Doesn't bother me a bit. Where are they buried?"

He pointed to the woods to the right, and through the trees we could see the fresh graves.

"There are no markers," Sophie said.

"No, most of the people killed in the raids were buried where they died and no one thought to put up markers."

"We'll put markers on their graves."

I turned to the agent, "Do you have their names?"

"Yes, they will be on the original claims papers."

We went back to town and closed the deal, then hurried back to our new home on Hawk Creek.

We worked hard to get the house in living condition before the snow came. We tore off the old roof and replaced it with new boards and shingles split from cedar trees. We covered the windows with oiled deerskin to let daylight in. We fixed the floor and the door and burned what remained of the mattress on the bed. We saved the frame and posts and made a new mattress from grass pulled from the meadow. I cleaned the chimney and replaced some of the stones in the fireplace. We built a fence around the yard in front of the barn, rebuilt the barn and covered it with sod. By the middle of October the house and farm were ready to be lived in.

Sophie had found a flock of chickens wandering around and began to feed them to keep them near. A stray cow showed up in our horse pasture. I didn't really want cows, but, what the hell. She wasn't making milk but I figured she might come in handy when the weather gets bad and we need meat.

We piled rocks from the river bottom on the graves of the people who had lived there. I carved their names on a slab of maple and nailed them to sticks that I drove into the ground at their graves. Satisfied with the job, I stood up and started walking away. I realized that I was walking by myself and turned around to see Sophie standing over the grave with her eyes shut and face lifted toward the sky.

"Soph?"

Then I realized she was saying a prayer to the Spirits so I quietly walked back to our cabin alone.

The day was warm and the trees had taken on their brilliant red, yellow, and gold colors and the air was filled with the sweet smell of poplar leaves and pine.

Down in the creek we cleared a small area of rocks and gravel and covered it with sand from a nearby lake, for bathing. After a day's work we went to the river and sat on the fine sand and talked and bathed each other. We had dried and dressed ourselves and were sitting on a blanket enjoying the cool fall air when we heard horses coming through the brush. We grabbed our rifles and went to the edge of the woods.

"Nice place ye got here," Sunkist hollered.

"Well, butter my butt and call me a biscuit!" Sophie laughed. "What brings you up this far, Sunkist?"

"We were just wandering around wasting time and come across this crick—never thought you two to be holed up here, Hawk. Figgered you and that fancy female you got would be curled up in some high-falootin' hotel in Mankato."

Posey swung a leg over her horse and jumped to the ground. She put her arms around Sophie and gave her a hug, then came and did the same for me.

"Damn," Sunkist said, "I ain't never seen her do that before. Sophie and Posey must'a made perdy good friends there at Wood Lake."

"She's very good at patching up bullet holes," Sophie said.

Sunkist came down from his horse and gave Sophie a hug. "That she is," he said.

"So what's going on with the Indians these days?" I asked.

"Sibley's got 'em penned up south of Lac Qui Parle. He's tryin' to gather up the warriors who was doin' the killin'. He's packin' all the white captives he can off to the fort for per'tection."

"He ain't chasing the Sioux up the valley?"

"Nope, he's cryin' fer more troops and supplies. Figger he misses his warm fire and hot meals."

"He must have enough men to go chasing Little Crow. Hell, when they skedaddled out of Wood Lake all the fight was beat out of most of 'em."

"Like I said, he ain't a fightin' man," Sunkist said. "He's taking all the credit for whippin' Little Crow, and he's only been in one battle—the one at Wood Lake—and it was the Third Minnesota boys whipped Little Crow there, not Sibley's army."

"Well, we're out of it now," I said, "and it's no concern to us anymore."

"You gonna fight if it starts up again?" Sunkist asked.

"I'll fight if it comes to my country but I ain't going lookin' for it. I figure I've been damn lucky to keep my hair this long and there ain't no point to pushing it."

"Word has it that Sibley's lookin' for scouts to ride north to see where Little Crow and his band are. Interested?

"Nope."

"Ye sign on with 'im and you'll be paid—might be enough to buy seed and animals."

"I ain't joinin' the army. That's the last word on that."

"Don't have to join the army. The governor says anyone who fights gets paid—even civilians, as long as they sign on."

"Well, that makes it more appealing, but I still don't want to go."

"Hawk, how are you gonna make a living out here? There ain't enough game to feed you and Sophie. And think about this—what are you gonna do when the babies start comin' along? How you gonna feed 'em?"

"Babies? We ain't having no babies. Not for a long time, anyhow."

"The way you two can tear up a bed you'd better give that some thinkin' before you go makin' any rash decisions," Sunkist said. "And somethin' else you should know—"

"I ain't joinin' no army."

"Remember your friend, Lorraine?"

"Yeah, what about her?"

"She went out to try to talk Little Crow into surrendering and she ain't been seen since. They think some brave took her and made her his wife."

"Lorraine let me know in no uncertain terms that she wants me to stay out of her affairs. That's the way I'm going to keep it. She probably chose that life anyway."

Lorraine was a Métis girl who traveled with the ox carts from Pembina to Saint Paul. She was beautiful, but in a different way than Sophie. Her hair was dark brown and she had large black eyes that made a man feel small when she talked to him. She carried herself like a schoolmarm—straight, tall and graceful.

She'd been sent to Montreal when she was a small child and was raised and schooled at a Catholic mission all her life until she came to Minnesota. Then she was sent to the reservation in the Minnesota Valley to teach the Indian children the ways of the white people. She said she didn't believe that could be done but she was determined to do her best.

She was too sophisticated for me. I loved Lorraine, but in a different way than I loved Sophie. Our differences didn't allow for anything more than a shaky friendship. She hated the fact that I carried a gun wherever I went and didn't seem to realize the need for it. And she corrected me when I said what she considered a bad word. She'd say, "There is no need to use that sort of language with me, Hawk."

I found her ways more entertaining than annoying and did what I could to aggravate her by being the ignorant hayseed she considered me to be. But she never got angry, she just rolled her black eyes back and walked away.

I saw her for the last time outside Fort Ridgely during a lull in the fighting. We said our good-byes and I never thought I'd ever see her again.

"You gonna let them Injuns keep her?" Sunkist asked. "You got any idea what yer sayin'?"

"Sunkist, I have a good woman here and I intend to keep her. Running off looking for someone who doesn't want me around just doesn't appeal to me right now."

"Sounds like you got yer mind made up."

"I do."

"Ye gottenything to eat in there?" Sunkist motioned toward the house.

"Not much, but you're welcome to what we have," Sophie said.

Without another word, Posey began pulling bundles from the pack horse and setting up a meal.

"I thought you were gonna eat our food."

"Don't worry, we will. Posey here thinks we should share what we have. That's the Indian way."

Just like the day I met these two, Posey put out fresh venison, herbs, roots and all sorts of food. How she had so much packed on that one horse, I'll never guess—one of those scary woman things. We sat for most of the night talking about the past and what the future might bring. Sunkist made a few more comments about going up looking for the Indians but I declined each time.

Later that night, after Sunkist and Posey had put up a shelter outside the cabin and settled in, Sophie and I slipped into bed and tried to be quiet.

"Hawk?"

"Hmm?"

"You might want to think about going after Lorraine. After all, she is a friend of yours."

"*Was* a friend of mine."

"Did she hurt you that badly that you'd leave her to the Indians?"

"Lorraine taught me a lesson. When someone doesn't want you around it's best to just stay away."

"Don't you know why she didn't want you around?"

"Yeah, I didn't fit into her crazy life. That's all there is to it."

"It sounds to me like she was falling in love with you and having you around made her question her own reasons for being here."

"Now, what the hell makes you think that?"

"Did she ever tell you to stay away?"

"No, not in so many words, but she sure did with actions."

"If a strong-willed woman like she is didn't want you around she would have said it straight out. Being a woman, I have a pretty good idea of what goes on in a woman's mind."

"You didn't even know her. How would you know what she thinks?"

"I saw her once in Mankato. She is a beautiful woman, but too damned tied up in her own world to get mixed up with men. You men can be a pain, you know."

"Beautiful ain't everything."

"I know that, Hawk."

"Well, I ain't going away and leavin' you here alone for God-knows-how-long."

"You're damn sure not going anywhere without me. I'm coming along."

"Okay, *if* we go, it's gonna be rough. There's going to be fighting and killing. You want to be part of that?"

She looked at me in silence.

"Damn, you are one stubborn woman."

"Uh-huh."

"We'll go and find Lorraine," I said.

Sophie rolled over and wrapped her arms and legs around me. "Thanks, Hawk, had a feeling you'd agree. Anything else I can persuade you into?"

Later, when I was about half asleep, I heard, "Ain't chuh glad you brought me along?"

Without opening my eyes or saying a word, I answered with a larger than necessary grin.

In the morning, Sunkist came out of his tent. "When do we leave?" he asked.

"And what makes you think we're going anywhere?"

"Call it instinct. When do we leave?"

"Damn, whenever you say. Maybe we should get ahold of Jake," I said. "He might want to be in on this."

"Jake should be here today. I talked to him before I came looking for you."

"So, you knew where to find me?"

"Course I did, Jake tole me."

"That was no instinct—that was more like a conspiracy."

Sunkist shrugged one shoulder, bobbed an eyebrow, and grinned.

"We're going to have to pack our things on our horses until we get a pack mule," I said to Sophie.

"Just get your camp together, we'll figger out how to carry it when Jake gets here."

Posey busied herself with putting a meal together for all of us while Sophie and I gathered our camp.

Around midday, we heard horses coming through the brush. Sunkist and I grabbed our rifles and slipped into the woods.

"Hellooo the camp!"

"That'll be Jake," Sunkist said.

We stepped out into the open and watched as Jake rode in. He was leading a loaded pack horse and two mules. One was the mule I'd left in my camp two months before.

"Brung you yer mule. Figgered you'd be needin' her."

"You guys had this all figgered out, didn't you? Well, what if I had refused to go? Then what?"

"Guess we never figgered on that," Jake said, "I ain't never seen a hawk yet that could sit on one branch for too long."

I looked at Sophie, "Am I that predictable?"

She replied with a grin.

"Gotta do something about that," I said.

Jake turned around and hollered, "It's them, come on out!"

A woman on horseback came out of the trees and walked up to us.

"Who's this now?" I asked.

"Hawk, meet Eve. Eve, my brother, Hawk."

"Nice to meet you." I looked at Jake and he smiled back. "Is she coming too?" I asked.

"Don't worry, big brother. She can handle herself."

"It's kinda late in the year for a picnic, ain't it?"

"This ain't gonna be no picnic, Hawk," Sunkist said. "We're gonna be ridin' hard and the women will be good to have along fer patchin' holes and such. Say, Soph," he said, as he took the reins of my mule, "you might think about getting a muzzle for that boy to wear at night. The noise kept us awake half the night."

"Hey, Sunkist," Sophie said.

He turned, "Whut?"

"Git used to it."

"Knew that was comin'."

"Where do we start?" I asked.

"We'll start by finding Sibley's camp and get signed up as scouts."

"I ain't joinin' no army."

"Would you risk your life for a friend?
Then you know why we must try."

7

CHAPTER SEVEN

IT WAS ABOUT HALFWAY THROUGH THE DAY when we finally got situated for traveling. We moved out toward the northwest following the rim of the valley. By sundown we could see the smoke from the fires at Sibley's camp across the valley. We stopped and set up our camps on a flat spot just over the rim.

"In the morning," Sunkist said, "we'll go in and talk with Sibley and see what he knows, if anything."

The night got as dark as the inside of a buffalo and there were no sounds except for an occasional field mouse scurrying around in the grass. I was awakened by a nudge on the end of my foot. I opened my eyes and saw Posey framed in the doorway with a finger to her lips, telling me to stay quiet. She motioned me out the door. I looked into the darkness but could see nothing. She pointed her finger to where Sunkist sat holding his rifle across his lap.

"What's up?" I whispered.

"Somethin' movin' out there," Sunkist said.

"Is Jake up?"

I felt a tap on my shoulder. I turned around with my heart in my throat and saw Jake's smiling face five inches from mine.

"I'm here, big brother."

Posey hissed and shushed us with her finger over her lips. Sophie's face came out through the flap of the shelter and I motioned her back inside. She came out wrapped in a blanket and knelt next to me.

"I told you to stay inside."

"What's going on?"

Realizing the futility of trying to tell her what to do, I said, "Posey hears something out there."

We heard a crash in the brush, a gunshot, and a grunt. The hammers on our rifles clicked back to full-cock. A voice came through the darkness almost loud enough to hear the words.

Sunkist said quietly, "Hold yer fire till we can see somethin' to shoot at."

Then it got quiet.

The wind picked up and made a soft sigh in the tall pine tree above us. Posey's head turned a little to one side as she listened for sounds. She signed to Sunkist that she was hearing someone talking. She communicated with sign and Sunkist translated for us.

"She hears voices but she can't tell what they're sayin'."

"Are they talking English?" I asked.

"Cain't tell—you boys got them dragoons loaded up?"

"Yep," Jake and I said at the same time.

We sat quietly through the night until the sky began to lighten in the east and we all quietly slipped behind whatever cover we could find.

"Think they're still there?"

"They're out there, all right. Be ready to shoot. I don't think there's too many of 'em—but it don't take that many of 'em neither."

We could hear voices now and rustling of the dry leaves. Our rifles were aimed toward the sounds.

Suddenly, a voice came from the brush. "Hello the camp. You be white men?"

"Who the hell are you and what do ye want from us?" Sunkist shouted.

"Scouts from Sibley's camp. We're comin' in—hold yer fire."

Five men stood up about fifty yards out and walked slowly to our camp. Six rifles from our camp were pointed at them as they came in. Four Springfield rifles and one strange-looking one were pointed at us. As they came into camp, all the guns were lowered and one of the men spoke.

"Sergeant Wambolt. Military scout for Sibley." Wambolt was a head taller than any of us and built like a Holstein bull.

"Name's Whistler. Folks call me Sunkist onna conna the sun burns my face so bad in the summer. Red Irish, ye see. You boys look a little hungry."

"We could use some food if you got extra."

"We ain't got nothin' extra but we got enough to feed you, I figger."

Wambolt turned and introduced his men, "This here's Private Sullivan, Torgerson, and privates Wells—they're brothers."

They were all good-sized men and looked capable of handling themselves in a fight. The privates stood forward and stuck out their hands. One of the Wells

SOPHIE'S HAWK

brothers said, "You look like you be brothers, too."

"Yeah," I said, "I'm Hawk Owen and this here's my brother, Jake."

"I'm Mike and this is my brother, Steve. Good to meet you."

Posey went to work making a meal for our guests. Eve poured water from her canteen over her hands, dried them on a white towel, and helped Posey. Sophie sat and watched. I looked at her and she looked at me and said, "Cooking ain't my strong suit."

"Just what is your strong suit?"

She smiled and raised an eyebrow at me with that devilish look in her blue eyes.

"Behave yourself," I said.

"How come you got your wimmin along?" Mike asked.

"Can't get rid of 'em," I said.

The scouts sat on the grass and ate until their stomachs bulged. "You gonna join Sibley's army?"

"I ain't joinin'—"

"Figgered to sign on as scouts," Sunkist interrupted.

"Sibley wants soldiers mostly, but he can use scouts, too, so long as they don't find no Injuns for him to fight with—afraid of getting his uniform dirty, I think. He's been sittin' in that camp for a month trying to get the Injuns to surrender. He's callin' it 'Camp Release'. He calls it that because all the prisoners the Injuns had were taken by the friendly Sissetons and Winnebagoes and turned over to him."

"He's got all of the captured whites in his camp?" Jake asked.

"The ones he got right off he sent to Fort Ridgely but there's still some there. Course, some of the prisoners are still with the Indians. He ain't got 'em all yet."

"You don't happen to know if there's a girl named Lorraine Bernier with them, do you?" I asked.

"Oh, so you're Hawk Owen and this is Jake. Hell yeah, I know who you are. Damn, fancy meeting you out here."

"Yeah, well, you know anything about the girl?"

"What girl?"

"The one I just asked you about."

"Oh, yeah. No, I don't know any of the names. We ain't allowed to get near the captives or the Injuns. Sibley's scared we'll be chasin' the squaws."

Sunkist started to move toward Wambolt, but Posey stopped him.

He looked at the Sergeant through his bushy red eyebrows and said, "I don't want to hear that word agin, you got it?"

"What word?"

"SQUAW!" he barked.

"Sorry, mister, I didn't mean no disrespect, it's just the common word used for Injun wimmin out here."

"Well it ain't no common word in this camp and I'm tellin' you, DON'T USE IT!"

"All right, okay, we won't use it." He turned to his squad and nodded. They all nodded back.

"Hey, Steve, what's that rifle yer packin'?" I asked.

"It's called a Henry's Repeating Rifle. Forty-four caliber—shoots fifteen times without reloading. Got 'er from an old drunk in Saint Cloud who needed a drink more than he needed a rifle. Paid twenty-five bucks for it."

"Shoots fifteen times?"

"Yeah. Here, take a look." He picked the rifle from the ground next to him and tossed it to me. I caught it, but it was so heavy I almost dropped it.

"See that lever underneath it? Pull that down and the shell in the chamber pops out, and when you pull it up, another one goes in. Slicker'n loon shit."

"Ain't never seen nothin' like this before. What'll they come up with next? Can you hit anything with it?"

"Well, they say it'll kill a man out to a thousand yards, but I don't think anyone could hit a man at that distance. Ain't no need to try anyway. If he's that far away he ain't nothin' to worry about. If he gets close I got fifteen chances to stop him. Gettin' fifteen shots in ten seconds makes a man feel perdy comfortable."

"Getting ammunition for it must be tough."

"It is, but I got a thousand rounds in my pack."

"Where do you come from, Steve?"

"Ottertail County—same place yer from. We heard about the Indians attacking yer farm and how they killed yer family."

"Yeah, well that was a long time ago. So, what brings you out here?"

"Well, Ma died a year ago and there wasn't much reason to hang around that place. Pa ran off twelve years ago—couldn't get along with Ma. We got no idea where he is, but we think he was headed this way."

"He was kind of a rounder," Mike said. "He couldn't fit in with people 'cause he wouldn't go along with what they thought he should be. We think he's dead, but we don't know for sure."

SOPHIE'S HAWK

"I think it's time to pack up and git over to Camp Release and talk to Sibley," Sunkist said. "You boys got horses?"

"Back at camp, but not here."

"How can you be scouts and not be on horseback?"

"Sibley wants to keep the horses back there for his soldier boys in case he's attacked. We're just patrolling the perimeter."

"You ain't soldiers?" I asked.

"Hell, no, we ain't soldiers, we're civilian scouts," Steve said.

"How come you call yourselves sergeant and privates then?"

"Sibley gave us those ranks. Makes him feel important to give out military ranks, I guess."

"What was that shot we heard last night?" Jake asked.

"Sullivan tripped over a stump and fell. His gun went off accidentally."

"You boys start walkin' back to camp. We'll catch up with you there," Sunkist said.

Sergeant Wambolt hollered, "ATTENNNN- HUT!"

Steve and Mike looked at each other and ignored the command.

"ABOUT FACE!"

Steve chuckled and grinned. He pointed his thumb over his shoulder at Wambolt and said, "He's regular army."

Then Sergeant Wambolt and his squad walked off toward Camp Release.

"Those boys look like a good bunch to have around," Jake said.

"We'll see about hookin' up with them after we get signed up. We know—" Sunkist said, holding his hand up to me, "you ain't joinin' no army. No need to say it agin."

We packed our camps and headed down the trail to the bottom of the valley. We found a fording place the army had built, crossed the river, and climbed up onto the prairie. The low rolling hills were bare of trees and covered in yellow grass.

"Hey, Jake," I said, "heard that pony of yours is the fastest in the valley."

"Best damn horse you ever seen."

"Well, I think my Brute can take 'im."

"Anytime you're ready, big brother."

We whipped our mounts into action and galloped hard across the grass. The Brute stretched out full front and back and took the lead. It seemed he knew he was in another race and put his heart into it. It wasn't long before Jake caught up and stayed next to me. I leaned over and whispered in The Brute's ear, "We can do it, handsome, that nag ain't got a chance against you."

Jake pulled ahead a length, then The Brute pulled up and got the front. Jake was laughing so hard I thought he'd fall off his horse. We galloped into Sibley's camp side-by-side.

Suddenly, a thousand men came out with rifles aimed at us. We pulled to a stop and hollered, "We be white men—don't shoot!"

"Hawk, fer crise sake, what the hell you tryin' to do—get yerself killed?"

"Hey, Sarge! Fancy meeting you here."

Sergeant Jones, the ordinance officer from Fort Ridgely, came storming over to us.

"Goddammit," he said, "things are scary enough around here without you two raisin' all kinds of hell."

"Just seein' who's got the best horse in the valley, Sarge."

"Well, do yer racin' somewhere else. You damn near got yer selves shot."

"Good to see you made it through the wars, Sarge."

"Wars ain't over yet. Governor Ramsey wants us to go out and bring in Little Crow and his bunch. You comin' along?"

"Nope, we're goin' chasin' a friend of ours. You know Lorraine Bernier?"

"Heard the name, but mostly connected with yours."

"Word has it that she's one of the captives. Maybe captured by one of the Indians."

"You can check Sibley's list of names. He wrote them all down in a book."

"Where's he at?"

Jones pointed toward a tent. "That's his camp. Scratch on the door before you go in, he might be taking a bath."

About that time, the rest of our group rode into camp.

"Well, who's got the fastest horse?" Sophie asked.

Jake said, "We're gonna have to run these critters a lot farther than that to see who's best."

"Let's go see Sibley," I said.

We rode to his tent and I scratched on the door.

"Enter."

"Hey, Henry," I said as I walked into the tent.

He looked up from his papers and said, "Aw, God. What the hell? Aren't things bad enough around here without you showing up?"

"Could be worse, Henry. I could have Jake here with me."

"Yeah, I need *that* like I need a chapped ass."

I opened the door to the tent and motioned Jake and Sunkist in. Sophie, Posey, and Eve followed them in. Sibley put his elbows on the desk and laid his face in his hands.

"Dear Lord, what did I ever do to deserve this?"

"Ye joined the army, Henry," I said.

"I wasn't asking you, Hawk. You're not here to join up, I hope. We've got enough trouble with the Indians."

"Ain't joining no army, but we want to join up as civilian scouts."

"Can you follow orders?"

"Yup, as long as they're the orders we want to hear."

"And just what are these orders you think you want to hear?"

"Order us to go out and find certain captives and bring them in."

"And this certain captive would be?"

"Lorraine Bernier."

"I might have known. Did Steven Riggs send you? He's worried about her, too."

"Yep," Sunkist said, "talked to him a couple'a weeks back. He's the one who asked us to go find 'er."

"You didn't tell me that," I said.

"You didn't ask."

"You got any idea where she might be, Henry?" I asked.

"Last I heard from one of the friendlies is that she's with a man called 'The Thief'. He's a mean one. She went out to try to talk Little Crow into surrendering and The Thief grabbed her up and made her his wife. Little Crow is not in a position to tell anyone they can't do what they want, so even if he knew about it, he couldn't do anything about it."

"Where'd they go? Any idea?"

"North. That's all I know, and that's just a guess."

"Sullivan, get in here!" Sibley hollered out.

Private Sullivan came through the door. "Yes, sir?"

"Hey, Sully," Jake said.

"Hey, Jake."

"Get these animals signed up as civilian scouts."

"You ain't scoutin' no more, Sully?" Sunkist asked.

"Naw, the Colonel wants me to be his clerk. That's okay—I ain't much for the outdoors thing, anyway."

"Nothin' wrong with that."

We got signed up and Sibley gave us our ranks. Sergeant James 'Sunkist' Whistler, Corporal Jacob 'Jake' Owen, and Private Harlan 'Hawk' Owen.

Sibley said, "What's the squaw's name?"

The room went silent and all eyes turned to Sunkist.

"She ain't no squaw," he growled.

"She is Indian, is she not?"

"She's my wife and I don't want you callin' her a squaw agin. I don't care if you are a Colonel in the goddamned army."

"I am sorry, Mister Whistler, but we are required to register all Indians, male and female."

"You ain't registering her." He took Posey's arm and led her out the door.

"He's a bit sensitive about that woman, Henry," I said. "I'd be careful."

"I can see that. Yer all a bunch of hotheads."

"I'd remember that too, Henry."

"Be on your way, Hawk. Try to leave some alive in your path, okay?"

"We ain't lookin' for trouble, Henry. Just out to find Lorraine. We want Sergeant Wambolt and the Wells boys and Torgerson to go with us."

"If they agree, you can take the Wells boys and Torgerson. Take Wambolt too, I don't need his kind around here. I need good soldiers and Wambolt is a troublemaker. They're all just as unruly as you are, so you're welcome to them."

"We'll take Wambolt as a military attachment."

"Hawk, I don't care if you take him as a pack animal—just take him."

"Where are they now?"

"How the hell do I know? I'm just the commander here. They're probably out there chasing the squaws around."

"Careful with that squaw thing, Henry—could cause you some serious health problems." Jake rested his hands on Sibley's desk, leaned over, and said, "I heard of a man who spent a week in a sickbed after calling Posey a squaw the second time."

"Right. Sorry."

We saluted Colonel Sibley. He sighed impatiently and returned a weak salute. We left his tent and joined Sunkist and Posey.

Camp Release was set up on a flat prairie. On one end, there were three hundred Indian camps mixed with tepees and shoddy shelters made from materials from the woods in the valley. On the other end was the army camp with their wedge tents and Sibley's tent in the middle. Soldiers on horseback patrolled the Indian camp.

　　　　　　　　　　　　　　　SOPHIE'S HAWK

"Hawk?" Sunkist said, sheepishly looking at the ground.

"Yeah?"

"Can I be the private?"

"Hey!" piped Jake, "I wanna be the private."

"Henry made me the private and I'm keeping it. You guys will just have to get comfortable with being what you are. "

"How about we all be privates? Wambolt can be the sergeant."

"I got a better idea," Sophie said, "let's make Posey the sergeant."

"Posey don't speak English," Sunkist said.

"Perfect."

We all saluted Sergeant Posey. She lowered her eyebrows and hissed at us.

"Let's go find those Wells boys."

Suddenly, we heard a commotion from across the camp. A group of soldiers were gathered around a fight involving civilians and soldiers.

"Lemme guess—that'll be the Wells boys and Torgerson," Sunkist said.

We walked over to the ring and pushed through the crowd. Steve had a private on the ground ready to smack his face with his fist. Mike was throwing another man at a third man. Torgerson was exchanging punches with a man whose face was already covered with blood from a broken nose. We strode to the middle and pushed the pugilists apart.

Sunkist had Steve's fist in his hand to stop him from dropping it in his adversary's face. "That'll do, boys. Looks like trouble jist follers you boys around."

"Aw, hell, Sunkist," Steve said, as he wiped blood from a split lip, "we was just teaching these soldier boys some manners. They figgered they was better'n us onna conna we ain't regular army. Guess we changed their minds about that, huh?"

The men they were fighting moved off to lick their wounds.

"If you boys are done here," Sunkist said, "I got a proposition fer ye."

"What's that?" Torgerson asked.

"Sibley says if you want to come chasin' Injuns you can join us."

"Anything's better than hangin' around this smelly camp. When do we leave?"

"Where's Wambolt?"

"Right here," Wambolt said from behind us. "I suppose you think I'm comin' with you."

"That's up to you, Sarge. If you like this military bullshit you can stay here. We're heading up the valley to find Little Crow. We'd like to have you along, though."

"Who's in charge? Sibley make any of you sergeant?"

"Yup," we all said at once and pointed at Posey. She bared her teeth and hissed at us again.

"Sibley didn't make no squ—uh, Injun woman no sergeant," he said with a quick glance at Sunkist.

"Wambolt, we don't need no sergeant. We all know what needs to be done and we can count on each other to do it," I said. "We don't need to be waiting around for someone to make a decision. You want to play sergeant, stay with Sibley. You want to do some hunting, you can come with us."

"Sounds good. I ain't got much use for Colonels, either. When do we leave?"

"As soon as we can get supplies—rations, ammunition, and powder."

"I can get you that."

"Yeah, good idea," I said, "you can be the sergeant long enough to get us plenty of supplies."

"I'll go talk to Sibley." Wambolt walked off and we sat down to eat.

Soon after, a wagon rolled up, interrupting our meal.

"We ain't takin' no wagon," I said "it would slow us down too much. What's in there, anyway?"

"Blankets, salted pork, dried beef, crackers, bread, lead bars, percussion caps and twenty pounds of powder," Wambolt said. "What the hell more do you want?"

"You could throw a couple of them Injun girls in there," Steve said.

"We'll take the blankets and dried beef and ammunition," Sunkist said. "Give the rest to those people over there." He pointed his thumb over his shoulder at the ragged Indians Sibley had fenced in.

"You serious?" Wambolt asked.

"Hell, yeah, I'm serious. We can feed ourselves out there better'n this, anytime. Posey here can find food on a frozen lake in the middle of winter. Besides that, them Injuns got contacts with the ones out on the prairie and they'll pass the word that we gave them food—makes for good relations."

After we had taken the supplies we wanted from the wagon, Wambolt told the driver to take it to the Indian camp.

There were about three hundred tepees clustered on the south side of Sibley's camp. The Indians were ragged and looked to be half starved. When the wagon pulled in, a crowd gathered around it and the food disappeared in less than a minute.

Sibley came out of his tent and hollered, "What the hell is going on here? That is the army's rations—not intended for the Indians."

Wambolt turned to Sibley and said, "Colonel, you issued that food to us to use. It ain't the army's no more. It's ours and we have done with it what we thought was best. We made good relations with the Indians. It's gone now and there ain't no reason to get uncorked about it."

Sibley stomped back toward his tent, grumbling. He stopped and turned, "Sergeant Wambolt, don't you come asking for any more rations. You have gotten all you will get."

"Sergeant Wambolt," I said, "you don't seem to like Colonel Sibley too much."

"I got no time for any of them damned army officers. They're all a bunch of idiots."

"Well, I don't know about all of them. I will admit there are some who should not be commanding fighting men."

"Yeah, I knew one of them. Damned coward, he was."

"Hey, Wambolt," Mike shouted, "we're all on a first name basis here, what's your first name?"

"Sergeant!" Wambolt barked. "Now, how do we find Little Crow?"

"Let's go ask the Indians," Jake said.

We walked over to the camp and found an Indian Jake knew as White Feather. He spoke broken English, as most of them did. He was chewing his last bite of salt pork when we sat down next to him.

"Good day, my friend," Jake said.

White Feather nodded his head in greeting.

"Do you know where Little Crow is camped?"

White Feather chewed his pork and looked Jake up and down.

"We are looking for a friend of ours. Can you help us?"

The Indian pointed to his mouth and looked at Jake. Apparently, his mother had taught him not to talk with his mouth full.

Peeking at the Indian from under his eyebrows, Jake pulled his pipe from his sidebag. He reached into the bag and pulled out his tobacco pouch, measured the correct amount and tamped it with his little finger. He then took a burning stick from the fire and held it to the pipe, puffed on it till it was smoking properly, all the while glancing up at the old Indian. The Indian watched him and chewed faster. Jake leaned back against the tepee pole with his feet stretched out in front of him and crossed at the ankle. He took a big pull from the pipe and inhaled deeply, then let it out slowly through his nose.

White Feather swallowed his pork with a loud gulp and stared at Jake's pipe. Jake handed it to the Indian who took it and pulled a lungful of smoke from it. "You look for Tao ya te duta?"

"Yes. We think he might have our friend. We will find her and bring her home."

"He has many warriors with him. It would be dangerous for you to go to his camp."

"We know that, but we have to try to bring her home."

"You are Pa Hin Sa. Many Indians will want to kill you. You cannot go there and come back alive."

"Would you risk your life for a friend, White Feather?"

"Yes. I have done it many times."

"Then you know why we must try."

"Little Crow is camped near The Lake That Talks. He is with Standing Buffalo. He tries to bring more Indians into the war, and defeat the white men, and chase them from our valley."

"Little Crow cannot defeat the white men," Jake said. "It's a war he can't win."

"Pa Hin Sa, I know that, and he knows that, but like you must find your friend, he must fight this war. It is something he must do."

"How many warriors does he have?"

"Maybe two hundred, but he loses them because the young men do not have faith in him as a chief. Tao ya te duta was against the war, but the young men said he is a coward, so he said he would lead them—and die with them."

"Will he talk to us if we go to him with a white flag?"

"You might not get that close to him. He has many angry soldiers with him."

"We must try. Thank you, my friend. We will see you again." Jake stood up and turned to leave.

"Pa Hin Sa—" White Feather said, as he held out Jake's pipe.

Jake tossed him a pouch of tobacco and said, "You keep it, my friend."

White Feather nodded and continued to smoke.

"Well? Where to?" I asked.

"Where is The Lake That Talks?" Sunkist asked.

"That's Lac Que Parle," Jake said.

"You know where that is?"

"North end of the valley, I was up there last year."

"Any idea where the camp might be?"

"Nope. That's big country up there."

"Wanna take a scout?"

"Be a good idea. You know one we can trust?"

"Let me go talk to Sibley," Jake said.

"Tell him we need a pack mule," Wambolt said. "Tell him I said so."

"We don't need a pack mule," I said.

"Yeah, we do. We're gonna pack our scout on it."

"I see."

Sunkist's face turned to the sky. He sniffed the air and turned around to look toward the tepees. He walked slowly to them and stood facing a young Indian woman.

"Barley Corn."

"My mother is Barley Corn. I am Snana."

"You look just like your mother. How old are you?"

"I am twenty-four winters. You are Sunkist?"

"I am Sunkist. Where is your mother?"

"Mother is gone to the agency at Red Wood."

"My heart is sad to hear that. I would like to see her."

"It is good that we have met," she said. "I have heard your name many times. Mother spoke of you each time she heard your name and it made her smile. You have a wife, Sunkist?"

"Yes. Her name is Posey. She is Cherokee."

"I am married to a man named Good Thunder. We belong to the Episcopal Mission. We had children but two of them died when they were very young. Do you have children, Sunkist?"

"No, we do not have children."

"That is sad. I had my mother bring me one of the white girls who was captured by the bad Indians. I adopted her to replace my little girl who died. I hid her in a hole in the ground inside my tepee when the bad Indians came, but Colonel Sibley took her away when he came. Her name is Mary Schwandt—I will not see her again."

"She will remember you saved her life—you will see her again."

Sunkist looked back over his shoulder and saw his people getting ready to ride.

"I must go now," he said. "I will see you again."

Jake came back leading a saddled mule.

"Hey Sarge, you seem to have some pull around here," he said. "I told Sibley we needed a mule, but he wasn't going to give us one until I said Wambolt wants it. He flipped his lid and told me to 'take the goddamn mule and go'."

Jake walked the mule over to White Feather. "Do you like it here, White Feather?"

"No."

"Do you want to come with us to find Little Crow?"

White Feather stood up. His head just kept going up and up and up. "We go now?" he asked.

He was taller than I had expected, thin as a beanpole and stood half-a-head taller than Wambolt. He was dressed in leggings and a breechclout with a long, dirty red shirt that reached almost to his knees. His legs were bowed about ten inches apart at the knees, and his moccasin-covered toes pointed inward. His hair was greased and hung in front of his face in strings. A large bent nose protruded from the center of his face like the cutting edge of a tomahawk. His lips were thick and scarred from numerous battles.

Jake looked at us and said, "We got us a guide."

"Sibley okay with that?"

"He's a little pissed at us for taking one of the Indians before he can try him in his court, but he gave me the okay. He thinks White Feather is too old to have been involved in the war."

White Feather stood close and Jake had to crane his neck to look up into his eyes.

"Do you have a horse, White Feather?"

White Feather looked down at Jake over the sagging skin under his eyes. "No, the army took all of our horses. I will walk."

"We brought a mule for you to ride."

"I will walk."

"Suit yourself. You can lead this mule or ride it, your choice."

It was getting dark and the Indians in the camp were singing and dancing by the light of the fire.

We moved to the edge of the camp and made our places for the night. Sunkist and Posey stayed up after we all had slipped into our robes—and they were still up when I crawled out.

"You didn't sleep?"

"Sure, we did. Sat right here and got plenty of sleep."

"The Wells boys up yet?"

"Nope. Gonna have to shake 'em out."

"Where're they at? I'll go get them," I said.

"They're over there sleeping on the ground. Let me go git 'em."

"Whatever you say."

"Watch this," Sunkist said with a grin.

He walked over to one of the bodies lying on the ground wrapped in a blanket. He kicked the man in the leg and yelled, "GIT UP, GOD-DAMMIT, WE

GOT PLACES TO GO!"

Mike rolled over and grumbled something. Sunkist grabbed the blanket and threw it off revealing a young Sioux girl wrapped around Mike.

"What the hell is this?" he demanded. "I thought Sibley outlawed pokin' the Indian girls."

Mike squinted up at Sunkist, yawned deeply and grumbled, "Sibley's in his tent. He don't know everything that goes on around here."

"You could get yer self in big trouble for this, you know."

"What's he gonna do, fire me?"

"Git out of them robes and let's git goin'."

Mike got up as the Indian girl wrestled with her clothing then stood and walked away.

"Mighty perdy girl you got there, Mike."

"Yeah, she ain't bad."

"Where's Steve and Torgerson?"

Mike pointed to a couple of bedrolls a few feet away.

"Is it safe to wake 'em?"

"I suspect they're perdy comfortable in them blankets."

Sunkist lifted the edge of Steve's blanket and peeked in.

"Damn, cain't none of you behave yourselves?" He kicked Steve's leg and yelled, "Unscrew that thing and git up! We gotta git movin'!"

Steve threw the blankets off and said, "Daylight already?"

"Yeah, it's daylight and I s'pose yer all rested up for the ride north."

"I'm ready when you are." He threw the blankets off the girl and shoved her away. She pulled herself together and walked off.

"That's no way to treat a lady."

"She got what she wanted."

"Let's go."

Torgerson was up and had his blankets rolled up.

"You slept alone?" Sunkist asked.

"My choice."

They came to where the rest of us were and sat down to a small breakfast.

Sophie said, "Mike, you bringing that girl with you?"

"Nope, hadn't planned on it."

"You can, if you want."

"She's just a girl. She can't be more than fifteen. I ain't taking a kid."

"She was old enough last night."

"Her Pa wouldn't let her go, anyway."

"Sophie," I said, "we don't need anymore wimmin along."

"I just thought he might want her company."

"Well, I don't," Mike said.

"Hawk," I heard from the right. I turned and saw a thin man sitting cross-legged on the ground in front of a small tent.

"Yeah? Do I know you?"

"'Course you know me. Zhaaaaawn," he said with a bit of sarcasm.

"Jean? Charbonneau?"

"Yeah, that's me. Guess I've changed a little."

"Yeah, I guess you have."

Charbonneau was the master of the ox cart train I followed from my home in Ottertail County to Saint Paul. At that time, he was tall and lean with brown skin and black eyes—the son of a French voyageur and a Cree Indian girl. Now, to look at my friend Jean was to be looking at the face of death. He was thin and pale and hunched over at the shoulders. His eyes were sunken into his head and ringed with dark circles. The skin on his face hung dry and lifeless like burlap.

"Jean, what the hell happened to you?"

"Last spring we were attacked by Ink pa duta's outlaws. They killed Henri and took his scalp. I don't know about Rolette. He might be dead, too. He got away but that don't mean nothin'. Rolette's old and fat. He ain't got a chance out there."

"He might be old and fat, Jean, but he's tougher'n oak bark. Smart, too. He ain't gonna let himself get killed."

"We can only hope and pray."

"What happened, Jean?"

"We were headin' to Pembina when the Injuns ambushed us. Henri took a couple of shots at them before he took an arrow through the chest. He died quick—musta went through his heart. I don't remember much of what happened, but I know I got a couple of shots off before I went down. I woke up in the back of a wagon on the way to Ink pa duta's camp. I was tied up inside a tepee and had no idea what was going on outside. The next day I was dragged out of the tent and stood in the middle of the camp tied hand and foot to a post. Every son-of-a-bitch that walked by hit me with a stick or threw rocks at me—one even came over and pissed on me. Hawk, I heard they have Lorraine."

"Yeah, that's what we're here for. We're going to find her and bring her home."

"I wish I could go with you, Hawk, but I don't think I can make it. I'm

78   SOPHIE'S HAWK

perdy busted up inside."

"We'll find her."

"I know you will, Hawk. Just be damn careful, okay?"

"Don't worry about that, Jean. I gotta go. I'll come back and see you before we leave."

"Do that, Hawk."

I walked away, wondering if I would ever see my friend Jean Charbonneau again.

"Hawk, who's driving the wagon?"

"Damn, never even thought about that. You're priceless, Soph."

Just then, Sully walked by.

"Where ye going, Sully?" Sophie asked.

"Gotta go wake up the Colonel."

"Do you know how to drive a team?"

"Sure."

"Well, git on that wagon—you're comin' with us."

"What about Sibley?"

"Sibley who?"

Sully shrugged his shoulders, glanced toward Sibley's tent, and climbed aboard the wagon. We packed our things and headed north.

Sophie rode up next to me. "Ye know what?"

"What?"

"Mike's in love with that girl."

"There you go again with that women's intuition thing. How the hell do you know that?"

"Watch him. He keeps looking back at her."

"Maybe he's just remembering last night."

"Exactly. He's remembering last night and probably the night before—and who knows how many other nights."

"Why did he say he didn't want her along, then?"

"He's like all you men—just too damn stubborn to admit your feelings."

I looked at her, knowing my next words could result in some considerable mental anguish, but just as I opened my mouth she leaned over, grabbed the front of my shirt and kissed me hard. The twinkle in her eyes told me she was just having fun messing with my head again.

"Sophie, don't you have somewhere to go?"

"As a matter of fact, I do have somewhere to go." She turned her horse around and rode toward Sibley's camp. I watched her ride away and chuckled, wondering who'd won that discussion.

"I'll be right back," she yelled back at me, "you keep going!"

I shook my head to get the confusion out and rode on. We rode for a half-mile before I heard the sound of hooves behind us. I saw Sophie and Mike's Indian girl riding up. Sophie left the girl with Mike and rode back to me.

"Now why did you have to go and do that? He didn't want her along."

"Hawk…" Sophie said, and pointed toward Mike and the girl. They were leaning sideways from their saddles and had their arms around each other, kissing.

"What do you think of woman's intuition now?"

"Scary, that's all—just scary."

"Let's get out of here, Sibley's really pissed now. You should have seen him. He came out of his tent and yelled at us to come back." She laughed and said, "He just threw his hands in the air and went back inside."

We rode through the day and camped next to a stream for the night. We took turns standing guard—I took the middle hours. The other men wanted the first shift or the last so they didn't have to be awakened during the night. We liked the middle hours because we knew we could crawl back into bed and sleep a little before the day got started. Sophie sat up with me and we talked softly. The sounds of the night were mixed with the snoring of the men.

The Milky Way stretched across the sky and the stars seemed so close you could have reached up and grabbed one to put in your pocket. A star fell, leaving a glowing trail halfway across the sky and Sophie whispered, "Close your eyes and make a wish."

"Make a wish?"

"Shhh—yeah, if you wish on a falling star your wish will come true."

I closed my eyes and tried to come up with a wish that hadn't already been granted.

"Don't tell me what you wished for, or it won't come true."

"My wish didn't come true."

"What do you mean it didn't come true?"

"You're still sitting here with all your clothes on."

Her eyes narrowed as she wrinkled her nose, "Animal."

We laid back on a blanket and stared into the glittering sky.

"Don't you wish sometimes you could go up there and see what those stars really are?" Sophie said softly. "There's an old story about a horse named Pegasus that had wings and could fly up there among the stars."

SOPHIE'S HAWK

"A flying horse? That's impossible."

She leaned up on her elbow and laid her cheek in her hand. She looked at me with raised eyebrows and said, "Haven't you ever seen a horse fly?"

"You set me up for that one."

"Yup," she said, then laid back down, radiant with the confirmation of superior intelligence.

"Soph?"

"Yes, Hawk?"

"If I were you, I wouldn't go around braggin' about being smarter than me."

"Pa Hin Sa, you are riding a trail
that will lead to your death."

C H A P T E R   E I G H T

STEVE CAME AND TOOK OVER the night watch. Sophie and I went back to our shelter and my wish came true.

Morning came and we crawled out of our robes and got ready for another monotonous day of riding. We had our breakfast of dried beef, biscuits and coffee. The camps were loaded onto the pack horses and we were ready to ride.

We suddenly heard a husky female voice shout, "ATTANnnnn—SHUT!"

Sophie stood next to Posey and said, "Well? You guys made her the Sergeant—snap to."

We looked at each other, snapped to attention, and saluted our Sergeant. Wambolt shook his head slowly and mumbled, "Ah, fer crise sake, I'm traveling with a bunch of children."

Sophie whispered something in Posey's ear.

Posey commanded, "MONT UP!"

At once, we mounted our horses and awaited the command to move out, but it didn't come.

"We didn't get to the next command," Sophie said. "Let's go."

I looked at Sunkist. "This could be a problem."

"You won't catch me arguing with her."

We rode off.

"Hey, Soph," Jake said, "did you teach her that?"

"Yeah, along with the other women."

Torgerson, Steve and White Feather rode out ahead. The Indian's long, thin legs hung down each side of the mule he was riding and his feet nearly dragged on the ground. His feet were becoming coated with the dust that rolled up from the grass. Mike and his girl held hands for most of the day. We rode without talking, hearing only the sound of hooves and the rattle of the wagon behind us.

In the distance, mounted Indians appeared and disappeared. They stayed far enough out so they weren't anything to be concerned about, but we knew we were being watched—we hoped by Indians from the friendly camps.

White Feather stopped us and pointed at a mounted Indian on top of a hill a quarter-mile away. Another Indian stood on the hill on the opposite side of the shallow valley between. Silhouetted against the blue sky, each wore a full head-dress of eagle feathers with a tail that hung off the side of the horse nearly to the ground. They wore nothing but the headdress, loincloth, and moccasins. Each of them held a colored cloth over his head that waved in the wind.

The white horses had no saddle, just a blanket, and a rope tied to the lower jaw for reins. Black circles had been painted on their shoulders and handprints on their rumps. Yellow lightning streaks were painted on the necks of both horses and feathers were tied in their manes and tails.

Simultaneously, the horses reared, dropped to the ground, and galloped off the top of the hill toward the bottom of the valley. The Indians leaned forward into the wind as they rode at full-gallop across the front of us, leaving clouds of light dust swirling behind them. They reached the bottom at the same time and passed each other as they splashed through a small stream. As they passed, they each dropped a cloth. The cloth swirled in the wind, then fluttered to the ground. They galloped up the hills and vanished as quickly as they had appeared.

"Steve! Mike!" Wambolt hollered, "Come with me!" He quickly turned his horse and galloped to the rear.

White Feather rode back to us and said, "We stay together now. Many Indians close. Maybe not all friendly."

"Let me tell you kids something," Wambolt said as he rode back to the group. "We all could have been killed back there. That impressive little display you saw there could have been a diversion. While you were all watching the show, we could have been attacked from the rear."

"Things getting exciting, Hawk?" Sophie asked.

"I'm feeling better right along, having the sergeant with us. You got fresh powder in your pan?"

"All ready to go," she said.

Torgerson rode in and said, "Party of Indians just over the hill."

"Form a line across the front," Wambolt said in a loud voice. "Sully, you stay back with the wagon and mules."

Sully smiled and shouted to Wambolt, "Riding behind these horses makes me think I'm looking at a couple of politicians." Then he laughed at his own joke.

Wambolt looked at him and shook his head slowly, "How long did it take you to come up with that one?"

We lined up side-by-side and rode up the hill. Atop the hill was a formation of mounted Indians facing us. One of them raised his hand as a sign of peaceful intentions. I rode out a few feet and halted with hand raised, palm forward. One of the Indians rode out at a walk to meet me.

Jake rode up next to me, "I'm going out there with you."

"Good, I can use the support right now."

"You boys be careful," Sunkist said. "If ye see anything that looks like an ambush, shoot first and ask questions after—and keep them dragoons handy."

We walked our horses out to meet the Indian. One more of their rank came out when they saw two of us coming. He wore only a breach clout and moccasins and a red headband with three eagle feathers standing from the back of his head. His long, black hair hung in tight braids down the front of his chest, almost to his waist. Across his lap he held an old double-barreled shotgun.

We covered the hundred yards between us in what seemed to be no time at all. Jake walked his horse past me to face the Indians. I started to stop him, thinking he might do something foolish, but he rode to the lead man and put out his hand.

"It is good to see you, Wabasha," he said.

Wabasha took Jake's hand and said, "It is good to see you are not killed, Jacob."

I rode up. "You two know each other?"

"Wabasha, this is my brother, Hawk. Hawk, meet Chief Wabasha."

I took his hand. "I have heard many good things about you, Wabasha. It is good to finally meet you."

He wore a dirty, light colored shirt buttoned to his neck, a black wool coat over that, and a blanket wrapped around his waist and draped over his left arm. He had on heavy wool trousers with ties around the legs just below the knees, and beaded moccasins on his feet. His hair had been cut short and just covered his ears. Across his lap he held a bow and three arrows.

His mouth was tight and turned down slightly at the corners. The angry look on his face made it hard to look into his eyes. His eyes were just narrow slits and held mine as he talked.

"If you have heard of me, then you have heard many bad things, too."

"I do not listen to the bad things people say about each other."

"Wabasha does not listen to *anything* a man says about another man," the Chief said. "We cannot know what is in a man's heart if we only hear his words.

Only when we see him do bad things can we know he is bad."

Jake looked at me with a slight grin on his face. "This ain't no ordinary man," he said. "He's smarter than both of us."

"You are looking for Little Crow?" Wabasha asked.

"Yes, but we are not looking for war. We only want to bring a friend home to her people."

"Little Crow left Tatanka Najin's camp two days ago. He is going north to Dakota country to Mini Wakan."

Realizing my ignorance of Indian names, Jake leaned toward me and said, "Standing Buffalo."

"I knew that—and the other word?"

"Mini Wakan—it means 'Spirit Lake'. White men call it 'Devil's Lake'."

I turned to Wabasha and asked, "Did he have white captives with him?"

"Yes."

"Women?"

"He has white women and Indian women. There is one who belongs to Wamonousa. She is mixed-blood. She is the one you are looking for. Wamonousa is a bad Indian. He would kill the woman before letting you take her."

"Do you know this Wamonousa?" I asked Jake.

"I've never met him, but I know *about* him. The name means 'The Thief'. They call him The Thief for reasons that should be obvious to most men."

"Is he with Little Crow?" I asked Wabasha.

"They broke away from Little Crow and went west to the plains. He will not stay there long. He goes there because he knows Sibley will not follow. Then he will go to the Missouri country for the winter. He cannot live on the plains in winter."

"Why are you not with him?"

"Little Crow has brought much trouble to the Indians. He came to Tatanka Najin's camp and demanded they join him. Tatanka Najin put his warriors before him. Little Crow was afraid to do battle. He burned some of their tepees, but he was afraid to kill any of their people."

"Why didn't he just kill him then and there?"

"Tatanka Najin does not want war with Little Crow, or with the white man. Wabasha does not want war. We wish to live in peace with all people."

"Were those your men we saw ride across in front of us?"

"Yes, they are my men. You have nothing to fear from them. We left presents for your women."

"What presents?"

"They left the colored cloth for them. We give back what some of my warriors took from the white women."

"Is that all they took?"

"You could not carry all that they took."

"Are you taking your people to Dakota?"

"I will go with my people to Sibley's camp and surrender. Sibley has promised he will not hang good men. We are good men and we will not be hanged."

"Did you fight in the war, Wabasha?"

"I was at Fort Ridgely and New Ulm. I was at the battle at Birch Coulee and Wood Lake. I was there because Little Crow would kill those who did not fight. I did not shoot any white men."

"Then you will not be hanged."

"If I am to be hanged, then I will go and be hanged. I do not fear the white man's rope. Many of my friends have gone to the Spirit World. It will be good to see them again."

"We will go now," I said. "Thank you for your help, Wabasha."

Without another word, the Indians reined their horses and went back to their people at a cantor and we rode back to ours.

"Well? Wha'd he say?" Sunkist asked.

"Lorraine's not with Little Crow. She's with a man called The Thief, heading out onto the plains."

"What about Little Crow?"

"He's going to Devil's Lake in Dakota country. Looks like he wants to get some of the other tribes to join him in his war."

"Well, let's go find 'im," Sunkist said. "Maybe he can tell us where The Thief went."

We turned our horses north and talked as we rode.

"That's gonna be damn dangerous, chasing Little Crow," Jake said. "He ain't peaceful like them guys are."

"Jake," Wambolt said, "we're not going to worry about what's dangerous and what's not. We've got a mission to complete and we'll ride straight into hell if we have to."

"Hell jiss might be where we'll find The Thief," Sunkist said.

"Well, we could tramp across Dakota and hope we run into The Thief, but by the time we find him we'll all be too old to do anything about it. We're out to find Lorraine and bring her back—young."

"Wabasha says The Thief will go to the Missouri for the winter. We might be able to find him there," I said.

"That's a bad place to chase Indians," Wambolt said. "They know the terrain and we don't—we'd be setting ourselves up for an ambush."

"If we're going to find Lorraine we're gonna have to take that chance," I said. "I say we try to find him on the prairie before he reaches the Missouri."

At the bottom of the valley they found the cloth left by the Indians. Eve stopped and leaned off the side of her horse to pull a dark blue scarf from a willow shoot next to the creek. The other cloth had fallen into the creek and caught on a twig, which kept it from drifting away. She climbed down from her horse and fished it out with a stick. She held the blue scarf up to the light and pulled the delicate material through her fingers. She looked up at Sophie.

"This is fine silk from the orient," she said with a smile. She draped the dry scarf over her saddle horn and handed the wet one up to Sophie on the end of the stick. "Here's one for you."

"It's beautiful, Eve, but you keep it," Sophie said.

"Best ye take it, Soph," Sunkist said. "It'd be an insult to Wabasha if you refused it."

We stayed the night in a hollow on top of a ridge that overlooked the prairie. Morning came and after breakfast we were ready to leave.

"ATTAN—SHUT!"

"Oh, yeah, forgot about that," I said, and snapped to attention.

"MONT UP!"

We mounted our horses.

"MOOOVE OTT!"

Jake cocked his head my way and said softly, "She's getting a little too good at that."

We moved out in single file with Torgerson, Steve and White Feather riding point.

"Hawk," Sophie said, "What's Torgerson's first name?"

"I don't know. Ask him."

Sophie rode ahead to Torgerson. They talked a while before she came back.

"His name is Matthew. He's married. His wife is back in Ottertail County."

"Married? What's he doing here?"

"He joined the civilian scouts so he wouldn't have to go fight in the south. He doesn't consider that war any of his concern."

"That's how I feel about it—none of my business. So, he's married, huh? I guess that explains why he slept alone that night."

Jake rode up next to us and said, "White Feather says he's seeing Indian sign—might be hostiles around so we should keep our eyes open."

"It's going to be dark soon," I said. "What say we find us a camp?"

We found a spot on top of a small hill where we were not likely to be surprised. Wambolt and the scouts gathered in a circle away from us. Posey began digging a small hole in the rocky ground.

"What's she digging?" I asked Sunkist.

"A hole."

"I can see that, but what's it for?"

"Fire," Posey said.

Sunkist and I looked at each other, surprised to hear Posey speaking English.

"WHAT?" we said together.

"Fire for cook."

Sunkist looked at her and said, "Where'd you learn that?"

She looked up at Sophie and Eve who were grinning at us.

"She decided she wanted to learn some English," Sophie said.

"And she is having fun doing it," Eve said. "She's quite intelligent."

"How'd you get her to speak English?" Sunkist asked. "She said she'd never do that."

"She wants to learn English so she can talk with the women," Sophie said. "She said her mother was wrong about all white men being evil."

"Jiss don't make a white woman out of her, okay?"

"Don't worry, she's making Indian women out of us."

I went to Sunkist and said, "We can't have a fire tonight."

"Sure we can. At least long enough to have a hot meal. She's diggin' it into the ground so's it don't show up when it gits dark. She'll keep it smolderin' through the night and we'll have fire in the mornin', too. B'sides," he said, "them Injuns know where we are and ever' move we make."

"What is that she's using for the fire?" Eve asked.

"Touchwood. It's the fungus that grows on the side of trees. Mostly popple and birch," Sunkist said. "It looks like a horse hoof stuck to the side of the tree. Some call it horseshoe fungus."

"Oh, I've seen that," Eve said. "We carved Christmas decorations with it when I was a girl."

"It makes a better fire than a decoration," Sunkist answered. "Once it's lit on one corner, a piece the size of yer hand will smolder all night. Posey keeps a leather bag of it tied to her saddle. When it's rainin' she keeps a small piece smolderin' in a buff'ler horn ready to build a fire."

"That simple, huh?"

"Yep. Nothin' to it. She keeps a mouse nest or bird nest in the bag with the horse hoof stuff. She takes some of that and lays it on the glowin' spot then blows on it till she's got a fire goin'."

"A thin sheet of birch bark works good to get the fire goin' too, Sunkist," I said.

"Hail, I know that. I was jiss gittin' to that."

"Do you know about this stuff, Jacob?" Eve asked.

"Yeah, my Uncle Robert did that. No smoke, no flame. I got a bunch of it in my saddlebag. In cold weather Uncle Robert used to dig a small hole in the ground and throw a few pieces in the bottom and get it smoldering. Then he'd sit close to the heat with a blanket wrapped around him and the hole and it would keep him warm all night."

"Very interesting," Eve said.

"Ye can turn it into charcoal, too," Sunkist added. "Ye bury it under the campfire and when ye dig it out it's black like burnt wood. Strike a spark to it with yer flint and steel and ye got yer fire goin'."

"It ain't that easy getting it to take a spark, Sunkist," Jake said.

"It is if ye know what the hell yer a-doin'."

"I can start a fire quicker'n you."

"Like hail you can."

"Gimme some of that charcoal—I'll show ye."

Sophie stepped up to Eve. "Eve, if you ask these guys about anything that has to do with survival you're probably going to start an argument."

"I can see that. I'll try to contain my curiosity."

Jake and Sunkist nearly wore out their flint and steel, scratching it over their bits of charcoal, trying to get it to burn. Posey took Sunkist's flint and steel, struck a spark and had the charcoal going in less than a minute.

"See? I tole you I could git it goin' quicker'n you," Sunkist said with a grin.

"You didn't get it goin', Posey did."

"It's my charcoal—don't make no difference if I had her do it. I wanted it burnin' and I got it goin' with my best fire starter."

"You cheated."

"Did not."

"Did too."

"Have you ever noticed that the wind always blows right at us?"
"Yeah, sometimes I wish it would blow at someone else for a change."

CHAPTER NINE

IN THE MORNING, after the now-expected commands from our sergeant, we were riding north. We followed a trail that went around two lakes and across a river. The hills became smaller and we were forced to travel over exposed ground more than I liked, but we saw no Indians. In the distance we could see the line of trees that told me we were close to the valley. We traveled until sundown and set our camp in the shallow valley of a small stream.

"In the morning we turn and follow the valley north," I said.

"We are in Indian country and must be very careful," White Feather said. "There will be bad Indians around and they know we are here."

"Have you seen sign, White Feather?"

He pointed toward the tree line at a column of smoke rising through the trees about three miles away.

"Best keep the fire low, Posey," I said.

Posey looked at Sophie. Sophie said something to her in Cherokee and Posey looked at me and nodded her head.

"You speak Cherokee already?" I asked Sophie.

"Enough to keep you guys guessing."

"You do that good enough in English."

Sunkist sat up suddenly and sniffed the air. White Feather stood and squinted his eyes to the east.

"What is it?" I asked.

"Dunno. The horses are gittin' skittish. Look at their ears—all turned east. Something's makin' 'em nervous."

Posey sat up and pointed at a bull elk walking through the trees.

"The horses will sense anything that moves long before we do—good to keep an eye on 'em."

Suddenly, a shot rang out. The elk stumbled and fell, got up and ran down the bluff and out of sight.

"Damn, someone shot the elk—someone close."

The three roughnecks, Steve, White Feather, and Torgerson had their rifles out and stared in the direction of the elk.

"Someone down there guttin' out an elk, I'll bet," Steve said.

"Yeah, well, we'll just leave him be. We got all the meat we need."

"I'm curious about who it might be. If he's white we might get some valuable information from him."

"Yeah," said Wambolt, "and if he's Injun he might get some valuable information about us—like what color hair we got."

"I say we leave well enough alone and just stay here and keep a watch," I said.

We kept watch through the night and in the morning we saddled up and headed north following the tree line. Two days' ride brought us to a small settlement in a low valley. We rode down the bluff and across a frozen swamp to the town. No one was out and it seemed like the town was deserted. We passed a few scattered buildings, a stable, and a blacksmith shop, then went straight to the trader's store.

"Where are we?" I asked the man behind the counter.

"Folks are calling it Brown's Valley—named it for Yoseph Brown," he said, with a strong Scandinavian accent.

It took me three steps to walk across the floor to the counter. Along the walls were shelves covered with more junk than I had ever seen in one building. To the right, a stack of broken feed sacks lay spilled and molding on the floor. Mouse droppings were as numerous as the grains of wheat. In front of the counter was firewood, split and tied in small bundles with twine. The building smelled like yesterday's coffee, tobacco, mold and rotted grain. Behind the counter was a doorway covered with a dirty sheet.

The storekeeper was clean-shaven, short, and fat. He wore dark blue striped wool trousers with wide suspenders that spread around his belly, a plaid shirt, and a well-seasoned bowler on his head. He had no chin and it was a straight line from the tip of his nose to his Adam's apple.

"I knew Brown," I said. "Good man."

"He's da von who started dis store back in tirty-eight. I youst vork for him while he's out scouting for Sipley's army." He reached over the counter and put out his hand. "Lloyd Erickson, here, and who might yew be?"

"Hawk Owen." I stuck out my hand.

"You boys youst passin' trew, den, or are yew planning on staying for a vhile?"

"We're making our way to Devil's Lake. How far do we have to go?"

"Youst a coupl'a veeks if da Indyuns don't get yew."

"That's a chance we'll have to take. You haven't had Indian troubles?"

"No, day stay avay from here. Diss iss Joe Brown's store—he vos gyud to da Indyuns."

"Not the Joe Brown I knew."

"Dat vos before da trouble started. He did a lot for da Indyuns. Dat man, Galbraith iss da von hew caused all da trouble—him and his crooket traders at da agencies."

"Seems to me it was the way all the white people treated the Indians."

"Vell, dat could be tew, but if Galbraith would'a giff them vhat day needed tew feed dare wives and kiddies, they wouldn't heff had tew go on da vorpat in da first place. Now, mister... Vot did yew say your name vos?"

"Hawk."

"Oh, ya, Hawk. Vie don't yew youst stay here for a coupl'a days. Vee got a coupl'a empty houses and gyud feed for da horses. Be gyud to have some comp'ny for a shange."

"Vee, I mean we, just might take you up on that," I said. "Is there a bathtub around here we could use?"

"Ya sure, yew betcha. Right in da back uff da store," he indicated with his finger over his left shoulder. "Da missus keeps vater hot for da men hew come in. Dey pay five cents for a batt. Dat okay vit yew, den?"

"Cheap at twice the price."

"Enny ting else yew need I got right here in da store. And, don't ye know, da missus puts up a fine hot dish if yew get hongry."

"That's gonna be hard to turn down. I'll get the boys and girls and we'll be back."

"Gyuude—vee vill be glad tew heff yew."

"Mister Erickson, you have a wife?"

"Ya, she iss a gyud voman. She iss out getting da firevood."

"I see."

I walked out the door and passed a man coming in. His face was covered with blood and his eyebrow was split open. Sunkist stood on the ground looking into the store and chewing on a strip of buffalo jerky.

"Said the bad word, huh?" I said as I passed him.

"Twice."

"Got a proposition for you, boys and girls," I said. "Mister Erickson has invited us to stay for a few days. Sleep in cabins, eat home-cooked food, and take a bath—what d'ya say?"

Eve spoke up first, "Stay."

"I say we move on," Wambolt said, "this place is a reg'lar target for hostile Injuns."

"Wambolt, if the Indians were going to attack this place they would have done it a long time ago. Besides, they got better taste than to take anything from *this* place."

Sophie whispered in Posey's ear.

"STAY!" Posey said.

The other women said, "Stay!" in unison.

"Looks like we're out-voted," I said.

"Well, I was gonna vote against staying," Mike said, "but I guess they knew that and voted against me."

Jake said, "Someone mentioned that a bath would be to my betterment, so I guess we'd better stay."

"Thanks, Jake," Eve said, patting him on the shoulder.

We all walked into the store and told Lloyd we'd be staying for a few days. Sophie carried her bag in with her.

"Come vit me," Lloyd said. "I'll take yew tew your cabin."

"Wait a minute," Steve said. "You got tobacco?"

"Ya sure, yew betcha."

"Got any chewing tobacco?"

"Ya sure, right over dare. Vee heff da plug or da bag."

Steve looked around and said, "Yer gonna have to find it for me. I doubt if I could find a hay wagon in that mess."

"I'll take some smokin' stuff," Jake said.

"Jake, you gave your pipe to White Feather."

"I've got three more—makes for good relations with the Indians."

We followed Lloyd out the door.

"You comin', Soph?"

"Go on ahead, I'll catch up."

Lloyd took us to three dirt-floored cabins. The doors were on the east side of the cabins, facing away from the wind. Poles were propped against the side of the buildings to keep the wind from blowing them over. Inside, was a bed, a chair, a small wood stove, and a lantern on a small table. On each end of the cabin was a small window.

I went to light the lantern and Lloyd said, "Da lanterns are dry, but I heff oil in da store."

"Yew heff da vood in da store tew, right?" Jake said.

"Ya sure, yew betcha. All shplit and bondled up for yew. Ten cents for a bondle."

"I think I'm seeing a pattern here," Jake said, "and I think I know why these cabins are empty."

"Mister Erickson, how much for the cabins?" I asked.

"Tew bits for da night. Dat okay vit yew den?"

"The women will go on the warpath if we leave now," I said, "so we'll pay for one night."

"Yew are velcome to stay as long as yew like."

"I'm sure we are. We'll be leaving in the morning."

The cabins were constructed of scrap lumber nailed to upright poles set in the ground. The slabs were round on one side and flat on the other. They didn't fit together too well and the cracks between them were filled with gray clay from the riverbanks. The roof was also made of scrap wood with sod laid over that.

Steve looked at the cabins and said, "I ain't payin' two bits to sleep in them things. The wind is liable to blow it over on top of me."

"I'll sleep in the barn for one night," Torgerson said, "looks to be warmer, anyhow."

The barn was cut into the side of the hill. It had a sod roof and log walls covering the front. The door was too low to walk through without bending over at the waist. It did look cozy, though.

Sunkist said, "We'd rather stay under the stars. Cain't see what's around you in them little shacks."

Jake and Eve took one cabin, Mike and Butterfly chose another, and Sophie and I took the third. I unloaded the animals and put them in the barn after paying Mister Erickson twenty-five cents each for hay and a handful of oats. Sophie was gone longer than I thought she should be. I built a fire in the stove with the wood I'd paid ten cents for and laid on the bed waiting for her. A sweet aroma filled the room when she walked in.

"Where have you been?" I asked.

"Got me a bath."

"I can tell."

She sat down next to me and waved her hair in front of my nose.

"Mmm," I closed my eyes as I started to pull her towards me.

"Your turn," she said as she bounced up off the bed.

"Right now?" I said, waking out of my dream state.

"I already paid for it—you should get over there while the water's warm."

I slid off the bed and headed for the door. I turned and asked, "How much?"

"Hawk, it's only five cents. I think we can afford that."

"And did you get soap?"

"Yes."

"How much?"

"As much as you need."

"How much did it cost?"

"Hawk, it's all paid for. Don't worry about it."

"How much for the soap?"

"Ten cents. But it's worth it. Just go and get your bath. I'll be waiting for you."

She looked up at me as she reclined on her side, moving her hand back and forth on the bed. That look was one of the most persuasive tools she had and she used it very effectively.

I went to get my bath.

I walked in and said, "I'm here for the bath Sophie paid for."

"Vell, you'll youst heff to vait, dare's someone in dare right now."

"Sophie paid for that bath. That was supposed to be for me."

"Vell Horst Yorgenson saw her coming out and he said he needed a batt right now. He's da stable vorker, don't ya know. He said he didn't even heff time for me to shange da vater. He vos in a hurry."

"The stable worker in a hurry to take a bath?"

"I don't ask nobody no qvestions," he said throwing his arms in the air and turning to go behind the counter, "I youst give dem vhat day vant."

"Well, I'll just stay right here and vait—I mean wait—for him to come out and for you to CHANGE THE VADER—water!"

"Heff it your vay, I don't care."

I sat on a flour barrel and waited for Horst to come out. The curtain flew open and Horst came out with a sheepish look on his face. He wore the same clothes he must have had on when he went in and didn't smell any better when he walked by me.

"Mister Erickson, how about you give me a pot and I'll take it back to the cabin and heat the water myself. I can take my bath there."

"Ya, I can do dat. Da pot will cost yew ten cents, dough."

"I don't want to buy it, I just want to borrow it."

"Oh no, it's not for sale, it belongs tew da missus. Ten cents to borrow it, tew."

"Gimme the damn pot."

He handed me a small tea kettle like my mother used back home. "Mister Erickson, this ain't big enough to heat bath water in. Gimme somethin' bigger."

"Dat vill cost more."

"LIKE HELL IT WILL!" I shouted at him. I slammed my hand on the counter to get his attention. "You got paid for the bath I didn't get and you're gonna give me a pot big enough for a bath. FREE! Got it?"

"Dare's no need to get opset, you can heff da pot for free." He threw his hands out again and said, "a man hess tew make a living somehow, don't ye know."

"Yeah, well, you can make a living without peeling the hide off a man, don't ye know!"

"I don't like dat kind of talk in my store, mister. Now yew youst take da pot and leave now or by gud I'll trow yew out my self. And bring it back ess soon ess yer done viddit."

I turned for the door and kicked it open.

"Det vill cost yew fiff-tycents if you broke my door," he shouted after me.

I muttered various obscenities as I walked away.

I went to the cabin and opened the door. Sophie was sitting on her heels on the bed wearing one of my shirts.

She looked up as I walked in and said, "Well, did you enjoy—" She waved her hand back and forth across her face. "Hawk, you didn't take a bath."

"That cheap bastard is damn lucky I didn't drown him in his own bathtub."

"What happened?"

"When I got there he had the damn stable worker in the tub. He said the man saw you come out and decided he needed a batt—bath, right now, and didn't want the water changed. There's something wrong with that man, Soph."

Sophie smiled, "You can still get your bath if you want."

"I ain't gettin' in the same tub he was in."

"You can take your bath right here—I'd be glad to help."

"This time I'm gonna take you up on that."

Sophie put water on the stove and built up the fire. She poured the water in a pan and told me to lie on the bed. We used up three pots of water taking my bath.

After the bath we got all sweaty again.

"Damn, I'm glad I brought you along," I said.

"You're supposed to let me ask before answering."

"Okay, ask."

"Ain't cha glad you brought me along?"

"Yeah, sometimes."

The next morning, we awoke to someone knocking on the door.

"Hello, in dare! It's time to get out uff da cabin. If yer not out in half a hour it vill cost you for anodder night."

I jumped out of bed and wrestled into my trousers and stomped to the door. I flung it open and grabbed Mister Erickson by the coat, "You get the hell away from here! We'll leave when we're damn good and ready."

He turned around and hollered, "Dat vill cost you for anodder night. Yew are not velcome to stay here inny MORE!"

"Such a hothead," Sophie said, smiling.

"Well, how much of that bullshit is a man supposed to take?"

"Why don't you come over here and let's get your mind on more… pleasant things?"

One knee went up onto the edge of the bed before I had time to think. Sophie wrapped her arms around me, threw me on my back and straddled me.

"Now, you don't really want to leave, do you?"

"Nope."

She laid her body flat on mine and wrapped her arms around my neck. We rolled over and over, side to side, and turned in all directions making love on the straw mattress.

Suddenly, the moment was broken by the sound of a loud crack as the side of the bed dropped and we rolled off the bed onto the floor. Sophie looked at me for a second, then we started laughing. We laughed so hard tears ran from our eyes.

An hour later, we heard another knock on the door.

"Oh, no. Not again."

"You guys up in there?" Jake hollered through the door.

"Yeah, I'm up."

"Allow me to rephrase that question—you guys out of bed?"

"We're coming. Don't wait—we'll catch up."

"Well when you're finished, please join us. We're leaving."

"You ready?" I asked.

"Ready when you are."

We got out of the broken bed, out the door, and mounted our horses.

Mister Erickson was standing by his store. "You owe me for anodder night in da cabin, mister!"

"Wait here," I said.

I turned The Brute towards the cabin and kicked him to a run. Erickson ran into the store and slammed the door behind him. I turned the horse around and went back to Sophie. From inside the store we could hear a woman's voice yelling at Mister Erickson.

"What would you have done if he hadn't run?"

"Hell, I don't know."

Our bunch was only a half-mile ahead of us and it didn't take long to catch up with them.

"Got any money left, Hawk?" Jake asked.

"Not a lot. I ain't never seen such a skinflint. He even wanted to charge Sophie for heating the bath water."

"He warmed Posey's bath water," Sunkist said.

"For free?"

"Sure. He called her the bad name and she threw him in the tub."

"Well, that was an interesting stop," Eve said.

"Did you get your bath, Eve?" I asked.

"Of course I did. A bath is worth anything you have to pay for it."

"Soap, too?"

She reached in her bag and brought out three bars of bath soap.

"You swiped his soap?"

"The prices he wants for this stuff, I think he still owes me two bars."

"You got a good one there, Jake," I said.

"Yeah, I know. Let's just hope she doesn't make us use that soap."

"It certainly wouldn't hurt you, Jacob."

"The way we smell right now an Indian could smell us across this valley."

"You smell good, Jacob."

"Yeah, I know. That's the problem. Injuns ain't used to such sweet smellin' things. Anything that smells as sweet as we do is like ringing a bell in his nose."

"Well, Jacob, I'm quite sure you will do your best to remedy that situation."

She put the soap back in her pouch, pulled her hand out and said, "Jake— think quick!" She tossed him two bags of tobacco and six clay pipes wrapped in a cloth.

"You swiped his pipes, too?"

"I figure he owes us," she said. "I'd trade all those pipes you have there for one bar of scented Castile soap."

"I like this woman," Sophie said, with a chuckle.

The air was cold and the wind blew straight into our faces.

"Hawk," Sophie said.

"Yeah?"

"Have you ever noticed that the wind always blows right at us?"

"Yeah, sometimes I wish it would blow at someone else for a change."

About halfway through the morning, Sunkist stopped and shushed us. White Feather rode at a walk towards us with Torgerson and Steve right behind him.

"What's up?" Wambolt asked.

"Smellin' Injuns," Sunkist said.

Posey sat straight up in her saddle with her chin up, testing the air.

"Check your weapons," Wambolt said.

I put a fresh cap on my Hawken.

Sophie lifted the frizzen to check the pan of her flintlock.

"Move out," Wambolt said. "Keep yer eyeballs skinned."

We walked in a loose circle keeping a distance between us. No one spoke or made a sound until Sunkist stopped us.

"Don't make no sudden moves—but there's Injuns on that hill yonder," he indicated with his eyes. "Spread out. They're up to no good or they'da let us see 'em."

Suddenly, a cloud of smoke erupted from the hilltop followed by the report of the guns.

"CHARGE!" yelled Wambolt.

Instantly, we kicked our horses and rode hell-bent toward the smoke cloud— yelling and screaming as we rode, firing our guns, and loading on the run. The Indians on the hilltop stood up and looked our way, then turned and ran down the hill away from us. We stayed on their tail till they reached a small stream where they had their horses tied. They swung up and were gone onto the high prairie in four different directions.

"Well, that was exciting," Eve said, as she tried to calm her horse. "What made you all attack them at the same time?"

"Hell, I don't know," I said, "but it worked."

"That's the best way to handle a situation like that," Wambolt said. "They weren't expecting us to turn on them and they didn't have time to reload their guns. They figgered we'd git down and trade shots with them."

"I think they will consider more carefully next time they try to ambush us," Eve said.

"Next time there'll be a hunnert of 'em, not jiss five," Sunkist said.

"Bring 'em on," Steve said, as he swung the lever on his Henry.

"May we stop for a while?" Eve asked, "I need to wash up."

"Yeah," I said. "I think we could all use a rest."

I turned to look for Sophie and saw her kneeling on the ground where the Indians had been when they fired on us. "Soph, come on we're going back to the wagon."

"Hawk, come over here."

I walked The Brute to Sophie. There on the ground was a young warrior who had been wounded in the chest. We hadn't seen him at first because he lay in the grass, concealed from sight.

"He's wounded pretty bad, Hawk."

I climbed off my horse and stood over the Indian. He had frothy blood oozing from a hole in the side of his chest.

"He ain't gonna make it, Soph. Let's go."

"Hawk, this is just a boy. We can't just walk away and leave him here."

"Guess you're right."

I called to Posey to come over. She knelt next to the boy and opened his shirt. She looked up at Sophie and turned her head side-to-side.

"We want him to live," Sophie said.

Posey reached into her sidebag and pulled out a rawhide parfleche. Inside was about a half-dozen different containers of bark, herbs, mosses, and pounded roots. She took one out, unfolded it, and pulled out a mass of gray-green material. She got to her feet, turned her head to the sky, and raised the bundle in both hands. She turned to all four corners of the earth, to the sky, and to the ground. At each position she silently chanted a prayer, then took a small piece and threw it up into the wind.

She got to her knees and rolled the medicine into a tight ball and with one finger pushed it into the wound. Instantly, the bleeding stopped. Then she rolled the boy over and pushed a ball into the hole in his back, and the bleeding stopped. Then she laid a burdock leaf over the wound and closed his shirt.

Sophie took Posey's hand and they walked away.

"Sunkist," I said, "what's going on?"

"My boy, you have just witnessed somethin' I've seen only once in my life. I took a Sioux arrow in the lungs a couple'a years back and Posey done the same thing fer me. I should'a been dead, but her medicine kept me goin'. That ritual Posey did there warn't no medicine any white doctor knows about. Hail, he wouldn't have the nerve to try it, if he did."

"What were the medicines she used?" I asked.

"She used special medicines that the Cherokee use, and said prayers to the Cherokee Spirits to heal the boy. Now all we can do is walk away from here and know that this boy is gonna heal up and live to fight us agin. We cain't stay and wait for 'im to heal, we have to believe and trust that he will, and leave 'im here. Let's go."

I looked down at the wounded Indian, put two fingers to my lips, and raised the index finger of my right hand in front of my face—making the sign for 'brother'. He looked up at me and nodded as I turned and walked away.

There was no need to discuss the reasons for healing an enemy soldier. We all knew that he was doing what he was supposed to do—fight white men. He was no different than we were. His moral convictions were as strong as ours, but the demands of his society were different. We all knew that if it were the other way around and it had been one of us wounded, the Indians would not have helped. That doesn't make them wrong—it only shows the difference in cultures.

To die in battle is the ultimate glory for a Sioux warrior. To the white man, death—by whatever means it comes—is something to be feared. We fought a party of Indian soldiers and we would do it again. The enemy was the single body made up of individuals. Together they are the enemy. Individually, each was a man with every right to live, and for that matter, the right to die.

It was then that I became aware of the
forty-thousand hooves pounding the ground.

IO

CHAPTER TEN

EVE POURED WATER from her canteen and washed her hands and face.
"Don't you people ever wash?"

"Wash what?"

"Your hands, your face—well, your bodies." We looked back and forth at
each other and shrugged.

"Guess we never give it a thought," Sunkist said.

We all washed on a regular basis, but she didn't have to know that. We were
a little more private about it, is all.

"We got about half the day left, let's git goin'," Sunkist said.

We gathered up the mules and pack horses and moved out. Night came
quickly and we found a hilltop to make our camp. We heard a shout from somewhere in the distance and looked up to see White Feather facing east on his mule
with his arms raised and his bow in one hand. He was looking at six Indians on
horseback about a half-mile away. They raised their arms to the sky, discharged
their guns, and shouted something we could hardly hear. Then, they turned and
walked over the hill and out of sight.

"What was that all about?"

White Feather looked down at me and said, "They are the ones we fought.
They have the wounded one and they tell us they are our friends. They will not
fight us again. They emptied their guns in the air to show that they are friendly
and will not attack."

"Well, that's a relief."

When night fell, I crawled into the canvas shelter and laid down next to
Sophie. She rolled away from me and said, "Goodnight, Hawk."

"No kiss goodnight?" She rolled her head over and kissed me on the cheek and rolled away from me.

"You mad about something?"

"No, just tired."

"Okay, goodnight."

I woke up in the morning and found Posey at the fire as usual, putting breakfast together. Sophie was still sleeping, so I went in and woke her.

"You coming for breakfast?"

"I'll be there in a minute, Hawk."

"We're gonna be moving soon so you'd better git up."

She came out of the tent and walked slowly to the fire and poured a cup of coffee. The usual morning smile was missing from her face and it seemed an effort for her to say good morning. I handed her a biscuit and she took one small bite, then set it down.

I was worried about her—she wasn't looking like herself. I moved close to her.

"Are you all right, Soph?"

"Don't worry about me. I'm fine."

She smiled with her mouth, but it didn't show in her eyes. She was quiet as we climbed onto our horses and moved out. Posey rode with Sophie behind the rest of the pack.

I rode up to Sunkist, "Something's really bothering Sophie."

"I see that. Y'ever seen 'er git this way b'fore?"

"Well, yeah—but not this bad."

"Hawk, sometimes women get that way for no reason at all. They get all crazy and crabby. Best thing you can do is to jiss stay clear of her for a few days and wait it out. She'll get over it."

"Well, what makes 'em get that way?"

"Well, hail. I don't know how to tell ye," he said. "She'll get this way about once a month, so you might as well jiss git used to it—ain't nothin' you can do to stop it. Posey gits that way sometimes, too, but she stays away from me to keep from bitin' my head off."

"Posey gets it, too?"

"Hail yeah, all women do. Watch the moon, when it goes into a certain phase you can expect it to happen. When it looks like it's comin', jiss stay clear of her. Don't ask no questions—and fer sure, don't try to make her smile." Then he said in a quieter voice, "And don't apologize for nothin', either." Then he stopped his horse and turned in his saddle. He looked at me and said, "And for damn sure, don't expect no roll in the blankets. That jist AIN'T gonna happen." He chuckled as he said, "Might be their way of lettin' us git our strength back. When this is over you'd best eat lots of fat meat—yer gonna need it."

"How long does it last?"

"Maybe a week. Jiss be patient, she'll get over it."

We rode through the next day and set our camp on another hilltop. Mike and his Indian girl sat together and giggled and laughed. Sophie stayed with the women and the men stayed together. I felt like I did when Ma was mad at me for some dumb thing I did and sat me in the corner facing the wall for half the day. With all these people around I still felt alone.

Sophie came and stood behind me and rubbed my shoulders. It made me feel better even though she didn't say anything, but when she walked away I felt alone again.

Night came and I set up the shelter. I crawled into the robes and waited for her to come in. She slid in beside me with all her clothes on and went to sleep with her back to me. I didn't sleep much that night, and in the morning I got up and crawled out of the tent, leaving her there.

She came out and said good morning to everyone, then sat down to her breakfast. The air was cold and frost had formed on the grass.

White Feather came to us, pointed to the north and said, "Pony tracks".

"How many?" Sunkist asked. White Feather held up ten fingers.

"Half of you pull the loads in your guns and put fresh in," Wambolt said. "When they're done, the rest of you do the same."

We mounted up and rode north with White Feather, Steve, and Torgerson fifty yards in front. The women were in the rear with Wambolt behind them. The sun was barely up when ten Indians on horseback rode at full-gallop over the hill to our right. Their guns left a trail of smoke churning in their wake. They were a hundred yards away when they came up.

"Steady, men!" Wambolt shouted. "Wait till you have a good target!"

It didn't take long for them to get within range and five of them dropped from their horses. White Feather, Steve, and Torgerson came up as we began our counter-charge. We hit their ranks and ran our horses right through them. I fired my dragoon point blank at one and he flipped off his horse backward with smoke coming off his shirt. I ducked a war club as we ran through them for another twenty-five yards, then we turned for another attack. They did the same. By now all guns were empty except Steve's Henry and Jake's and my dragoons. Steve had his reins wrapped around the saddle horn and was shooting and jacking that lever-gun faster than all of us together could load and shoot. The Indians broke to our right and left and kept going.

Suddenly, Sophie kicked her horse and took off after them. She'd loaded her rifle and was aiming at the rear-most Indian. Her rifle went off and the Indian slumped forward. He stayed on his horse for another fifty yards, then toppled to the ground. We all kicked our horses and went after Sophie. Jake's horse and mine took the lead and caught Sophie at a dead-run trying to reload her rifle. I grabbed her reins and pulled her to a stop.

"Sophie, fer crise sake, stop this—yer gonna get yourself killed!"

"Hawk, why didn't you let me go? I had them on the run!"

"We all had them on the run before you took off after them. Now come back to the group, you can't wipe out the whole Sioux nation by yourself."

She jerked the reins to the side and rode away leaving me to watch her go. We rode at a gallop back to the group with Sophie in front. I followed without getting too close—I'd kept my scalp this long and was not ready to give it up to an irrational woman, no matter how I felt about her.

When we got back to the group I walked over to Sunkist.

"Sunkist, she's sick or something."

"Posey's takin' her away fer a while. She'll come back feelin' better."

"Where they going?"

"Jist off by themselves. Posey'll take good care of her, don't worry."

Steve, Mike, and Torgerson were out checking the bodies of the dead Indians and gathering up what powder and lead they had. The guns they carried were mostly old trade guns and double-barreled shotguns. They rammed the muzzles into the dirt and bent the barrels over so they couldn't be picked up and used against us again.

The next three days were pure hell, I kept turning in the saddle and looking behind me to see if the two women where there.

We stopped for the night. I was sitting on a fallen log with Sunkist when Mike's girl came, knelt in front of me and sat on her heels.

She looked up at me with liquid brown eyes, "Hawk, you miss Soapy?"

I didn't know she could speak English because she and Mike stayed away from the rest of us except when we were traveling.

"You speak English?" I asked.

"Yes, I speak little white man talk. Sultan teach."

Mike stood next to her, smiling. "I taught her all the words she needs to know," Mike said. He looked down at her, "Who am I?"

"You are Great Sultan of Plains," she replied.

"That's right, and don't you forget it."

"What's her name, Mike?"

"Her Sioux name is Kimi Mila. It means 'Butterfly'."

"She's a perdy little butterfly," I said. "How about we call her Butterfly?"

"We already do," Mike said.

"Hawk," Butterfly said, "you miss Soapy?"

"Yeah. Yeah, I do."

She looked up at Mike. Her eyes were big and black and turned up on the outside corners like a cat.

"Sultan, we go bring Soapy to Hawk?"

"Yes. We'll go bring Soapy to Hawk—but we don't know where they are," he said with appropriate but exaggerated gestures.

"I find Soapy," Butterfly said.

"You don't need to do that," I said, "she'll come back when she's ready."

"We'll go get her."

"I'm staying here," I said. "Two men out of camp is one too many."

They walked away, mounted their horses and left camp.

Just before sundown the next day, they came into camp. I led Sophie's horse to our camp and helped her down. We stood face-to-face and I looked into her eyes.

"Are you all right?"

"I'm fine, Hawk."

I put my hands behind her neck, under her hair, and pulled her to me, "I love you, Sophie."

She smiled and wrapped her arms around me. We kissed long and hard. The others turned and walked away.

Our shelter was a canvas stretched over a framework of poles, open on one side facing the rising moon. We had a buffalo robe to lay on and wool blankets for covers. I led her inside and we laid down on the bed. I pulled the robe up to our necks and wrapped my arms around her. I kissed her lightly on the lips and pressed my body tight against hers. I knew by the way she was pressing her body to mine that she wanted me as much as I wanted her.

Her lips were soft and warm, and sweeter than the candy in Mister Belleair's store. Her hair smelled like spring rain as I nuzzled my face into her neck and kissed her under her ear. She sat up and lifted her buckskin shirt and cotton undershirt over her head and lay down against me. My hands were shaking so hard I couldn't get my shirt off.

She laughed softly and helped me pull it over my head. When we were completely undressed, she laid back and a look of complete relaxation came over her face. She closed her eyes and stretched out on the buffalo robe. Her body moved slowly as her fingers and toes dug into the soft fur.

"Umm," she whispered, "this feels so soft and sensuous."

I loved the way she seemed to enjoy everything she experienced, like it was the first time. She wrapped her arms around me and rolled me over to lay herself on top of me. Then kneeling with one leg on each side of me, she sat up and smiled down at me and ran her fingernails over my chest, raising goose bumps on my skin.

Sophie's face was even more beautiful in the moonlight and her eyes glowed like the light from a lantern through blue glass marbles. She looked at me and smiled as I traced the outline of her breasts with the tips of my fingers. The soft blue light from the moon outlined her shape and I watched as her breasts responded to the cool air. I tried to tell her how I felt, but words just seemed to get in the way.

"Sophie, you are so—"

"Shhh." She gently touched my lips with her finger, leaned over, and kissed me. Without letting go, we explored each other with hands and mouths leaving no part untouched.

Then, finally, when our bodies had to answer to a need so desperate that only the other could satisfy, the world around us disappeared. Nothing physical existed. Nothing was important, not even our bodies. They served us only in a way that allowed two separate beings to share one single emotion.

The next thing I was aware of was the light playing on the insides of my eyelids and I opened them slowly as the image of Sophie took form.

"Good morning, sleepyhead."

"Mornin'—been up long?'

"No, and you?" She smirked as her gaze ran down my body. "Looks like we got ourselves some company."

My gaze met hers, "Yeah, and it ain't nice to keep company waitin'."

"In that case, Hawk Owen, I intend to show our company some real hospitality."

"HAWK! You awake?" Jake shouted from behind our tent.

I jumped at the sound and said, "Yeah, I'm up."

"Yeah, I'll bet you are. Git up, we gotta git going."

I looked at Sophie, "Later?"

SOPHIE'S HAWK

"Does a horse fly?"

I kissed her on the cheek and crawled out from under the robes. It was cold, and heavy frost lay on the ground. I'd brought our clothes in from the cold and laid them under our blankets next to me to keep them warm through the night.

"Better get dressed before you get up, Soph, it's cold."

Her muffled voice told me her face was still buried in the blankets, "I don't want to get up."

"Well, I'm not gonna argue about it. I did learn a few things this past week. Come out when you're ready."

"I'll be there in a minute."

"Everything all right in there, Hawk?" Jake asked.

"Couldn't be better, Jake."

"Posey's got biscuits and coffee goin'," Jake said. "We're headin' out as soon as everyone's ready."

Sophie came out of the tent and walked to the group. Her eyes closed as she raised her face to the wind and drew in a deep breath of fresh, cool air. She moved with smooth, easygoing steps and held her face to the sky while running her fingers through her hair. She bent down and kissed me on the cheek, then poured herself a cup of coffee.

"Gude mo'ning, Soapy," Posey said.

"Good morning, Posey."

Posey almost smiled.

"Let's git goin', boys and girls—time's a'wastin'," Sunkist said.

Though the morning was cold, I took my coat off to let the rising sun warm my back and Sophie did the same. It's a good thing The Brute had his eye on the road because my eyes were focused on the woman riding beside me. To look away from her required a deliberate effort, and anything that involved conscious thought was beyond the limits of my abilities at that point.

Jake had been teaching us to speak the Sioux language with Butterfly's help. We practiced as we rode and soon we could communicate fairly well. Sophie learned the Cherokee language while Posey learned English. Mike learned the Sioux language quickly from Butterfly and taught her the English words he wanted her to know. He neglected to tell her that some of the words he was teaching her were vulgar and repulsive, but they got along very well with that arrangement.

We also practiced Indian sign language, which was fairly easy because it's mostly gestures that everyone uses every day without knowing it. Indian sign was pretty much universal among the tribes because they had to use it to trade with other tribes and cultures.

"Sophie, how did you get that bruise on your leg?" I asked. She turned her horse and came around to the other side of me and lifted her shirttail to show a ragged hole in her pant leg.

"Is that a bullet hole? You got hit?"

"Just enough to rip my pants and burn the skin a little—and piss me off. It's nothing to worry about. Posey looked at it and said not to worry about it."

"Damn, Soph, I never even thought about you getting hit. I guess it was too scary to think about."

"I guess that's why I got so crazy when those Indians attacked us."

"From now on when we get in trouble you stay behind me, okay?"

"I'll not walk behind you, nor in front of you. I'll walk beside you. I read that somewhere—I like it."

I moved The Brute closer to her, put my hand behind her neck, pulled her close and kissed her.

In the north we saw a dust cloud rising over the hills. We turned our horses to a depression and got down to the ground to wait for them to get close enough to see.

White Feather rode up and said, "Many horses come."

"How many?"

"Many. Maybe one hundred."

"Damn, this could be trouble," Sunkist said.

Wambolt, always the soldier, said, "Check your loads and stay down."

As the column drew near we could see that they were not Indians, but Métis. They had two dozen carts pulled by small horses, oxen, and mules. The shrill squeal of the wheels made shivers run up and down my spine.

"Stay awake," Wambolt said. "All Métis are not friendly to whites. They've got troubles with the Canadian government and are not inclined to be friendly with white people."

I spoke up in their defense, "I knew some Métis and they were a hell of a lot more friendly than most white men I've met."

"Hawk, those people you knew were trading with the whites for survival— they had to be friendly. These people are wild as Injuns. Probably on a buffalo hunt."

"Let's give them their dues and not start anything."

"Just stay down and maybe they won't even see us."

"Hell, they already know we're here," Jake said. "They know where we are better than we do."

They rode closer at a walk. The squealing of their wheels got louder and more obnoxious as they came on. A man rode out with his hand held high.

"Looks like they want a parley," I said.

"Who's goin' out to talk?"

"I'll go," I said. "I've dealt with Métis before and they might know some of the people I knew."

"I'll go with you," Jake said.

We climbed onto our horses and made the fifty-yard ride to meet with the Métis.

A man walked his horse up to us. "You are Pa Hin Sa?"

"We are Pa Hin Sa."

"I am Patrick. These are my people. We are told you are looking for your friend, Lorraine."

"Word gets around fast out here."

"The Indians say when Pa Hin Sa moves—someone will die."

"We're not looking for war, we only want to find Lorraine and bring her home."

"Another is also looking for Lorraine. She has a brother called Bon Cheval who is out to kill the man who has her."

"The Thief?"

"You know of him?"

"I know *about* him," I replied.

"He is a bad man and very dangerous. You will have to kill him to take what is his."

"We'll do what we have to," I said. "Do you know where Bon Cheval is now?"

"He has gone west to the grass prairies," Patrick said. "That is where The Thief has gone. Winter will be hard on the plains—very cold, and a wind that does not stop. You would do well to find shelter and wait it out. Even now the sky tells us that winter is coming." He pointed to the west at a dark, gray sky that warned of snow. "We will camp in the valley west of here until this storm blows over. You are welcome to stay with us as long as you need."

The air had become colder as the day wore on. There was a sharpness to the cold that told us snow was coming and that we would have to find shelter soon.

"Thank you, my friend. We'll talk with the others and probably take you up on your offer. We have our own food and shelter so we won't be any bother to you."

"Our camp is open to you and you are welcome to what we have. Bon Cheval has told us you are good men and we welcome you."

Jake turned to me and asked, "You know this Bon Cheval?"

"He's Lorraine's brother. He traveled with us to Saint Paul last year."

"Hawk, I must tell you," Patrick said. "Jean Charbonneau, Henri, Bon Cheval and Joe Rolette came back to Saint Paul in the spring and on their way back to Pembina, Indians attacked them. Henri was killed and Jean Charbonneau was taken prisoner. He is with the Winnebago and is probably still alive."

"Yes, I know. I talked to him at Camp Release."

"Then he is still alive. That is good to hear."

"He's alive, but I don't know for how long. He's in pretty bad shape."

"We will say prayers for him," Patrick said.

"What about Rolette?"

"Joseph Rolette escaped and hasn't been seen. People say he is out hunting Indians—but he is too old and too fat to fight Indians. He will be killed."

"I doubt that. He may be old and fat, but that man has iron in his veins and he's too smart to get himself in too much trouble," I said. "We'll go now and talk later."

"Yes, follow our trail and come camp with us."

Jake and I rode back to our group.

"What the hell kind of a name is 'Patrick' for an Indian?" Jake asked.

"Métis are not all Indian. They're a mix of Indian and damn near every nationality that comes over from the old country. Most of them are French and Scottish, but the Irish did their share of bringing mixed-bloods into the world, too. My guess is Patrick is half Irish."

"Tell me about these people you know," Jake said.

"Bon Cheval means 'Good Horse'. He's French and Cree Indian. He was one of the riders who escorted our ox cart train from Elk River to Saint Paul. The man's an animal—he doesn't sleep, except on his horse, and eats damn near anything he can take a bite out of. I'm glad I'm not one of the Indians he's after. He can load that Lemans rifle of his four times a minute—and he don't miss."

"And Charbonneau?"

"The master of the train—middle-aged and tough as a keg of nails. He was a trapper and guide in the old fur trade days out west. Kinda like Sunkist. In fact, Sunkist reminds me of him—tough and world smart."

"Who's the other one?"

"Rolette? You don't want to know Rolette," I said. "He was some kind of politician before Minnesota became a state back in fifty-eight. His father's the one who cut the trails from Pembina to Saint Paul when the ox cart trains started moving trade goods between the two settlements. In fact, he blazed the trail we're on right now.

"He's a good man but his mouth never rests. He's always got to be talking. I like the guy, but I can take only so much of his talking. He rode dogsleds from Pembina to Saint Paul to sit in on the territorial government meetings. Sometimes he walked the entire six hundred miles on snowshoes and moccasins. When Minnesota became a state, Pembina became part of the Dakota Territory and Rolette couldn't be a representative anymore. He thinks they made it part of Dakota Territory just to get rid of him. That could be, I don't know, but Rolette's an honest man and they don't have much use for his kind in Saint Paul. The cold doesn't bother him. I saw him chop a hole in the ice once, and take a bath when it was twenty below. That's why I doubt if any Indian could take him out."

"Sounds like some people we should have with us," Jake said.

"Good Horse and Charbonneau, maybe, but Rolette would drive everyone nuts with his constant chatter. And the truth is, he probably *is* too old and fat to be much good in a close fight."

"Storm coming, Hawk," Sunkist said as we road into camp. "Best we find some shelter."

"Those Métis invited us to share their camp. I say we go for it."

"Can they be trusted?"

"They know all about us and why we're here, and they know some of the people I knew. I say we trust them and go to their camp."

Wambolt spoke up and said, "Those people are half-Indian and Indians can't be trusted."

"They're hunting their winter meat—not white men, Wambolt. They got their women with 'em and all the things for hunting buffalo. I think you're being too cautious."

"We'll go there, but I'm tellin' you now—I don't like it."

"I think we should go," Steve said. "Those Métis wimmin are damn perdy."

"Those women belong to the men," Sunkist said, "and they don't do sharin'."

"It don't hurt nothin' to look."

"Jist try to behave yerself."

We mounted our horses and rode out to find the Metis. We found them camped in a ravine and we set up our tents off to one side. The Metis men busied themselves cleaning guns and taking care of the livestock while the women set up the camp. Their shelters were small tepees set randomly around the grounds with a fire at each of them and one large fire in the center of the camp. A copper pot was hung on a tripod over the fire and a stew was set to boil.

One cart was turned topside-down with the wheels pulled off. A man stopped working on a new axle he was making and leaned over the upturned cart to watch us ride in. He nodded our way without showing any emotion but curiosity. We rode through the camp and found the people sitting or lying on the ground while one of the women from each family prepared the meal. We accepted the invitation from Patrick and his family to join them.

After the meal, several fires were built in front of the tents and small groups gathered for conversation and music. Fiddles and guitars came out and the singing began. Some old French songs were sung and some Irish sailing tunes—some bawdy saloon songs and even a few religious melodies. Women danced and whirled sending their long full dresses fanning out and wrapping around their legs as they stopped to turn the other way. Hands clapped the rhythm and laughter rang throughout the camp.

The wind picked up and light snow started to fall. The parties quieted to small talk and soon everyone went into their shelters carrying heated rocks for warmth.

It snowed through the night and when we crawled out of the tent there was a four-inch layer on the ground. The sky was overcast and the temperature had fallen. Our water cans had a layer of ice on top and the cold air bit into my freshly-shaven face. I kept a full mustache, I figured a little extra warmth wouldn't hurt.

"Well, looks like winter's here," Jake said.

"That's okay with me—makes for cozier sleeping conditions," Sophie said as she glanced over at me.

"Hail, you two never sleep enny way," Sunkist grumbled.

We stayed in that camp for two more days. Riders went out looking for buffalo sign while the rest of us enjoyed the company and warm meals.

One night, as we lay quietly in our tent, Sophie peeked out the door. "Hawk, look," she said, "the moon is beautiful."

"What phase is it in?"

"Half," she said as she turned toward me. "Why?"

"Just wondering."

I woke the next morning to sunshine coming through the canvas. Sophie was lying on her side with her head propped on one hand, looking at me.

"Have you been looking at me all night?"

"I'm waiting for an answer."

"Answer to what?"

"Why did you ask what phase the moon was in?"

"When it gets to three-quarters waning, I'm headin' fer the hills."

A rider came in at a gallop, *"La vache, la vache!"*

"La vache, la vache!" echoed through the camp and fifty men ran for their horses.

"What's going on?" I shouted.

One of the men running by said, *"La vache!* Buffalo! Get your horse and come with us, we will kill many buffalo for the winter!"

I'd never considered hunting buffalo from horseback but this seemed like a good time to try it. The few that I had killed were taken from the cover of thick brush and hollows in the ground.

"Soph, I'm going buffalo hunting. You stay with the women."

"Hawk," she said, as she ran for her horse. "If you think for one minute I'm gonna miss this, you're crazier than I thought!"

"I should'a known better," I muttered.

She was saddled and riding as fast as the rest of us. I wasn't sure what was going to happen next, so I kept the reins tight on The Brute so he wouldn't run past the Métis. We stopped and formed a line at the crest of a hill. Patrick looked around to see if everyone was ready. He held his rifle high and when all were set, he dropped his arm. Some of the men made the sign of the cross across their chests and we started off at a walk.

As soon as we crossed the top of the hill the buffalo spotted us and turned our way with their heads lowered. We moved towards them slowly until, as if one huge living thing, they turned and stampeded away from us. The men yelled and raised their rifles in the air and we were off at a hard gallop. We ran full-tilt over the snow, directly at the herd.

There must have been ten thousand buffalo in that herd. It didn't take long for the Métis to catch them. Then the shooting started. The Brute ran to the herd and took a position on the right shoulder of a cow. He stayed next to her as I lowered my Hawken and fired from about two feet distance. Her front legs buckled and she buried her muzzle in the snow, rolled end-over-end, then lay dead. I had an awful time reloading that rifle with The Brute running so hard and jumping small dips in the ground. His head was stretched out before him— he thought he was in another race and he loved it. The wind blew the powder away from my barrel, so I had to put the horn right on the muzzle and hope to get enough powder down the bore to make my next shot. The minie ball went down easily and I tamped it down on the powder. The Brute came next to another cow, I fired into her and she dropped like the first.

The excitement had me in a world all my own, until I suddenly realized Sophie was no longer with me. I looked around and saw her in the middle of the herd.

"Sophie!" I shouted. "Get to the outside of the herd, you'll get killed!"

It was then that I became aware of the thunder from the forty thousand hooves pounding the ground. My voice was completely drowned out by the roar. She couldn't hear me and stayed where she was. I turned The Brute into the herd and rode hard to get to her. She was leaning forward over the horse's neck with her feet in the stirrups extended outward, laughing and yelling. I waved my gun in the air to get her attention and pointed to the outside of the herd.

We ran with the herd and slowly made our way to the outside. Thick black horns came so close we could have reached out and touched them. The musty smell of buffalo mixed with dust and churned-up snow made it hard to breathe as we came to the edge of the herd and turned out onto open ground.

"I should've told you to stay at the edge of the herd, Soph," I said as we slowed to a cantor. "If your horse would'a stumbled, you both would'a have been trampled to death."

"You're right, I should have realized that."

"You mean I'm right for a change?"

"This time—but don't get use to it," she said with a grin.

"Where's your rifle?"

"I dropped it back there somewhere trying to get it loaded. I got a buffalo, though," she said. "I think I did, anyway."

The thunder of stampeding hooves disappeared over the hill a half-mile away. Dead and dying buffalo lay all around. Three wounded cows walked their last steps. One dropped to its knees and toppled sideways. A big bull stood a hundred yards from us, looking our way, scraping dirt and snow with his front hoof and tossing sod with his horns. His black, beady eyes glared with rage and blood poured from a hole in the side of his chest. We watched to see if he was going to charge.

"Let's walk around and see if I can get a side-on shot at him."

We walked our horses around to our right and the bull turned with us following us with his eyes. Bloody slobber ran from his nose and mouth and flew over his shaggy head when he shook. I knew that trying to drive a bullet through the front of that massive scull was useless.

"Walk your horse around to that side. I'll go to the other side and maybe I can get a shot at him."

He was fifty yards from us now and he turned as we walked our horses around to each side of him. First he watched me, then turned to watch Sophie. I had to get close because the bullet probably wouldn't have the power to take him down from that range. As we got closer, he began to get more violent with his snorting, bellowing and pawing at the dirt. He was looking at Sophie when I saw his rear end drop a bit.

"GET OUT OF THERE!" I shouted.

Sophie kicked her horse and took off away from the bull. He charged at her with surprising speed. I kicked The Brute and took off after him. The animal chased Sophie for a quick twenty-five yards, then stopped and turned towards me. Sophie made a wide turn and rode at a cantor back my direction. The bull turned side-to-side watching each of us as we moved around him. Suddenly, he took off after Sophie again. She was quick to kick her horse and easily pulled away from him. The buffalo stopped. She galloped around to get the bull between us, then stopped. She waved my way, then kicked her horse and ran directly at the buffalo. She made a circle around him about twenty yards away and the bull took off after her.

She ran her horse past me and hollered, "Take your best shot!"

I stood my ground until the bull was nearly on me. I fired a shot that hit him too high. He turned toward me and The Brute instinctively turned away and easily outran him.

Sophie was sitting high in her saddle and grinning as she came around and got close enough to get the animal's attention. He turned on her. Sophie's horse seemed to be having fun playing cat-and-mouse with the beast. She slowed her horse to lead the buffalo behind her. I turned The Brute and came up next to him and held close. By this time, the bull was running slower and having trouble keeping his feet under him. He stayed with Sophie and made turns toward me trying to hook The Brute with his horns, but The Brute was quick to turn with him and avoided the attacks. I thought about just breaking off the chase to let him go and die in his own time, but that could mean hours of suffering, so we stayed with him. I loaded the Hawken heavy with an extra load of powder and a minie ball, then leveled the muzzle to a point just behind his left ear and jerked the trigger. Dirt, dust, and smoke exploded from the thick hair on his great head and the buffalo's front feet went out from under him. He collapsed and slid on the snow for ten feet before coming to a stop. Smoke from my rifle rolled from the hair. He lay on his side kicking for a minute before finally settling into the deep sleep of death.

Sophie came back to me and we stood looking at the huge mass of buffalo lying there.

"What a magnificent animal," she said.

"Let's go finish those two off," I said. "They'll die soon, anyway."

We rode to the side of the cow. I put a minie behind her ear and she went down. I did the same for the other.

"Now what?" Sophie asked.

"Now we go looking for your rifle."

The trail left by the buffalo was a hundred yards wide and the ground was torn up like a sod plow had gone over it. It was obvious there was little or no chance of finding Sophie's gun. Over the hill we could see carts and people coming, so we walked our horses to meet them.

"Have any fun, Hawk?" one of the Metis asked.

"Haven't had that much excitement since Birch Coolie."

"Birch Coolie?"

"Never mind."

"You was at Birch Coolie?"

"I was there and don't care to talk about it." I said.

"Perdy bad, I hear."

I walked away, not wanting to remember the sixteen men who died and the thirteen who were wounded. That battle raged for thirty-six hours without food or water. The Indians kept up a steady fire so we were helpless to feed ourselves or get water for the wounded. All of our horses had been killed in the first two hours of fighting. I didn't want to remember the sounds of dying men and the words of grown men crying for their mothers—the screams of wounded horses, the terrible smell of death that will be forever in my mind, and the man who was so scared that he had to be threatened with death to make him stop crying, "Oh my God! Oh my God! Oh my God!" over and over.

I shook the memory from my mind and turned to Sophie, "They're here to cut up the meat and pack it for winter."

The hunters came over the hill on their way back to the camp, laughing and shouting, racing their horses, and raising hell as only the Métis can. The women unloaded the carts and began setting up camp on the spot. Fires were lit with racks made of saplings built over them to dry the meat. The meat was cut into thin strips and hung in the smoke.

I walked over to Steve, "How many'd you get, Steve?"

"Just a couple," he held up an old Springfield rifle. "This thing don't load too good on horseback."

"Where's your Henry?"

"I don't hunt with that. The cartridges are too precious. That thing is for tight situations when I need to shoot fast—like when those Injuns attacked us back there. I'm not sure it's powerful enough for buffalo, anyway."

"Ah, I see. I suppose we should go back and get our camps—we'll be needing 'em."

"Yer camps are here, Hawk," Patrick said. "The women brought them in."

"Well, that was nice of them."

"Your women—not ours."

"Oh. Well it was nice of them, too."

"Yes, it was."

Someone shouted from horseback, "Anyone lose a rifle?"

"Here!" Sophie shouted, and held her hand up.

He rode over and handed it to her. "Looks like there's been some improvements done on it. You can shoot around corners now."

I took the rifle—or what was left of it. It had no stock and no lock and the barrel was bent in two different directions.

"Hope you guys got a gunsmith with you." He laughed and rode away.

"Steve and Torgerson!" I shouted.

They came over, "Yeah?"

"Remember those Indians' guns you busted up back there? We won't be doing that anymore."

"We kept a couple of them. Fifty caliber cap locks, they are. We got their ammo, too."

I looked at Sophie, "There you go, you got yerself another gun."

"I'm sorry about your rifle, Hawk."

"You didn't get hurt—that's what counts."

"You have run buff' before, Hawk?" Patrick asked.

"Nope, that was the first time. I always killed them from cover."

"Well, that horse of yours has. He knows how to pick out the cows and stays right beside them till you shoot. Good horse you got there."

"The Brute's one of the best."

"Hawk," Sophie said, "why do you call your horse The Brute?"

"Because that's what he is—a brute. If you'd seen him beat me up when I was trying to break him, you'd know that."

After three days of watching the women dry meat, we got itchy feet and were ready to move on.

I walked over to Patrick to tell him we'd be moving out in the morning.

"Hawk, if I were you I would not try going out on the prairie until spring. It is a hard place and not many survive the winter there. Even the Indians go to better places."

"Where would that be?"

"Most of them hunt buffalo here on the prairie and move south to the Missouri. There is shelter there and wood for fires. In Dakota there is very little wood. It would be better for you go to the valley for the winter."

"We won't be going back till we find Lorraine," I said.

"Then stay in the hill country. Without shelter, the flats north of here will kill you in the winter."

"What about Indians?"

"Indians attacked Fort Abercrombie in September. They will not attack there again. That would be a good place for you to spend the winter. There are houses and supplies there. Most of the Indians have moved out of the country now and are not much of a problem in the winter. They have enough to do to keep themselves fed."

"Most of them? What about the rest?"

"Hawk, you are in Indian country. You will see Indians everywhere you look. Some of them are peaceful, but some are still fighting the war they started in August. Little Crow is moving up to Devil's Lake and he knows you are coming. He also knows you are not looking for war with him and that you only wish to find your friend. But I warn you, The Thief also knows you are coming and he knows you want his woman—he will not give her up alive."

"Thank you for telling me these things, Patrick, but we will go after her until we find her—dead or alive."

"She means a lot to you and your people."

"She does, and we will find her. How far is Abercrombie from here?"

"Four days' ride—three if you ride hard. But there will be no grass for your horses and no food for you unless you stay in the valley, but you will find Indians in the valley."

"I'll talk to my friends and decide what we'll do."

"Have a good voyage, my friend. We will say prayers for your safe journey."

"Prayers would be nice, but some of that buffalo meat would be good, too."

"Yes, of course. You helped get the meat and you are welcome to what you need."

"Thank you."

I went back to our people and told them we'd be moving to find a winter home in the morning.

"Now," I said, "we can go to the valley and rough it out for the winter, or we can go to Fort Abercrombie and stay in houses."

"How far is that?" Sophie asked.

"Three or four days' ride if the weather stays good."

"So close to a hot bath and a warm bed," Eve said.

"Yeah, I suspect we'd all enjoy that."

"If we go to the fort we'll have to stay in the valley and probably see Indians— friendly and not-so-friendly. If we stay on the flats our horses will be half-starved by the time we get there."

"I'm for roughing it in the valley," Steve said.

"Me, too," Mike said.

"Our horses are our main concern, right now," said Wambolt. "We have to think about them first. If they go under, we all go under. I say we take the valley."

"We can move up the valley all the way to the fort," I said. "It'll be tough going but we'll stay alive."

"What do you say, Torgerson?"

"It really doesn't matter what you guys decide. I'm just following along."

"Sunkist?"

"We'll be jist fine in the valley. Posey ain't much for fort life and I ain't neither. But we can make it wherever you decide."

"Okay, Sophie, how about the women?"

"You need to ask? They have hot baths and warm beds at the fort."

"So," I said, "we go to the valley and move north to Abercrombie. All agreed?"

"Let's git goin'," Sunkist said.

We packed our camps and Posey gave the order to "MONT UP!"

Just then, Patrick came over leading a mule loaded with buffalo meat. "Here is your share of the meat. It will keep through the winter and will not spoil. Have a safe journey, my friends."

"Thank you, Patrick. We'll see you down the road."

"Good-bye, Pa Hin Sa," he said and walked away.

The way he said good-bye sounded too final, but I brushed it off, nodded at Posey and said, "Let's move."

"MOVE OTT!" came the order, and we started off to the east and back to the Minnesota Valley.

Between them there was nothing—a chasm that,
from where we rode, appeared to have no bottom.

 CHAPTER ELEVEN

SNOW BLEW ACROSS the ground in waves. For two days we traveled with our coats pulled up around our faces. The ground was as flat as a griddle and not a living thing could be seen.

Jake rode up to me, "Remember that shawl Ma used to wear when she read the Bible to us?"

"Yeah, I remember it."

"That snow drifting across the ground makes me think of it."

"Funny you should say that, I was just thinking the same thing."

We found a dry, shallow creek bed just deep enough to crouch down out of the wind for the night. We were setting up our shelters when suddenly I heard a sound that took me back to Birch Coolie—the sound of a bullet thumping into human flesh. Immediately, the sound of a rifle came from the tree line two hundred yards to the east of us.

"I'm hit!" Mike said.

"GET DOWN!" Wambolt yelled.

We all hit the ground. The ditch was too shallow and we had to stay in a crouched posture to stay hidden. Mike was lying on the ground with blood flowing from a wound just above his left breast.

"Hmmm," he said, "this kinda hurts." Then his face turned white, he let out a groan and his head dropped back. Butterfly screamed and got down next to him, crying loudly. Posey scrambled over and ripped Mike's coat open to reveal a hole in his chest. She turned him over and found no exit wound.

"Bullet in Sultan," she said.

Butterfly was crying and holding Mike's head in her lap.

Posey said something to Sophie in Cherokee. Then we heard the sound of a shot and a bullet whistled overhead and skipped across the prairie behind us.

"There!" Jake said, pointing directly into the wind, "The smoke from his gun."

"Sunkist!" Sophie said, "I don't know what she's saying, she's talking too fast."

"She said he's still alive, but we need to git that bullet out."

Another bullet popped into the dirt behind us.

"I can see his smoke but can't get a bead on him," Jake said.

Another puff of smoke erupted from the place where the shooting was coming from.

Mike, still unconscious, moaned as Posey pushed a thin knife into the wound. She made a small cut in the flesh, slid a finger in alongside the knife and pulled a fifty caliber round ball out of the wound.

"Fifty caliber should have gone clear through. Whoever is doing the shooting either doesn't know how to use that rifle or he's just too far away for it to be effective," Jake said.

Another bullet hit the dirt, this time in the bank behind us. Suddenly, shooting started from our hideout. One shot followed the other as Steve jacked his Henry and filled the air with lead.

"Steve!" I yelled. "You can't see anything to shoot at—what the hell are you doing?"

"If I can get enough bullets out there he might bump into one of 'em," he said as he loaded shells into his rifle. "If he ain't dead, he's a little nervous right now." He pressed his cheek tight against the cold stock and peered over the sights of his rifle across the open prairie. "Come on, you son-of-a-bitch, shoot again."

Nothing happened. The shooting had stopped.

"You might have got him, Steve."

"Nah, I doubt it. But if I get a good bead on him, he's coyote bait."

"How far out there ye think he is?"

"Figger about two hundred yards."

"That should be easy to do with that thing."

"I can hit a man-sized target at four hundred yards on a good day, and two hundred yards on *any* kinda day. This wind doesn't help much, but shooting straight into it I should be able to get close enough. His smoke comes straight at us so we don't have to guess where he's hiding."

Posey and Sophie worked on Mike and soon had his wound patched up. Posey went to Butterfly and held her in her arms. She spoke to her softly and Butterfly smiled through her tears.

"Sultan be okay," she said to us.

It had been quiet long enough for us to think the sniper had left, when a bullet smacked into the dirt to our right.

"Dammit!" Wambolt yelled. "Get down!"

"Did you see the smoke, Steve?"

"No, he must have changed his position."

Another shot came in and one of the mules jumped, brayed, and ran off onto the prairie.

"Never mind the mule," Wambolt said. "We'll find him when this is over—if he's not dead."

Jake fired his Hawken. "You get a bead on him, Jake?"

"I did, but not a good one. Two hundred yards is a long haul for this fifty-four—just wanted to get my two cents-worth in."

Jake looked around and said, "Where's White Feather?"

I looked around and saw no sign of White Feather. "Where the hell'd he go?"

Jake pointed to a track in the snow that led away from our camp. It went out a few feet and disappeared in the grass.

"He's right out there in the grass on his belly making his way to the sniper."

I could see nothing. The grass was only about a foot tall but it was thick enough to hide a man.

"Is he going after him?"

"I guess—he's got his bow with him."

A bullet went over our heads and Sophie laughed. I looked over and saw her with a shirt hung on a forked stick holding it up for the sniper to shoot at.

"Watch for the smoke when I hold it up again," she said. "I'll give him time to reload."

Sophie held the shirt up in the wind. The sniper fired and missed the shirt. Five rifles fired at the same time at the puff of smoke. Dirt flew all around where the sniper was, but we saw nobody there.

Two hundred yards out, an Indian raised up onto his knees with his rifle to his shoulder, aiming at our camp. Steve's Henry barked. The Indian's arms dropped to his side. He stood there on his knees, looking down at his shirt, then toppled face first into the snow.

"Got 'im," he said. "If I got this figgered right, that slug went right through the middle of his chest. Hopefully, that's the end of that."

"Someone will have to go out there and make sure he's dead," Jake said.

"White Feather is out there, he can do it."

Suddenly, White Feather jumped up and ran toward the trees. The brush on the edge of the woods was so thick I thought he'd get hurt when he hit it, but he simply disappeared from sight at a dead run. We watched and waited till White Feather came out of the trees holding up a scalp. I motioned him back and he came at a trot carrying the Indian's rifle and scalp.

The gun the Indian had was an old Lemans rifle.

"Lemme see that gun," Sunkist said.

He took it and looked down the bore.

"Ain't no damn wonder he couldn't hit nothin', this thing's shot out. The damn fool—he'd never hit nothin' at that range even if the gun was good."

"Well, bust it up and bury it, we won't be needin' it," I said.

"White Feather," Sophie asked. "May I ask how old you are?"

"Maybe sixty summers."

"You're in pretty good shape for sixty."

He handed the scalp to Steve and said, "You keep. You kill bad Indian."

"Where'd the bullet hit?" Steve asked.

White Feather put his finger in the middle of his chest, "Here."

"Do you know who he was, White Feather?"

"He is called 'Kills Spotted Buffalo'. He is from Little Crow's village. He never could shoot too good."

"We're glad of that. How'd he git that name?"

"He shoot Myrick's milk cow. He has broken leg. He try to be the one to kill Pa Hin Sa before he die, I think."

"I say we head for the trees and take a few days to let Mike rest," I said, and they all agreed.

We carried Mike to the trees on a blanket stretched between our horses. Posey and Sunkist put up a shelter made from saplings and canvas for Mike and Butterfly.

They found a thicket of hazel brush and cleared a circle in the middle of it. Then they stripped the lower branches from the stalks around the circle and bent them till they met at the top about five feet from the ground and tied them together. They gathered more sticks and laid them over the sides of the shelter and laid canvas over that. The shelter was made so that it closed on all sides with a small vent at the top and a small canvas flap for an entrance.

Posey built a fire pit outside the tent and surrounded it with rocks. When the rocks heated she carried them inside the tent and poured water over them to warm the tent. She sent Butterfly out and stripped Mike to his bare chest, then

SOPHIE'S HAWK

filled the tent with steam.

We kept two people on guard through the three nights we stayed there. Mike slept most of the time while Posey and Butterfly took care of him. One or the other stayed in the shelter with him at all times. Posey made potions from roots and bark, which helped to relieve the pain and prevent fever.

After three days of doctoring I went inside. "How ye feelin', Mike?"

"I'm fine. It only hurts when I laugh."

"We need to get moving before the weather turns worse. You can ride in the wagon if you want."

"I can ride."

"Are you sure? That's a bad hit you took there."

"Ma taught us to ignore pain. She said it'll make us tough."

"Yeah, well, tough is one thing but we don't want that hole to start bleeding again."

"Hawk, I'd rather be on my horse than ride in the wagon, okay?"

"Have it your way, but if you start feeling bad just jump in the wagon for a while."

"Will do."

We took down our camp and loaded the mules and headed up the valley. "How you doin', Mike?"

"Oh, I'm just havin' a good ole time. Just keep moving."

"You were damn lucky back there."

"I was? Getting shot is lucky?"

"You were lucky you had all those clothes on. Your sheepskin vest and that coat slowed the bullet, otherwise it would have gone clear through."

"Posey knows how to take care of a wound, that's for sure."

"She's a good woman to have around."

Two more days brought us to another settlement. We stood on a ridge and looked down into the town. Several small buildings were scattered over a piece of high ground with smoke pouring from the chimneys. A few horses and wagons moved slowly up the main street.

"Anyone got a reason to go in?" I asked.

"I say we keep moving," Wambolt said. "Can't see anything down there that would interest any of us."

"Okay with me," I said.

We turned our horses north and kept moving. The town disappeared behind us and the prairies opened in front of us. It looked as if we could ride forever without finding anything but flat ground, snow, and wind. The horizon ahead of us was a black line where the land met the sky and not a hill or valley in sight. To the east the black line of the trees along the Minnesota Valley showed the western rim, and across a wide gap the eastern rim showed as a second black line. Between them there was nothing—a chasm that from where we rode, appeared to have no bottom.

Another long day's ride brought us to Fort Abercrombie. Two soldiers from the fort came out to meet us.

"You be Hawk Owen?"

"Nope. James Whistler. People call me Sunkist onna conna the sun burns my face so bad in the summer. Red Irish, ye see." He pointed at me and said, "That's Hawk Owen."

He caught me with my hand between my legs trying to scratch an itch that had developed between me and the saddle.

"Mister Owen, I'm Private Kaufman. Captain Vander Horck told us to keep an eye out for your company and bring you in as soon as you arrived. He's got a message for you from General Sibley."

"General? Sibley's a General now?"

"Yep."

Kaufman grinned at me as we rode to the fort.

"What are you grinnin' at?"

"Vander Horck told us to watch for a bunch of redheads traveling with women. I ain't never seen so many redheads in one place before." Then he added, "They'd make a nice show piece on some brave's tepee wall."

"That's the last time we'll hear that, right?"

Kaufman's face turned red and he lowered his head, obviously embarrassed at his remark. "Yes, sir. I didn't mean no harm." He tipped his hat at the women and said, "Nice to meet you, ladies." His head was bald except for a ring of bright red hair around the sides and back.

Kaufman was about thirty-five years old and heavily muscled. His face was clean-shaven and he looked as though he might be a bit bashful.

"Them Injuns take a shot at you, Kaufman, and you can bet it won't be for your scalp," Jake said.

He looked at Jake from the corner of his eye. "I guess there's good things to say about most anything."

"How long you been in the army, Kaufman?"

"My name's Lee."

"So, how long you been in the army, Lee?"

"About a year. They keep sending me all over the country—I don't like it much."

"Why do you stay in?"

"I'm a blacksmith. I'm hoping to be stationed somewhere where they'll let me stay."

"A blacksmith? Do you fix guns, too?"

"Sure, that's what I like best."

"Soph!" I shouted. "You still got that buffalo gun of yours?"

"Yes, it's on the mule. Why?"

"Lee here's a gunsmith. Maybe he can fix it for you."

"I'll give it to him when we get to the fort."

As we rode into the fort, men were busy putting up cabins and walls around the perimeter. Private Kaufman led us to Captain Vander Horck's quarters. Sergeant Wambolt led the way in followed by Jake, Sunkist, and me.

Wambolt saluted Vander Horck and said, "Sergeant Wambolt reporting, sir."

Vander Horck stood and returned the salute with quick, deliberate movements. "Welcome to our fort, Sergeant."

"Thank you, sir. Private Kaufman said you wanted to see us."

"Which one of you is Private Owen?"

"That's me, Captain."

"Mister Owen, General Sibley has sent orders for you to find Little Crow's camp and try to convince him to surrender. I have the order right here." He opened a drawer in his desk and pulled out two envelopes.

"Why me? I'm just the private here."

"Read this," he said, then handed me an envelope.

"What is it?" I asked.

"It's addressed to you, personally. You may open it now or later."

"I'll open it later, if you don't mind," I said, not wishing the captain to know how limited I was with my reading skills.

"As you wish."

"Sibley wants us to go into Little Crow's camp?"

"Yes, he says you are probably the only person crazy enough to try it."

"Sounds like he's trying to get rid of me," I said.

"Owen, our scouts have followed your trip up here and, by the sounds of it, you have left quite a mess in your trail. I only wish I had men like yours in my command. I have mostly green soldiers whose only experience with Indian fighting is what they received here a couple of months ago. We held the fort but only because of the cannon we have."

"So, how do we find Little Crow?"

"Reports say that Standing Buffalo is moving his camp to Devil's Lake for the winter. Little Crow is out on the prairie somewhere."

"We were hoping to spend the winter here. They tell me trying to winter on the prairie is suicide."

"We'll be glad to have you. You can learn more about Little Crow during the winter. Knowing your enemy is the best weapon you can have."

"Do you have quarters for the women?"

"Yes, we had a train of emigrants come through here last spring on their way to Montana and they put up shelters. They're a little primitive, but they're warm. My men are building more living quarters and putting up a palisade around the fort. You may have one or as many of the houses as you need. Of course, you will have to do your share of the work."

"That's fine with me. I don't expect anything free."

"Oh, Owen—I have another letter for you from Brown's Valley. Mister Erickson has claimed that you owe him six bits for a night in his cabins and two dollars for a broken bed."

Jake, Sunkist, and I broke out laughing then Vander Horck joined in, "Should I ask how the bed was broken?"

"Use your imagination," Jake said, glancing and nodding his head at Sophie and me.

"You send him a message saying that he still owes Sophie for a bath."

"Will do. We have had our times with Mister Erickson."

"Where do we stay, Captain?"

"Find an empty cabin and move in."

"Just like that? Just move in?"

"Of course, this is a military outpost and you, being military men, are entitled."

"Captain," I said, "we ain't in the—"

Sunkist put his hand over my mouth and said, "Thank you, Captain. We're gonna take you up on that."

"Mister Owen—"

"Call me Hawk."

"Very well, then. Hawk, you are military. Read that order you have in your hand."

"I'll read it later."

"As you wish, but read it soon. It contains special orders for you."

"Sibley probably wants me to attack Little Crow single-handed."

"I suspect General Sibley has a sense of humor such as that."

Then he told Kaufman to take us to our cabins. I opened the envelope from Sibley but I couldn't read it because it was written in long hand, so I handed it to Sophie to read for me.

Her mouth went into a wide grin.

"Wait here—I'll be right back." She walked out the door and suddenly I felt like a sheep on his way to slaughter. She came back with the entire group behind her. They lined up with wide smiles on their faces, stood straight and tall, and saluted me smartly.

"What the hell is this?" I said.

Jake handed me the letter and said, "Seems our friend, General Sibley has a better sense of humor than we thought."

"Why? What does it say?"

Sophie took the letter, squared her shoulders and with authority read, "It says…

> *Sir,*
>
> *Due to service above and beyond the call of duty, and by authority of the office of the Governor of Minnesota, I hereby appoint Private Harlan "Hawk" Owen the field rank of Lieutenant of Volunteers in the United States Army.*
>
> *—Alexander Ramsey*

…and it's signed by Governor Ramsey, himself," Sophie said.

"Yer in the army, Hawk," Jake said.

"No, I'm not."

"Yeah, you are. Sibley says so."

"I ain't in no damned army!"

"I know you don't like it, Hawk," Sophie said, "but the fact is, you are a lieutenant in Sibley's army."

"Gimme that paper," I said. I grabbed it, tore it into small pieces and threw it in the stove. "There. I ain't seen no paper, have you?"

"Yep. We all saw it, Lieutenant."

Sophie put her arms around me and motioned the others out the door. They turned and left us alone.

"Does that letter really say that?"

"That is what it says—you're a lieutenant in the army."

"Soph, I can't live like soldiers do."

"Hawk, you've been drafted and I'm afraid that if you don't abide by the rules they can send you to prison."

"That's what I mean—I can't live by their rules."

"I think Sibley knows that, so don't worry too much about it."

"I have to go and talk to the Captain," I said.

"I'll go with you."

I opened Captain Vander Horck's door without knocking and said, "Captain, I need to talk to you about this lieutenant thing. I'm not in the army and I don't want to be."

The captain leaned his elbows on his desk and looked up at me.

"Mister Owen, why are you so adamant about being in the army? What do you see that's so repulsive about it?"

"I like to do my own thinking. I don't need someone telling me when to jump and how high. We followed Captain Marsh to the Redwood Ferry because he was an officer in the army."

"Captain Marsh was a very good officer, Mister—"

"He maybe knew how to fight the confederates in the south," I interrupted, "but he didn't know doodley-squat about fighting Indians."

"Not many of us did before this recent trouble," Vander Horck said.

"If we'd had a man like Sunkist or Jake in charge when we went down to the river that day, those Indians never would have been able to ambush us like they did. Being in the army don't make a man a better fighter, it makes him a better follower—someone who'll follow orders no matter how damn stupid they are."

"Relax, Hawk. You are not in the regular army. You are a lieutenant in the volunteer army. That means you can get out whenever you wish."

"Okay, I wish now."

"There are some benefits to your position you might want to consider before doing anything too drastic."

"Benefits to being in the army? You'll have to explain that one."

"As an officer you are entitled to quarters in any military post. You have access to rations and ammunition just like any regular military officer. You can also have soldiers assigned to your command from the regular army. This could be a great advantage to you."

"We don't need soldiers. We can make it without them."

"You can also have artillery assigned to you. Does that change things any?"

"Artillery? You mean cannons?"

"Yes, Lieutenant—cannons."

"Now that sounds more like it. And men to shoot them?"

"Of course. There's no use sending field pieces out if you don't have men who know how to use them."

I looked at Sophie. "This is sounding better all the time."

She smiled and winked at me.

"I ain't wearin' no uniform," I said to the Captain.

"Hawk, look around you. Do you see any uniforms?" he asked. "The army cannot provide uniforms. You will supply your own clothing. But, Lieutenant, you will be subject to orders sent from General Sibley. So far you have all of the orders he has for you, and I suspect they are orders you can follow. Just find Little Crow and talk with him."

"Our main reason for being here is to find a friend and bring her home alive."

"You can continue with that mission and do what Sibley has ordered. You will most likely meet up with Little Crow, anyway."

"All right, Captain. We'll do it. We'll start when the weather warms up."

"We have scouts out keeping a close eye on the Indian movements. All we know now is that Standing Buffalo and his band are moving up to Devil's Lake. They have about two hundred tents, which means that many fighting men. Standing Buffalo claims to have had nothing to do with the war and can be considered peaceful. However, Little Crow is the leader of the war and he is very dangerous. He has moved out onto the plains with about thirty lodges. Our mixed-bloods tell us that he's trying to recruit allies for his war, but is not being successful. Standing Buffalo ran him out of his camp and told him to leave his land and leave him at peace. We have no idea where Little Crow is now, but we think he is moving toward the Missouri to talk with the Indians there."

"How far is it to Devil's Lake? I should go there and talk to Standing Buffalo before going after Little Crow."

"It's well over two hundred miles of rough traveling. A winter trip is not advisable. It would be best to wait until spring, at least then you will have buffalo to feed on."

For the next month we stayed in the fort and entertained ourselves as best we could. On the east side of the compound we found a billiards room and spent much of our time there learning the finer points of a game the soldiers called 'pool'. Under the tutelage of Private Marv Hurwitz, Sophie got good at the game much more quickly than I did. The soldiers lined up and waited their turns to try to beat her at the game. Most of the time, I just sat and watched.

On Christmas Day, a celebration was held and some of the men exchanged gifts. We, of course, had nothing to exchange but quick glances.

On the twenty-seventh of December we got word that thirty-eight Sioux had been hanged at Mankato and the remaining Indians were being sent to Fort Snelling until the government could decide what to do with them. Captain Vander Horck had everyone on high security guard in case of an attack, but none came and life gradually resumed its monotonous course.

We made several trips outside the fort but seldom went far enough to have to stay out through the night.

The billiards room became the favorite place for the soldiers to spend time through the winter months.

Sunkist and Posey were gone most of the time because, as he said, "I don't take much to fort life."

. . .

The old man rocked back in his chair and breathed a deep sigh.

"Dad, are you all right?"

"Give me a few minutes to catch my breath. I want to tell you about Sophie."

"You just start when you're ready, Mister Owen," the reporter said.

"Can I get you anything, Dad?"

"Some lemonade might be nice."

Lorraine went to the house and came back with a pitcher and glasses and poured each of them a serving.

The old man sipped from his glass with trembling lips and continued.

"Hold that thought, I need a beer. Want one?"
She looked straight at me without saying a word.
"Dumb question, huh?"

12

CHAPTER TWELVE

SOPHIE AND I STAYED IN THE FORT and helped with the construction of the houses and other buildings.

One night, while we were in bed after a good day's work, I said, "You know, Soph, I don't know anything about your past, where you came from or where you've been—I don't even know your last name."

"You don't know my last name?"

"Crazy, ain't it? I've just called you Sophie all this time. Guess it never crossed my mind until now."

"Well, it's Boisvert. Sophie Boisvert. It's French. When it's read, people pronounce it 'Boyz vert', but it's 'Bwa-vair'."

"Boisvert, I like it. That was your husband's name?"

"No—that's my original name. I won't use *his* name."

"What was it?"

"Swanson."

"So, where did you come from?"

"Do you want to hear the whole story?"

"Yeah, all of it."

"Okay, well, I'm told that sometime in eighteen thirty-eight a man called Johnson came to Saint Paul and built a cabin on the bank of the river. They tell me that he came from the Grand Portage area where he was involved with the fur traders. I just know he came from there, but I don't know any more than that. I doubt if I'll ever get there to find out—maybe it's best that way.

"He had a woman and a baby living with him. People naturally assumed the woman was his wife."

ARVID LLOYD WILLIAMS
BONNIE SHALLBETTER

135

"And that baby was you?"

"Yes, I believe so. It was obvious to the people in town that they had previously moved in a higher bracket of society. Their manners were refined and elegant and their clothes were fashionable and expensive. They stayed by themselves most of the time and people started to wonder about them because he had no source of income to support his high living. You know how people talk."

"Yeah, I know. That's just one reason not to hang around places like that—too damn many people with not enough to do."

"Then one stormy night, a man knocked on our door. He'd spent the evening at Pig's Eye's Tavern and asked for shelter for the night. People would do that sometimes. No one ever turned a stranger out on a bad night in those days—except for my father. And ye know what, Hawk? That man was found frozen to death the next day. That convinced his neighbors that my 'supposed' father was some sort of criminal on the run and they requested that the military at Fort Snelling investigate and arrest him. Well, the military couldn't find anything to arrest him for."

"That's hard to believe. The army can find a reason to arrest anyone for anything."

"Anyway, the people whined and howled so much that they finally sold their claim and cabin to a man named James Clewett. Then they moved down the Mississippi to another town. No one knows where they went. I was just a baby at the time. The people in the town demanded I be taken away from them and turned over to the orphanage. I heard he didn't put up much of a struggle when they took the baby, so he probably *was* hiding and didn't want people to know where he was."

"That makes sense."

"But then, he might have wanted the baby to have a better life than he could offer, too—no one knows for sure. That's how I ended up in the orphanage."

"Hold that thought, I need a beer. Want one?"

She looked straight at me without saying a word. "Dumb question, huh? Ah, be right back."

We settled in with our beer and she went on with her story.

"I spent most of my childhood putting up with stuffy nuns and priests until I was about fifteen. I got my schooling there and learned about reading, writing, and arithmetic. Believe me, it was no picnic living in that orphanage. Every day we were out of bed and dressed before sunrise, then off to church. We said the rosary for two hours every day." She took a big swig of beer. "Then out to work in the gardens or in the field for some farmer all day long. Along with all of this, we had to keep the orphanage spotless and ourselves just as clean."

"That's more than any man can take. You're one tough woman, Soph. Here's to one tough woman."

We raised our mugs and touched them together, spilling some of the golden liquid.

"Hey, careful! You're wasting the good stuff!"

"Sorry, just got carried away. Go on."

"Now, where was I?"

"Right here with me."

"They tried to teach us that the female body is sinful to look at, so when we took our baths we did it with our nightshirts on."

"Seems like a waste of a nightshirt."

"When we started to grow into women we were trussed up in girdles to keep our breasts from showing. They were called the 'devil's pillows' and we were taught that if a man saw them, he would want to use them."

"Well, they got that lesson right—won't get any arguing from me." I took another gulp of beer, wiped my mouth on my sleeve, then let out a belch.

"Oh, that was lovely, Hawk—done?"

"Yup."

"I couldn't figure out why God would make a woman's body so beautiful and then not want anyone to see it. That just didn't make sense to me."

"Me either. You know what does make sense?"

"What?"

"Another beer—want one? Oops—I did it again. Some things just don't need askin'." I came back with both mugs topped off and Sophie continued her story.

"Anyway, we were in bed when the sun went down and up before sunrise, just like the birds—but we weren't singing like birds. Then I was sent to live with some people in town who ran a laundry and was made to work for them until I was eighteen. I was pretty good with numbers, so a man hired me to work for him in his lumberyard taking care of his books and keeping his finances in order. While I worked for him I met lots of people who came in to deal with him for lumber. I was always asked to sit in on the meetings and keep records of what was said.

"One of the men who came in was a tall, good-looking man who always dressed nicely and seemed to have very pleasant manners. One day he asked me to go to dinner with him and a romance started from there. He treated me so kind and generous and eventually asked me to marry him. I said yes. That was a big mistake. As soon as I was his wife, everything changed. Then I was his possession. I was told how to dress and how to walk, and even how to talk. He even sent me to beauty parlors to get my hair done and told them how he wanted it."

"He was a brave man. He probably hadn't figured out yet what a tough woman you are. See? I learn quickly—better'n pushin' up daisies."

"He wanted me to change from what I am, to what he wanted me to be. He took me to his meetings and paraded me around like a prize horse. I was nothing more than a decoration on his arm. We'd go to meetings and he'd introduce me to a new client with a smug, 'Hello, I'm Robert Swanson and this is my beautiful wife, Sophia.' I told him that my name was *not* Sophia, it's *Sophie.* 'I know that, my dear', he'd say, 'but Sophia sounds so much more elegant'."

"Wasn't too smart, was he? Guess some people jiss like playin' with fire. Makes army life sound a helluva lot less dangerous."

"Yeah, he was too busy being self-absorbed to notice or care about anything other than himself. I wasn't cut out for high society and all the bullshit that goes with it. Don't get me wrong—I do like getting dressed up once in a while, but I don't like being told how or when.

"At parties, the men would stand in little circles bragging about how much money they had. Most of them were lying anyway—I know he was—and the women stood around flashing their jewels, trying to impress each other.

"He could have had money if he'd put it in the bank instead of spending it on needless junk to impress his business friends. He paid four hundred dollars for a gun built in England, just to show it off. Then he'd throw it in the closet and never look at it again until some rich guy came around that he wanted to impress. Hell, he didn't know anything about guns. He wouldn't know the end of a pistol if it was aimed right at him.

"When people came to our house, he'd start showing all the things he owned— his books, which he never read, his guns, his fancy furniture, the paintings on his walls, and the fine chinaware and silverware. Then, if I happen to be in the room—and it suited him—he'd say, 'And this is my beautiful wife, Sophia.' Gawd, I hated that! I was no different than one of his fancy objects on display.

"He'd walk around with his nose up some rich lumberman's ass trying to make believe he knew something about lumber. He knew how to sell it to the farmers around Saint Paul for a big profit all right, but the big guys knew how to manipulate him into buying their lumber for big profits for themselves. I tried to tell him they were making a fool of him, but he got mad and told me to stay out of his affairs. Well, that was fine with me. I decided to just sit back and let him spend his money on jewels and fancy clothes for me till I could find a way out. I figured it would be an investment for *my* future."

"Zoph? Jiss want you to know that I would never do that to you."

She looked at me while trying to take a sip of beer and nearly spit it out. "Hawk, I don't think that will be a problem I'll have to worry about."

"N-n-nope."

"Anyway, one night he was having trouble trying to arrange a huge merger with some big shot. He walked over to me, took my arm and led me to the side. 'Sophia, I need that contract but I can't get him to agree to my terms, I need your help. If I don't get this, I'll go broke.' When he said this to me he was squeezing my arm and speaking through his teeth, 'I know you can make it happen.' I remember telling him to let go of my arm. Then I reminded him that he wanted me out of his affairs. And now he was asking for my help, so I asked him what he had in mind. You know what he said?"

I could tell she was getting angry as she told this part of her story, so I just said, "Uh-uh."

"He said, 'I want you to sleep with him.' That was the last straw. I jumped back from him and yelled in front of all his phony-assed friends, 'What! You want me to sleep with that slob? I'm not a goddamed whore, you bastard—not for you or anyone else! I don't care how bad you need that contract!' I slapped him hard across the face and stormed out of there."

"Hot damn, Soph! Wish I could'a been there to see that one." This was followed by a loud hiccup.

"Oh great," Sophie mumbled. "Now he's got the hiccups."

"Bleeeze go on."

"As I was saying—I went to a friend's house for the night. I didn't care that he didn't know where I was. When I came back the next day, he told me to pack my things and leave. Well, I knew he was the one who was getting out because I had seen his things disappearing from his closet for a couple of months. After that night none of the lumbermen would have anything to do with him. He was broke with no way to get out of debt and was skipping the country."

"I gan't imagine you hookin' up with someone like that."

"Well, he was a real sweet-talker at first and knew how to get the things that he wanted. He prided himself on that fact. I think that's what really bothered him about that deal, because he couldn't do it and needed me, and it hurt his precious pride."

She took a long swig of beer and sighed, "That seems like such a long time ago—I don't even like talking about it, it makes me so angry. I might as well finish the story, though. How much beer do we have left? It's not quite as bad with a wet whistle."

I laughed at the way she enjoyed a good beer—or two. "You keep talkin', I'll (hiccup) han'le the refreshments."

"Well, all the while he was packing his junk, I was hiding the jewels and clothes that he'd bought for me. When he left, the bank came and took the house we lived in and the store he owned. They left me with nothing. I had the fancy clothes and jewels, but I couldn't sell them because if the bank found out I had them, they'd take them away from me to pay off his debts. After that, no one wanted anything to do with me, especially the high society women I knew from the lumbermen's club. I took a job serving dinners in a restaurant for a while until they found out who I was and fired me. Apparently, the rich people put the word out about me being a divorced woman—and the fact that I was an orphan didn't help, either."

"Scandalous, Zoph."

"Yeah, real damn shocking. With those kinds of labels on me, I was an undesirable in all the neighborhoods except for places like Linda's 'Dance Academy'."

"Ah, yes—a place where a man can find all the pleasures of life— *including* dance."

"Anyway, that's when I met Linda. She ran the academy and asked if I needed a job. She came from a life similar to mine and understood what it was like. Even though Linda realized I wasn't cut out for a job 'teaching dance', she let me stay to do the cleaning and serve drinks to the customers. But the pay was not enough to live on and the day you walked in, I had reluctantly decided to try the profession."

"Mankind will never know the service they missed—and I'm glad of it."

"Me too, Hawk. That's just not me, but when you're desperate, you sometimes do things you wouldn't normally consider doing. Linda knew you were shy and Jean told her it would be your first time, so she put us together. She knew you wouldn't do anything to hurt me and if I backed out, it would be okay. When I left there I went to work washing clothes in a laundry. Linda came to me one day and told me that someone had shot Robert to death. As far as I know, they never found out who did it. I wanted to find that person and give him a reward."

"I'm surprised it wasn't you—you sure it wasn't? I'd better watch my back from now on."

"Probably not a bad idea."

"You have my undivided attention. Pleeeze… hup… go on."

"One day an old German guy named Herb Ringot came to me and offered me a job in his restaurant in Shakopee. It was far away from all the phony people around me, so I took the job. We got in his wagon that very day. Soon after that, you and I crossed paths again."

I downed the last bit of beer in my mug and looked at her, "So… wuzz yer lass name agin?"

"Boisvert"

"French, right?"

"Right. It's the name they gave me in the orphanage. I think it's my real name, but I'm not sure. I like it though—sounds exotic."

"I like it, too."

"What do you say we take a walk? I need to get up and get movin'."

"Yeah, lead the way—I'm right behind you. Um, kinda like walkin' behind you enna way."

. . .

Lorraine came out of the house.

"Mister Holcombe, Dad is getting tired. Shall we have a bite to eat before we continue?"

"Yes, I think we could all use a break."

"I'm not tired, Lorraine. Let's keep going with this," the old man said. "I need to get this said. You can bring the food out here if you're hungry."

"If you're sure that's what you want."

"Yes, I think we should keep going."

"Dad?"

He raised his hand and motioned her to the house. Lorraine looked at him curiously and turned to leave.

*"The white man's promises are like a hole
in the ground that has no bottom."*

13

C H A P T E R   T H I R T E E N

THE FORT WAS QUIET except for the clang of Kaufman's hammer in the blacksmith shop. Scouts came and went, reporting what they had learned about Little Crow's band. Little Crow had gone to the valley of the Missouri hoping to get support from the plains tribes to the south and west. Some of the Indian leaders were pulling away from him because of the problems of feeding a large group of travelers, and because some of them realized the futility of continuing the war without help from other tribes.

No one knew anything about The Thief. He had separated from Little Crow early in the winter with a small number of followers. Reports from the scouts said that there were still small bands of Indians moving around the Big Woods and in areas east of the Minnesota River.

We heard of attacks on farms and small settlements but they were so random that we didn't know where to start looking for the Indians. People built walls around the towns and put up barricades to ward off any attacks. The entire state was on the alert for Indian troubles. Saint Cloud, Clearwater, Henderson, Long Prairie, and Forest City all built fortifications. Nearly every town between Little Falls and Glencoe had built stockades and formed volunteer militia. They took on names like the Guards, Rifles, and Rangers, the Le Sueur Tigers, and the Saint Peter Frontier Avengers.

In the north, citizens were flocking into Fort Ripley under the threat of Chippewa chief, Hole-in-the-Day. It was rumored that Hole-in-the-Day and Little Crow planned the outbreak together. There was no substance to the rumor but people were taking no chances and did what they could to protect themselves.

Kaufman came to me one day in February carrying Sophie's rifle.

"Hawk, I got your gun done."

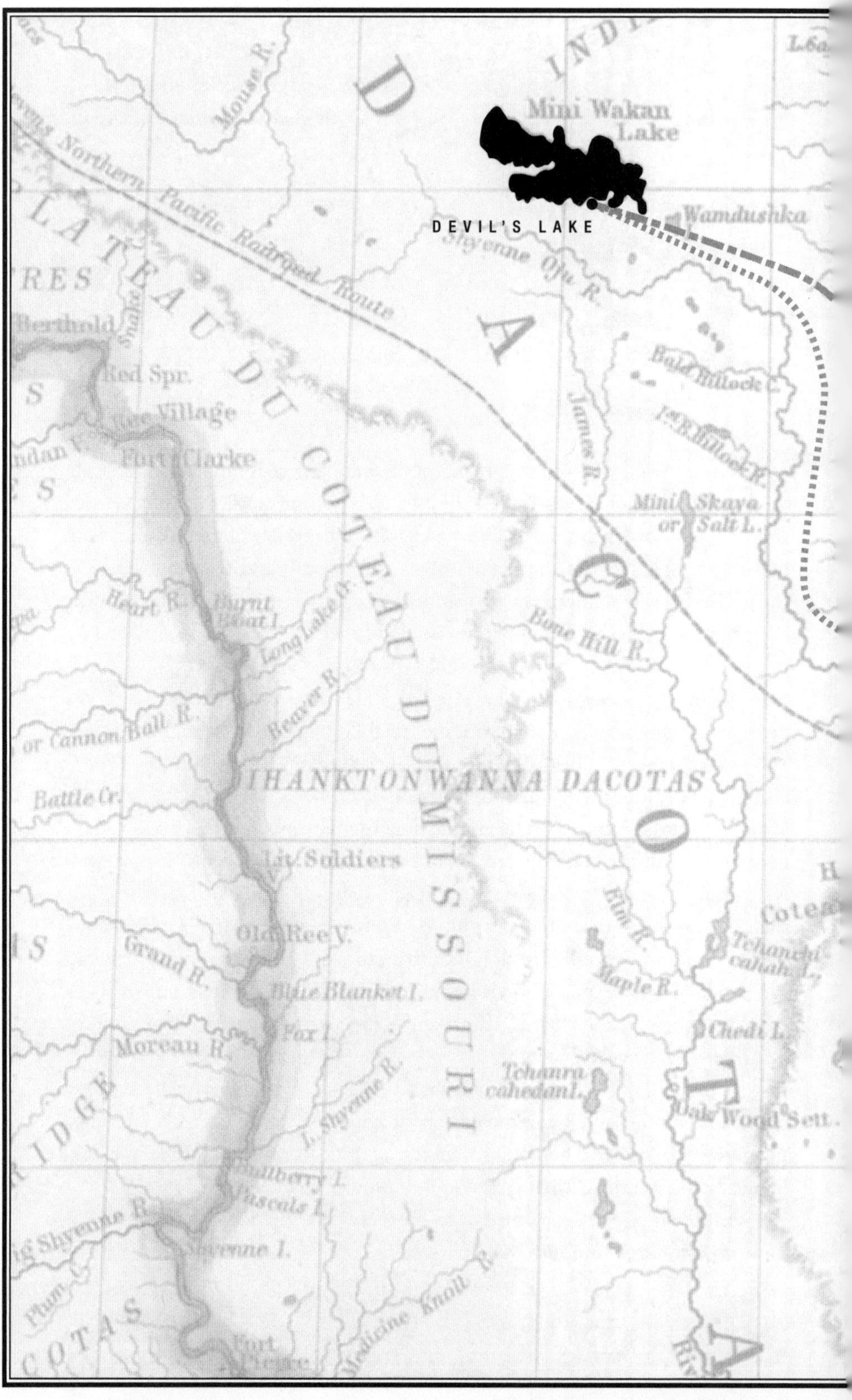
DEVIL'S LAKE
Mini Wakan Lake
Wamdushka
Northern Pacific Railroad Route
Mouse R.
Shyenne Oju R.
Bald Hillock C.
James R.
Mini Skaya or Salt L.
Bone Hill R.
Red Spr.
Village
Fort Clarke
Heart R.
Burnt Boat I.
Long Lake R.
Beaver R.
Cannon Ball R.
Battle Cr.
IHANKTONWANNA DACOTAS
COTEAU DU COTEAU DU MISSOURI
Old Ree V.
Grand R.
Blue Blanket I.
Fox I.
Moreau R.
Tchanra cahedan L.
Maple R.
Elm R.
Chedi L.
Oak Wood Sett.
L. Shyenne R.
Pascals I.
Big Shyenne R.
Shyenne I.
Plum C.
Medicine Knoll R.
Fort Pierre

PEMBINA

Swamp R.

RED LAKE R.

RED

Douglass

Clear Water R.

Mitcha

Sand Hill R.

RED RIVER

Sarsfield
Wild Rice

BRECKENRIDGE

Fayette

Silvanna

JOURNEY THROUGH
MINNESOTA &
DAKOTA TERRITORY

1863-64

·········· WESTWARD TREK

━ ▪ ━ ▪ ━ TRAIL HOME

━ ━ ━ ━ WAR TRAIL

FORT ABERCROMBIE

**EMIGRANTS
CROSSING**

• OTTER TAIL LAKE

LAKE TRAVERSE

• **Brown's Valley**

BIG STONE
LAKE

• **Hawk Creek**

CAMP RELEASE

MINNESOTA RIVER

PLATEAU

BROWN

"You fixed it?'

"Sure. I can fix anything."

"Let me see that thing." I took it and looked it over.

"I got a stock and a lock off an old Tennessee rifle from the warehouse. It was shot out and wasn't no good no more. That one was a cap lock so I took the lock off that and put it on this one. It ain't no flinner no more, it's a cap lock now."

The barrel on the rifle was straight but covered with hammer dents. The lock plate was tight in its recess but there was a large gap between the iron and the wood. The stock didn't fit the barrel and I could see where Lee had used his folding knife to fit the barrel into the wood.

"Have you fired it yet?" I asked.

"Nope, I figgered you'd want to shoot it first."

"Tell you what, let's tie it into the crotch of a tree and fire it with a string first."

"Hawk, it'll shoot. I fixed it."

"Yeah, well, I just want to be sure which end of it is most dangerous."

Kaufman was clearly disappointed at my distrust in his abilities but I insisted that we test it first and he reluctantly agreed. He loaded the gun with some trouble getting the bullet down the bore. I took it to a small tree and lashed it tight. A string tied to the trigger would fire it. I capped it and followed the string back about twenty-five feet.

"You want to pull the string, or should I?" I asked.

"You do it."

I gave the string a jerk and the gun went off with a horrific explosion. A cloud of white smoke erupted from the gun and enveloped the entire tree. My ears rang like a church bell as the wind carried the cloud down the valley. I turned to look at Kaufman. He had moved back about ten feet and stood looking at the mess in the tree with his hands over his ears.

"What the heck happened?" he said with a tremble in his voice.

"She blew up, Lee. How much powder did you stick in 'er?"

"I don't know. Just a handful."

"Well, it seems to have been a little too much."

I walked over and picked the remains of my Tennessee Rifle off the ground. The barrel had split into three strips of steel that were peeled back like dandelion leaves separating it from the breach plug and leaving the threads bare. The stock was shattered back to the lock, bark was blown off the tree limbs, and slivers of iron stuck out of the wood.

"Want to try to fix it, Lee?"

"Musta been bad iron in the barrel," he said.

"Yeah, musta been. Oh well, good thing one of us wasn't holding it."

"Hawk!" someone shouted. "The captain wants to see you."

"Lee, take this thing and make horseshoes out of it. I won't be needing it anymore."

"I'm sorry, Hawk. I didn't mean to—"

"Forget it, Lee. No one got hurt and we learned a big lesson here."

Kaufman took the rifle and walked away. I could see that he was hurting, but there was nothing I could think of to say to make him feel better.

"Lee," I said, "that was an old gun. It should have been thrown away a long time ago. It wasn't your fault it blew up."

He just looked at me and turned away.

I went to the captain's quarters.

"You wanted to see me, Captain?"

"Hawk, the scouts say that Little Crow is back at Devil's Lake. If you want to talk with him, now is the time. He won't be there long, Standing Buffalo won't let him stay with his camp. If you want to go, I'll send a detachment of troops with you."

"It'll take me ten days to get there and from what I've seen on that flat ground, there ain't nothin' for the animals to feed on. If I can get a wagonload of hay and some rations for me and my men, we can make it."

"You can take whatever you need. You'll go, then?"

"No time like the present."

"When can you be ready?"

"I'm ready now. I'll get the men together and we can move out in the morning."

"Good. I'll have your hay and rations and a twelve-pounder cannon ready, with a crew to use it."

"We won't be needing the cannon this time, Captain. It would just make the peaceful Indians nervous."

"Very well, then. I'll see you in the morning."

I sent Steve and Mike out to find Sunkist and Posey. We gathered in my cabin and I told them what was happening.

"The women will have to stay here," I said.

"Hawk," Sunkist said, "having women in the group will show Little Crow that we are on a peaceful mission, and they might come in handy for patchin' up leaks in yer hide. Besides, there ain't no way in hell yer gonna make 'em stay behind enny way."

Knowing that Sunkist was right, I said, "Be ready to ride at sun-up."

Sophie and I talked into the night.

"How did I get so lucky to have a woman like you, Soph?"

"Damned if I know. I guess you're a lot like me. You don't need fancy toys and games to make you feel important. You seem to be content with what you have."

"I've got you, what more could a man want?"

"Well, I'd feel much better if you had one of those sixteen-shootin' rifles like Steve's got."

"Yeah, I guess that would be one thing."

She swung her legs off the bed and started to get up. "Close your eyes, Hawk."

"What for?"

"Just close your eyes."

I closed my eyes and felt something cold land on my stomach. I jumped and grabbed it off of me. In my hand was a brand new Henry rifle.

"What the hell's this?"

"It's yours, Hawk. I got it from the sutler's store today."

"I didn't know there were any of these around here."

"Yup, they're becoming more and more popular with the settlers. Got a thousand rounds for it, too."

I took her in my arms and the rest of the night was spent showing her my appreciation.

Morning came too quickly and we packed our camps and went to the captain's quarters.

"We're ready to ride, Captain."

"Good. I have ten good men ready to ride with you and a wagon loaded with hay and rations. Hope you like salted pork."

"It'll do in a pinch, but we don't really need the troops and I'd rather not have them along. This is a peaceful mission and having them along will make the Indians nervous."

"Lieutenant, this is a military mission and the troops will be going. No argument."

"Have it your way. But tell them to stay behind us."

"Done."

"How do we get there?"

"Just follow the emigrant road a little north of west and cross Wild Rice Creek. You'll be on the flats for about four days, then you'll hit the hill country. Keep moving west till you come to the valley of the Sheyenne River. There, the river will be flowing north. The emigrants built a ford there and, as long as the river hasn't washed it out, you shouldn't have any trouble getting across. You'll be in the country called the 'Big Bend of the Sheyenne'. Go west till you find the river again. There, the current will be running south. Follow the river upstream for about six days. When the river turns straight west, you'll turn straight north. It'll take you to Devil's Lake. You should be seeing plenty of Indians around there, most will be from Standing Buffalo's band. But be damn careful—Little Crow is out there and The Thief could be there as well."

We left the fort and headed out onto the cold, forbidding plains of Dakota country.

Steve rode up next to me and said, "What'cha got there, Hawk?"

"Sophie bought me this Henry rifle." I held it up to show it to him. It had a long hexagon barrel, a beautifully polished brass frame, and a fine-grained walnut shoulder stock.

"Ye like it?"

"So far, I do. You'll have to show me how to use it, though."

"Yeah, I told Sophie I would."

"You knew I was gettin' this?

"Sure, I helped her pick it out while you were talking to Vander Horck."

"Git otta here."

Steve walked his horse away with a grin on his face.

We followed the road the emigrants built while on their way to the Montana gold fields. Travel was easy the first hundred miles. White Feather knew the road to Devil's Lake and could find safe, comfortable camp spots. The prairie was flat and bare except for small patches of trees along the east side of creek beds and frozen water holes. Travel was slow and very monotonous. We saw small herds of buffalo and a few foxes and coyotes, but no Indians.

On the forth day we crossed the Sheyenne River, then White Feather turned us north.

"We're supposed to stay with the river," I said.

"I know this country," he said. "We will get to Devil's Lake faster this way. Save us many days. The river does not go straight. We go cross-country between the turns."

"Okay, you're the boss—lead the way."

"If there are Indians they will stay close to the river, so traveling this way is better. They will not be on the plains."

The hills got higher and we started seeing lakes and streams. The weather turned cold and halfway through each day we had to stop and build a fire to warm up. In the hills, the air was just as cold but the wind wasn't as strong. The snow was deeper which made travel more difficult for the horses.

"Hawk," Sunkist said, "we got comp'ny."

I looked to my right and saw a party of twenty Indians about two hundred yards away traveling parallel to our course, and another party of twenty to our left.

"I would imagine we're surrounded," I said.

"Yup, jiss keep walkin' and don't look skeert. And Hawk—don't look behind us."

"It's kinda hard not to be scared right now."

"Time to put out a white flag—let 'em know we're peaceable."

Eve pulled out a white scarf and tied the corner to her rifle barrel. She set the stock on her leg so the flag stood above her. The Indians didn't seem to notice.

"How does she keep those things so white?" I asked Sophie.

"*Why* does she keep those things so white?" she said.

Eve turned to us and said, "They stay white because I don't let them get dirty."

"I guess that makes sense."

"White Feather, do you know these men?"

"No, I do not."

"How far are we from Devil's Lake?"

"We are close. We will see the lake soon. I think these men are peaceful."

"How do you know that?"

"They have women with them."

I hadn't noticed the women because all of the Indians were wrapped in blankets and coats. The Indians rode at a walk with blankets pulled tightly around them. Two of the horses had travois trailing behind.

"Do you think someone should go out and talk with them?"

"They will come to us when they are ready."

We kept our course and walked slowly. I sent Mike and Butterfly ahead to tell Steve and Torgerson to come back to the group.

As we climbed and crossed a small hill we saw the lake stretched out before us as far as the eye could see. The Indian escort moved close and stopped about thirty yards away. A man walked his horse toward us and said, "You are Hawk?"

"Nope, my name's Sunkist." He pointed at me. "That's Hawk."

The Indian looked back and forth between us with a curious look on his face. He shrugged his shoulders and came to me.

"You are Hawk?"

"I am Hawk."

"Come with us. We will take you to Standing Buffalo."

"Lead the way."

The forest was close on both sides of the trail. There were a dozen mounted Indians in front of us and more than that behind us. We were boxed in with nowhere to go if something should happen. Around a bend we came out of the forest and into a large clearing. Two hundred yards ahead, we saw a camp of about thirty tepees. Suddenly, there was a commotion among the tepees and three braves rode out at a fast gallop. One of our escorts rode out to meet them and yelled something in Dakota. The rider stopped and waited for us to come close.

"Feeling a little vulnerable, Jake?" I asked.

"Just a little," he said.

"Relax, boys," Sunkist said. "If they was gonna do enna thin' they would'a done it a long time back."

One of the new riders moved his horse close to mine and looked me in the eye. He held a double-barreled shotgun across his lap with the muzzle pointed in my direction. He kept his gaze on me as we rode on. I held my eyes on his, trying not to show any fear. Suddenly, he smacked his horse with a quirt and took off with a high-pitched scream that almost made me jump out of the saddle. I took a deep breath and looked over at Jake.

"Feelin' a little vulnerable there, Hawk?" he asked with a forced smile.

"Not just a little," I said.

The rest of the walk into camp was done in absolute silence. People lined up on both sides of the road and watched us ride in. Children stood behind their mothers, and young boys strutted out in front of us, as if daring one of us to walk on them. A boy about thirteen years old stepped out in front of Sunkist. Sunkist kicked his horse and almost ran the boy down. The boy jumped out of the way just in time.

"Damn li'l brats," Sunkist said. "One of them little varmints gits in front of ye, jiss run 'im over."

"You lookin' to get us killed?" I asked.

"They ain't gonna let you run 'em down, they're just seein' if you got the guts to do it."

We were led to a tepee in the center of the camp and motioned to step down. One of the men who led us there went into the tepee. A moment later, a woman came out and held the entrance flap open. She pointed at me and motioned for me to go into the tent.

"Looks like they jiss want Hawk to go in," Sunkist said.

"Jake, you come with me."

"They just want you in there."

"Jiss go on in, Jake," Sunkist said, "and don't give 'em any notion you might change yer mind."

A brave stepped in front of Jake to stop him. Jake put his hand on the man's chest and pushed him aside, then turned to face him. The man got a surprised look on his face and took a step back. We went into the tent. Standing Buffalo sat cross-legged with three warriors on each side of him. He wore a blue blanket around his shoulders, leather leggings, and beaded moccasins. On his head he wore a headband made of soft doeskin with twelve eagle feathers standing straight up, and four ermine tails hanging down on each side of his face. A circle of white was painted around his left eye and outlined with black. His eyes showed an intelligent man and his face showed a stern, but friendly personality.

He motioned us to sit. A young warrior pulled a pipe made of red catlinite from a beaded bag and handed it to the chief. The woman lit it with an ember from the fire. The chief held the pipe high, saying a prayer of thanks. He held it up to the north, south, east, and west, and to the sky and to the earth. He took four pulls and handed it to each of the men beside him. They handed it back and he took another pull, then handed it to me. I took four puffs and tried unsuccessfully to stifle a cough, then handed it to Jake. Jake took four big drags from it, inhaling the smoke and letting it out through his nose, then handed it back to the chief.

"You leave your women outside," the chief said. "Bring them in."

My legs were sore from being on a horse for ten days and I groaned as I stood. I went to the door and motioned Eve and Sophie in. Sunkist and Posey came in behind them. The chief nodded to each of them as they entered.

Inside the tepee it was warm and spacious enough for all of us to stand. The smoke from the fire gathered at the top of the tepee and slowly made its way through the opening at the top. In the dim light we could see the walls were hung with bows and lances, and on one side, a buffalo skin shield with twelve scalps tied to the outside edges. It was painted with the crude figure of a buffalo, and a hunter on his horse holding a lance, ready to be driven into the buffalo.

Standing Buffalo looked at Sophie and said, "Situpsa, welcome."

Jake and Butterfly exchanged smiles.

"What was that all about?" I asked Jake.

"Tell ye later."

Sophie said, "I believe he thinks I'm someone else."

"No," Jake said, "he knows who you are."

"How would he know who I am?" she whispered.

"Tell ye later."

We could hear activity from outside—children laughed, dogs barked and men and women talked as they walked by. A rider ran through the camp on his horse and we heard cheers from women and children. From somewhere in the distance we heard a gunshot. Inside, the tepee was silent except for the occasional crackle of the fire.

Standing Buffalo raised his hand toward me. "Hawk, you are here to talk with Little Crow?"

"Yes. Can you make arrangements for me to meet him?"

"I have sent messengers to his camp."

"Will he talk?"

"He will talk. Little Crow is in this war because he has to be, not because he wants to be. It will do no good to try to talk him into surrendering. He knows that he will be hanged if the whites catch him."

"I will talk with him."

"The Thief is not with him."

"You know that?"

"Yes. The Thief left Little Crow's camp and is moving east across the Big Sioux River and back into Minnesota. He will not start the war again. He only wants to stay away from Sibley's army."

"Standing Buffalo, you claim to be peaceful with the whites. Why do you run to the prairies?"

"I am a young man, but I have always felt friendly toward the whites because they were kind to my father. Little Crow has brought me into great danger without my knowing of it beforehand. By killing the whites it is just as if he had shot me down from ambush. The Lower Indians feel very bad because we have all got into trouble—but I feel worse, because I know that neither I, nor my people have killed any whites, and yet we suffer for the guilty.

I was out buffalo hunting and I felt as if I was dead when I heard of the outbreak, and feel so now. We all know that the Indians cannot live without the aid of the white man. We had our reservation at Big Stone Lake. Little Crow sent word to my young men to come down, and that he had plenty of oxen, and horses, and goods, and powder, and lead. But now we see nothing. We went back to Big Stone Lake and left Little Crow to fight the whites. We can no longer hunt the buffalo and the deer to feed our women and children. The white man has killed all of the deer and buffalo and we have to go far into the prairie to find enough meat."

"But you did not fight. Why do you run?"

Sophie leaned toward Sunkist and said quietly, "Would it be proper for the women to leave now?"

"Yes, the women may go," Standing Buffalo said. "They should not be here when men are talking of war."

Sophie and the other women left the tent. I heard a commotion outside and started get up to see what was happening.

The chief motioned me to sit, "It is good. No harm will come to Situpsa."

After a couple more glances toward the door I asked the chief, "Why do you not surrender to Sibley?"

"Four young men from Red Middle Voice's camp killed the settlers at Acton. Then they went and told their chief of it. The Indians knew the white men would take revenge for the killings because women were killed and there would be war."

"Sibley has promised protection for the Indians who were not involved in the killing."

"Do not talk to me of the promises of white men. They have made too many promises and not kept any of them. The white men used our women for their pleasure and promised to feed the children when they came, but they did not. The children are white and Indian, but they are neither to the white men. When a mixed-blood wants to own land, he is an Indian. When he wants annuities, he is a white man. The white man's promises are like a hole in the ground that has no bottom. There is nothing there for the Indians. I cannot condemn the Sioux for going to war. If the white man had been treated like the Indian, he would have gone to war a long time before the Indians did."

"That is true, my friend. But not all whites are that way. Some of us do not care about money and property. We can be trusted."

"What you say is true, Hawk, but how do we know who to trust? To learn who can be trusted we first have to trust. The white man has lied to us and taken all that we had. We have nothing left to trust him with. He has taken it all.

"Fighting this war has done what the white men would do sooner or later. They will take what land we have and run us out onto the prairies to freeze and starve. That is the reason I did not fight in the war. I know we will have no place to call home. We will be running from the white armies until our women and children die—then the Dakota will be no more."

"Chief, I hope that it's not that way, but I think you're right. Little Crow has done the wrong thing by being in this war. I feel your sorrow for your people."

"For the Indian, it is better to starve while we are free rather than starve on a reservation where there is no food. Promises will not fill our stomachs. It does no good to talk about these things when the damage has been done. If the white men would have listened to our cries and felt the pain of our women and children, they would have given us our rations. Now it is too late for talking.

"I am finished," the chief said, then started to stand. "You will stay and eat with us?"

"Yes, of course. Friends should eat together like brothers."

We stood and Standing Buffalo extended his hand. I took it and he said, "You are welcome in my camp, brother Cetan."

"Thank you, brother."

Young Indian girls surrounded Sophie and Eve and laughed and talked with them as best they could. Butterfly and Posey sat back and watched.

"Hawk," Sophie said, "these children are beautiful. I'm having a wonderful time with them."

"They seem to like you, too."

"We're not leaving, are we?"

"No, we'll stay for a while. Standing Buffalo has invited us to dinner."

"Good, I'm getting hungry." She stood and started toward me.

"Situpsa!" the girls shouted as she walked away from them. Sophie turned and gave them a curtsy, then turned back to me.

"All right, just what does 'Situpsa' mean?"

"I don't know, ask Butterfly. Where's Jake and the boys?"

"They're over there."

She pointed at a large group of men standing in a circle watching something going on in the middle. I walked over and made my way to the center to see what was happening.

Jake, Sunkist, Mike, and Steve were kneeling on the edge of a blanket trading with the Indian men. Jake was the obvious favorite with his pipes. Steve had empty copper shells from his Henry rifle that the women urged their men to trade for. Knives and hatchets were on the blanket as well as furs and blankets and all sorts of decorated leather clothing.

All of the trading was done with hand signs and no one spoke. One of the Indian men put out a full buckskin shirt and leggings. A man laid out a butcher knife to trade, but it was refused. Another put out three arrows and they were refused. A handful of beads was refused. The man with the arrows laid out three more arrows and again they were rejected. Each of the men laid something on the blanket to trade, but with a wave of his hand he refused them all. Then he pointed at Steve's rifle.

Steve shook his head. "Not a chance," he said.

The Indian laid out a pair of beaded moccasins, but Steve held fast. A fine, strong bow was offered. Steve picked up the rifle and held it to his chest as if he were holding a baby. The Indian stood and stomped away.

"Did he really think I'd trade off my rifle?"

"I guess so."

"I think I'm done here. I got better things to do than this." He stood and walked away.

That night when the sun went down we gathered around a cook fire with the chief and his family. We had a meal of boiled buffalo hump, wild rice, corn, potatoes, and sweet wild cherries that had been packed in glass jars. The cherries were most likely plunder from the attacks on white settlements.

A fire was built in the middle of camp and a large elkskin drum was brought out. The drummers took their places and started a soft rhythm. People began circling the fire and chanting. The sound became louder and more intense until I could feel the throb in my chest.

A small Indian child approached Sophie. She must have been around seven years of age. She had long dark hair and large brown eyes that reminded me of a fawn. She held in her outstretched arms a long, beautiful red shawl. It was draped over her arms and long fringes made of ribbon decorated the ends and hung down on each side. She walked toward Sophie with her arms still extended, stopped in front of her and said, "Situpsa take."

Sophie bent down slightly and looked at the child. As she took the shawl she said in her new-found Dakota language, *"This is beautiful, may I ask your name?"*

"My name is 'Walks With Grace.' It is for you, so that you can dance the butterfly dance with my people."

"Walks With Grace, will you wait here? I will be right back."

The little girl stood with her arms at her side and moved her body in a small circle to follow Sophie as she walked over to me and whispered in my ear. I nodded and reached into my belt pouch and handed something to her.

Sophie walked back to the child, bent down and said, *"This is for you, Walks With Grace."*

The girl looked down at the colorful dark blue bead that was placed in her hand. Her eyes got big for a moment, mesmerized by the small object. She looked up at Sophie and smiled slightly.

We watched her walk away and sit down to watch the dance that was about to begin.

"Now I understand why she is called, 'Walks With Grace'," Sophie said, admiringly.

Just then, the low booming sound of the drums began their deep heartbeat rhythm, ba BOOM, ba BOOM, ba BOOM. This was accompanied by the higher chanting of men's voices. There were six men seated cross-legged around the four-foot drum playing at the same time. Each beat was performed in perfect unison—one single beat perfectly blended. The combination of drum and voice gave a haunting feeling that was easy to get lost in. It was an ancient sound capable of sending your mind into another world, another time, long ago.

I watched as several women in long dresses moved to the middle of the dancing circle. Each dress was decorated differently and flared out at the bottom to accent movement. Some wore colorful beaded moccasins and feathers in their hair. The dancers moved in a large circle, stepping lightly as each toe came forward to touch the ground. Their bodies moved straight up and down as they bounced lightly, feeling the rhythm of the drums. Their shawls swirled out from their bodies as they danced, commanding attention.

The young men were dressed much more brilliantly than the women. They had adorned themselves in brightly colored feathers, war shirts, breach clouts, and beaded moccasins. Their hair was greased, combed and braided, and decorated with brightly colored feathers and strips of colored cloth. They wore necklaces of brass beads, copper rifle shells and bone. Arm bands circled their upper arms, and attached to some of these was the wing of a large bird.

The breach clouts, decorated by the women with fanciful patterns, were tied around the waist with a leather belt. Feathers, strips of fur and cloth were attached to the belt. Some of the men had sleigh bells tied around their ankles that jingled in time with the music. Their faces were painted with black or white clay. Their bodies had been painted with handprints on their chests and legs. Some of the men were covered with paint from their heads to their feet. Each of them carried a favorite weapon—a lance, bow, war club or tomahawk.

In this vibrant costume they danced—turning and whirling—bowing at the waist—jumping high, bringing their knees up to meet their chest. They shouted loudly, each trying to out-perform the other. Their movements were as graceful as deer playing in the grass. Some strutted and bowed at the waist, reminding me of male prairie chickens doing their spring dance, vying for the females' attention.

I could feel Sophie behind me moving with the rhythm. She put the red shawl around her shoulders over her buckskins and joined the others. They all moved together in a large circle, but each individual responded differently, letting the drums tell their bodies how to move. Sophie danced around the circle, feeling the rhythm. She closed her eyes and twirled, holding the shawl at arm's length, bringing her knee up, skipping on the other foot, then softly stepping down to repeat the step with the other foot. I watched as the shawl flew out behind her, sending each ribbon dancing with the wind. Her arms went up overhead on either side of her face, then straight back down like butterfly wings. She crouched slightly, then dipped to one side with her arms still extended, then dipped to the other side.

I watched her as she danced to the primal sound and had no doubt she could really fly. The world seemed to disappear when music touched her life. It spoke to her and she could do nothing else until she responded in her own way.

The other dancers backed away and stood around the edges watching. They bounced on their toes and clapped their hands in time with the music as Sophie continued to dance. As the drums slowed their rhythm, Sophie slowed hers and stood bouncing lightly up and down, head down and arms at her sides until the sound of the drums completely faded and only the dancers remained.

She looked at me, smiled, and sat down next to me. I didn't know what to say. I was in company with the most exciting woman in the world.

The women came to Sophie one at a time and tied feathers and strips of brightly colored cloth in her hair, and put beads around her neck. She smiled when they said, "*Lila wiya waste*," and thanked each of them.

She turned to me and said, "Why are they doing this, Hawk?"

"They're honoring you as a very special person."

"They called me a beautiful woman," she said with a shy smile.

"Yeah, Situpsa, you are a beautiful woman."

"I still don't know what that name means," she said.

"Didn't Butterfly tell you?"

"She doesn't know either. At least she said she doesn't know."

A small dog came into the middle of the crowd. A boy kicked it and chased it away.

Sophie jumped up and yelled at the boy, "Oh, don't do that! You'll hurt him!"

She ran after the dog and caught it in the snow outside the camp and brought it in. It was a mangy black and white mutt with floppy ears and long scruffy hair. She held it on her lap and scratched its ears while she talked to it.

Standing Buffalo smiled and said, "Situpsa holds the dog like it is a child."

"She seems to have taken a liking to that one," I said.

"I do not understand. Why would she like a dog?"

"Some people like dogs. Most white people have them, some for hunting, some for protection, and some just for companions."

"I know white people keep dogs, but I did not know they could be companions."

"Dogs are more faithful to their owners than some people are to their families. No matter what you do to a dog, he will be your friend. He will protect your children and your women when they are threatened."

The dog became excited at having so much attention and Sophie laughed at his violent tail-wagging.

The chief laughed and said, "That is situpsa."

"There's that name again. Chief, what does it mean, please?"

The chief pointed at the dog.

"I'm a dog?"

He laughed, "No, you are not a dog—look." He pointed at the dog's tail wagging back and forth, "Situpsa."

"Tail?"

The chief said, "I don't know how to say it in white man talk. I think it means 'wagging tail'."

Jake and the rest of the men had joined us by then and when they heard the chief, they broke out laughing.

Jake said, "The name means 'wag-tail'. I think he likes the way you wag your tail when you walk."

"I do not," she said, trying to look angry.

"Yeah, you do, Soph," I said, "and I like it."

"Well, I'll just have to work on that, now, won't I?"

A little Indian girl stood close to Sophie and looked at the dog in her lap. Her eyes were wide and she had a somber look on her little round face.

"Is this your puppy?" Sophie asked the little girl.

"She does not know white man talk," the chief said. "Yes, it is her dog."

Sophie kissed the dog on the top of its head and handed it to the little girl. The girl smiled and ran off with the puppy biting at her heels.

We stood and started to our tents. Sophie turned to the chief and said, "Chief, may we have some of those delicious cherries?"

"Yes, take what you like. They will freeze and the glass jars will break if they are not eaten. The Indian way is better."

"What is the Indian way?"

"Our women dry the cherries in the sun and they will not spoil or break jars in the cold."

Sophie walked out of the circle with a jar of cherries in her hand. She glanced back at us with a smile, slapped herself on the butt and walked away with an exaggerated swing.

We walked to the tepee that Standing Buffalo had arranged for our stay. The floor was covered with robes and woven reed mats and a fire burned in the center. On one side a pile of skins and blankets were laid out for a bed. I was first to get out of my clothes and lay down. Sophie slipped in beside me and curled up next to me with her head on my shoulder.

"They're nothing like the wild Indians we've been hearing about," she said.

"Not at all."

"Want a cherry?"

"Yup, open 'em up."

She opened the jar and took a cherry out and placed it in her navel and smiled at me. "There's your cherry."

I went to pick it up but she pushed my hand away, "No hands."

It didn't take me long to figure out how to get that cherry. So I bent down and picked it up with my teeth.

"Another one?"

"Keep 'em coming."

After half a jar, she took a cherry between her teeth and offered it to me. I bent down toward her lips and plucked the fruit with my teeth from hers. I bit into the cherry, causing it to burst, sending the sweet red juice down over her lips and down toward her neck. It made a path as it trickled down and I instinctively bent down. My tongue followed the trail of sweetness from the hollow at the base of her throat, up her neck, over her chin and finally to her lips. As we kissed she passed the cherry from her mouth to mine in a playful game. She popped a couple more cherries into her mouth, then rolled on top of me and continued chewing. I heard a garbled attempt at what sounded like words.

"What?" I said, looking at her with bewildered amusement.

She then raised her chin, forcefully spit a couple pits over my head, swallowed, then passed her tongue over her teeth with a slight sucking sound and said, "Tasty little things."

All I could do was laugh as I held her close.

During the night, I heard a noise from outside that woke me. Sophie was sleeping on her side with her back pressed against me. I pulled her closer and she responded with a soft moan. Her skin felt warm to the touch as my hands softly caressed her.

The only indication of time passing was the light of the full moon coming through the smoke hole at the top of the tepee moving slowly across the floor. Deep, contented sleep soon fell upon us, the kind that comes only when two people have been completely satisfied.

As my eyelids struggled to open, I noticed the moonlight had been replaced by sunlight. Sophie and I were in the same position we were in when we fell asleep. She groaned and stretched like a cat and in her low morning voice, said, "Good morning."

"Morning already?" I grumbled.

"Yeah, no sense in wasting it on all this needless talk, what do you say we start putting the 'good' into morning?"

I did what any man would do in that situation. An hour later I crawled out of the tent to find the Indians about their business of cooking breakfast and dragging their bedding out to freshen up in the cold March air. Sophie came out of the tepee, stretched, and gave me a kiss on the cheek.

"Will we be leaving today?"

"I think so. Little Crow won't stay close for long."

I walked over to where Steve was sitting on the ground cleaning his Henry, "You spend a lot of time cleaning that thing, Steve."

"Yeah, it should be cleaned every time you shoot it."

"You haven't been shooting have you?"

"No, it got kinda dirty last night."

"What happened?"

"Remember that Injun who tried to trade me for this gun? Well, he figgered he could get it for free. When he thought I was asleep he came into my camp and tried to take it."

"What happened?"

"I wasn't asleep and he didn't get it. We scuffled a little and he ran off."

"So, everything is all right?"

"Far as I'm concerned—he'll have a tough time getting it now with a broken arm."

"You broke his arm? How the hell'd you do that?"

"Dunno, I punched him and he fell. I heard it snap."

"I think we should go talk to Standing Buffalo and find out where Little Crow is."

"Good morning, Chief. I trust you slept well."

"Yes, Hawk, I slept well—better than your friend here." He turned toward Steve, "My warriors have been told to cause no trouble. The man who tried to take your gun has been punished. You will have no more trouble from him."

"Come with me, Hawk," he said. I followed him to his tepee and went inside.

"If you are to see Little Crow, you must go today. He is moving his band north to Canada to find land for himself and his people. He will not wait for you. I have a man who will take you to him. He wants only you to go—not your friends. You must wear nothing but a blanket."

"Why just a blanket?"

"You cannot carry weapons if you only wear a blanket."

"This could be a trap, Chief."

"Little Crow has given his word that he will talk with you and no harm will come to you or your people. He is a man of his word and can be trusted. He will meet with you on the open prairie, alone."

"When do we leave?"

"My man is ready now. Good-bye my brother, I will not see you again."

"Good-bye, my brother. And thank you for your hospitality."

"Then we were defeated and I knew it was the last time.
I gathered my people and we left our valley."

14

CHAPTER FOURTEEN

I TURNED AND WALKED to where the rest of the group was saddling their horses and loading the pack animals.

"Little Crow wants to see me alone."

"What if it's a trap?" Sophie said. "You know your reputation—they'll kill you on sight."

"Standing Buffalo has assured me that I will not be harmed. Little Crow has promised and he is a man of his word. I have to trust him."

"Well, make sure your guns are loaded."

"I won't be taking any guns—neither will he."

"You be damn careful, Hawk."

"Worry if you have to, but I'll be back." I started to take off my clothes.

"What in the world are you doing?" she asked.

"I have to go naked. He figures I can't carry weapons if I'm naked."

"You'll freeze to death."

"I can wear a blanket."

"Well, *that* makes me feel much better."

The cool air felt good on my skin but it wasn't long before I could tell that this was not going to be an enjoyable experience.

I kissed Sophie on the lips and said, "I'll be back tonight." I rode off with the Indian guide onto the open prairie.

The first time I saw Little Crow was at Fort Ridgely in the summer of eighteen sixty-two. I was with John Other Day when he came into the fort. Mister Other Day had told me that Little Crow was a bad man and was not to be trusted. I remembered the way Little Crow looked at me as he walked by. Other Day told me that Little Crow knew Jake and that he knew he was my brother. At that time, Jake and I had made a bad name for ourselves with the Indians by fighting and killing some of Ink Pa Duta's band of renegades.

I saw Little Crow again at the Yellow Medicine Agency when he came to council with Agent Galbraith. He had gone there to convince Galbraith to give the Indians the rations he had in his warehouse. Little Crow recognized me and had called me Tse tan wake wa mani—his grandfather's name. It meant, 'The Hawk That Hunts Walking'.

I rode with the Indian guide for two miles before finding Little Crow sitting on the top of a small hill. The top of the hill was bare but surrounded by trees and underbrush. I couldn't see more than fifty yards in any direction and I felt a little vulnerable.

Little Crow sat with a red blanket wrapped around his shoulders. When he saw us coming he dropped the blanket and sat before us dressed only in the band of feathers that he wore around his head. We stopped about twenty-five yards from where he sat and I climbed down from The Brute. His eyes stayed on me as I walked up to him. He stood up, completely naked for all the world to see and offered his hand. He was taller than me and stood straight as a stick, looking into my eyes as if he could see right into my mind.

I dropped the blanket from around me and took his hand.

"You come with no guns, Hawk."

"I was told you wanted to talk. We do not need guns to talk. If you wanted to fight you should have said so."

"You would come to me if I wanted to fight you?"

"Yes."

"I do not know if you are a brave man or a fool," he said, showing his well-known egotism.

"They are sometimes the same, Little Crow."

He snickered and said, "Yes, Hawk, they are. You are wise for so young. Sit with me and smoke."

I sat cross-legged on the blanket facing him.

He lit a pipe and took a puff, then handed it to me.

"This is Indian ritual that has become custom for us. I see no reason for it," he said, and laid the pipe on the snow.

Little Crow sat cross-legged with his hands on his thighs. I sat with my hands folded between my thighs. He looked into my eyes and pressed his hands down on his thighs twice. I didn't know the meaning of this so I just looked back at him. Again he pressed his hands down on his thighs, this time with more enthusiasm. He nodded his head. Then I got the message and put my hands on my thighs, exposing myself to the elements. Apparently, there was to be nothing hidden in this conference.

In the fall, when the air turns cold, the white-tailed buck's antlers harden and grow. Not so with men. Sitting naked in the cold air is not a good time for men to be showing off the size of their antlers.

Little Crow nodded and said, "What is it you wish to talk about, Hawk?"

"General Sibley has given me orders to talk you into surrendering."

"You know I cannot surrender. I would be hanged the same day if I were not shot first."

"Then you will not surrender?"

"No, I will not."

"Well, that's out of the way. Now for the real reason I'm here—do you know where The Thief is?"

"I have heard that you are looking for Lorraine Bernier. She is with The Thief. Lorraine Bernier came to us with the same request as you. She wanted us to surrender to Sibley and bring in the captives we have. She said Sibley would not hang the Indians who surrender peacefully. I do not believe that and refused to surrender.

"At the time, The Thief and his warriors were with us. He told me that he wished Lorraine to be his wife. I did not want him to do that."

"Couldn't you stop him?"

"The Thief's men were all fully grown and had been in many battles with the Chippewa. My warriors were boys, I had nothing to say about it. The Thief took Lorraine by the arm and dragged her to his tent and made her his wife."

"Where will he go?" I asked.

"He is going back to Minnesota to the Big Woods for the winter. I think he will stay there if he can, it is better living there in the winter than on the prairie."

"Do you know Lorraine?"

"I have seen her. I have seen you with her many times. I saw you when you talked to her near Fort Ridgely. My braves wanted to attack Reverend Riggs and the refugees, but I would not allow it. There were only women and children and old men there and nothing for the Indians to steal."

"They didn't have much."

"No. They had no guns and they had no food. I told the braves that they were leaving the valley and that is what we wanted of the white men. We wanted them to leave our valley and never come back.

"You were sad when you left her. She is the reason you came to talk with me. You must love her very much."

"She's a friend I've known for a long time."

"But there is Situpsa now, and you love her. You are indeed a very brave man. Why do you not take them both for your wife?"

"That is not the white man's way. We take only one wife."

"I see that you and your men have your wives with you. You did not bring Situpsa with you to see me. Were you afraid for her?"

"Standing Buffalo told me that you wanted to see me alone."

"That is true, but if you had brought Situpsa with you I would have welcomed her. She is respected by the Indians because she can defeat the Pa Hin Sa."

His comment was a little embarrassing for me, but all too true.

"Is there anything you don't know about me?"

"I know everything about you and your brother. It is my business to know my enemy."

"I am not your enemy, Little Crow. I come here in peace."

"This is true, but someday we may meet in battle, then I must kill you or you must kill me."

"It would be an honor to die at the hands of a man like you, Little Crow."

"I have said the same many times about you and your brother. Many of my braves have tried to kill Pa Hin Sa and now they are dead."

"You seem to be an intelligent man, Little Crow. Why did you get into this foolish war?"

"You are right, Hawk, this *is* a fool's war. I know the white man will own all of this country. He takes what he wants even if he has to shoot a man in the back to get it—or starve a man from his home as he has done to the Dakota.

"The white man has the paper that talks. The Indian cannot read what it says. He makes us sign the paper before he is finished putting words on it. He says he will do this and he will do that, but then changes the paper to the way he wants it, and we have nothing to say about it.

"The white chiefs have cheated us many times. We never got what was promised us when we signed our names to the papers. We were promised food, but when it came it was spoiled. The white men will not eat it, so that is what they give us to feed our women and children."

I sat and listened quietly, trying to ignore the cold that was creeping into my bones.

"They have taken our land, our hunting grounds, and even our traditions

166

and religion. They take our children and make Christians of them and tell them they cannot speak their own language. This is wrong. Why is the white man's religion better than ours?"

The cold air was getting through my skin and into my body. I struggled to fight off the tendency to shiver until I saw Little Crow shiver slightly and felt a little better.

He continued, "The traders who cheat us when the annuity money comes call themselves Christians. They lie when they say that we owe them more money than we do. The Christian officer who gives out the money does not ask for proof—he just hands the money to the trader. We wanted Agent Galbraith to keep the traders away from the tables so they could not take our money."

Little Crow's arms went up to cross over his chest.

"The traders said if they cannot sit at the tables the Indians could not have any more credit. I told them we will pay our debts with the money we get, but the trader, Myrick, said we can 'go eat grass'."

"That is not what Myrick said. He said you 'cannot eat grass' and that you need the traders to feed yourselves. I was there, remember?"

"Yes, I know you were there, and I know that is not what Myrick said, but that is what the other Indians heard him say. They were very angry and wanted to go to war and kill Myrick there."

Little Crow stood and walked in a circle as he talked. It looked to me like a good way to warm up, so I waited a few moments before I stood and did the same.

"Agent Galbraith said he would send food to the Lower Agency Indians, but he did not. Galbraith says he is a Christian, too. He goes to church, but he lies and starves women and children."

Little Crow was shifting his weight from one foot to the other as he talked. I knew that the cold ground was getting to his feet because the ground had my feet nearly numb.

He continued, "I have been to your churches, Hawk. They teach us to love one another. Why must the Indians love one another when the white men, who say they are Christians, cheat and steal from one another? Why does one man have a house full of food he does not need while his neighbor starves? I do not understand this. Are your God's commandments written only for certain people?"

The wind blew a blast of cold air over us and Little Crow sat on his blanket and continued talking.

"The white man takes all he can get, whether he needs it or not. The Indian shares what he has with all of the band. Is that not a better way?"

I had heard of Little Crow's passion for speech-making but this one had already gone longer than I wanted.

"Before the white man came to this country there were no rich people. All people were the same. There were no poor people. All people were the same. There is no word in the Dakota language that means 'poor'. The white man came to our country and now all the Indians are poor, but we are poor only because we have less than the white man. Before the white man came, our women and children had full stomachs. Then the white man came with his way that he says is better, and our women and children starve. If the white man's way is better, why do we starve?"

At this most inopportune time my stomach grumbled.

Little Crow paused, glanced down and continued, "There are poor people because rich men like Sibley and Ramsey and Galbraith have all the money. Why do they not share it with all of their people? Then there would be no poor people—white or Indian. We would all be the same.

"I went to the white man's church the day before the attack on the Lower Agency. I wanted to hear words from the minister that would help me prevent this war. But he talked only of white men's sinful ways. If the preacher knows that the white men are sinners, why does he not ask his God to make them right?"

"I can't answer that, Little Crow, but I know what you are saying is true. I have seen it too. But this war is not the answer. It will only lead to your end. Wouldn't it have been easier to try to fit in with the white man than to fight him?"

"Hawk, many of the Indians became farmers. They were taking care of themselves but the white men wanted the land. The papers were brought out that said that the Indian did not own this land—his land is over there. So he was made to move from his warm house and leave his crops where he planted them."

"I could use one of those warm houses right now," I said.

"If you are cold, why do you not put your blanket on your shoulders?"

"No, I'm all right. Go ahead and put yours on if you like."

"I do not feel the cold. I will leave my blanket on the ground."

I couldn't help thinking how stupid this was—two grown men sitting in the cold air trying to prove to each other how tough they are.

"The white man uses our land for his houses and takes our wood for his fires, but he does not pay us for it. It is our land, do we not have the right to be paid for what they use? The land was given to us in the treaties the president signed. Why is it not our land if the chief of all the white men said it should be?

SOPHIE'S HAWK

Is your president so weak he cannot make his soldiers do as he tells them? If he is weak they should make another man president. That is the way it is done by the Indians."

I saw a shiver go through the chief and his lower jaw was starting to shake. I thought about pulling my blanket up but didn't want to be the one to break down first.

"I am a chief and I talked to the young men. I tried to tell them to wait for the annuity payments to arrive, but they did not want to wait. I told them that the white men are like the locusts that come and eat their crops in the spring— they are too many to fight. I told the young men that they are like children and the white men will wipe them out. I told them that if they kill one white man, ten will come to take his place. If they kill one hundred white men, ten times that many will come and take his place.

"I have seen the cities in the east. I have seen the thousands of men there and the big guns and the armies. They are like the leaves on the trees when they drop in the fall and come back even more in the spring. The Dakota cannot fight the white men and win. I told the young men they are like dogs in the hot moon when they run mad and snap at their own shadows. 'You are full of the white man's devil water', I told them, but the young men would not listen.

"Some of the chiefs wanted war. Red Middle Voice, Shakopee, Medicine Bottle, and The Thief all wanted war, but I did not. They said I was a coward and afraid of the white men. I am not a coward. I have fought the Chippewa in many battles. I have eagle feathers and scalps to show that I am not a coward. I am their chief and I would lead them in war and die with them.

"I was the one who could make fighting men of them and help them win the war. They needed a chief and asked me to do it. I am a chief, and they would know this, and I would be chief of all the Dakota. So I said I will fight and die with them. They said all of the soldiers were fighting with their brothers in the south. There were not enough here to stop us."

Little Crow apparently liked the fact that he was a chief.

"When we attacked the agency at Red Wood, I watched the killing but I saw no fighting—just murder of men without guns, and women and children being carried away. Myrick was killed and his mouth was filled with grass. Then the Indians said, 'Now look who is eating grass!' When the young men saw that they had the white people scared and running away, they stopped killing and started to take things from the stores and homes.

"Some of the Indians were running past the stables but they did not shoot the men who worked there. I said to them, 'If you are going to fight this war, then fight. If you only want to steal from the white men, then don't kill.' They said they are fighting, but I know they were just killing and stealing and I said to them, 'What are you doing? Why do you not shoot these men?' Then they turned and shot the men. "These were not the warriors I was supposed to lead, they were angry boys trying to show how brave they were by killing old men and babies and women."

Little Crow paused, looked at me, and nodded. "It is cold," he said as he pulled his blanket over his shoulders.

"After the agency attack we saw the troops coming from Fort Ridgely. I told the Indians to hide behind the trees, and when the soldiers got on the ferry to cross the river, to shoot them. They did what I told them and we defeated Captain Marsh."

"I was there, Little Crow, and so was my brother. We were very lucky to get out alive."

"Yes, I saw you. You fought like the warriors my men should have been. I did not want you to die. This country needs more men like you and your brother."

The blankets on our shoulders did little good as the wind picked up and drove the cold deeper into our bodies.

"I made a good plan and we defeated Captain Marsh and his army. I could have done it again but the young men would not listen. All of the Indians went separate ways, and killed and stole without leaders. I could not control them. I was a chief but I did not have men who could fight.

"After defeating Captain Marsh, I wanted them to go and attack the fort, but the young men were afraid. We could have taken the fort that day, but Lieutenant Sheehan came with soldiers and Galbraith came with soldiers. Then it was too late.

"When we fought at Fort Ridgely, they ran back to the woods like scared rabbits each time the big guns would shoot. I was angry and tried to make them act like brave Dakota. They wanted to go fight in New Ulm. There were no big guns and there were more things to steal."

I stifled a yawn.

"We could have taken Fort Ridgely at the second battle with one good attack but the boys who were fighting were afraid. I made a grand plan to attack the fort, but the young men would not follow the plan. It was like trying to lead mosquitoes in summer."

My mind began to wander to the hot summer days when we complained about the heat and took off as many of our clothes as was decent. I remembered

S O P H I E ' S   H A W K

that hot night Sophie and I went and cooled off in the creek. I found it necessary to pull my blanket over my lap.

Little Crow spoiled the moment. "At Wood Lake we could have defeated Sibley and his troops but Sibley was not a warrior. He did not have guards on the flanks to see us surrounding him. He did not have control of his men and some of them went off to steal potatoes from the Indians' gardens. We were discovered and the battle started before we wanted it to."

He glanced down and saw my fingers drumming on my leg. I pulled my hand under the blanket and he continued.

"Sibley was there but he did not fight. Instead he blew the bugle to call his men back. They did not come back. They stayed and fought like soldiers. Then I knew we were defeated and it was the last time. I gathered my people and we left our valley. I knew we would be chased out of Minnesota or be killed, so we left while we were still alive."

I yawned, but he didn't seem to notice.

"I went to the tribes south and west of here to find warriors to help in this war. When we came to their camp they attacked us and killed six of my men. We are outlaws in our own country. We are not welcome in our own land. The young men who wanted this war caused that. They are the ones who are to blame for the trouble, not Little Crow."

I looked up at the sun and said, "It's getting late."

"I was respected by the white leaders. I hunted deer and buffalo with Sibley and we were friends. Now I am the one he is hunting. Henry Sibley knows I am a good man, but still he hunts me like the coyote."

"Little Crow," I asked, "where can I find The Thief?"

"He is on the other side of the valley in the Big Woods by the lake called 'Otter Tail'. He has women and children and not many fighting men. His warriors are all brave men. He knows you are coming and will be ready when you find him. He will have warriors out watching for you and they will kill you if they can. The one who kills Pa Hin Sa will be made a chief. That will make all of the young men want to be the one who kills you.

"The Thief knows you are here and he knows everything you do. You and your men are on a fool's mission. The Thief is a very dangerous man. He will have you and all of your party killed, if he can.

"The man called Sunkist I have known for many years. I knew him when we were children and I heard his name many times when I was in the west. He was in the mountains with the man called Liver Eater. The man Sunkist will be in great danger. He has been in the mountains many years and it would be good to listen to what he says, as if he were a chief.

"If The Thief can take your women he will kill them all. It is the Indian way to kill the women and children to make the men crazy so they will be easier to kill."

"I plan on leaving them at Fort Abercrombie when we cross the river."

"That would be best," Little Crow said. "Now it is time to say good-bye. I will take my people north and never see Minnesota again for war."

"Little Crow, why are you telling me these things about The Thief?"

"The Thief abandoned me and my men when we needed him most. He took with him all of our food and left us alone on the prairie to die like dogs. He is a traitor and he must die."

"It was good to talk with you, Little Crow. If you are going to Canada there is no reason for Sibley to know where you are and I will say nothing to him about it."

"It makes no difference if he knows or not, someday we will be found and killed. Good-bye, Cetan."

"Good-bye, Little Crow."

He stood, pulled his blanket tighter around his shoulders and turned away. He walked over the hill and out of sight. My mind searched all of the things he had said and I came to the conclusion that Little Crow was a good man. It is too bad he had to get caught up in that stupid war. He might have been the one to make things work between the white men and the Indians. He was wise about the ways of the whites and educated enough to know when he was being cheated. He was strong enough to stand up for what he thought was right and had a good concept of right and wrong in both worlds.

What is right in the Indian world is not necessarily right in the white man's world, and what is wrong in the Indian world is not necessarily wrong in the white man's world. It is wrong in the Indian world to let your neighbor starve when you have plenty of food to share. But in the white man's world it is the way things are done.

I walked back and got on my horse and started back to our people. I saw them coming my way. Sophie saw me and came to me at a gallop, carrying my clothes. I got down from my horse and slipped into my long underwear and buckskins, then put a heavy coat over that.

"You must be freezing," she said.

"Got a little chill, that's all. I just want to get away from here. The

Indians gone?"

"Yes, they left right after you did. Sunkist said you'd want to get moving, so we packed up and left, too. Are we headed west?"

"No. Little Crow said The Thief is going back to Minnesota."

"You mean we came all this way for nothing?"

"Looks like it."

"How do you know Little Crow is telling you the truth?"

"We don't."

We walked toward the rest of the people.

"Goin' to the Missouri?" Sunkist asked.

"No. We're going back to Minnesota."

"What's goin' on?"

"Little Crow and Standing Buffalo said The Thief is going back to Minnesota."

They turned their horses around and we headed east. Sunkist came to me and said, "You sure he's goin' east? Little Crow could be lyin' to protect 'im."

"Nah, he's going east."

"Well, yer the boss."

Sophie and I rode behind the rest of the column as they followed our trail back toward the valley.

"You're awfully quiet, Hawk," Sophie said. "Is everything all right?"

"Yeah, everything's all right. I'm just thinking about what Little Crow said."

"What did he say that bothers you?"

"Nothing in particular."

The sun was low and the air grew colder, so we stopped to make camp for the night. While the women were busy making a meal, the men took care of the horses and cleaned their guns.

Jake sat down next to me, "What's going on, Hawk? Why so quiet?"

"Little Crow says we need to protect our women. The Thief will try to kill them. We're not going to say anything to the women except that they are to stay in the middle of the party. We're going to keep them boxed in so they can't be picked off by snipers."

Sunkist and the rest of the men listened in.

"We'll keep the soldiers and ourselves around the women. And if they ask why, just tell them it's best that way. They don't need to know anything more then that."

"Hawk," Sunkist said, "yer really worried about the wimmin, ain't cha? That's why yer goin' back to the valley, right?"

"Right."

"Ye ain't gonna chase The Thief out to the prairies?"

"Right now I'm not worried about The Thief. We gotta think about the women."

"Guess yer right about that," Sunkist said.

"Let's get some sleep and move out as soon as we can see in the morning."

Morning came and we packed up. We walked slowly, keeping an eye on the skyline and in the grass and trees around us. The women rode in the middle of the column surrounded by the men.

"White Feather," I said. "I want to get on the prairie as soon as we can."

"There is no cover for us on the prairie."

"There's no cover for the Indians, either."

"We will go straight to Abercrombie. We will not follow the river."

"Sergeant Mayhew," Wambolt said, "send two of your best men to the right as flankers about fifty yards out—and two to the left, the same distance. Tell them to stay in sight of the column."

Sergeant Mayhew turned to his men, "Taylor, you heard what the man said—you and Kaufman take the right flank. Brown, you and Kline take the left, and keep your eyes peeled. Any sign of Injuns, come back to the column and report. Don't start shooting."

"I didn't know Kaufman was with us," I said.

"Yeah, Vander Horck said to take him along. You didn't see him because he stays by himself and stays quiet. Kinda shy, I guess."

"Well, is he any good out here? I know he don't know nothin' about guns."

"Hawk," Mayhew said, "it hurts me to tell you this, but that's exactly why Vander Horck sent him. He ain't got much time for a man like Kaufman. He's a little slow but he's a damn good man. He'll do all right."

"Why did you send him out on flank? We need good eyes out there."

"The boy needs to feel like he's contributing. He'll fight as good as any of us just to show he can."

"Sarge, we have to look out for the women and do everything we can to protect them."

"You want me to bring him in, Lieutenant?"

"No, just keep an eye on him—and stop with that 'lieutenant' thing."

"Yes sir," he said, with a smart salute.

"And stop with that bullshit saluting, too."

"Just having fun, Hawk, they told me you don't want to be a lieutenant. I won't do it again—bad policy in the field, anyway. It tells anyone that's looking who's in charge, and you got enough troubles without that."

"Steve, you and White Feather take the point. The rest of us will stay around the women."

"I'll take rear guard," Wambolt said.

"Good idea, wish I'd thought of that."

We rode through the day and camped in a draw that night. Sophie and I set up a small tent under the largest oak in the draw. Willows and scrub oaks surrounded us. At the bottom of the draw a small stream lay motionless in its bed. We laid down on a buffalo robe and pulled blankets over ourselves. Sophie pulled herself tighter against me.

"Hawk, what's going on? Why are the men staying so close to the women?"

"We're just keeping you safe from snipers. I doubt if we'll see any before we get back to Abercrombie anyway, but we're not taking any chances."

"You didn't stay this close before, what's changed?"

"I told you —"

"Dammit, Hawk. I know you better than that. Something is different. You're too quiet and you're just laying here looking at the top of the tent. Now what the hell is it?"

"All right," I said as I turned to face her. "Little Crow told me The Thief will try to kill our women first. That way he can pick us off easier when we go crazy."

"I thought it was something like that."

"When we get back to Abercrombie you and the women will stay there. And I'm not suggesting—I'm telling you."

"Is Sunkist going to leave Posey there, too?"

"That will be up to him—but I don't suppose he has much to say in the matter where she's concerned."

She pulled back a little and looked into my eyes. "Hawk, you know me well enough to know that I'm not going to just stay there and let you run off without me. You'd have to tie me to a post to keep me there."

"Then that's exactly what I'll do. I ain't taking you out to those woods to be a target for The Thief. I love you and I don't want you hurt."

"I love you, too, Hawk—but I *am* going with you."

"You'll slow us down."

"Oh, come on. I can ride just as far as you can in a day, and you know it."

"Yeah, I know. Dammit, Soph, I wish we hadn't taken on this chase."

"No you don't. You and these men are in your glory out here getting shot at. You wouldn't live a year scratching in the dirt trying to make corn grow."

"S'pose you're right about that, too. Let's get some sleep. We'll talk in the morning."

"Morning is promised to no one, Hawk."

*"Colonel, you're a goddamned coward.
I'm taking my men and going to that fight."*

15

C H A P T E R   F I F T E E N

WE TRAVELED FOR THREE DAYS without seeing anything but melt-
ing snow and washed-out creek beds. March was coming to a close and the weather
was warming. We were able to travel in shirts most of the time but at night it
got cold.

On the fourth day out a snowstorm hit. Heavy, wet snow fell and covered
the ground. The wind picked up and built drifts behind every stick of grass and
bump on the ground. It got so deep that the horses had trouble pulling the wagon.
We were on flat ground and the wind was vicious. We unloaded the wagon, turned
it on its side for shelter, and huddled together behind it like puppies in a basket.
Sunkist and Posey sat together outside the shelter under a buffalo robe with their
backs to the wind. The snow blew in and covered them so they could barely be
seen. Building a fire was impossible so we shared our body heat until the wind
died down shortly after dark.

A man sat down next to me. "Lieutenant, my name's Chester Rockholt."

Rockholt was a tall, thin man with a pencil-thin mustache. He wore ragged
clothes, heavy army boots, and a wide-brimmed hat that should have been thrown
away years ago.

"Hey, Chester. Call me Hawk," I said and offered my hand.

"Hawk, did Sibley talk to you about Wambolt?"

"Nope, and I didn't ask. I kinda got the impression he's not real fond of
him, but that's his problem and it's got nothin' to do with me."

"You're not curious about why he's not fond of him?"

"Nope, seems Wambolt ain't real affectionate toward Sibley, either."

"There's a reason for that."

"Sounds like you got a story to tell."

"Well, I just figure you should know. He ain't no criminal or nothin' like that, he just can't take orders from stupid people—and that covers just about all them damned army officers." He glanced quickly at me and continued, "Are you familiar with the Third Minnesota Regiment and their troubles?"

"The Third were the ones who beat up on Little Crow at Wood Lake. They seemed to be good soldiers."

"They are—each and every one of them. They just had a bad commander there at Murfreesboro, Tennessee. Chicken-livered coward, he was."

"If the Third was in the war in the south, why are they up here fighting Indians? It seems to me that once they have an army they'd keep them where they need them most."

"That's what you need to hear. Sergeant Wambolt is a damn good soldier. He just got mixed up with the wrong commander—colonel named Lester."

"Lester? What's his last name?"

"That is his last name, Colonel Henry Lester. When the Third Regiment was formed at Fort Snelling in sixty-one, Colonel Lester was assigned commander right off. They had a lot of good men signed on with that outfit from all around the state. He drilled and trained them to be the best fighting unit in the south.

"They were moved to Louisville, Kentucky, then to Belmont with the Ninth Michigan Regiment to guard the railroad while the rest of the brigade went to Murfreesboro. I don't think the army had the confidence in Colonel Lester they should have had, and I think that's why they left them behind. I'm no army officer and I don't try to guess why they do things, but it seems to me that after all that training, the Third should have had the opportunity to go fight the war."

He turned his head toward me.

"Now I ask you," he said. "If the Third was so damn good, why in the world would they be sitting there guarding a railroad? Why weren't they marching to Murfreesboro with the rest of the brigade?"

"You ain't lookin' to me for an answer, I hope."

"Naw, just asking the same question Wambolt asked. He wanted to go to Murfreesboro but Lester seemed content where he was. In April of sixty-two we got orders to march to Pikeville to find a company of rebel cavalry that was supposed to be camped there. We marched eighty miles over the Cumberland Mountains. The road was good but Lester kept us at a slow march and we stopped every few miles to rest. Hell, we could have made twenty miles a day with no problem, but he said he wanted his men in top condition when they met the enemy. Wambolt tried to get him to move faster but Lester kept saying, 'I want

178   SOPHIE'S HAWK

these troops in top condition when we find the enemy'."

Rockholt chuckled to himself.

"One day, they heard a rifle go off and Lester damn near shit his pants. From somewhere down in the woods he hollered an order to take cover. Well, we didn't really need to be told to take cover—it's kind of a natural thing to do when someone starts shooting at you. Everything was quiet except for some yelling at the front of the column and Lester was nowhere to be found. After a bit, a soldier came through the woods and said that someone accidentally shot Private Stewart through the chest.

"Lester came up out of the brush and had a fit. He screamed and yelled at that poor soldier till he damn near passed out. Wambolt got a hold of him and dragged him off to the side and got him calmed down. He told him it was an accident, that the boy didn't do anything wrong. Lester came uncorked and yelled at the soldier for walking around with a loaded gun. 'That's dangerous,' he said. 'People get killed doing that!' We couldn't believe he said such a stupid thing. We all had our guns loaded, fer da cripes sake—we were in a war. A gun ain't much good if it ain't loaded.

"Lester just looked at Wambolt with his mouth hanging open, his lips were moving but he wasn't making no sound. He cleared his throat and stammered with all the authority he could muster, 'Well, you make sure these men practice all the rules of safety from now on. I don't want anymore men killed in my regiment.' Wambolt just looked at him and said, 'Right, Colonel. We'll be real careful not to hurt anyone in this war'."

"What about the guy who got shot?"

"The bullet went through both his lungs, but somehow he made it. By the time we got to Pikeville the Confederates were gone. Lester said they must have heard the Third Minnesota was on its way. Wambolt said they most likely ran out of rations waiting for us. From there we went to Murfreesboro, Tennessee. That's where it all went to hell. We set up our camp in town, then Lester split his forces leaving the Ninth Michigan and about eighty men of the Seventh Pennsylvania Cavalry at the first camp. He moved his Third Minnesota Regiment and the artillery about a mile and a half northwest. One company of the Ninth Michigan was posted as provost guard at the old courthouse. There were about nine hundred-fifty men stationed there at the time.

"About that time, Brigadier General Crittenden showed up. He called a meeting with Colonel Lester and asked why he had separated his forces. The reason Lester gave was that he couldn't find a campsite with enough water for the entire brigade. Crittenden didn't want the forces to be separated like they were, so he took Lieutenant Duffield to look for water. They found enough water for five thousand men, then went back to Lester and raised all kinds of hell. He inspected the rest of the brigade, trying to figure out why Lester did some of the things he did—nothing was done according to the way it was supposed to be done.

"July thirteenth, Confederate General Nathan B. Forrest surrounded our pickets at daybreak and captured them without firing a shot. Then he attacked the camp of the Seventh Pennsylvania Cavalry and pushed into the Courthouse Square and the streets of town. They over-ran the cavalry camp, then attacked the courthouse and the Ninth Michigan. The Ninth was ready for them and after a few hours of fighting, they beat them back about three hundred yards.

"Wambolt and the company he was with, sat at their camp listening to the battle going on in town. The rebs were beating hell out of the Ninth and Wambolt wanted to go up there and help them. Lester ordered Wambolt to form his troops and be ready to move out. Wambolt called his men together, formed a battle line and moved forward. About a quarter-mile out, they were ambushed by a woods-full of rebs. Lester stopped the march and ordered the artillery to open fire on the woods. A small force of rebel cavalry attacked them from the left, but when they saw Lester's artillery, they broke off the attack and ran back to the woods. Lester ordered his men to halt and stay where they were.

"From where we were we could see the smoke from the battle and black smoke from burning buildings, but Lester still wouldn't order us to march. The rebs were killing the Ninth and Wambolt was getting pissed. He yelled at Lester, 'Let's go get them johnnie rebs, for Christ's sake!' Lester got mad and told Wambolt that *he's* charge of this company and he'll decide when and whom to attack. Then he ordered Wambolt to get back in ranks and await orders.

"A man from the Michigan camp came in with a dispatch from Colonel Parkhurst, commander of the Michigan boys. Lester read the letter, then tore it to pieces and threw it on the ground. He was mad because he thought Parkhurst wanted him to send his troops up there to do his fighting for him. Wambolt put his face close to Lester and asked if we were going to go fight now. Lester used the excuse that he had no idea how many troops they had up there, and until he had a positive number he was not going to risk the loss of his entire company in a reckless attack. He said he needed numbers so he could draw a plan of attack.

"Wambolt glared at Lester and accused him of being scared. He looked him in the eye and said, 'You're scared you're gonna get shot.' Lester ordered Wambolt

SOPHIE'S HAWK

back to ranks or he'd have him busted to private and have him digging latrines. Wambolt put his face up to Lester's, looked into his eyes and called him a goddamned coward. Then he told him he was taking his men and going to that fight and told Lester he could just sit there and shiver like the goddamned coward he was. Wambolt stormed off, leaving the colonel standing with his mouth hanging open.

"A second letter came from the courthouse requesting reinforcements and was again ignored. Wambolt heard about it and gathered a small group of men and left the camp to get into the battle. No one saw or heard from them until after the battle.

"After holding the town for nearly eight solid hours of hard fighting, Colonel Parkhurst was overwhelmed and had to surrender his force. A full three hours of that battle was in direct defense of the courthouse. They didn't surrender until the courthouse was set on fire and they had no choice. They lost eleven men killed, eighty-six wounded and thirty-six missing. Colonel Lester lost none of his men and later bragged about it.

"Lester went to see Colonel Duffield who'd been wounded in the battle. He went under a flag of truce and got close enough to see the whole confederate force and decided it was too large to fight. He didn't know that the Rebels were standing back because of his cannons. He also didn't know that, with those cannons, he might have beat the rebs and chased them back to Chattanooga.

"Lester wanted to surrender to the rebs, but to do that he needed a vote from his officers, so he called a meeting. About that time, Wambolt and his squad returned from the fight. He hadn't lost any of his men and they'd only fired a few shots before the Michigan Company surrendered and the fight was over.

"Someone told Wambolt that Lester was in conference with the company commanders and was going to surrender us to the rebs. Wambolt blew up again and stomped over to the table where the officers were talking. He yelled at Lester and told him that we weren't going to surrender to nobody. Lester reminded him that he was not an officer *yet* and he was not welcome at the table.

"There was a time when Lester wanted to make Sergeant Wambolt a lieutenant, but the army wouldn't give him any more officers than he already had. That attitude was about to change. Wambolt would have been a damned good officer if he'd had the chance. Wambolt agreed that he was not an officer and added, 'I ain't no goddamned coward, either'.

"Lester accused Wambolt of insolence and threatened to have him arrested for insubordination, then ordered him away from the table. Wambolt softened his voice and told Lester that all we wanted was the right to get into that battle and do what we came there for. Then he asked the colonel not to surrender his men before they've had a chance to fight. Lester called in his guards and had Wambolt removed from the meeting. After about fifteen minutes, Captain Hoit, the company commander, came to Wambolt and told him they'd voted to fight.

"Wambolt immediately began gathering the troops together, organizing the battalion with all four guns and all the cavalry and infantry for one massive attack.

"Wambolt saw some of the officers and Colonel Lester gathering at the table again. He started to walk over but the colonel's guards stopped him. He asked the guard what the meeting was about. The guard said all he knew was that Lester told him to keep him away from the table. Wambolt watched as the officers talked and didn't like what he was seeing. They stood and saluted Lester, then went to their companies. The camp got quiet and Captain Hoit came and said that Colonel Lester had taken another vote and decided to surrender the company to the rebs. He said he didn't like it, but that's the way it was.

"Wambolt was furious and asked how in the hell Lester had pulled that off. Captain Hoit told him that Lester had called another meeting of a few officers that he knew would vote to surrender and kept it secret from the rest of them— otherwise he never would have gotten the vote to surrender and he knew it.

"Wambolt went into a conniption fit. He shoved the guards away from him and stormed over to Lester. He was screaming at Lester, wanting to know how the hell he'd pulled that off. Lester got to his feet and called for his guards but none of the guards would come to his aid. They stood and watched Wambolt yelling and shaking his fist at Lester. His face was red and the veins on his neck stood out as his temper flared. Finally, two privates went to him and pulled him away, but before they could get him clear, Wambolt hit Lester in the face and knocked him backward onto his chair. The chair collapsed and he tipped over backwards to the ground. He got to his feet slowly as he screamed at his guards to arrest Wambolt for striking an officer in the United States Army.

"Lester got his surrender and the rebs took our guns and cannons, and all of the equipment they could carry. They burned the wagons and tore up the railroad, then burned the railroad bridge and cut the telegraph wire.

"The battalion was gathered up, sent to McMinnville, Tennessee and paroled on condition they wouldn't fight in the war until they could be exchanged. The wounded men were left at Murfreesboro until they could recover, then they were supposed to surrender. Lester and his officers were sent to Knoxville. After being declared exchanged, the Third was paroled and sent to Minnesota to fight in the Indian wars until they could prove they were fit to fight the rebs.

"Sergeant Wambolt was called to testify against Colonel Lester and told the whole story. The army wouldn't let Lester press assault charges against Wambolt, probably because it would not look good to have a sergeant bring such a disgraceful affair to the public's attention. They did, however, pass the word around that he was a troublemaker. That's what Sibley meant when he said he didn't need that kind of man around. Sibley's got some things in his military record that he doesn't want the public to know, too."

"Were you there?" I asked.

"Yeah, I was in the Third Minnesota Regiment when we were surrendered to General Nathan Forest."

"So, is Wambolt still with the Third Minnesota?"

"No, the Third was recalled and sent back to fight in the south."

"And they didn't want Wambolt down there, right?"

"Right. They figured he'd be less trouble to the officers here fighting Indians."

"Well, Wambolt is certainly no trouble to us. In fact, it's kinda comforting to have him around. He knows what he's doing and he ain't afraid to get into it with the Indians."

. . .

The old man paused to light his pipe.

"I'm tired. We'll continue this in the morning."

"Of course, Mister Owen, you get some rest. Miss Biegler and I will go to the cabin and go through what we have so far. We're not going to print the story about Sergeant Wambolt—we only want stories about the Sioux Conflict."

"No," Hawk said, "that story goes in or we'll stop this interview right here."

"But, Mister Owen—"

"Wambolt's story goes in—or you can get up and leave right now."

"Very well, Mister Owen, we'll use it."

A light rain was falling the next morning when the reporters came out of the cabin. The old man sat next to the grave wearing a heavy elkskin coat and a wide-brimmed hat.

Lorraine went to him, "Come in, Dad, you're going to catch cold."

The old man looked up at her, "I'm not worried about gettin' a damn cold," he grumbled. "Let's go in. We need to finish this."

"We're ready when you are, Mister Owen."

"Where were we?" He asked.

Abigail looked back on her notes and said, "You were on the prairies of Dakota in a snowstorm."

"Oh yes, I remember that storm all too well..."

She lay on the ground with blood running from her side.
"Hawk—I'm hit bad."

16

CHAPTER SIXTEEN

WE STAYED BEHIND THE WAGON till daylight and started on our way.

"Sunkist," I said, "the hay and rations are about gone from the wagon. Why don't we put the supplies on our horses and leave the wagon here?"

"I say we load the supplies on the horses and keep pullin' the wagon—might come in handy later on."

The weather had warmed and the spring snow was melting and running in the streams. There were puddles of water everywhere and we had to pass through many of them. The mud was thick and black and stuck to the wagon wheels and the horses' hooves. We had to stop and scrape it off from time-to-time so they could walk. The wagon was empty, making it much easier for the horses to pull.

We climbed above the low, waterlogged ground onto a higher prairie where the going was a little easier. We camped alongside a shallow creek bed. The creek was filled with water but there were banks on each side where we could find cover if needed.

In the morning, we left our camp and moved away from the creek. We liked the open prairie where there was little chance of being surprised. There were small rises in the ground that could not be seen from horseback.

A shot rang out from behind one of the rises. Private Meyer fell sideways from his horse. The bullet went through the middle of his chest and killed him instantly.

"Don't panic!" Sunkist yelled. "Move your horses in a random pattern and keep moving—and stay close to the women!"

"What about Meyer?" Sophie asked with concern in her voice.

"Sophie," Sunkist said. "Meyer's dead. We cain't do nothin' for 'im now. Jiss keep movin' and don't walk in a straight line." He turned in the saddle and shouted, "Mayhew! Go tell those men out there to split up so they can cover more ground."

Suddenly, fire came from a small ridge to the left. One of the left flankers dropped from his horse. We were on flat ground with nowhere to hide, so we whipped our horses and headed forward at a gallop. Fire continued from the ridge but we had opened the distance enough that it had no more effect. I could see a line of trees to our right.

"Head for the trees!" I shouted.

"Hawk!" Wambolt hollered back at me, "There might be Indians in those trees."

"If there were, they would've attacked from there, not from the ridge."

We turned our horses into a shallow draw where we dismounted and took up positions facing the enemy. I pulled the dragoon from the saddle and handed it to Sophie.

"Here, you keep this. You know how to handle it and if the fight gets close, use it."

I also gave her the Hawken, knowing it was a much better weapon than the one she had. I had my Henry and had little use for the dragoon.

The dry grass from last summer stood tall enough to give the Indians all the cover they needed. We lay in the ditch and watched the Indians crawl slowly toward us through the grass.

"Hold your fire till they get close," Sunkist whispered. "Wait till you're sure of a kill before firing—one kill for each shot."

An Indian rose to his knees with his rifle to his shoulder and Steve's Henry barked. The Indian fell on his face. The metallic sound of that lever gun operating was comforting as he jacked another shell into the chamber.

We saw no movement after that and started to think they had moved away. But suddenly, the shooting started again. Their bullets flew high overhead at first then started to drop in amongst us. They could see no more to shoot at than we could, but they kept firing.

"Taylor, you and Kaufman go up the crik to that bend and watch for anyone crossing," Mayhew said. "If you see 'em—kill 'em. Brown, you take Profant and go downstream."

Suddenly, the Indians stood and came at us at a run, screaming and yelling. There weren't more than twenty of them, but they came fast. They'd shoot and drop to their knees to reload. They were fast with their reloading and were quickly up and at us again.

"FIRE!" Wambolt shouted. All of our guns went off and an Indian dropped for each shot. Our fire stopped the charge and made the Indians drop to the ground for cover. The sounds of rifle fire came from the left as Kaufman and Taylor got into the fight.

Just as Sunkist had expected, the Indians had moved a party around to get behind us. Wambolt and Mike sloshed through the creek to the bank on the opposite side to watch for Indians to the rear. Again, the Indians jumped up and made a rush at us. They were only about forty yards from us now and made great targets. Each time we fired, their numbers dropped. Steve and I kept up a steady fire with the Henrys and made any movement by an Indian his last.

Suddenly, as if from nowhere, a band of Indians on horseback appeared from the east.

"We're in trouble now," Jake said.

My heart began to beat hard and I had a feeling that this was the last fight. The Indians came at full-gallop directly at us. I was about to take one out when White Feather put his hand on top of my rifle.

"Do not shoot."

The riders turned their direction from us to the Indians we were fighting. They hit their ranks and fired their guns and bows into our attackers, sending them running in all directions.

"What the hell is this?" I said.

"They are the ones who attacked us before," White Feather said. "Your women saved the life of one of them and now they have saved us."

"Well, I'll be damned."

"They have paid their debt."

"Will they follow us to the fort?"

"No, they have done what they must do. They will not come back."

The Indians didn't stop, but kept running until they were gone and out of sight. Then it got quiet. No Indians were to be seen and silence took over.

"What do ye think, Hawk?" Jake said. "Think they're gone?"

"Yeah, they're gone. Indians don't like being at a disadvantage."

We stayed in our positions a short while before getting up to move.

I looked around, "Is everyone all right?"

"Seems we came out of it alive this time," Jake said.

Brown and Profant came in from the right.

"You boys all right?" I asked.

"Yep, you guys had all the fun. We didn't see nothin'."

"Let's go see where Kaufman and Taylor are," I said.

We walked up the wash till we came to Kaufman. He was sitting on the ground with his rifle across his lap, staring at Taylor's dead body.

"He's dead, Hawk."

I took him by the arm and tried to lift him to his feet.

"Come on, Lee. There's nothing you can do for him now."

"He's dead, Hawk."

"We know that, Lee, now git up and get moving. We'll bury him right here."

"How come he had to get killed, Hawk?" He looked at me with tear-filled eyes.

"Lee, he died fighting like a soldier. Now get on your feet and get goin'."

Kaufman just sat there.

"Lee, if we don't get out of here we're all gonna die. Now get off your ass and let's go." I took one arm and Jake took the other and we lifted him to his feet and led him back to the company.

"You gonna bury him, Hawk?" Kaufman asked, looking back over his shoulder.

"They're digging his grave right now, Lee. Don't worry about it."

"I ain't never seen a guy git killed before."

"I know it's hard, Lee, but that's the way things are out here. Men die."

We took Kaufman and handed him over to Sergeant Mayhew.

"When we get back to Abercrombie," I said, "he stays there."

"Guess you're right, Hawk. He never should have come in the first place."

We gathered our horses and wagon and started across the prairie. The terrain was becoming flat and the hills and valleys slowly disappeared behind us. Lines of cottonwood trees in the distance revealed the occasional creek bed or low, wet ground. We rode quietly. The squeak of saddle leather, the plod of the horses' hooves, and the rattle of the empty wagon made it almost impossible to stay awake. I rode close to Sophie and each of the men stayed by his woman. Wambolt and White Feather rode about fifty yards in front of the rest of the troop. Visibility was almost endless across the flat plains, so we had the flankers come in and ride with the rest of us around the women.

Far off in the distance a buffalo appeared as a black speck against the horizon. A light wind blew steadily from the west, making the grass appear as waves on a golden lake. The sky was blue with occasional white billowy summertime clouds drifting lazily overhead. I followed a cloud's shadow as it moved slowly over the ground and tried to see which cloud was making the shadow. The ride

SOPHIE'S HAWK

had become monotonous and everyone was having trouble staying awake in the saddle. Some of the soldiers dismounted and walked next to their horses. I tried to make the decision to do the same, but at that point, decision-making, planning, and the execution of a sequence of proceedings were not within the bounds of my abilities.

From my half-conscious state, I heard the sound of a rifle and a bullet passing overhead—then another shot and the sound of lead hitting flesh. The sting of buckshot hitting my right thigh brought me to my senses in time to see Wambolt tumble from his horse. I turned side-to-side to find where the shooting was coming from, when suddenly I heard another bullet thump into flesh. Sophie's face went blank and her eyes suddenly came to me, then she slumped forward on her saddle. I was about ten feet from her and tried to turn The Brute toward her but the shooting had become steady and the animal, in his panic, would not respond to the reins. Sophie leaned to the right and slid from her horse to the ground.

I jumped from the saddle and ran to her. She lay on the ground with blood running from her side.

"Hawk—I'm hit bad," she said.

I lost control. I screamed at her, "God, no—Sophie! Oh, dear God—how bad is it?" I was suddenly panic-stricken. My hands shook and my voice trembled. I turned and yelled, "Posey—Sophie's hit!"

Posey was already there and knocked me aside with a swing of her arm as she ripped Sophie's coat open to show a large hole in her side.

I leaned down and kissed Sophie on the mouth and cried, "Please don't die, Sophie! Oh, God—please don't die."

Posey pushed me away from Sophie and said, "Go!" pointing her finger away.

Sunkist came and pulled me away from her. "Hawk, let Posey do her medicine. If Sophie's gonna live through this, you're gonna have to stay out of the way. Go see about Wambolt."

He pulled me backward away from Sophie. I ran to where Wambolt lay on the ground. My hands trembled uncontrollably as I opened his coat to find frothy blood pumping from the wound in the side of his chest. He tried to talk, but blood shot from his mouth and only a sickening gurgle came out. He looked at me with panic in his eyes. His face turned blue as he tried to speak, then his head dropped back and his sightless eyes stared at the sky.

Sergeant Wambolt was dead.

Sophie was unconscious while Posey and Eve worked on the wound. Tears flowed from both women's eyes as they worked. Posey wiped the tears away with her sleeve and continued to work on Sophie.

I was unaware of the fighting going on until the clatter of rifle fire filled my ears and brought me out of my panic. I jumped onto The Brute and whipped him to a hard gallop toward the Indians. Jake yelled for me to stop, but I was out of my mind and was determined to kill each one of those goddamn Indians single-handedly.

Soon the rest of the company was right behind me charging at the enemy. We hit their ranks firing our rifles point blank. I flew off The Brute and hit a standing man with my full body, driving the stone tomahawk into his head at the same time. We fought hand-to-hand, using our rifles as clubs as we tore into them like a pack of hungry wolves on a wild pig. I held my rifle in one hand and my tomahawk in the other, swinging them round and round, clubbing any Indian that got close. Jake jumped from his horse and flew through the air, connecting with two Indians, knocking them down. He fought with his hammer-like fists breaking face bones and killing with a slam on the nose.

The Indians were in a state of panic to see these insane men butchering them almost at will. They hardly fought back, but got to their knees and allowed themselves to be slaughtered.

The fighting stopped and the survivors took off and ran across the grass like the devil himself was on their tail—and the devil *was* after them—it was Jake, Sunkist, Steve, Mike, Torgerson, Mayhew and a crazed lunatic swinging a stone tomahawk. The soldiers behind us fired at the escaping Indians and kept them at a dead run until they were out of sight.

Jake came to me and pulled me off a dead man I was chopping at with the tomahawk. "Come on, Hawk. He's already deader than he needs to be."

Sunkist stood over a dead Indian, panting like a mad dog. "Take scalps," he said in a hoarse whisper.

"I damn sure will," I said, and ripped the scalps off three of the savages and looped them through my belt.

"Now, cut saplins and hang them scalps high so them Injuns can see 'em," Sunkist said, in a voice that sounded more like a growl.

I had never heard that tone in Sunkist's voice before, and to hear it now raised goosebumps on my skin. His eyes were slits and his mouth was tight like a knife-cut across his face and it hardly moved when he talked. Then he stopped, stretched himself tall and straight, took a deep breath into his barrel chest and settled to a comfortable stance.

"They ain't gonna bother us no more," he said. "They're scared and they know they're in trouble with the Pa Hin Sa. Jake, that was good, you smashin' their faces in like that. That was one of the things ye did that made 'em afraid of ye. They think you cain't be killed."

I turned and ran The Brute hard back to Sophie. Sunkist followed close behind.

Sophie lay on the cold ground with blankets over her. Her face was white, but still as beautiful as ever.

I laid my hand on Posey's shoulder.

"She's alive, Hawk," Eve said. "Posey got the bleeding stopped."

I knelt by her side, smoothed her hair, and looked down at her face. Tears flowed from my eyes. Sunkist knelt beside me and I laid my head on his shoulder and cried, "Goddamn it, Sunkist, I don't want her to die."

"Hawk, she's a strong woman. If anyone can come out of this alive, Sophie can. Posey knows what she's doin'. Come on, we gotta git her to the fort."

I straightened myself up, dried my face and asked, "Did we lose anymore men?"

"Kaufman's dead," Sunkist said. "He came with us when we attacked the Indians and took a ball through the chest. He died proud."

"Anyone else?"

"Yeah, Wambolt and two of the soldiers. I didn't know their names."

I went to Wambolt's body. I didn't want his scalp taken so I cut his hair off to the roots and held it up to the wind. We dug a grave next to his body, laid his blanket over him and buried him. I sent one of the soldiers ahead to alert the post surgeon that we had wounded coming in.

We laid Sophie on a blanket stretched around poles and lifted her into the wagon and moved out.

"Sully," I said, "you take it easy on them horses and try to stay on smooth ground."

"Hawk, there is no smooth ground out here."

"I know, Sully—just take it easy, okay?

"Do the best I can, Hawk."

We were on ground now that was as flat as a kitchen table and there was no chance of being surprised by any more Indians. We could see buffalo on the horizon twelve miles away. The country was so big it seemed like we would never come to the end of the grass. Thirteen scalps flew in the wind above the wagon.

Posey and I stayed close to Sophie. We traveled slowly to soften the ride for her. She'd open her eyes once in a while, but there was no sign that she was seeing anything.

Mayhew rode up next to me.

"Hawk, I was with Kaufman when he died. He said you made him proud to be a soldier. He told me to give you this." He handed me a large Bowie knife with a moose antler handle and the picture of a hawk engraved on the polished blade. "He wanted you to have it so you will know that he is a good blacksmith."

"I have to admit I wasn't sure, but now I know he was. Thanks. Mayhew, you coming with us after the Thief? We could sure use a man like you."

"Nope. I rode with Sibley for a while chasing Injuns out on the plains. I've had my fill of it and I'm goin' back to Grand Marais. Got me a claim up there and I figger on bein' a rich man in a couple'a years."

"Rich on what?"

"D'ruther not say. We got enough people hangin' around up there waitin' to get rich."

"Well, if you change your mind, just know we'd like to have you along," I said, and went back to Sophie.

That night we camped in a small patch of woods. I stayed awake next to the wagon through the night with Sunkist and Posey by my side. Sophie woke up in the night and called my name.

"I'm here, Sophie."

"Hawk, how bad is it?"

"Posey and Eve got you patched up and said you're going to be all right. You sleep now, and we'll have you at the fort tomorrow."

"I love you, Hawk," she whispered with her eyes closed.

I broke down and started crying again. I leaned down, put my arm around her head and kissed her on the lips. Her face turned a little toward me and, even in this difficult time she showed a hint of that perpetual smile.

Late the next day we arrived at Fort Abercrombie. The surgeon met us at the gate and directed the wagon to his quarters. The surgeon had us lay her on a bed. He opened the bandages to look at the wound.

"Who did the patchwork?" he asked.

"Sunkist's wife."

"Is she a trained surgeon?"

"No, she's a Cherokee Indian."

"Well, if she ever wants a job as a surgeon she can work for me anytime. It's going to take a while for her to heal up but I think she'll make it. The squaw did a good job."

"Doctor," I interrupted, "I need you right now, but if you ever call Posey a squaw again, you're the one who's going to be needing a surgeon."

"Beg pardon?"

"Posey is the woman who helped Sophie. She is a woman, a damn good woman, and you will not call her squaw again."

"I'm sorry, Mister Owen. I meant no disrespect."

"I know that, Doctor. No harm done."

"You'd better leave now. She needs to rest."

"Let me know if anything changes."

I kissed Sophie on the lips and walked out the door. I found the rest of the people standing around waiting for me.

"She gonna be all right, Hawk?" Jake asked, wiping a tear from his cheek.

"She's got to be—I ain't gonna think nothin' else."

I stepped up to Posey, put my arms around her and kissed her on the cheek. "Thank you, Posey."

She hugged me back and smiled, "Sophie be okay."

I nodded my head, "I know."

We walked our horses to the barn and threw down hay for them, then walked in a group to our cabins.

"I'm going out after The Thief," I said.

"When do we leave?" Steve asked.

"I'm doing this alone."

"Hawk," Sunkist said, "you cain't go up against 'em alone. You got no idea how many they are, and don't know where to find 'em enna ways."

"Sunkist, this is my fight now and I'm going to do it alone. I don't want anyone else getting killed for something that I started."

"We came and found *you*, remember?"

"Yeah, well, if I hadn't got mixed up with Lorraine none of this would have happened."

"Well," Jake said, "I ain't gonna stand here and argue about this. Hawk, you ain't going alone and that's the way it stands."

"Well, you guys do what you want. As soon as I know Sophie's gonna be all right, I'm headin' out whether you're ready or not."

"Hawk," Sunkist growled with fire in his green eyes, "we was born ready. You jiss say the word."

The next morning I was up before the sun and went to the hospital to see Sophie. She was in the bed just as the surgeon had put her the night before. She was breathing softly and her face had come back to its normal color. I leaned down and kissed her lips.

Her eyes opened and she smiled at me, "Ain't cha glad you brought me along, Hawk?"

"No, Sophie, I'm not glad I brought you along. When you get out of here we're going back to Hawk Creek. We'll set up a farm or a sawmill or something."

She closed her eyes and took a deep breath.

"I need to sleep now," she said.

"Yes, you sleep. I'll come back later." I bent down and kissed her on the lips.

As I was turning to go, I heard her say, "Hawk, don't worry, I'm not going to leave you."

I found the surgeon sitting at his desk. "She's going to be all right, ain't she?"

"Yes, Hawk. She'll be just fine."

"Anything I can do to help?"

"Yes, there is one thing you can do."

"Name it—anything."

"Stay out of here and let her rest."

"I guess that makes sense. Let me know if anything changes."

"You asked that before and I said I would. Now, off with you—and quit worrying, she's going to be all right."

"Thank you."

"Hawk," the surgeon added, "what is this that the Indian woman used on the wounds?" He opened a cloth and showed me the balls of moss he'd taken from Sophie's wound.

"I don't know. It's something she uses to stop bleeding."

"I'm going to send it to Saint Paul and have it analyzed. Medical people have the highest respect for Indian medicines and this may be something that could be useful."

"Don't bother, that stuff is used along with Cherokee religion. I doubt if a white surgeon would be able to make it work."

"Nevertheless, I'm sending it in."

"Well, I hope they learn something from it."

"We always learn something from our studies. Unfortunately, we often learn that we can't use the specimen."

"Well, good luck."

"What did the surgeon say?" Jake asked.

"He said it'll be a couple of days before he could tell anything."

"Then you won't be leaving for a couple of days, right?"

"Right. You guys just relax, I'll let you know when I'm ready."

"Yeah, sure, Hawk—you let us know."

We went to Captain Vander Horck's quarters to give him our report.

"Little Crow is moving into Canada to find land for his people," I told him. "He won't be coming back to Minnesota."

"You demanded his surrender?"

"I didn't demand anything. I asked him if he would surrender and he said no."

"And that is the end of it?"

"That's all there is, Captain."

"Hawk, General Sibley has sent orders —"

"Captain, you take any orders from Sibley and throw them in the fire. I'm going after The Thief and Sibley's got nothin' to say about it."

"General Sibley sent orders for you to go to the Big Woods and search out and destroy any hostiles you find there."

"Those orders I will follow."

"He also said to give you the supplies you'll be needing."

"All I need is ammo. You got that?"

"Yep—lead bars and minie balls and ammunition for your Henrys."

"I'll take the bullets but I won't be stopping long enough to run ball."

"Hawk," he said, "I'm sorry about Sophie. Anything you need to find The Thief is yours—just name it."

"Thanks, Captain. I think I've got what I need."

"Injuns, hail yeah, they's runnin' all over the gud damn country. They don't bother me none though onna conna they think I'm nuts."

17 CHAPTER SEVENTEEN

THAT NIGHT I DIDN'T SLEEP. I couldn't get the thought of tracking down The Thief and his band out of my mind. I pictured myself charging in with a tomahawk in one hand and Kaufman's Bowie in the other, slashing and chopping as I went through their camp. I could see them running from this bulletproof, indestructible maniac with the devil on his team.

Then I got realistic. I knew I needed to make plans that included a real killable man with real weaknesses and limitations. I was determined to do this alone, so in the middle of the night I wrapped some supplies in a blanket and went to the stable for The Brute. I saddled him up and walked him out the door. My heart nearly jumped out of my chest when I saw a group of men on horseback in front of me.

"Guess you forgot to give the word, huh, Hawk?" Jake said.

"Yeah, I guess. How did you know I was going?"

"Like I said before, I ain't seen a hawk yet that could sit on one branch for too long, and a hawk that has a rabbit in sight don't wait around. That's you, Hawk. Let's go."

"White Feather, do you know how to get to the Big Woods?"

"Yes, I have hunted there many times."

"Any idea where The Thief might hole up?"

"I know of camping places the Indians use, but The Thief will not go there, he will find new places to camp."

"Well, either way, we have to get to the woods before we can find him."

"The Thief will find us. He probably knows we are leaving right now."

We rode out of the fort and down the hill to the ferry, crossed the river and out onto the flats. We rode until the sun started to lighten the eastern sky and

Sunkist called a halt.

"Git down and stretch yer legs. Let the horses graze for a while and take a nap. We got a long way to ride."

It was then that I noticed that Jake, Mike, Sullivan and White Feather were all carrying Henry rifles and had their muskets tied to their saddles.

"Where'd all them Henrys come from?" I asked.

"We asked Vander Horck for 'em," Jake said. "He got 'em from the sutler. He says Sibley said we could have all the guns and ammo we needed. Don't figure he meant Henrys, but then Vander Horck bent the rules a little and bought all they had in the store. Got a bag of shells for each of 'em, too."

"Well, that'll make things a little easier. The Thief damn sure ain't figgerin' on taking on six Henrys. You didn't want one, Sunkist?"

"Been shootin' this Springfield for a lotta years—kinda got attached to 'er. You boys best lay down for a spell. I'll keep an eye peeled."

I didn't sleep long, so when I woke up I walked over and sat with Sunkist.

"How'd you get the women to stay behind?" I asked.

"They didn't want to come along. They wanted to stay with Sophie."

"Good, I don't want her to be alone."

"Worried about her?"

"Can't get her out of my mind. Damn, I hope she's all right."

"She'll be fine, Hawk. Go clean that rifle or something—git somethin' else goin' in yer head."

"Don't want nothin' else going in my head."

"You gonna be up for a while, then?" he asked.

"Yeah, you get some sleep."

I sat on the ground thinking about the times I'd had with Sophie. The time I met her in the 'dance studio' when she wanted to give me a bath but I didn't want her to. I had never had a woman before and didn't know what to do—and I didn't want a woman that way, anyway. I was in love with Lorraine at the time and Sophie didn't fit into the plan. I told her that I didn't think it was right that she be there when I was taking a bath, and that I should just get out of the tub and leave. She said to me, "You're a decent man aren't you, Hawk?" I said I was.

Then she got serious and told me that she was a decent woman and didn't belong there. We both left and went our separate ways. I met her again in Mankato while she was working in a restaurant. I didn't know at that time that she was going to be such a big part of my life.

I saw her again when I was in the hospital after being wounded by some young Indians trying to take my scalp. She nursed me back to health and I stayed in her house for three weeks. That's when I fell in love with her. I was still looking for Jake at the time and couldn't stay.

The next time I saw her was when we were in Mankato looking for some thieves who were looting homes after the Indian wars. She came away with me and has been with me ever since. She was the joy of my life, always laughing and having fun—always making jokes with me because I can be so ignorant sometimes—but always showing me that she loves me. Tears ran down my face as I sat there with the image of her beautiful face before me.

"You all right, Hawk?" Jake asked, waking me from my thoughts.

"Yeah, I'm okay." I wiped the tears from my eyes and stood up.

"Maybe we should get moving, the boys are up and ready. Come on, we'll talk while we ride."

The men rode ahead of us, knowing we were talking about Sophie.

"I know what yer goin' through, Hawk," Jake said. "I went through this a couple of times."

I knew what he was talking about. He was remembering finding Ma dead and his Indian girl, Sisoka, being shot.

"Yeah, but Sophie ain't gonna die," I said. "She's gonna be all right. She's got to be."

He reached out and slapped my shoulder. "Sophie's gonna be all right. Come on—let's catch up with the others."

. . .

The old man paused and stared at the floor. A tear dripped off the end of his nose.

"God, that was hard," he said softly.

Abigail and Mister Holcombe swallowed hard to keep their tears from flowing.

. . .

At sundown we found the Otter Tail River and followed it up-stream to the falls. An old man came out of a shelter cut into the side of a bank. He was dressed in worn-out buckskin trousers, old, dirty moccasins and a plaid shirt that looked like it hadn't been washed in years.

"Where ye boys headed?" he asked with a toothless grin.

"We're lookin' for Injuns. Ye seen any?"

"Injuns! Hail yeah, they're runnin' all over the gud damn country—the woods south of here is full of the damn critters. They don't bother me none though, onna conna they think I'm nuts."

"I wonder why they think that—what's yer name, old timer?"

"Wells. They call me Grampaw Wells. Don't know what mu front name is, ain't been called that in a coon's age. Mostly they jiss call me Grampaw—been called a bunch of other names, though. Wanna hear some of 'em?"

"No thanks, we can imagine," Sunkist said.

"What are you doin' sittin' out here in the middle of nowhere?" Jake asked.

"Nothin'."

"Nothing?"

"That's what I said, ain't it? Nothin'. I jiss sit out here in the sun and whittle till mu gud damn fingers near fall off, then I go in and sleep a spell."

"Don't you get people to come and visit?"

"Hail, the last people I saw was wagons movin' up the road gittin' away from the Injuns, er headin' out to Montanee lookin' fer gold." He looked at the ground, spit and said quietly, "Damn fools." Then his head came up and he said loudly, "There ain't no gud damn gold in Montanee."

"Now, how do you know that?"

"Y'ever heard of any gold out there? Why the hail would there be gold out there? Ain't nothin' but rocks an mount'ns."

"You been out there, old man?"

"Yep, buncha years back—me and another guy." The old man paused and looked at the ground and scratched his shaggy beard. "Now what the hail was his name? Aw hail, don't matter none enna ways. He's dead now. He went through the ice checkin' his traps—the damn fool. I tole 'im not tuh go out there."

"Anyone else come though here?"

"Huh?" He looked up at me like I had just woke him from a deep sleep. "Oh," he said, "no, ain't been no one through here lately—Injun or white. Coupla years back, some fellers come and measured the ground. They figgered on buildin' a town around here but the damn redskins skeered 'em away. Hea, hea, hea. Don't know what the hail they'd wanna build a town out in this gud damn county fer enna ways. Ain't nothin' here but me and the Injuns and the gud damn coyotes— and ain't none of us worth a pinch o' shit."

"You know an Indian named The Thief?"

"Hail, they's all a bunch of thieves, ever gud damn one of 'em. Steal the skin off'n yer smelly feet if ye'd let 'em."

"The one we're looking for is named 'The Thief'. You know anything about him?"

"Nope, don't know none of 'em. I jiss sit here in mu mansion and let the whorl pass me by. Don't give one squirt about the whole gud damn thing. Far as I'm concerned they can burn the whole gud damn whorl down and start over." He looked at the ground and spit.

"Who's they?" Jake asked, smiling at the old man.

"Now how the hail do I know? Ever'one ye talk to got some god or some other gud damn spook they think is to blame for all this mess."

"Seems you've got a bad attitude, Mister Wells."

"Attitude! I'll say attitude. By Jesus, let me tell you about attitude. Back in Otter Tail country where I came from they—"

"Grampaw," Sunkist said, "is there a place we can git across this river?"

"Yep, this here's the Otter Tail River. Canadians built a ford 'bout three mile downstream, ye kin cross there if it ain't worshed out."

"Thanks, Gramps." Sunkist turned to us. "Let's go afore the ole geezer starts carvin' us up with that butcher knife."

We turned our horses and started to walk away.

"Eddy Evans!" Grampaw shouted. "That's what his name was. Eddy Evans!"

"Who was Eddy Evans?" Mike asked.

"The feller I went to Montanee with. Crazier'n a gopher in a graveyard, he was."

Steve looked at Mike and said, "Don't even think it."

Then I realized that they were from Otter Tail County where Grampaw was from, and their name was Wells.

I said nothing.

I could see Steve and Mike talking as we moved south into the hill country.

A voice came through the forest.
"Hawk, I am the one who killed your woman."

18 CHAPTER EIGHTEEN

WE TRAVELED FOR ANOTHER DAY and camped in a draw for the night. Sometime during the night I was awakened by a voice far off in the forest. It was a high-pitched voice shouting something I couldn't hear well enough to make out the words. Sunkist was standing next to a tree with his Springfield at chest level, peering into the darkness. I stood and quietly walked to him.

"What is that? Wasn't no coyote."

"Injuns playing their scare games with us. They're gonna do that till they're dead. They call from somewhere and say things that's supposed to make us skittish and piss us off."

"Well, so far it's working—what an eerie sound."

"It's the way the sound travels in the cold air and echoes off the trees. We're gonna to have to keep two men on guard all the time from here on."

Suddenly, I felt a tap on my shoulder. I jumped and let out a short cry, then whirled around to see White Feather standing right behind me.

"You scared the livin' shit out of me!"

"You are afraid. It is good. Men who are not afraid die young. We have Indians all around us. I do not know if they are from The Thief's band, but they are there. We must stay awake."

"How close are they?"

"There are none close, but they are following us wherever we go."

"I figgered that," Sunkist said. "They'll wait till we let our guard down before tryin' anything."

"How the hell are we gonna fight them in this timber? They can be anywhere."

"So can we, Hawk."

Suddenly, Sunkist raised his face to the wind.

"What?" I whispered.

"Injuns."

"Close?"

"Yeah, close."

A voice came through the forest, "Hawk, I am the one who killed your woman. Come and get me!"

The voice came just once and I couldn't tell from which direction.

"Easy, Hawk. He's just tryin' to make you mad and go runnin' around the woods like a skeert turkey." Sunkist said, "Ye gotta learn not to listen to that, it's just skeer tactics, that's all."

I turned to White Feather but he had disappeared.

"How the hell does he do that? He shows up and disappears without a sound."

"All them Injuns can do that. They're just as good in the woods as a deer. And that, mu boy, is why we have to stay watchful all the time. Work yerself up to where you can feel someone around you. You don't have to see 'em or hear 'em, you can just feel 'em around you—jiss like when you can feel someone lookin' at ye."

"Yeah, Ma used to do that with us when she didn't want Pa to know. She'd just stare at us till she got our attention. Sometimes I'd want to ask her a question or say something to her, and when I looked up she was already looking at me waiting to hear what I had to say. Sometimes she'd even answer the question before I asked it."

"That's the way it works—jiss feel 'em. Watch this." He focused his eyes on Jake who was talking with the others.

Shortly, Jake began to fidget and turned to Sunkist.

"What?"

"See? That's how it works."

Jake walked over, "You want something?"

"No, just learnin' the boy about gettin' someone's attention without sound."

Jake walked back to his place without comment.

The sound of tom-toms came through the forest and made me think about Sophie's dance at Standing Buffalo's camp. I had to get her out of my mind if I was going to stay alive.

"Can you tell where the drums are coming from?" I asked Sunkist. I could tell as well as he could, but just had to say something to get Sophie off my mind.

"Yeah, but don't know how far off, might be on the other side of that hill or half a mile away."

"Wanna go see?"

"Figgered you'd say that. So did they. They'd like us to come lookin' fer 'em. We're gonna let them come to us."

The sound of a big drum started a deep boommmm, boommmm, boommmm echoing through the forest like far off thunder. The drum waited for the echo off the trees to die before sounding. The sound was almost pleasant to hear for a while, but soon became irritating.

"When I find that drum," Jake said, "I'm going to shove it up somebody's ass."

The rest of the men laid down and went to sleep. Sunkist and I stayed awake and listened. It was silent except for the drum and an occasional chirp from a night bird or the rustle of a field mouse in the leaves on the ground. The tiny sounds made the night seem even more silent. I heard a leaf fall from a tree and the snap of a twig. Soon the sky in the east started to lighten and the breeze picked up in the treetops. The air was cool and smelled like rain. Far off in the distance, thunder rumbled.

We heard the rustling of leaves in the dark. I stiffened up and raised my rifle.

"Jist a deer," Sunkist whispered. "Ye can tell by the way he makes sounds. If it was an Injun, he wouldn't be makin' no sounds. Deer can be completely silent when they wanna be, but when they think there ain't nothin' to be worried about, they can make as much noise as we can. Hawk, why don't cha lay down and git some shut-eye, I can handle this."

I lay on the ground with my blanket wrapped around me and tried to sleep. My mind went to Sophie. I wanted to be with her and hold her in my arms and kiss her. I wanted her to be with me among these beautiful trees and experience with her the beauty of nature. I wanted to hear her laugh and watch as she studied one interesting tree or flower and then go to another. I wanted to hear her call me over to look at the peculiar leaf, or rock, or blade of grass that caught her eye, or the hole in the base of a tree where some animal had laid claim to make its home.

I awoke to the sounds of the men saddling their horses and getting ready to travel. The drums had stopped and the forest was waking with the sounds of robins and cardinals. Crows called from their perches sounding like they were calling, HAWK, HAWK, HAWK. Small birds flittered from tree to tree, pecking at the bugs and seeds. A nuthatch lit on a tree trunk close to me and hopped around it as if there was no gravity for him to be concerned about. Upside-down was as easy a way to move as any other.

"Where we goin' from here?" Jake asked softly.

I answered in a whisper, "South, I guess. I'm just following White Feather."

As we entered the Big Woods there was an immediate feeling in one's soul that echoed the reverence of the forest—an unconscious response that one did not have to think about, it just happened. Breathing slowed, voices softened, and any spoken word came out as a whisper. It was nature's cathedral—without doors, without windows, a place of peace and reflection.

The ground was rough with hills and valleys, creeks, rivers, and small mud holes. Maples, oaks, elms, and basswoods towered above us. Some of their trunks were so thick it would take three men to wrap their arms around them. I rode past a fallen log that lay decaying on the forest floor, covered from end to end with moss and mushrooms. It was large enough that, if one crawled inside, it could offer protection from rain and wind and enemy.

The canopy at the top of the trees was so thick that it shut out the sunlight so the woods seemed to be in twilight even at high noon. Nothing grew on the forest floor but small shrubs and thin grass and we could see for fifty yards through the trees.

Where a tree had died and fallen, it left a hole in the canopy and sunlight was allowed to hit the ground. Small seedlings took advantage of the sunlight and sprouted and grew.

Small potholes dotted the floor at different elevations, making me wonder why the higher ponds didn't drain into the lower ones. I'd see a pond to the right of the trail and look down the hill to the left and see another pond.

Ferns and wildflowers grew on the floor. Trillium grew all around, turning the ground white like patches of snow. Mushrooms of a hundred varieties clung to the sides of the fallen trees. Some were dull gray or brown and some showed bright red, yellow and gold. Some were beautiful to look at, but there were those so hideous that, even with their bright colors, a man would not dare get close.

Sunkist rode up next to me, "Some of them there mushrooms ye can eat—but some of 'em can kill you in a minute. Deadly poison, they are. But then," he said with a slight grin, "some of 'em will send you on one hellava a vision quest. Best to stay clear of 'em all."

Once again, thunder rumbled in the distance. The sky was clouding over and rain was on the way. The rocky ground made it almost impossible to stay quiet and the air was heavy with the smells of the deep, damp woods in the spring. We saw no deer or rabbits or squirrels—nothing but small birds. The wind made

SOPHIE'S HAWK

a low moan as it moved the tops of the trees. Near the forest floor it was as still and damp as the air in Ma's kitchen. You could feel the silence. We moved without words, looking up and down, taken in by the quiet beauty of the woods. The click of the horses' hooves and the creak of saddle leather, normally unnoticed, were now all too obvious.

Around midday, a light mist began to wet the woods. We stopped for hot coffee and some rest in a deep draw. We dug our canvas ponchos out and slipped them over ourselves.

It was not necessary to try to hide our presence because the Indians knew where we were. Because of the openness and silence of the forest floor, the Indians couldn't get near us without being seen or heard—nor could we effectively hide from them. The sound of hooves clicking on the rocks was replaced by the sound of hooves splashing through mud puddles.

White Feather scouted ahead watching for potential ambush spots. From what I could see this whole area was a good ambush place. We walked slowly between the hills, keeping a distance between us. Nothing gave any indication that Indians were around, until we came to White Feather sitting cross-legged, leaning against a big maple tree. Both hands held his pipe to his mouth.

"What's up?" Sunkist asked.

With a quick twist of his wrist and without looking up from his pipe, White Feather pointed his thumb up the trail. Ahead, about thirty yards, we saw a dead hawk pinioned on a small tree that had been sharpened to a point. I walked over to it and pulled it off the tree.

"How long since they did this?" I asked.

"It was still warm when I found it. They are watching. What will you do?"

I pulled my patch knife from the sheath, opened the body of the hawk, pulled out the heart and cut the veins. I held it high and turned around slowly, offering it to the six sacred directions, then dropped it in my mouth and swallowed it.

"Now what the hell'd you go and do that for?" Mike asked. "Yer an animal, Hawk."

White Feather watched with no more emotion than to nod his approval.

"That was good, Hawk," Jake said. "They'll like that."

"Why the hell did he do that?" Mike asked again.

"The Indians believe that eating the heart of an animal will give the man its spirit," Jake explained.

I took the tail feathers, then buried the carcass with a ceremony I made up as I went. Some of the feathers went into my hatband and the rest into my side pouch.

"That's real perdy, Hawk," Mike said.

"Thanks."

The next day, the rain had stopped and heavy fog lay at the bottom of each valley and draw. Mosquitoes swarmed around us so thick that we had to pull our ponchos up over our heads for protection. Our trail led us into heavier brush and trees. Willow, sumac, hazelbrush and ironwood closed in around us. The floor of the woods was covered with a thick mat of leaves, grass, and broken trees. Visibility was down to a few feet, which was good and bad—we couldn't see the Indians, and they couldn't see us. We knew, however, that they were following every turn we made. We tried to follow game trails where we could and more often had to push our way through the brush.

From the top of a hill we could see a thunderstorm in the distance. Lightning flashed and thunder rolled. Dark streamers of rain hung from the clouds like a gray curtain.

White Feather came to us and said, "We are in the hunting woods. Here we will find The Thief—or he will find us."

We found two more hawks and I swallowed the hearts and pulled the tail feathers out of each of them and slipped them into my pouch. Again, I buried the remains with the made-up ceremony, hoping the Indians were watching. As we rode, I pulled each of the tail feathers from my pouch and slipped a blue bead over the shaft—for Sophie. I planned on giving them to her when we got back. We came to a fourth hawk that had been killed and stuck on the branch of a tree. It had been cut open. I reached in and found the heart.

"Someone give me a piece of meat," I said.

"What's up?" Jake asked.

"This one ain't attached. I think it's poisoned."

Jake slipped me a piece of jerked buffalo meat and I dropped it into my mouth, chewed it, and swallowed it.

Immediately, drums started. The deep boom of the thunder-drum echoed through the trees in a low, continuous hum.

"There's that damn drum again," Jake said. "If that thing is supposed to piss us off, it's working just fine."

"Take it easy, Jake," Sunkist said. "That's jist what they want it to do."

White Feather had decorated himself with grass and small leafy sticks to camouflage himself while he prowled silently through the woods.

A strange feeling came over me like someone was watching me. I turned in the saddle to look back.

"How far ye figger he is behind us?" Sunkist said quietly.

"You feel it, too?"

"Been smellin' that critter fer half a mile."

"You guys keep movin'," I said.

I tied my Henry to the saddle, covered myself with leafy branches and filled my hatband with grass. I let the party get ahead of me before dropping off The Brute and slipping into a heavy alder patch. Jake turned and looked back at me, then I saw him say something to Sunkist. Sunkist glanced back and kept moving. I figured they knew what I was up to.

I rubbed my face and hands with mud. I then crawled through the brush to a freshly-fallen tree and sat in the middle of the branches to wait. I watched a deer browsing on the new leaves and saw his head come up and turn to look over his back in my direction. In a flash, he jumped and disappeared into the brush.

I didn't have to wait long before I heard a soft rustling of dry leaves behind me. I had Kaufman's Bowie knife in my left hand and my dragoon in my right. The sounds got closer and I knew something was moving my way—it was either another browsing deer or an Indian hunting. I sat perfectly still and only moved my eyes. Very slowly, I turned my head to the left and, about twenty feet away, an Indian appeared. He carried a shotgun and a scalping knife. He moved slowly, slightly crouched at the waist and his eyes squinted as they searched the forest.

I snapped a dead twig and he stopped to listen. I snapped another one. I could have shot him right there and then, but I wanted him to see me before he died. I pulled the hammer back and the metallic click-click-click stopped him in his tracks. He suddenly tightened up, stood, and turned toward me. I stood up with the dragoon leveled at his chest. His mouth dropped open and his eyes got big and he knew he was dead when he started to pull up his shotgun. The big pistol roared and recoiled heavily. White smoke engulfed the man as my bullet ripped through his heart and shattered his spine.

The blast echoed through the forest as he dropped to the ground dead. I stayed still for a while, thinking there might be more Indians, but none came. I walked to the quivering body. He lay on his back two feet behind where he stood before the bullet hit him. I took his scalp, then reached into my pouch, pulled out a hawk feather with a blue bead and stood it in the hole in his chest. I loaded the empty chamber in the dragoon, all the while watching and listening before starting back to the group. I moved as slowly and quietly as I could, looking at each blade of grass and twig in the forest. I had just hidden from an Indian well enough to get within killing distance and I knew someone could very easily do the same to me.

I suddenly felt eyes on me. It sent chills up my spine and I instinctively dove behind a fallen log. I got into a crouch and waited to see what was going to happen. In a small patch of brush, I could see what appeared to be the form of a crouching man—but I knew that the forest can play tricks on a man's eyes and he can see just about anything his imagination can create. I studied the form for a short time before deciding it was not a man, then looked away. I was about to move again, but turned one more time to look at the imaginary man in the patch of alder. The form was not there. A chill went through me, thinking that I might have been that close to death but had escaped, for whatever reason.

It was late afternoon and the air was becoming cold. Suddenly, I heard voices ahead of me. I got down on my belly and listened but couldn't make out any words. Moving inches at a time, I crawled toward the sounds, feeling the ground for anything that could snap or rustle and give me away. I could feel my heart beating heavily in my chest and my breathing became deep and irregular. Fear was taking control of me but I knew I had to control it—or die.

I slithered like a snake with the dragoon out ahead of me. Suddenly, the ground next to me exploded and showered me with leaves and dirt. A load roar stormed through my ears and a sharp pain shot through my chest. My heart stopped for an instant, then began a rapid, lopsided beat. I rolled to the side to get away from the violent uproar happening a foot from my head. Dirt and grass burned my eyes when I caught a glimpse of a ruffed grouse as it flew away and glided downward into the dense branches of a fallen tree fifty yards away. Before the grouse landed, I heard the familiar sounds of Henry rifles being cocked. I lay in the grass trying to get my heart to stop hammering in my chest and my hands to stop trembling. I felt a lump growing in my throat, like I was about to cry.

I knew the sound of a Henry rifle working, but I also knew that we were not the only people in the world who had them. I stayed in my position for what seemed like an eternity. A shiver went through my body as I felt a tick crawling up my leg, but I didn't dare do anything about it.

Then I heard Sunkist's voice. "Friend er foe, come on in, we're ready fer ye!"

"It's me—Hawk."

"Well, bring that scelp in here so we can see it."

I walked into the camp, took a seat next to Jake and raised my pant leg to remove the tick.

"Had some fun out there, I see."

"Yeah, somehow I knew he was there and it made me nervous."

I felt another tick crawling up my neck so I picked it off, took aim, and launched it into the air with my fingers, then smiled.

"Figured that was what you was up to. Sunkist knew it, too."

"Ye got that power I was tellin' you about. Ye didn't have to see him or hear him, ye jiss kinda knew he was there," Sunkist said as he pulled a tick off his leg.

"Yeah, it's a kind of a feeling you can't get away from."

"I think fear puts that extra feelin' in a man. A self-pr'tection thing, mebbe."

"Hawk," Jake said, as he picked a tick off of his neck and pinched it between his thumbnail and index finger. "I wasn't much worried about you comin' back alive. You been sneaking up on deer and elk all yer life—but don't make a habit of goin' off by yerself, okay?"

"Ain't makin' no promises, Jake. Except I will promise you we'll get Lorraine back, one way or another. You guys listen up," I said. "There's another one out there. I saw him looking at me through the brush. I got no idea who he is or why he didn't kill me when he had the chance—but I know he's there."

"Yeah," Sunkist said. "I felt it too. Kinda spooky, but I have a feelin' he ain't after us."

My confidence in myself and our troop was at a peak. Lorraine was close and in a few days we would have her and be on our way home.

The evening was spent pulling wood ticks from our bodies and checking each other for the ones we couldn't see. It was spring and the ticks were out in full force with an army of their own.

Sunkist held a tick in his fingers, looked at it and grumbled, "Wood ticks are the most despicable little critters God ever put on this earth. They can send a chill through the biggest, meanest, toughest man on the planet. They're dang near indestructible—vulnerable only to knives, tomahawks, guns, fire and hungry little tweety-birds—and I see no justification fer their existence a'tall."

He pinched the tick hard between his fingernails and flicked it into the fire.

. . .

Miss Biegler rubbed her leg through her cotton dress and then around the back of her neck. "It makes my skin crawl just thinking about those horrible little creatures," she said.

I reached into my side bag and pulled out a handful of hawk feathers.
"Here, take some of these and leave one with each
Indian you kill—it's for Sophie."

19 CHAPTER NINETEEN

WHITE FEATHER CAME INTO CAMP the next morning and said, "I have found The Thief's camp. He is two miles south of here by the lake. He has about thirty men with him and a few women. I know some of these warriors and they are the best. We will not all come out of this alive."

"Yeah, we will, White Feather," Sunkist said. "We gotta go in there knowin' we're comin' out alive, or there ain't no reason to go in a'tall. If you think you cain't do somethin', ye failed before ye started."

"Will he stay where he is, White Feather?"

"Yes, maybe three days. He is making jerky and drying food. He has scouts out and many guards around the camp. It will be hard to get to him."

"Lorraine?"

"He has one small bark shelter built in the middle of his camp and a guard at the door. She is in there, I think."

"Can you draw a picture of his camp?"

White Feather picked up a stick and began drawing in the dirt. He drew the shape of tepees with straight lines and round shapes to show wigwams. He showed six wigwams and three tepees circled around the bark shelter in the center.

"Do you know where the sentries are?"

"No. They are all around the camp."

"Well? What do you think, Sunkist? A night time full-out attack?"

"We try that, and Lorraine would be dead before we took a second shot. We're gonna have to get in there and take her out without The Thief knowin' she's gone."

Sunkist's nose went in the air. "Someone comin'. Get hid."

We led our horses to the underbrush and waited.

"He ain't Injun," Sunkist said, "he's white. How the hell did a white man git this far with his scelp still on his haid?"

"How do you know he's white?"

"Well, cain't ye see him? He's right over there under that fallen tree." He indicated the direction with his eyes and a nod of his head. "He sees *you*."

"Hawk—" A soft low voice came from the brush.

I didn't answer, but lowered myself behind a log. I thought for sure that I was sitting on the front sight blade of some Indian's rifle.

"Hawk—" It came again, a little louder.

"Damn!" I said, and peered over the log, "Good Horse, that you?"

He raised up onto his knees and looked at us. He was thin as a sapling and his beard was thick and black. His eyes were slits below his eyebrows and could only be seen by the glint from the sun. His complexion was dark brown. His black hair was tied in a knot behind his neck and hung almost to his waist. His clothes were ragged buckskin trousers and a leather shirt blackened by sweat and grease.

"You know him?" Jake asked.

"Yeah, that's Bon Cheval, Lorraine's brother. I told you about him when we were with the Métis."

"Oh—that Good Horse. You said he'd be good to have around, right?"

"Damn glad he's on our side. He's probably worth five good men."

"Well, bring 'im in and let's have us a look," Sunkist said.

With a short motion of my hand I told him to come in. He dropped into the brush and disappeared. A grunt came from behind us and we all jumped at once and turned around to see Good Horse crouched in the dogwoods directly behind us.

"Now, how the hell did he do that?" I asked.

"Beats hell otta me," Sunkist said.

Good Horse held up a finger as if telling us to wait, then disappeared into the brush.

Sunkist looked hard at the man. "Kinda reminds me of a feller I knew back in thirty-two. Feller called his self 'Moon'. Tall and lean like that, and tougher'n a keg o' nails. Sometimes, when he got in a fix, the guy could turn his self into an animal—not really an animal, mind ye, he jist fought like one.

"We was lookin' fer beaver up on the Snake River and got ourselves in a scrape with a mess of Blackfoot. We was behind a pile of logs that we'd set up to fight 'em off. But they was too damn many of 'em and they got around a'hind

SOPHIE'S HAWK

us. Ole Moon turnt his self around and started hissin' and snarlin' at them red critters and showin' his teeth and slappin' at 'em with his hands helt like they was claws. He sounded scary-like, like a wrathful badger.

"He threw his gun to the ground and charged the whole damn bunch. There musta been fifteen of 'em. Then he broke the charge and stooped low to the ground and hissed and snarled at 'em agin. Them Injuns' horses was skeert and raisin' all kinda hell and they couldn't get 'em to stand still enough to get off a shot at ole Moon. They musta figgered he was tetched in the head. N'Injun is skeert of a body what's been tetched by the White Painted Lady.

"Ole Moon was almost laid on the ground with his knuckles in the dirt and his hind legs was cocked like he was ready to spring on 'em like a badger. He snarled and snapped his teeth at 'em till one of them Injuns raised his rifle to take a shot. Moon run at him on all fours and sprang off'n the ground clear over the Injuns horse—took him off the horse and chewed the throat outta that red coon. The rest of the Blackfoot saw that and took off whoopin' and hollerin' to high heaven. We never had no trouble with the Blackfoot after that. They kinda left us be."

Good Horse came back with his pack in his hand.

Sunkist looked deep into his eyes. "You be Moon?"

Good Horse turned to me, "Hawk, Lorraine is in the camp just a short way from here. She is not well and we need to get her out of there."

"That's why we're here, any suggestions on how to do that?"

"The Thief will be hard to fight. His men are scattered all around the hills and an attack would not work. We will have to kill them one at a time."

"How 'bout we set up sentries and pick 'em off with sniper fire?" I asked.

"We can do that until The Thief figures out what we are doing, then he will kill Lorraine—and he will do it slowly where we can watch. We will make his men come to us."

"How we do that?"

"Let them know where we are and wait for them."

"Don't you think they already know where we are?" Jake asked.

"Yes, he knows where we are—but he does not know that we know where he is."

"So, we make them think we're here and when they come to us, we go to the camp and get Lorraine," I said.

"That's what I was trying to say."

"I'll git the fire goin'," Sunkist said.

"Make lots of smoke," Good Horse said, "so they think they're coming to a trap."

"Why would you want them to think it's a trap?" Mike asked.

"They will think we are all here to fight them. They will send more men here and leave fewer in their camp."

"I'm goin' to the camp," I said.

"You ain't goin' nowhere without me," Jake said.

"And I must go," Good Horse said. "The rest will stay and fight here when they come."

"I'll stay behind and help these boys," Sunkist said. "We ain't gonna let them Injuns have no fun a'tall."

"The men going to the camp will start tonight when it gets dark," Good Horse said. "Keep the fire burning all night to guide the Indians here. They will not be able to resist such foolish white men who build big fires at night."

"White Feather," I said, "can you get a fast horse for Lorraine to ride?"

"You will have a good horse for her to ride."

"You gonna walk again?"

"Where I go, I will not need a horse," White Feather said, as he walked away.

I reached into my side bag and pulled out a handful of hawk feathers. "Here, take some of these and leave one with each Indian you kill—it's for Sophie."

"Good idea, Hawk—let 'em know who they're dealin' with," Sunkist said.

"I just hope we don't have enough feathers to mark 'em all," Mike said.

Evening came and Good Horse, Jake, and I started through the forest. We came close enough to their camp to see the light from their fires. Good Horse pulled us together.

"Now," he said in a whisper, "we will come into the camp from three sides. I will go around to the other side. Hawk, you go straight in. Jacob, you go to the left. We will make our way in separately. You will know when I am there, then you will move in."

I walked slowly and carefully, keeping my eyes moving. The moon was throwing enough light to see the outline of the trees and underbrush. We had plenty of time to get to the camp before the sun came up.

A movement caught my eye and I focused on an Indian about fifty yards away sitting on a log, stretching and yawning. He was faced away from me and didn't seem to be wide-awake. I got on my belly and turned into a snake. Very slowly I made my way through the grass toward him. When I got close I could see his head bobbing as he tried to stay awake. It was easy to get behind him and touch his shoulder with the point of the knife. His head came up slowly as he realized that something had touched him. I touched him again and he sprang to his feet and turned around just as Kaufman's Bowie connected with his forehead and split through the scull. He fell instantly and lay on the ground shaking and quivering. I took his scalp and stood a hawk feather with the blue bead in the split head.

I didn't think there would be any sentries between this one and the camp, so I moved a little faster. The back of the shelter was facing me and it was easy to move through the tall grass to get to it. The top of the shelter was only about five feet from the ground. Hoping to get Lorraine's attention, I scratched on the bark covering and dropped a hawk feather through the smoke hole.

I heard a noise to the right and turned to look, but saw nothing. The guard at the wigwam stood and walked to the side where I could see him. Suddenly, he realized he wasn't alone and started to turn. He didn't make the full turn before the big Bowie cleaved his head from ear-to-ear.

Shooting started from the edge of the camp and Indians came out of their shelters with bows and arrows and guns. Jake stood behind a tree levering his Henry and sending the Indians for cover. Good Horse came into camp at a full run swinging a war club and killing anyone who got in his path. He leaped from one enemy to the next, coming five feet off the ground at times, and screaming a terrible war cry. The camp was in total confusion and terror.

I ran around to the front of the shelter and crashed through the door just as an Indian was about to kill Lorraine with a stone war club. I fired my Henry point blank at the back of his head and he dropped on top of Lorraine. I threw him off, grabbed Lorraine by the arm and pulled her out the door without giving her a chance to get her balance.

As we cleared the door we saw Indians coming at us with clubs and lances. I leveled the Henry and began firing their way. Most of the shots went wild but enough connected to stop them and they turned and ran away from us—right into Jake's rifle. I pulled Lorraine to a run around the back of the wigwam towards the woods. I stopped when we hit the heavy timber and told her to stay there, then I went back to the camp. Before I got there, the shooting had stopped and I didn't see Good Horse or Jake anywhere. The Indians had completely abandoned the camp.

I ran back to where I had left Lorraine and sat on the ground next to her. She was thin and pale, her once beautiful, dark brown hair hung in strings and her black eyes were surrounded with dark circles. She was barefoot and wore a tattered leather dress.

"Hawk," she said, "I knew you'd come. I prayed every day that you would come and find me. The Lord has answered my prayers."

"Lorraine, Sunkist answered Steven Riggs' prayers."

"But the Lord worked through Steven Riggs."

"You haven't changed, have you?" The sounds of fighting were now coming from the direction of the trap we'd set. "Come on, we gotta get out of here."

We crept back into the woods and started toward our camp two miles away. She was good in the woods and made no sound even though it was difficult for her to keep up a fast pace in her weakened condition. I had to get her to a safe place before getting into the battle raging around us.

Suddenly, an Indian crashed through the brush to the left. He slid to a stop when he saw us and went into a crouch, knife in hand. He stared into my eyes waiting for me to come to him to fight. I didn't go to him—I sent a forty-four caliber slug from the Henry to do my fighting. The slug won. I quickly pulled a feather from my pouch and stuck it in the hole in his chest.

I grabbed Lorraine's arm and took off through the woods.

She stopped. "Hawk, give me that pistol. I can do my part."

I looked at her, remembering all the times she had scolded me for carrying guns everywhere I went.

"Well, give me the damned gun! I know how to use it."

Lorraine was a woman who would never have used words like that when I knew her. She had gotten after me many times for saying words she thought were bad. I was completely surprised by her actions and handed her the dragoon. She turned it up and looked into the front of the cylinder to make sure it was loaded. I took the pouch with the ammo for the dragoon from my shoulder and slipped it over hers, and we were off and running again.

There were sounds of shooting coming from two different directions. Some came from the direction of The Thief's camp and some from the ambush we'd set up. I led Lorraine to a creek bed and told her to wait there until I came back.

"I will *not* stay here. I will come with you."

"Women," I said. "Do whatever you want. I don't have time to argue. Let's go."

We were getting closer to the shooting and I knew we would soon be in it. I saw an Indian hiding behind a tree ahead of us, and rather than shooting and giving away our position, I ran up behind him and, just as he turned toward me, I smacked his head with the stone tomahawk.

I could hear the rifles going off in the distance. The sound echoed through the cool morning air as the shooting slowed until only an occasional shot was heard. We moved in and found the men behind the barricades they'd put up.

"Sunkist!" I shouted into the camp.

"Yeah—here, Hawk."

"We're comin' in."

"Come on in. Don't trip over the Injuns."

"Everyone okay?"

"Yep, we whipped 'em good. Hey, Lorraine."

"Hello, Sunkist."

"Them Injuns will think twice before comin' here to visit agin," Sunkist said.

"What about Good Horse?" Mike asked.

"Bon Cheval is here?" Lorraine asked. "I heard he was killed last fall."

"Nope, he's around here somewhere."

"We must go and find him."

"Lorraine, you ain't goin' nowhere. You're staying right here. Good Horse will come in when he's ready."

"Hawk, *ain't* is not a word."

"It ain't?"

The woods had become quiet and the birds were singing in the trees. A soft, warm wind began to carry the rotten egg smell of burnt powder from the air, and the sweet smell of spring took its place.

"We gotta stay alert, them Injuns ain't done yet," Sunkist said. "We got The Thief's woman and he ain't gonna stop till he gets her back."

"Where's White Feather?" I asked.

"He ain't come in yet. He'll be here."

Good Horse appeared in front of us and walked to Lorraine. They hugged and talked.

He came to me and said, "Thank you, Hawk."

"It ain't all my doing. Thank these men around you, none of us did it alone."

He tipped his hat and nodded a silent thank you to the group.

"Ain't no trouble a'tall," Sunkist said.

Good Horse stepped into the woods and disappeared.

"Where's he going?" I asked.

"I ain't got no idea," Mike said. "He's probably going hunting."

"All right you guys, you can stop now," Lorraine said.

"Stop what? We ain't doin' nothin' wrong."

"Stop saying *ain't*."

I turned to the men and said, "I want you guys to stop using the word 'ain't'. Lorraine says it ain't even a word."

She moved in front of me with the dragoon in her hand hanging down at her side. She put her face inches from mine and looked square into my eyes. I heard the metallic click-click-click as she pulled back the hammer of the big pistol.

I held her gaze and without moving said to the others, "I'm going looking for White Feather. It's probably a lot less dangerous out there. Anyone comin' along?"

"I'll go with ye," Sunkist said. "I ain't been on a good hunt fer a long time."

"Let's go."

"Right behind ye, big brother," Jake said from directly behind me. "Ye ain't leavin' me behind." I jumped and turned.

"Dammit, Jake! I wish you wouldn't do that. How'd you get back here so quick?"

"Do what?"

"Sneakin' up behind me like that."

"Learned it from you, big brother. I saw that you had Lorraine and I figgered I'd come back here and plant me a few hawk feathers. Got me a nice little garden started."

"Okay, let's go, but stay in sight of each other."

A tom-tom started somewhere in the woods. We moved in a line towards the Indian camp with Jake to my right and Sunkist to the left. Slowly and silently we moved.

A voice came from somewhere in the forest. "Hawk! You have my woman. You will die!"

I stopped and shouted back, "I am here, come and get me! Or are you a woman who is afraid to fight me?"

I listened, but no sound came.

I motioned to move on. Jake was walking just below a ridge of timber. I was in the bottom of the small valley and Sunkist was halfway up the other side.

Suddenly, I heard Jake hiss at me. I looked up and he motioned me to come to him. Sunkist looked down at us and Jake motioned for him to come. We crouched down and peeked over the top of the hill at a band of six warriors squatted on the ground in a wash, forty feet below. One of them was drawing a map in the dirt.

"Got that Henry ready, Jake?" I whispered.

"Ready when you are."

"You start on the right, I'll take the left."

They were about forty yards away and downhill from us. We leveled the sights on them and I said, "Now!"

We both fired at the same time and two warriors fell. We jacked the rifles and two more fell. Sunkist fired and another dropped. Jake and I chased the last man into the woods with several shots, but he got away.

"Let's move," Sunkist said. "They'll be on us like flies."

We ran to the thick brush, scampered under it, then crawled about fifty feet and laid down in a dry wash. We heard Indians running close but they didn't see us and ran by.

"How the hell are we going to find White Feather out here?" Jake said. "If he's alive he'll be moving and we can only hope he moves towards us."

The voice in the forest came again.

"I am looking at you, Hawk. I could kill you now."

We dropped to the ground, each facing a different direction.

"Hawk, he can't see you—if he could he would have shot you."

"Are we trying to read an irrational mind, Jake?"

"No, I'm guessing at the thoughts of a man scared shitless."

Suddenly, something hit the side of my neck. It felt like I'd been struck with a flat board. It knocked me senseless for a moment, but the sound of Jake's rifle brought me out of it enough to realize I had just been shot.

Sunkist scrambled over Jake.

"How bad ye hit?"

"I don't know. Take a look."

He turned me to my side and pulled my neck scarf down.

"Jiss cut a gash in yer hide. Didn't do no permanent damage that I can see. Yer kerchief is trash, though."

"Kinda hurts."

"I suppose it does. Bullets have a habit of doin' that."

"You all right, Hawk?" Jake asked.

"Yeah, I'll live."

"We gotta do somethin'," Sunkist said, "we're like sittin' ducks in these woods."

"Let's get down to the Indian camp and if White Feather ain't there we'll head back," I said. "Trying to find him in these woods is stupid."

We started out slowly, staying in the underbrush as much as we could. We had crawled about a hundred yards toward the camp when Sunkist stopped us.

He was in a couch, peering through the brush ahead of us.

"What is it?" I asked.

"Don't know, but I think we've found White Feather."

Sunkist pointed at what looked like a man standing against a tree. We got to the ground and moved closer. I felt my stomach turn over. White Feather's body was lashed to the tree and his head hung down on his chest. He'd been scalped and horribly beaten and two arrows stood out from his abdomen. Tears burned my eyes and my hands trembled as I began untying the ropes that held him there. His head came up slowly and he looked at me through eyes that were nearly swollen shut.

"Now you have a horse for Lorraine to ride," he said.

"Oh, God. White Feather, I am so sorry," I whispered.

"Do not be sorry for me, Cetan. I do not die of starvation in a prison. I die a Sioux warrior's death, and for that I thank you, my brother."

The old warrior looked into my eyes, then his head dropped.

I stood silently for a moment then heard myself say, "We'll bury him here."

"No time for that, Hawk," Sunkist said. "We got Injuns on our tail."

"Sunkist, we'll bury him here."

"Guess you're right. Wouldn't be right to leave 'im like this."

We buried White Feather in a shallow grave and went to meet the rest of the men and Lorraine. We saddled up and started back to Fort Abercrombie.

I had the feeling again that we were being followed, so I told the rest of them to keep going. I dropped off The Brute and hid in the thickets to wait. It was a very short wait before I heard leaves rustling on the forest floor. Then I saw the hideous face of The Thief and another warrior moving my way. When he was about ten feet away, I stepped out in front of him.

"So," he said, "we finally meet, Hawk. You have chased me for a long way just to die."

"It ain't me who's gonna die, you son-of-a-bitch."

He stood taller than me and was thin-boned and scarred from the many battles he'd been in. He wore a breach clout and a dirty white shirt that hung below his thighs showing his bone-thin legs and simple moccasins. The young warrior with him brought up his shotgun. The Thief knocked it down, then turned and shot the young man through the chest.

"This is my fight, I do not need him."

He threw his rifle aside and pulled his scalping knife. This was going to be hand-to-hand and that was fine with me. I tossed the Henry to the ground and pulled Kaufman's Bowie from the sheath at my back.

He looked at the big knife and laughed. "You cannot fight with such a big knife."

"Come and find out if I can fight with this knife, Wamanousa."

"Your friend, White Feather, died a brave man. He did not cry out when I took his scalp."

He flipped the scalp at his belt with his fingers.

I didn't look at the movement, but said, "Come and die."

He charged me with his knife and I dodged him and struck him on the back with the heavy handle of my knife. He instantly turned and came at me again. I hit him on the end of the nose with my left fist, which stopped him in his tracks. He stood in a crouch with blood running from his nose and waited for me to come to him. I held the big knife low with the point aimed at his guts. We circled and suddenly he jumped at me, knocking me to the ground. He was on top of me in a flash, ready to shove his knife into my chest, but a quick slam on the side of his head knocked him off. I jumped to my feet an instant after he did and caught the point of his knife in my side. I whirled around and the edge of my knife cut a gash across the front of his shirt and into the gaunt flesh of his chest.

He was bleeding hard and we were both gasping for breath as he came at me again. I thrust my knife forward and he ran right into it. The blade sank into him just below his ribs on the right side and I felt it scrape across bone as it went through. Dark red blood poured heavily from the wound. He stopped and looked down at the wound, then at me, and came at me again. This time I hammered the handle on the top of his head and he fell to the ground. I jumped on top of him and was ready to shove the knife into his chest, when he pulled a pistol from behind him and fired a round that hit me in the left hip. I fell to the side, thinking I was dead. He slowly rolled to the side and stood over me. Dark blood flowed freely and parts of his guts hung from the gaping wound in his belly.

The world was going dark around me as I looked up at his evil, grinning face. Thoughts of Sophie raced through my mind. I was about to die and I knew it. Dying was not as bad as the thought of never seeing Sophie again.

I heard The Thief say, "Now, my good friend, you will die." I heard the blast and the world was suddenly shrouded in a white cloud. I waited to feel the bullet hit me, but instead I saw The Thief fall to the ground next to me.

I rolled over and saw Lorraine standing a few feet away with a smoking dragoon in her hand. She walked to The Thief and with both hands on the pistol, aimed it between his legs and slowly pulled the hammer back. The Thief lay on the ground looking up at her.

Hatred showed clearly in her eyes as she said, "Now, you god-damned bastard, go to hell and live with the devil."

She pointed the pistol at his head and pulled the trigger. The pistol recoiled and The Thief's head exploded—his body jerked nearly off the ground. The Thief was dead.

. . .

Abigail reached out and touched the old man's shoulder, "Are you all right, Mister Owen?"

"Yes. I just need to lie down for a bit."

"We'll have some tea and continue this when you're ready," Lorraine said.

"Don't let me sleep too long. I have to finish this."

"There is more? Mister Owen, we have a very good story here already."

"There's a lot more to tell and I want the records straight. We'll finish this later."

The old man went to his bedroom and Lorraine went to the kitchen to make sandwiches and tea. The reporters sat together in the cool fall air and compared notes.

An hour later, he came from the bedroom and took his chair on the porch. The rain had stopped, the sky had cleared, and mosquitoes came in hordes.

"Dad, we'll have to go inside or these mosquitoes will eat us alive."

The old man slowly raised himself from the chair and moved inside. They sat in a half-circle in front of the fireplace.

"Would you like to continue, Mister Owen?"

A man turned to me and said,
"Les voyageurs n'avaient jamais vu des petits loups."

20 CHAPTER TWENTY

I WOKE UP ON A TRAVOIS behind Jake's horse. Lorraine rode next to me and when she saw my eyes open she said, "Back with the quick, I see."

I couldn't answer but tried real hard to smile.

For the next two days I was in and out of consciousness and didn't see much of the country. We stopped at the mansion of Grampaw Wells for the night.

"Figger you boys foun' the Injuns," he said. "I tole you they was all over the woods, but ye didn't listen, did ye? Ye had to go see fer yerself."

"Yeah," Jake said, "we found 'em, and they won't be botherin' nobody no more." He raised the scalp of The Thief and shook it like a rag.

"Hail, they never bothered me no how—skeered of me onna conna me bein' nuts an all."

"Grampaw," Steve said, "where do you come from?"

"Come from right here in Otter Tail County, tin years ago."

"Where'd you live?"

"Didn't I jiss tell ye? Otter Tail County."

"Yeah, but *where* in Otter Tail County?"

"Don't wanna talk about that, son." He turned his head and started to walk away. "Got me some bad memories of them days."

"Were you married to a woman named Martha?"

He stopped and turned to looked at Steve and slowly said, "How the hell did you know that?"

Steve pointed at a leather satchel on the ground next to Grampaw. On the front of the satchel was printed the initials, K.J.W.

"Is that the bag Martha made for you?"

"Yeah, it is," he said softly.

"Wanna come with us, Grampaw?" Mike asked.

"No son, I think I'll just stay here. I've kinda gotten used to being alone and not worryin' about anyone but myself."

"You ain't nuts, are you?"

"No, I'm not nuts. It just keeps people from asking stupid questions I don't have answers to."

"Do you know who you're talking to?"

"I didn't know until just now."

"Pa, leave all this here and come with us."

"You mean that?"

"We know you had your reasons, Pa."

"I've got an old black mule out there somewhere. I guess she'll take me where we're going. She's the only female I've got, so I take care of her."

"You never did find another woman, Pa?" Steve asked with a grin.

"Oh, I had some women friends, none of them worked out, though. Some were beautiful, some intelligent, some fun to be with, but none of them had it all." He got quiet and stared off in the distance. "There was one, though. She was all of those things. Pretty as a spring rain, smart as a whip, and more fun than a shootin' match. She was always smiling and laughing and she never had both feet on the ground at the same time."

The old man got quiet. He looked at the ground and said, "Damn, I loved that girl. Maybe someday I'll find someone like her, but I doubt it. She really was one of a kind." He looked up at Steve and said, "Ye know, Steve, I think I'd just like to have someone to be with—someone to be in love with and do things with. That's all I want."

"Maybe someday you'll find her, Pa. Come on, let's get some sleep."

Grampaw went into his dugout and came out with a handful of papers.

"What's all that, Pa?"

"I've been keeping a journal. I'm thinking maybe I'll write a book someday."

The next two days were the longest days of my life. I laid on that travois watching the sky go by and watching the high flying birds and the hawks circling in their endless hunt for survival. I saw hawks so high that I knew they could see both Sophie and me, but it would take another day for me to get to her. The pain in my side got worse as the days went on and I couldn't get up from the travois without help. Lorraine did the patchwork on me but she said I needed a surgeon to get the bullet out.

We arrived at the fort and Jake took me straight to the surgeon. They laid me on a bed next to Sophie's.

She opened her eyes and said, "My God, Hawk! And you were worried about *me*. Are you all right? What happened?"

"Just a little encounter with a bullet—nothin' to worry about. I guess lead and flesh don't make a perdy sight."

"And how are you doing, Soph?" Jake asked.

"Doc says I'm healing up just fine. I can thank Posey for much of that. I feel stronger each day and the pain is easing up. I'll be back in the saddle giving you hell in no time."

"Runnin' buffalo for me again?"

"Oh, something new will come along to try."

"Guess ye can't keep a good woman down… but I'll keep tryin'." I gave her a wink.

"I can see you haven't lost your sense of humor. I know you don't feel much like talking right now, but someday I'd like to hear the whole story."

"Hey Doc, can you pull this bed closer to her?"

Jake and Sunkist each took a corner and slid the bed to rest against Sophie's. I reached out and took her hand.

"Did you get Lorraine?" she asked.

"Yeah, we got Lorraine—and The Thief is dead."

"Did everyone make it out?"

"White Feather died."

"Oh, Hawk, I am so sorry. I know he was a true friend."

"Sophie, remember when you said you'd like to take a trip to Grand Marais and look into your past?"

"Yes, I remember. But that was more a dream."

"Dreams can come true, you know."

"You mean it? I'd love that. Let's do it."

"Yup," I said, "then we'll come back to the valley and our home on Hawk Creek for the rest of our lives."

The whole gang came in the door.

Sophie started to sit up but dropped back onto the bed. She raised her hand out toward Lorraine.

"Hi, Lorraine, I'm Sophie. It's a pleasure to finally meet you."

Lorraine took her hand. "Sophie, I'm sorry for what happened."

"Every road has a few puddles," Sophie said.

Lorraine chuckled softly. "I wouldn't call this a few puddles."

She leaned down and kissed Sophie on the cheek. "Thank you, Sophie."

Lorraine came and stood by my bed. "Hawk, I don't know how to thank you for all you've done."

"No thanks needed, Lorraine. I wouldn't be here if you hadn't showed up when you did."

She leaned over and put her arms around my neck and touched her face against mine. "I love you, Hawk."

I put my arm around her shoulders. "I love you, too."

She stood and wiped tears from her cheek. "Well, I guess this is good-bye."

"Not good-bye, Lorraine—"

"No, of course not," she said with a smile. "See you down the road."

"Where will you go from here?" Sophie asked.

"Bon Cheval is coming back to Yellow Medicine with me. I'm going to open a new school for the Indian children—one of my own, without the government telling me what to teach."

"The children will be in good hands," Sophie said, then turned to the Wells boys.

"What are you guys up to?" Sophie asked.

"We're heading back to Otter Tail County," Steve said. "We came to say good-bye."

"Do you have to run off so fast?" Sophie asked.

"We got some father-and-son catching up to do."

"I guess I can understand that," I said. "You guys stay in touch and if there's anything we can do for you, you just holler and we'll come a-runnin'."

"Will do," Steve said. "We'll be seeing you guys again."

They shook hands with all the men and shared hugs with the women—and walked out of our lives.

We stayed at Fort Abercrombie for another month. Sunkist and Posey and Jake and Eve stayed with us. The surgeon had dug the bullet out of my hip and gave me a pair of crutches to use till I could walk on my own. He said the bone had been shattered close to the joint and would take a long while to mend. We watched as the fort was turned into a real fort with walls around it and buildings inside.

Captain Vander Horck came to me one day in late June.

"Hawk, there's a brigade of canoes going south tomorrow. I can arrange for you and Sophie to ride as far as Fort Ridgely, if you'd like."

"What do you think, Soph?"

"I don't think either of us is ready to ride that far on a horse and I'd really like to get back to our cabin."

"It would be easier on both of you to ride in canoes than in a wagon or on horseback," Vander Horck said.

"We'll see what Sunkist wants to do," I said, "but I doubt if he'll want to ride in a canoe."

Sunkist and Posey had built a shelter in the trees a half-mile from the fort. We sent a soldier out to bring them in.

Sunkist came in and said, "Heard you two was takin' a canoe ride."

"Yeah, we're thinking about it. We're kinda anxious to get back to our cabin. You comin' along?"

"I ain't been in a canoe fer tin years. Didn't like it much then —and don't know why I'd like it now. How 'bout we jiss tag along on dry ground?"

"Mister Whistler," Vander Horck said, "you cannot ride where they will be going. If you wish to accompany them you will have to take the wagon roads that follow the river south."

"Figgered that. We'll take the horses and mules and string them down to yer place. We can meet up somewhere down-river, mebbe Brown's Valley. I'm sure Old Man Erickson will be jiss tickled to see us."

Just then Jake came in, "What's goin' on?"

"Sophie and I are taking canoes down to Hawk Creek. You and Sunkist are following along with the animals and our gear. Sound good to you?"

"Sounds like a plan. Gettin' tired of sittin' around this place anyway. When do we leave?"

"First light tomorrow."

"That don't give us much time to get packed, but we'll be ready."

"It's settled then. We'll be in canoes and you'll be on dry ground. Leave when yer ready and we'll see you in Brown's Valley."

At sunrise the next day we were at the waterfront looking at six canoes being loaded with packs and bales. The canoes were about twenty-five feet long and had four French-Canadian voyageurs to paddle each of them.

The men were short with thick black hair that hung to their shoulders. They were clean-shaven and wore brightly colored shirts and dull colored pants that came to their knees. Stockings covered their lower legs from the bottom of the pants to the simple moccasins on their feet. On their heads were hats of different styles—a wide-brimmed hat on one and a knit stocking cap on another.

Three of the canoes were made of cedar strips and three were made of birch bark. One of the canoe men came and looked us up and down, then pointed to Sophie.

"Come, you ride here." He pointed at one of the birch bark canoes. Sophie started to walk to the canoe but the man took her arm. "Wait." He pushed the canoe out into the water and three men climbed in and held it against the current. The man put his arm around Sophie's back and one under her knees and lifted her off the ground.

"Hey!" she yelped.

"No, no!" the startled Frenchman said. "I put you in canoe—you not walk in water—I walk in water."

She put her arms around his neck, pulled herself close and looked at me over his broad shoulder.

"Now *this* is service," she said with a toothy grin.

Then a man took my arm and pointed at one of the cedar strip boats.

"You ride with me."

I waited for him to carry me to the boat but he started toward the water and turned around. With a look of impatience he motioned me to come and get in. That was all right with me. I didn't want to be carried anyway.

Coming from Otter Tail County, I was familiar with boats, but they were bigger and heavier and much more stable than the narrow canoes we were about to ride in. Sophie sat in the canoe and watched me with a concerned look as I fumbled around trying to get comfortable. She sat on a soft bale with a larger one behind her to lean against.

"I wish you'd sit down," she said, "you're making me nervous."

My seat was not nearly as comfortable as hers. My legs had to be curled under me, which made my hip hurt from the minute I sat down. My rifle lay next to me, and a leather pouch hung at my side with a hundred rounds of ammunition. Sophie kept her dragoon in a small pack in front of her on the floor of the canoe.

A man in a gray suit came down to the water and said something in French to the man who had helped Sophie into the canoe. The Frenchman picked him up and carried him to the canoe at the end of the line and sat him on a bale in the center.

The Frenchmen got into the canoes and the man in the suit said loudly, *"Allons nous!"*

Immediately, and in perfect unison, the paddles dipped into the water and the men pulled. The force of the first pull on the paddles nearly threw me backwards off my seat. They paddled hard until we were out in the main stream.

Suddenly, the man in the front of the first canoe began to sing, *"En roulant ma boula roulant… en roulant ma bou–la."*

All the men joined in and repeated the line in a round. Then the first man sang, *"Derriere ches nous y a t'en etang,"* and the rest responded with, *"En roulant ma boula.."* So it went through the morning.

The canoes were turned into still water every so often and the men sat back and smoked their pipes. Then, without saying a word, they took up their paddles and pulled us back into the stream.

The sun lay like half of a red disk just below the horizon and the world was shrouded in deep red. The clouds glowed with brilliant shades of red, yellow, and orange. Above them, the sky was a deep blue that faded to white at the horizon and streaks of sunlight beamed skyward from behind the clouds. The only sound I heard was the light splash of the paddles. Even the crickets and frogs had become silent as if they, too, were awed by the spectacle of a Minnesota sunset.

We pulled up to the shore and had no sooner stopped when hoards of mosquitoes swarmed around us. Sophie climbed out of the canoe with a blanket over her head and ran through the water to shore.

The Frenchmen didn't seem to notice the mosquitoes as they unloaded the canoes and carried them out of the water and onto dry land. The canoes were tipped on their sides and canvas was drawn over them to form shelters. The cook started a fire and put a large pot of water on to boil.

The man in the suit sat away from us writing in his book. He didn't talk to anyone except to answer an occasional question or pass out orders. The voyageurs had set up his tent before unloading the canoes. The entry was covered with fine cheesecloth to keep the mosquitoes out.

The evening grew cooler and the mosquitoes stopped tormenting us. The cook banged his wooden spoon on the side of the copper pot and the men rushed in to fill their cups. One of the voyageurs brought Sophie and me each a large cup of thick pea soup that was swimming in grease, gray dumplings and an assortment of unidentifiable ingredients—most of them dead.

When we'd finished eating we sat around the fire listening to tall tales about the old days. A man who seemed to be a little older than the rest raised a hand and said in a loud voice, *"Ecouter moi!"*

The men stopped talking and turned their attention to him. The pain of rheumatism showed clearly on his face as he raised himself slowly to his feet and stepped into the firelight.

"I am Joseph Jardin," he said in a loud voice. "You have heard my name, no? I have paddled de canoe for tirty-five years. I paddle for Le Bourgeois at Hudson's Bay and de American Fur Company, and for *la bon homme,* Michael Cadotte."

With exaggerated gestures he re-lived each of his experiences.

"I paddle from sunrise to midnight and never stop or slow down. I could run any *sault* and my canoe never got broke. De rain, or de snow, or de heat or de cold, never mean a ting to me. One day was like de other. De flies and de mosquitoes did not bite me because they knew I was a great canoe man.

"I sing a hundred *chansons* and my voice is heard a mile away. I carry two packs on my back up any hill or across any swamp in *de pays d'en haut.* I drink weeskey with *L'oeil de Cochon* for tree days and never get drunk. I eat rats, and mice, squirrels and dogs and feesh and de bark off de trees. I could go for tree days without drinking water. I fight *le loup, l'oures, le chat sauvage, a la peau-rouge* and keeled them all. I never break a bone or get sick. I was a great canoe man and never turned away from my work, and I would do it all again if I was not so old."

A man turned to me and said, "*Les voyageurs n'avaient jamais vu des petits loups.*"

Sophie laughed out loud.

"You understood that?" I asked.

"Yeah, I've heard it before about the voyageurs. It means, 'the voyageurs never see a small wolf'."

After the storytelling they all rolled out their blankets and began to disappear for the night. One man came to our tent with an armload of cedar boughs and laid them on the ground where Sophie would be sleeping. I looked at him curiously.

"This keep *les moustique* away from *la fille,*" he said.

"Where's mine?" I said jokingly.

He looked at me with his head tipped to the side and a wondering look in his eye, "Monsieur?"

"Never mind."

The man in the suit sat quietly away from the rest, alone at a small table. He sat at an angle to the table with one knee draped over the other. The toe of his dangling foot tapped at the air as if keeping rhythm to some unheard music. By the light of an oil lamp he scratched his pen across the pages of his leatherbound book. He stopped and paged back to read something he had written. He picked up a cigar and took a puff then laid it on the edge of the table. He then picked up his pen, dipped it in the ink bottle and drew a line through something. Then he took a puff of his cigar and went back to writing. He paid no attention to the voyageurs, or us.

He wore a black suit over a white blouse with ruffles that completely covered his neck, and a satin bowtie with the ends tucked into the front of his jackt. The round-topped bowler on his head did little to hide the small double focus glasses on the end of his nose.

The Frenchman looked over at him and said quietly, "*Il etait Bourgeois. Il vas pas nous parler.*"

Realizing I couldn't speak French, he paused, searching his mind for English words.

"He tink we are de animals for do his work. He not talk with us."

"Pretty high and mighty, huh?"

He looked at me curiously, then walked off. Apparently, he could see no reason to fritter away valuable sleep-time attempting conversation with someone so ignorant he can't even speak French.

Not once did I see a man take his paddle out of the water for rest.
They kept up the rhythm until the sun was high in the sky.

21

CHAPTER
TWENTY-ONE

IN THE MORNING, the canoes were loaded before sunrise. We pushed off into the river and the first thrust of the paddles left the mosquitoes behind. Few songs were sung, but the paddling never slowed. So far, the countryside had been flat with nothing to see but cattails and bulrushes. We paddled through swamps so thick that we had to duck our heads to keep from being swatted by the passing reeds. Everything was quiet except for an occasional, *"kon-ka-reeeee,"* of a red-winged blackbird from some unknown place in the swamp. Eventually, we came upon a huge opening. Lake Traverse stretched as far as the eye could see. The avant turned us to the west side of the lake and pulled us to shore.

The men passed around pemmican and ate until it was gone. They must have eaten five pounds of meat and grease each. When they finished eating they walked to the edge of the lake and drank water, washed their faces, and wet their hair. We were put into our canoes and the voyageurs sank their paddles deep and pulled with all their strength. The force of the first pull nearly took my hat off, but then the canoes settled into a smooth ride and skimmed over the water easily.

The voyageurs' arms pulled and their backs bent forward-and-back as they made long strokes with their paddles. A song erupted from the avant, *"Le lendemain que je me suis mari… ma femme a voulu me battre."* The quick words and stepped-up tempo had the voyageurs laughing and pulling on the paddles to the rhythm. They kept up the rhythm until the sun was high in the sky.

Although most of them were in the waning years of the life of a voyageur, they laughed and told stories like children. A voyageur was very fortunate to live past his fiftieth year and these men were pushing that age pretty hard. Their skin was brown and wrinkled from years of exposure to sun, wind, rain and cold. Their legs were bent in almost grotesque shapes from being curled underneath them from sun up to sun down. Their upper bodies were heavily muscled and their arms were thick and powerful. Their hands were like oak bark, rough and wrinkled, and their fingers were bent and crooked from rheumatism or from being broken at one time or another. If not for the pity of it, their walking gait would be comical—more like a duck than a human being.

I watched as one man got up and started toward the woods. As he walked behind the circle of men he turned around and casually kicked one of the men in the ribs, then continued on his way. Black eyes peered from beneath thick, black eyebrows and the man's ever-present smile was wide, showing broad yellowed teeth—if he had teeth at all. They laughed at most anything and often rolled over backwards laughing at some joke or story we couldn't understand. Even though we couldn't understand their language, we laughed with them simply because their jocularity was so contagious.

The man in the suit, still as clean as when we started the trip, sat by himself writing in his journal and ignoring the grown-up children's laughter.

"How long will we be here?" Sophie asked the voyageur next to her.

"We will stay here until the Bourgeois say we go."

"Well, I'm going down to the lake for a swim. He can call me when he's ready. Coming, Hawk?"

"Right behind you."

Sophie ran to the water and stripped off her outer layer of clothes and dove in. I stood on the shore watching her splash around in the water. All she had on her was her shirt that covered her not quite to her knees. Her hair was wet and hung over her face.

"What cha waitin' for?" she yelled. "Come on, ye big chicken!"

I kicked off my moccasins, pulled my shirt off and waded out to her. She splashed water at me and I jumped at the coldness of it on my chest. I dove head-first into the cold water. She bobbed herself over to me and wrapped her arms around my neck.

"Doesn't this feel wonderful?"

"Yeah," I said sarcastically, "just great."

We kissed as she held me tightly to her.

"How ye feelin', Soph?"

"You tell me," she said and pushed my hands down her back to her bottom.

"Yeah, yer right. It *is* wonderful."

She smiled, kissed me again and tipped backwards away from me. Neither of us was in any shape to get too rambunctious, so we swam around and played for a while and got out. Sophie wrapped a towel around herself and I picked up my shirt and moccasins and we went back to camp.

After a half-day of rest we were back on the lake.

We paddled leisurely till we entered the river at the end of the lake. A short time later we came to Brown's Valley. The small settlement lay back from the river on the east side.

As we stood on a road that led to Brown's Valley, the avant came to us and said, "Do you know what this place is?"

I looked at Sophie and she looked at me.

"Is this something special?" I asked.

"Yes," he said with a wide smile. "This is the beginning of the Minnesota River, and the beginning of the Bois Des Sioux River." He pointed to the river that we had just come off of and said, "That water runs north to Hudson's Bay." Then he turned around and pointed to the water on the other side of the road. "That water runs south to the Gulf of Mexico."

"How can that be?" I asked.

"All of the water on that side of this road runs downhill to the north, and all of the water on *that* side of the road runs downhill to the south. Everything from here is downhill."

Sophie said, "I think I'm going to have to learn all of this a little at a time. Where does the Bois Des Sioux end up?"

"De Bois Des Sioux starts here and when the Otter Tail River joins it at Breckenridge, it becomes the Red River of the North. Then it runs all the way to Hudson's Bay."

After the canoes were unloaded and camp set up, the voyageurs disappeared into their tents, or down to the river to bathe. The next time we saw them they were dressed to the hilt with brightly colored shirts, clean trousers, clean socks, and brightly beaded moccasins on their feet. Their faces were shaven and their hair was combed out. They all wore red knit caps with the tassel hanging to the right. They had their pipes tied with leather thongs to the other side of their caps. Around the neck they each wore strings of bright glass beads and a tobacco pouch. Each wore a brightly colored woven sash around his middle, and attached to the sash was a small knife and a beaded pouch that hung down the front. They came at us strutting like roosters and walking with that curious gait common to the voyageurs.

They came to Sophie and each in turn bowed and gave her a light kiss on the hand.

The avant came to her last and said, "The men tell me to say they will miss you, Sophie."

Then he took her shoulders and leaned forward and kissed her on both cheeks. A smile crossed her lips and she kissed him on the cheek. The group of voyageurs let out a whoop, jumped up and down, clapped their hands, and pointed their fingers at the man who had just gotten a kiss from a lady. Then they went off to town singing and laughing like a bunch of children.

He came to me and shook my hand and said "*Au revoir, Monsieur Hawk Owen, et bonne chance.*"

. . .

"Dad, are you getting tired?" Lorraine asked softly.

"Yes. I think we should go to bed and finish this tomorrow."

The old Indian fighter rose from his chair slowly and stood for a moment, then turned and walked to his bedroom.

"Miss Owen," Mister Holcombe said, "I'm a little worried about your father. He doesn't look well."

"Dad will tell us when he's too tired to go on. I think he wants to get this interview over with as quickly as we can."

"We'll go to the cabin. Call us when he's awake and ready to continue."

"He will be up early. He likes to sit with Mother in the morning. They always sat on this porch and watched the sun come up, then went down to the river for a morning swim and a bath. Mother has been gone for almost a month and he hasn't missed a day sitting with her in the morning."

"We'll go to bed now and you call us when he gets up."

"Good night, Mister Holcombe—Miss Biegler."

"Good night."

"Oh, ya. I alvays heff da hotdish ready fer da traff'lers."

22

"GOOD MORNING, Mister Owen."
"Where did we leave off?"
"You were just landing at Brown's Valley."
"Oh, yes."

. . .

We had just gotten out of the canoes when a man dressed in a suit came to meet us.

"Well, you made it. How was the ride?"

"I like horses a lot better than canoes," I said.

"It was nice," Sophie said. "The voyageurs were wonderful, too."

"Yeah, you can say that. They waited on you hand-and-foot."

"One of the benefits of my gender."

"My name is Henry Blakely," the man said. "I run the general store in town. Come with me, we have quarters ready for you."

"At Mister Erickson's? No thanks, we can't afford that."

"You know Mister Erickson?"

"Yeah, we know him."

"You won't be staying there. I have a house right in town you will be using until we can find a way to get you back home."

"Who's doing all of this?"

"Captain Vander Horck from Fort Abercrombie. He says the army will be paying for it."

"Why would the army pay to get me home?"

"Mister Owen, I wouldn't ask any questions, it might make them wonder the same thing. Vander Horck said you and your troop did enough this past spring to earn you the rights of an officer in the United States Army."

We were put aboard a four-seat buggy and taken to town. We passed Mister Erickson's store but he was not to be seen.

"Mister Erickson is having problems keeping that store alive," Mister Blakely said.

"I'm not surprised."

"He's losing money and keeps raising his prices to make up for it, but each time he raises the prices, fewer people come in. He complains about it endlessly and people keep telling him to bring the prices down, but he won't. Someone set fire to the cabins he had out back so now he can't make any money from those, either. That was all profit for him."

"Well, ain't that Joseph Brown's store, anyway? Why doesn't he do something about it?"

"Brown hasn't been here to see what's going on. He's out in Dakota chasing Little Crow with Sibley."

"Little Crow ain't in Dakota," I said. "He's in Canada."

"How do you know that?"

"I just spent a week with Canadian voyageurs. They seem to know everything."

"Voyageurs are nothing but over-aged children and you can't put stock in anything they say."

"Well, that may be true, but this time I know they're right. I talked with Little Crow myself and he told me he was going to Canada."

"When did you talk with Little Crow?"

"Last spring, out by Devil's Lake."

"Did you tell Vander Horck about this?"

"Vander Horck knows I talked to Little Crow. Henry Sibley sent me out there to talk him into surrendering."

"And were you successful?"

"No."

"Did you tell Vander Horck that Little Crow was going to Canada?"

"I did, but I don't think he believed me any more than you do."

"Are you a friend of Little Crow's?"

"We've been on opposite sides in a few battles."

"But are you a friend of his?"

"I think that if he and I were able, we could be very good friends."

"You are very good at dodging my questions, Mister Owen."

"Mister Blakely, I have never sat down to dinner with Little Crow. We have seen each other from a distance but until last spring we had never had a one-on-one conversation. I may be a friend to him, but I am also an enemy of his. Friends can be enemies in war. In the south, brothers are fighting against their brothers but after the war they will be friends again. A friend is a person you can trust and respect. I would trust Little Crow's word much sooner than I would most white men I've met out here."

"Yes," he said. "I suppose you are right."

He snapped the reins and we headed towards town. He drove us to a frame house with a small yard around it.

"This will be yours for as long as you need it."

"We won't be needing it for long, Mister Blakely," Sophie said. "We're on our way home."

"I'll see what we can arrange for your transportation."

We carried our bags into the house. It was plainly decorated with a kitchen and a living room and a bedroom in the back. I sat at the kitchen table while Sophie went through the cupboards for any kind of food. There was none.

She turned, looked at me and said, "Negative on the food situation. You want to go see if there's a place to eat in this town?"

"Yeah, it's either eat or go to bed. I'm not real particular which, right now."

Sophie came and sat at the table with me. She laid her face in her hands and leaned her elbows on the table.

"Ye know what, Hawk? As much as I dislike Mister Erickson, I think we should go and pay him what we really do owe him."

"And how much is that?"

"Well, I guess I don't really know. We paid for the bath and the wood and the cabin. Hey, all we should owe him for is a broken bed."

"And how much do you think that bed was worth?"

"That night—priceless."

"Yeah, it was, wasn't it?" I said, smiling toward the floor, lost in thought.

"How about we give him ten dollars for it?"

"How about we give the money to Mister Blakely to give to him. That way we won't have to see the old skinflint."

"Why, Mister Hawk Owen, are you afraid of Mister Erickson?"

"I'm not afraid of him, it's just that if we go looking for trouble, it's bound to find us."

"Come on, Hawk, let's go see him. Maybe he's got some of that hotdish he promised us."

I looked at her and saw that she was serious. "Okay, we'll go. But we'll go in, give him the money, then leave. We'll get some hotdish, too, while we're there."

We walked out the door and headed to Mister Erickson's store. We found him standing behind the counter reading the *Saint Paul Pioneer*.

"Hello, Mister Erickson," Sophie said, with a mischievous look in her eye.

He looked up slowly and when he saw us, his eyes got wide and his mouth dropped open.

"Vell, so yew heff come beck. I never taught I vould ever see yew tew again."

"Yeah, we came back to pay you for the bed that got broke."

"Oh," he said with a wave of his hand. "Neffer mind dat. Dat bed vos no gyud enny vay."

"Mister Erickson, we broke the bed and we think we should pay you for it."

"Oh no, yew don't owe me nodding. It vos a pleasure to heff yew stay here."

I looked at Sophie and she looked at me.

"Mister Erickson," Sophie said. "When we left here you were madder than a wet hen. What's changed?"

"It iss nodding. I heff decided to get out uff dis store and go beck to Saint Paul."

"What made you decide that?"

"Vell, vit the missus gone now dare isn't nodding to keep me here. She vos da one hew ran diss store, not me."

"Your wife is gone? Where?"

"Oh, yew didn't know? My Helga passed avay a mont beck. She iss buried out in da beck."

"Oh, Mister Erickson we are so sorry to hear that."

"No, it's all right. I tink she made most uff da problems here anyvay. She vanted tew make tew much money and ven da prices vent up da people shtopped coming in. Now the store iss ruined and dare iss nodding to keep me here."

"Why don't you stay here and get the store going again? You can do it. Just be good to your customers and charge them a fair price—they'll come back."

"Da people in diss town don't like me. Day vill neffer come beck."

"Mister Erickson, I'm sorry, but did you ever consider that it might not have been you that people disliked? Didn't you say Helga was the one who kept raising the prices?"

"Ya, I know. Yew are right about dat. She vos a hard voman."

"Here's the twenty dollars we owe you. It would be nice to see you get this store back in shape. You don't need anyone telling you how to treat people. You're a good man, Mister Erickson. If you stay, this store will become one of the best in town."

He put up a hand and turned his head to the side, "Oh no, yew don't heff tew do dat."

"We want to," Sophie said as she laid the money on the counter.

Mister Erickson glanced at Sophie, then at the money, then he slowly picked up the twenty dollars.

"Vell, maybe I'll take it and buy some stock for da store." He slipped the money into the cash box and said, "Tank yew."

"Now, do you have any of that delicious hotdish you promised us last time we were here?"

"Oh, ya. I alvays heff da hotdish ready fer da traff'lers."

"That's great. We'd appreciate some—we're starving."

Mister Erickson went to the back and came out with two large glass plates heaping with tomato hotdish.

"Dat vill be ten cents."

I looked at Sophie. She was staring at Mister Erickson.

Suddenly he broke out laughing.

"I vos youst making a choke," he laughed. "Yew two eat ass much ass you like and ven dat iss gone, I can get yew more—it von't cost yew nodding."

Sophie laughed and leaned over the table and kissed Mister Erickson on the cheek. His face turned pink and his blue eyes twinkled.

"Uff da!" he said with a giggle. "Tank yew."

"Mister Erickson—"

"Please, call me Lloyd."

"Okay, Lloyd. This hotdish is wonderful. How much of it do you have?"

"Oh, I heff a full pot uff it—eat up or it vill go to vaste."

"I'm not thinking of us eating it, I'm thinking of the people in this town coming here for hotdish tonight."

"But—"

"Lloyd, all you have to do is show these people that things are changing in this store and they will come in. You'll have more business than you can handle."

He looked at her curiously and a smile came over his face.

"Yew know, it youst might vork." He pulled at the extra skin under his chin and looked at the counter. "Ya—by golly, I tink I'll do it." His eyes searched the ceiling. "Free hotdish vonce a veek at Lloyd Erickson's store—maybe on Sundays after shurch," he said, mostly to himself. "Ya," he said softly, "dat vill vork." He slapped his hand on the counter, "Ya, by golly, dat *vill* vork!" Then he leaned over the counter to Sophie and whispered, "But don't tell Helga, she wouldn't like it." He snickered with his hand over his mouth.

"Mister Erickson, you don't have to give it out for free, just make the price as low as you can without losing money."

"Ya, dat iss better. How much?"

"Five cents a plate."

"Oh, dat vould be tew much—tree cents a plate."

"Sounds like you're on your way to big profits."

We left Mister Erickson's store and walked back to the house.

"Think he'll do the hotdish feed?" I asked.

"I'm hoping to be gone from here before we can find out."

During the night, a thunderstorm passed over. Rain pounded the house and lightning flashed all around us. Thunder rolled.

When we came out of the house the ground was soaked and puddles stood all through the town. Nothing moved but the smoke from a few chimneys. The sky was dull gray and a fine drizzle fell. Mosquitoes swarmed around us and drove us back into the house.

"Looks like we're fenced in for a while," Sophie said as she closed the door. She leaned back on it and said with that sly smile, "Gee, whatever will we do now?"

"Well," I said, "I'm going back to bed. Comin' along?"

"Ouuu, you're such a sweet talker."

She beat me to the bedroom and flopped on the bed. "Ou!" she said, holding her side, "I forgot about that in all the excitement."

I climbed onto the bed and lay next to her with her head on my shoulder. The air was cool so we pulled the blankets up to our necks and wrapped up in each other's arms.

"How's the hip?"

"Sore as hell today—must be the damp weather."

"I hope that doesn't become a permanent problem for you."

"Naw, I think it'll heal in time. I'm not gonna worry about it right now, though."

She kissed me on the mouth. "Guess there's no reason to get another twenty dollars out. Unfortunately, this bed is going to stay intact tonight."

We lay in bed talking and snoozing for most of the day.

Someone knocked on the door.

I got up, pulled my trousers on and went to open it. There, in the rain stood

Mister Erickson, covered with a canvas poncho.

"Lloyd! What the hell are you doing out in this rain?"

"I saw dat yew tew vas cyooped up in here and I brought yew some hotdish."

"Well, that was awfully nice of you."

He handed it to me and said, "Dat vill be ten cents." Then he laughed and waved a hand at me, "I am youst making anodder choke."

"Come on in before you catch your death."

"Oh, tank yew, but youst for a minute. I heff customers in da store and I heff tew get beck. I heff hett people coming in all day—even in da rain."

Mister Erickson walked into the cabin.

"Hi dare, Sophie, gyud to see yew."

Sophie sat on her heels on the bed with a blanket pulled over her. "Hi, Mister Erickson. Thank you for the hotdish."

"Oh no, tank yew for safing my store."

"Come in and sit for a while."

"Oh no, I heff to get beck. Da vidow Halverson iss over dare helping vit da store."

"Missus Halverson?"

"Ya, she is da vidow dat liffs down da street. She hess been coming over dare and helping me vit da hotdish." He giggled and put his hand over his mouth and said, "I tink she likes me."

"Well, good for you. I didn't think it would take you long to find a good woman."

Mister Erickson turned and peeped out the door to make sure no one was listening. Then he turned back to Sophie, "She vants me tew come and stay vit her at her house."

"Well?"

"Oh, I don't know," he said with a wave of his hand, "vhat vould da people tink?"

"You can't always be worried about what others will say, that will only drive you crazy. You have to do what makes *you* happy."

"Ya, dat iss right. Ya, by golly, I tink I'll dew it." He wrinkled his nose and bobbed his head, "But I'll vait a little vhile." He reached for the doorknob, "I better get back tew da store. Tank yew." He quickly turned, walked out the door and disappeared in the rain.

"That crafty old devil, he's already got himself a woman," I said.

"Yeah, it's kinda cute, those two old birds nesting up."

"Want some hotdish?" I asked.

"Ya sure, yew betcha. I'm starfing."

Later in the day another knock sounded on the door.

"Hawk! You up?" It was Jake's voice we heard. I scrambled to get my pants on and went to the door.

I turned to Sophie and said, "Better git up—it's Jake!" She swung her legs off the bed and stood facing the door.

"Soph—get dressed!"

We heard another knock.

"Hawk, I know yer in there—open up."

She took a robe and pulled it around her.

"Happy now?"

"Sometimes you drive me nuts."

I opened the door and Jake and Eve walked in.

"Hey, big brother. Have a little trouble getting to the door?"

"Not me, it was her," I said pointing my thumb at Sophie.

She smiled at Jake and nodded her head toward me.

"He loves me."

Sophie gave Jake and Eve a hug, "Glad to see you guys."

"You guys made it in pretty good time," Jake said. "We thought we'd be waiting for you."

"Those Frenchmen know how to paddle a canoe, that's for sure. Where's Sunkist?"

"He's out there sitting on his horse like the sun's shining," Jake said. "Got a piece of news for ye, Hawk. Little Crow is dead."

"How'd that happen?"

"Well, the way the story goes, he came back to Minnesota last month to steal horses for himself and his son. They stopped in a berry patch and a farmer named Nathan Lansom shot him from a corn field."

"Little Crow let a farmer get close enough to shoot him? I doubt that."

"That's the way the story goes."

"Little Crow was smarter than that. He'd never get that close to a town he raided—and he'd *never* let himself get ambushed by some farmer."

"I'm just telling you what I heard," Jake said with a shake of his head.

"How do they know it was Little Crow?"

"He had the scars on both his arms from when he was wounded by his brothers fighting about who should be chief."

"Was Little Crow the only Indian who was ever wounded in the arms?"

"Well, I don't suppose he was the only one, but the people in town identified the body—people who claimed to know him."

"Everyone claims to have known Little Crow. People like to say things like that to make themselves look important. What else?"

"After Lansom shot Little Crow he ran to town and told people about it. The next day they all went out there and found the body. They had no idea who they had at that time. He was scalped, then dragged into town and through the streets. Kids stuffed firecrackers in his ears and nose and set them off. They threw mud on him and kicked and beat the body, then threw it in the gut pile behind the slaughterhouse. It laid there for a couple of days before it was finally identified."

"Now, how in the hell could anyone identify a body two days after it's been mutilated like that?"

"Guess yer right about that, Hawk."

"You say Lansom didn't know who it was he shot at?"

"Nope."

"Jake, Lansom and Little Crow were friends. Little Crow stayed at his house and ate meals with him. How could he not know who it was he shot at? He would have had to be close enough to Little Crow to identify him in order to hit him with a bullet. It just don't add up, Jake."

"That's true, but Henry Sibley sent a letter to Ramsey reporting Little Crow's death."

"Did Sibley see the body?"

"Nope, not that I know of."

"You do know Sibley wanted to be dismissed from the war, don't you?"

"Yeah, we all know that."

"What better way to get out than to have the enemy dead?" I said.

"True, but figure this out. His son, Wowinapa, was captured and he told the whole story. He said that his father was killed, and that he was there when it happened."

"But, think about this, li'l brother—Little Crow heard the news that someone claimed to have shot him and they believe he's dead. Little Crow is a smart man. He might have figured it this way—'Let the foolish white man think I am dead. They will not search for a dead man'."

"You believe that, don't you, Hawk?"

"I don't know what to believe—but I don't believe Little Crow would be careless enough to let a farmer shoot him from ambush. He knew that Indians were fair game at that time and would be shot on sight. He'd never let a thing

ARVID LLOYD WILLIAMS
BONNIE SHALLBETTER

247

like that happen. Besides, he told me he was going to Canada and never coming back to Minnesota."

"You got a good point there, Hawk. Maybe Little Crow ain't dead. Maybe he's living happily somewhere in the north country. It does make you wonder though, don't it?"

"Damn sure does."

I pointed my thumb toward the door. "S'pose we aught to bring him in outta the rain?"

"Probably."

I went to the door and saw Sunkist and Posey sitting on their horses, looking at me. The rain was just a light drizzle—just enough to keep everything wet.

"Well, don't just sit there in the rain, come on in."

He raised his hat and looked up.

"Oh, is it raining?" He swung his foot across in front of him and jumped to the ground, splashing mud onto his horse's legs. Posey did the same and they came into the house. He pulled his hat from his head and slapped it across his leg. "Wish someone woulda tole me it was rainin'."

Sophie went to Posey and gave her a hug.

"Hey, Posey."

"Hello, Soapy."

"We'll have to work on that name," Sophie said quietly.

"Ye got any grub in this fancy joint?" Sunkist asked as he looked up, down, and around the room.

"No, but we can go to Mister Erickson's store and get some," I said.

"I hope you brought plenty of cash if yer goin' over there," Jake said.

"Oh no, he's a changed man," Sophie said. "I'll bet he'd give you hotdish for free."

"Yeah, and maybe a buffalo will surrender some steaks, too."

"We'll fix you up," Sophie said.

"Yeah," I said, "I'll get you some hotdish right now."

When I came back with the pot of hotdish they were all sitting at the table with forks in their hands.

"You guys hungry?"

"Jiss put that grub right here on the table."

Sunkist filled his plate and leaned his head over it, scooped the food directly into his mouth and swallowed it with a minimum of time wasted chewing. One swallow hadn't hit his stomach before the next was on its way down. His plate was clean by the time the others had taken their second mouthful.

He wiped his sleeve across his mouth and belched. "Gotteny more?"

"Not right now, maybe later."

"Sunkist," Sophie said, "do you believe Little Crow is dead?"

"Hail no, he ain't dead. A farmer ambush Little Crow? Not likely—he'll be back. You guys ridin' down to Hawk Crick in canoes?"

"Not if we can find another way to go," I said.

"Ye feel good enough to ride in the wagon? We got a canvas we can throw over the top to keep the sun and rain out. Mostly rain, from what I hear."

"That sounds like a good idea to me," Sophie said.

"Me too. When do we leave?"

"First light?"

"We'll be ready."

"You two ready at the same time we are?" Jake said. "That'd be a first."

"We'll be there," I said.

"Done. We'll be back first light," Sunkist said.

"Where you going?"

"Dunno, but I know I ain't stayin' in this box all night."

"If you have room, Eve and I might like to sleep under a roof for a night," Jake said.

"Sure, we've got plenty of room. In fact, Sunkist, why don't you and Posey stay, too?"

"Hail, I ain't slept under no roof since—" He glanced at Posey who was looking at him with a stern eye. "Umm, well now, what do you think, Posey?"

Posey pulled a chair out from under the table, sat down and looked up at Sunkist.

"Well, there ye go," he said with exaggerated cheer and a gesture toward Posey, "looks like we stay here fer the night."

"Good," Sophie said. "Hawk, do we have any beer?"

"Um, sorry—no beer."

In the morning we got right to work packing our belongings and loading the wagon. Sunkist walked to the stable to get the mules and horses. He came back leading the riding horses and pack mules, and a big horse in harness that no one had seen before. It was brown and white paint, thickly built with heavily-boned legs, a deep wide chest, and enormous muscles around his hindquarters and shoulders. His neck was thick and beautifully arched with a thick white mane. He had wide-set eyes that sparked with intelligence. He stood taller than The

Brute, and Sophie's horse, Gorgeous.

"Wow," I said, "where'd ye git that thing?"

"The wagon horses was wore out so I traded the hostler fer this one, even up."

"Why in the hell would he trade a horse like this for a couple of worn-out ones?"

"Says this one's too hard to feed. He's too small fer pullin' heavy loads and too big for ridin'. I figger he's jiss about right fer anything a man can hitch 'im to."

"He kinda looks like them big draft horses they use for pullin' freight wagons down by Saint Paul," I said.

"Yup, that's ezzac'ly what he is. Half ridin' stock and half Belgian heavy workhorse."

"Well, hitch 'im up and let's see what he can do."

Sunkist backed the horse to the wagon and hooked up the lines. "Who's drivin' the wagon?" he asked.

"Well, since Sophie and I are riding we might as well do the drivin'."

"Well, git on up there and let's go."

I started to get a foot into the spoke of the wagon wheel but couldn't quite make it. Sunkist came up behind me and wrapped a hand around my belt on each side of my pants.

"Ready?"

I looked down and saw that he intended to help me get aboard the wagon.

"Ready," I said.

Suddenly my belt went up and my pants pulled up higher in the crotch than was comfortable and I sailed upward and dropped into the seat of the wagon. I sat there wondering what the hell had just happened. I shifted around a little on the seat to re-adjust my britches and suddenly felt Sophie land in the seat next to me. I looked around the wagon in a sort of daze before taking the reins in hand.

"Well?" Sunkist said from behind us.

"Yup!" I snapped the reins and the horse began walking. He didn't pull or even lean into the weight. He simply walked forward and the wagon followed.

"Y'all go ahead on, I'll catch up," he said and turned back toward the barn.

"I think Sunkist made a good trade here," Sophie said.

"I think you're right."

"Ye think he's a rider?"

"Dunno, might be. He's docile enough."

"I'm going to ride him."

"Sophie, as big as this horse is and as small as you are, you could make a bed on his back and sleep there."

"Well, at least it's not going to cost me twenty bucks."

We heard a horse coming up from behind and turned just in time to see Sunkist throw a big saddle in the wagon.

"Looks to me like he's been rode before."

"Yup, looks that way," Sophie said with a grin.

. . .

Lorraine came out to the porch with a tray of sandwiches and a pitcher of beer.

"It's lunch time," she said. "Everyone here likes beer, I hope."

Mister Holcombe reached out and took a glass. Abigail did the same.

"You'll notice there are sandwiches there, too," Lorraine said with a smile.

She poured a mug of beer and handed it to the old man. He took it with trembling hands and brought it to his lips.

He wrinkled his nose, "This ain't nothin' like the beer Jake used to make." He turned the mug up and swallowed the beer down. His gaze wandered beyond the porch toward the creek. He raised his mug, "Here's to you, my dear Sophie."

They all raised their glasses and the room grew silent as Lorraine swallowed hard to fight back the tears.

"Let's go for a little walk, Dad."

He rose from his chair and stepped from the porch. They walked to the front of the house and headed down the road.

The old man walked slowly, leaning heavily on his cane. Lorraine stopped, took his arm, and looked into his eyes.

"How are you feeling?"

"We should get back to the house and get on with the story," he said.

Back on the porch, the old man lowered himself into the chair. He tipped his head back and closed his eyes.

"Mister Owen?"

"Yeah, I'm awake… just thinking."

"You can eat June bugs, you know."

23

CHAPTER
TWENTY-THREE

WE MOVED SOUTHEAST on the government road for the day and pulled into a patch of trees for the night. The next morning we were moving before the sun was up. The road followed the Minnesota Valley and often came right to the edge. We stopped to look at the beauty of the valley stretched out before us. About halfway through the day we saw smoke rising in the east a mile away.

"Looks like a perdy big fire goin' yonder," Sunkist said.

"S'pose we should go see if there's anything we can do?"

"You figgerin' on gettin' in some Injun fightin' on this trip, Jake?"

"Nope, hadn't planned on it, but I'm gonna ride over there and see what's happening."

"You be damn careful," Sunkist said. "There's still Injuns roamin' these parts."

"I'll keep an eye skinned," Jake said and kicked his horse to a gallop. Eve kicked hers and they rode off toward the smoke. They disappeared behind the grass and short foliage that covered the rolling hills of the countryside.

Suddenly, we heard shooting from their direction and Jake and Eve came over the hill at full-gallop. They leaned into the wind as they came on. Jake was hollering something we couldn't hear and waving his hat, telling us to get moving. Then they turned and rode away from us to the north.

"Injuns!" Sunkist yelled. "Whip that critter and let's get the hell outta here!"

I snapped the reins hard across the horse's rump. He took off and ran as if the wagon wasn't there, each jump taking him fifteen feet. The huge hooves thundered and shook the ground and kicked up rocks and gravel. The wind blew through Sophie's hair and she had a wide grin on her face as she held onto the wagon seat with both hands.

Jake and Eve lured the Indians away from us until they were out of sight.

We ran the wagon until the distant sounds of shooting stopped then we slowed to a walk. I turned and saw Jake and Eve coming up on us from behind. As they came alongside us, a dozen Indians appeared in the distance, whooping and hollering.

"Keep that animal runnin'," Jake yelled, "they're still comin'!" Again, I snapped the reins and the horse jumped to a gallop. Jake came alongside the wagon and hollered, "Damn, that horse can run!"

We made for a grove of trees but before we could get there the Indians broke off the chase.

Sunkist rode up and said, "Looks like we got us one hell of a horse here."

"What's his name?" Sophie asked.

"Ye don't name the meat, Soph," Sunkist said as he walked on ahead.

"That wasn't funny, Sunkist." She looked at me and said, "I'm gonna call him 'Dan'."

"Who?"

"The horse."

"Why 'Dan'?"

"He puts my mind to this big guy named Dan who tended the gardens at the orphanage. He was such a sweet old guy. All of the girls just loved him."

The road took us along Big Stone Lake and down through Ortonville and Odessa. We camped five miles further down the road on the rim of the valley.

"Isn't it beautiful?"

"Yeah, I love this valley."

We looked quietly over the three mile-wide chasm. The geese were restless, anticipating the fall migration. Flocks of thousands came in and landed for the night in the lakes and ponds.

We set our tent so we could look at the valley through an opening in the brush. We lay on our stomachs resting our chins in our hands. The sun went down and we could see a few campfires flickering across the valley.

"Do you suppose they can see our fire?" Sophie asked.

"If we can see theirs they must be able to see ours."

Sophie got up and went to the fire. She took her blanket and held it up between the fire and the valley. She lowered it for a moment, then raised it, and lowered it again. She did this a few times, then lay down on the bed disappointed.

"If they saw it, they didn't know what I was doing."

"Did you really expect to get an answer?"

"No, but it would have been fun—never hurts to try."

We stared out over the valley till we began to doze off.

"I'm going to bed," Sophie said and slithered backwards into the tent.

"Soph—come out here."

She came out of the tent and I pointed at what appeared to be firelight flashing in the distance.

"Someone saw me!"

She grabbed her blanket and held it up to the fire and lowered it twice, then stood back and looked across the valley.

The fire across the valley went out, then re-lit twice.

"Hawk, did you see that? We're communicating across miles!"

"Pretty good, Soph." I smiled at her child-like excitement.

They signaled back and forth a few times. The last one was a long light, followed by two short lights—then the fun stopped.

"Yer good, Soph."

She smiled and kissed me, then we laid down for the night.

In the morning, I looked over to see Sophie with her head propped up on her hand, looking at me. I focused my eyes and looked straight into hers.

"Who do you suppose that was across the valley?" she asked.

"Probably some Sioux war party lookin' for scalps."

"It was not."

"Nah, I doubt it. Just some crazy female playing with the fire, most likely."

She slapped me on the chest and said, "Git up—ye ain't much good to me here."

We crawled out of the tent and fanned the embers in the fire pit until we had a small fire going. Sophie put water in the pot and a handful of coffee and we sat back waiting for it to boil. Sunkist walked over and sat down.

"How you two doin'?"

"Much better, thanks," Sophie said. "At least I am."

"Yeah, me too," I said. "How come no one's movin'?"

"We figgered on givin' you two a rest. We'll stay here for the day and move out tomorrow—nice spot and there's a little crick runnin' yonder ye can take yerself a bath, if ye want. Posey's down there right now."

Sophie stood then went into the tent and came out with a towel and a bundle of clean clothes. "See ye."

"Ye got yer self a good woman there, Hawk."

"Yeah. I don't think I could find a better woman anywhere in the world."

"'Sept maybe Posey," he said quietly.

I looked at him and said, "You trying to start an argument?"

"We kin argue about it all ye want, but it won't do ye no good."

"An endless discussion."

"Hawk, I doubt there's a better bunch of women on the entire frontier."

"I'll have to agree with you there."

Sunkist raised his nose to the wind, looked around and quickly stood up. "Someone comin'."

I looked in the direction he was staring and saw the horses all turned to the northwest with their ears cocked.

"Soph!" I yelled, "Get back here!"

I walked to the horses and looked down the road. There was a group of Indians walking slowly our way. Jake and I grabbed our rifles and moved toward them.

"Relax boys, them's friendlies," Sunkist said.

"How do you know that?"

"They's Chippaways."

An old woman, two young girls, and a boy stood looking at us. They nestled close and stared at our guns. They were dressed in cotton clothes, moccasins, and blankets. The older woman had a turkey feather tied in her hair.

Sunkist walked to them and held up his hand.

"You speak English?"

The old woman looked into his eyes and shook her head, 'no'.

"You know these are Chippewa?"

"Ye can tell by the flower pattern on their beading and the way the baskets is made."

"Friendly then, right?"

"Well, if they ain't friendly they ain't stupid enough to make trouble with three men holdin' guns."

Posey came and stood next to Sunkist.

She held her hand up with the fingers open and her palm toward them and waved her fingers back and forth. Then she pointed one finger to the sky and moved it in a circle.

Sunkist translated, "She asked where they come from."

The young girl stood forward and signed 'two' with her fingers, and then 'moons' by forming a cup shape with her index finger and thumb, then pointed north.

"They come from away up in the north country—two moons' journey."

"Why are they here?" I asked.

Posey signed with the five fingers extended, pointed at the Indians with her index finger, then at the ground.

The young girl put two fingers to her eyes then wrapped her arms around herself and turned side-to-side.

"They come to see family."

The young woman then signed with her open hand across her stomach.

Sunkist turned and motioned them to follow him.

We went back to our camp and Posey began pulling food from the wagon to make a meal for the Chippawas. They sat quietly with blankets pulled tightly around them and watched as Posey and Eve worked. When the food was ready the older woman took a pinch of meat and stood up. She held it high and murmured a prayer to each of the six sacred directions—the north, south, east and west, and to the sky and the earth. She buried the meat in the ground then they sat and ate the meal with their fingers.

Keeping her eyes on the Indians, Sophie leaned toward Posey and whispered, "What are their names?"

Posey pointed at the old one, "She 'Crow Woman'." Then she pointed at one of the young girls, "She 'Dream Talker'. She is medicine woman. These— grandchildren," she said, pointing at the boy and girl.

"Are they going home?"

"Yes. They not stay."

When the Chippewa finished their meal they walked to the stream and washed themselves, then continued their journey home.

We stayed through the day, mending what needed mending and washing our clothes.

"Hawk, I want to ride that horse," Sophie said

"Yer crazy, ye know—I'll saddle him up."

I threw a thick blanket on the horse, then pulled the heavy saddle from the wagon. The giant horse stood perfectly still while I pulled the cinch tight and adjusted the stirrup leather.

"There you go. Hop up."

Sophie looked like a small child next to that big horse. She looked up at the saddle far above her head and said, "Yeah right, I'll just hop on up there."

She raised one foot to the stirrup and tried to jump up. Sunkist and Jake stood by watching and smiling. I put my hand on her butt and pushed her up onto the big animal. Her legs were spread almost straight out. Her feet still didn't reach the stirrups, even though I had shortened the leather, so I pulled them up another notch. She sat holding the reins and rocked from one side to the other, pulling up on the legs of her leather pants. Then she touched her heels to his flanks and the horse walked forward slowly.

She walked him for a short distance and turned back to me and said, "He doesn't respond to the reins!"

"I think that one you have to drive like he's pulling a wagon—he doesn't neck-rein."

She tried it and it worked. She turned him in figure-eights and came back to me.

"I'm gonna run him."

"Go ahead."

She kicked him and he took off with a jump. She had a hold on the saddle horn and stayed with him. He ran at a cantor for a short distance. When she kicked him again he opened up to full-gallop. His heavy feet pounded the ground and his white mane streamed back in her face. She turned him around in a wide circle through the grass and came back to us.

"This is the smoothest horse I've ever been on," she said.

"Better than your horse?"

She glanced over at her horse, Gorgeous. Then she leaned off the saddle and said softly, "Don't tell her, but yes, he's smoother than she is. He's not nearly as comfortable, though." She wrinkled her nose, "He's a little too wide for me."

"I noticed."

"My turn," Sunkist said.

He lowered the stirrups and slipped a foot in, swung his leg over and sat high and stately, like an army general. He grabbed the saddle horn and kicked the horse hard. The horse took off from a standing start to full-gallop in one jump. Sunkist almost rolled off his back but stayed with him. He leaned forward in the saddle and kicked the animal. He rode out a hundred yards and disappeared behind a patch of sumac.

Suddenly, he sprang from behind the brush at a dead run, "Git'cher goddamn guns—we got company a-comin'!"

He came up to us and pulled back on the reins and the horse locked all four feet and slid to a stop. We ran back to the wagon and pulled our guns out and hit the ground. Suddenly, a band of Sioux came screaming out from behind the sumac. Some had repeating rifles and some had shotguns. There were no bows and arrows. Their faces were painted for war and they came at us on foot—running and screaming that terrible war cry that sends chills through the most experienced Indian fighter. Jake's Henry went off and one Sioux fell. All of our guns fired and more

SOPHIE'S HAWK

Indians dropped. They kept coming. There were about twenty in the pack and were determined to take us, but we were determined not to be taken. Jake got up and ran to the right to get himself on their flank. I couldn't run so I stayed where I was, behind the wagon, jacking my rifle and pulling the trigger as fast as I could fix my sights. The Indians slowed but kept up a steady advance.

"Damn!" I heard from Sunkist. He lay on his side looking at a stream of blood coming from the top of his left shoulder. "Aw, hail, it's jist a scratch."

"Stay low!" I shouted.

Jake began firing from his position and the Indians stopped. They lay in the grass and fired from about fifty yards out. Jake stood and ran toward them, firing his Henry. He ran a few feet and dropped to the ground, rolled over once and fired from the prone position. The continuous fire from our rifles kept them down.

Shooting started from behind as Sunkist and Posey fired their Springfields and marched ahead, standing bold and upright, walking toward the Indians. The Indians' fire was slow and most of the shots went over our heads. The bullets made a quick crackling sound as they cut through the grass around us. Shotgun pellets dropped harmlessly around us. Jake got up and made another dash, then dropped. We heard a whoop from the Indians and they all got up and ran to the rear. Jake took aim and dropped one as he ran away. We chased them with bullets till they were out of sight.

We sat to catch our breath and reload our rifles.

"Damn, where the hail did they come from?" Sunkist said.

He held a rifle in his hand as he rummaged through the dead Indians.

"That was that party that chased us from the farm they burned out," Jake said. "They musta been following us."

"Why were they on foot instead of on their horses?" Eve asked.

"'Cause they cain't hide sittin' on top of a horse."

Sunkist dug through the side bags and pouches as if he were looking for something in particular.

"What are you looking for, Sunkist?" Jake asked.

He held up a rifle and said, "Got me a Spencer here. They're usin' 'em down south 'ginst the rebs. One of these boys was shootin' this thing," he grabbed a leather bag and looked inside, "so he's gotta have ammunition fer it somewhere."

He pulled a belt off an Indian, flipping him from his belly to his back.

"Yeah," he said. "Here it is, looks to be a fifty-two caliber. Hot damn, we got us another repeater."

He walked over to us and handed it to Sophie.

She took it and said, "Sunkist, I have no idea how to use this thing."

"I can show ye. That gun's almost as good as them Henrys we been shootin'. Whoever was shootin' this thing didn't know how to use it or we'da been in a lot more hot water than we figgered on."

"What do you mean by that?" Eve asked.

"He was a loadin' and a shootin' one round at a time when he could'a been spittin' seven shots, one right after the other."

"My Henry holds sixteen shots," I said in defense of my rifle.

"Yeah, but that's only forty-four caliber, this here's fifty-two."

"I doubt if the guy that gets hit with either one of 'em will stop to measure the bullet to see if he should fall down or not," Jake said.

"I'll show ye how to use this thing, Soph—you'll be damn glad to have it."

"Why don't you give it to Posey?"

"She don't want it. I made her that Springfield about three years ago and she won't shoot nothin' else."

"I got an idea we should be goin' after that bunch of Chippewa," Jake said.

"Do you think they had something to do with this?" Eve asked.

"No, I doubt it, but if them Sioux find them, they're dead meat."

"Either way, we need to find 'em," I said.

"Hawk, you cain't ride and neither can Sophie," Sunkist said. "And I ain't so damn sure I can ride right now. We're gonna have to forget about them Chippaway and move on."

"Yeah, I guess you're right."

We went through the bodies, taking guns and weapons.

"Hawk," Sophie said, "these are just boys."

"John Other Day told me once that if these boys are old enough to kill like Sioux warriors—they're old enough to die like Sioux warriors."

Two of the Indians had forty-four caliber Remington pistols with round ball ammunition and extra cylinders. I took one and gave the other to Sophie.

Jake walked out to the Indian he had picked off and bent over him. He rolled him over, undid the belt and took a pistol from him.

"Hey, Hawk!" he yelled, "where the hell did an Indian come up with something like this?"

"What'cha got there?"

"It's a forty-four Colt's Walker. Biggest damn pistol you ever saw."

"Lemme see that thing."

I took it from Jake's hand and lifted it. It was heavier than the dragoon. It had a nine-inch barrel and a massive six-shot cylinder. It was a little rusted but the hammer worked and the cylinder turned smoothly.

"How the hell you gonna carry this thing?" I asked.

"Strap it to Sunkist's saddle."

"What the hell do I want that thing fer?" Sunkist asked.

"No one wants it?" Jake asked.

"Nope."

He looked at it once and tossed it over the bank of the valley.

Posey was standing behind Sunkist, working on his shoulder as he talked.

"Sunkist," Sophie said. "That's more than just a scratch."

The bullet had struck just behind the shoulder bone and traveled downward under his skin. A blue streak ran from the back of his shoulder to the bottom of his rib cage. The bullet lodged there and made a lump under the skin.

Posey stepped out from behind him, "I take bullet out."

"Aw hail, jiss leave it there," he said. "It ain't the only one I got in me."

"No," she said, "we take out. Not good to have bullet in you."

"Do what ye have to then."

"Hawk," Sophie said, "shouldn't we bury these Indians?"

"I think we should load up and get the hell outta here," Sunkist said. "The rest of the Indians will come and pick up the bodies and bury 'em."

"Then they'll be back on our trail," Jake said. "I say we high-tail it outta here while we can."

"Sunkist, your horse is down!" Sophie yelled. She ran over to the horse and knelt down. Dark red blood ran from a hole in his side just behind the ribs.

Sunkist walked up, "Damn, got his liver." He knelt down and stroked the horse's neck. "Ye ain't gonna make it, ol' horse." Then he turned and looked up at us, "Git back to the wagon."

We turned and quietly walked away.

A shot made us jump.

Sunkist came back and said, "Don't ever wanna do that agin."

Sophie touched his face, "I'm sorry, Sunkist."

"Guess I'll be a-ridin' Dan fer a while."

"You'll ride in the wagon till we get to our house."

"Yeah, guess that'd be best."

We picked up three repeating rifles and the ammunition for each and threw them in the wagon. We jammed the muzzles of the shotguns in the dirt and bent the barrels in the crotch of a tree.

Sunkist and Posey went to their tent. We heard a groan from inside and knew that Posey was cutting on Sunkist.

We packed the wagon and Sunkist and Posey came out of the tent.

"How you doing, Sunkist?" Sophie asked.

"Aw, hail that weren't nothin'," he said. His face was white as one of Eve's handkerchiefs and his green eyes were bloodshot. He lifted himself up into the wagon without using his left hand.

We moved slowly south for the rest of the day and camped in a patch of willows for the night, taking turns on watch. Sunkist and Posey stayed inside their tent away from the group. Throughout the night we could hear soft sounds coming from their tent as Posey nursed him. He never complained about the wound but we could all see that he was hurting. His face had lost some of its normal sunburned color and his movements were slower, but his sense of humor stayed with him through it all.

In another day we were on the road leading to our log home on Hawk Creek. We rode in and found everything in place and undisturbed.

"Sunkist, why don't you and Posey stay here till you're feeling better?" Sophie said. "It would be better than trying to sleep on the ground."

"No, we got us a nice little place down by Sacred Heart Crick. We'll be all right there. We'll take that horse with us. They tell me horse meat is the best thing fer healin' wounds."

Sophie's hand instinctively flashed out and slapped him on the left shoulder. Suddenly realizing that she had hit him on the wounded shoulder, she jumped back and put her hands to her mouth and cried, "Oh my God, Sunkist. I forgot about your shoulder! Are you all right?" In a state of panic and remorse she stepped toward him then backed away. She wanted to touch him and make him know she didn't mean to hurt him. "I'm so sorry."

"Aw hail li'l gurl, I been hit harder by June bugs bumpin' into me."

She stepped close and stretched up to kiss him on the cheek, but with a quick glance at the sore shoulder, backed away.

"Stop worryin' about it," he said, "I hardly even felt it."

She came close and took his hands. "No more about horse meat, right?"

"Okay li'l gurl, whatever you say."

"Thanks," she said and turned to walk away.

"But each of them hams on that horse weighs more 'an you do."

Sophie turned quickly and feigned a punch. Sunkist jumped, bent his body to the side and pulled his bad shoulder away from the expected pain.

"June bugs, huh?" she said with a grin, "musta been one hell of a June bug."

"Watch it li'l gurl, I'll be takin' some pieces off'n you."

"Yeah, you'd like that wouldn't you?"

"Naw, I kinda like ye."

"You can eat June bugs, ye know."

"Yeah, I know, but they get in mu teeth."

"You won't have any teeth to worry about if you keep talking about eating horse meat."

Sunkist chuckled.

"You guys moving out tomorrow?" Jake asked Sunkist.

"No, I think we'll be headin' out right away. Kinda like to git back home and settle in for a while."

"How about you, Jake?" I asked.

"We're goin' back to Courtland and see what's left of our place. How about you? Got any big plans?"

"We were talking about going up to Grand Marais in the spring, see what's up there."

"Ye comin' back here?" Sunkist asked.

"That's the plan."

"Well, you ain't goin' nowhere without me," Jake said.

"Count me in," Sunkist said. "We'll bring that horse, too." He looked at Sophie and added, "To pull the wagon."

We walked them out to their horses and wagon. Sophie walked to the front of the wagon and rubbed Dan's nose. "You stay away from that man. You can't pull a wagon with one ham missing."

We shared hugs and shook hands. We watched until they were out of sight and quietly went into the cabin.

Sophie had a tear in her eye when she said, "I'm really going to miss them."

She came to me and put her arms around me and I wrapped mine around her. We stood that way for a while, then lay down together on the bed.

"How you feeling?" she asked.

"Feel like I could whip a wild cat."

"Prove it."

. . .

Lorraine turned to the reporters, "Dad is finished with the story."

"Is that the end?"

"Oh, no. There is much more to tell."

"Can you tell us the rest of it?"

"Yes, Mother talked about it endlessly. We'll continue another time."

"Thank you, Miss Owen. We'll go back to Saint Paul and write this up. We'll come back when you're ready."

"Thank you, Mister Holcombe. I'll get in touch with you."

"Good-bye, Miss Owen."

The reporters walked out the door and started their automobile and drove away.

24

THE OLD MAN SHIFTED IN THE ROCKER and it gave a responsive dry creak. It sounded just about as weary as his bones felt. His mind drifted again, as it had done so often lately, to the days when his body was his friend. Back then he never had to tell his body what to do, it responded automatically to the slightest thought. Now it felt more like a stranger with no regard to the man inside or his feelings and thoughts.

His hand reached out instinctively to touch Sophie's dress nestled over the arm of the old rocker. This small gesture seemed like the only thing he did not have to think about or concentrate on. It happened with such frequency that it had become rote—something necessary, like breathing. Just the touch of the soft cotton and the thought of the woman who once graced it always resulted in tears.

He lifted a corner of the dress to his face and inhaled slowly. His eyes closed and his face softened as the vision of Sophie wearing the dress appeared. He could feel the emotion of the young man on that hot summer day when he watched a single bead of sweat trickle down the front of her dress and disappear.

He let out a soft, involuntary sigh that woke him from this intimate memory. His face changed back to the face of a man who willingly awaits the freedom of death.

He swallowed hard and said, "Lorraine, I'm tired now. Let me sleep."

Lorraine walked over and kissed him on the forehead, "You let me know if you need anything, Dad."

"I will," he responded with a forced whisper.

Lorraine kissed him on the forehead again and said, "Good-bye Dad." He heard the door to his room being quietly closed as Lorraine made her exit.

He opened his eyes to look out the window. The sun was just about to set. *Sophie's favorite time of the day*, he thought to himself. He remembered her telling him that there was a few brief moments before the sun would set, when the tops of the trees would capture the soft reds, oranges, and pinks of the descending sun. The whole world seemed momentarily transformed by this soft illumination. It happened so quickly that if one was not observant, one would miss it entirely.

He had learned so much from her, nothing real important, but it was these smaller things that seemed to enrich his life. The ache that gripped his mind and body from being without Sophie was like a hunger or thirst that could never be satisfied. It dragged on his body, bringing it down, pushing on him, forcing him to relent to its power.

At that moment, his mind quite effortlessly made its last decision. He sat alone in the manner in which every soul leaves its earthly bonds. His last breath left him, and with no further information telling his body what to do, his head slumped forward onto his chest. His arms released their resting position and dropped to the outsides of the armrests. A feeling of complete lightness and freedom embraced his soul.

He looked down at the scene below him, at the shell of the man he used to be. It was as though he did not recognize that old man sitting there alone. It was then he became aware that his hip no longer hurt and the thought of using that cane seemed odd to him.

He felt he was being drawn to a light that was more magnificent than anything he had ever experienced. It seemed to envelope him in love, carrying him on an invisible wave toward the heavens.

Suddenly, as though a warm wind was hitting his face, a feeling of familiarity so strong, so indistinguishable from his own thoughts and feelings, passed through him and the scent of soft spring rain enveloped him… *Sophie?*

At that moment, their souls passed through each other. He felt every move, every thought, every feeling she had ever had. He could feel her smile. It was no longer something physical, but a feeling that echoed her very soul. Although he was not physically crying, his spirit cried out with a joy and intensity of which he had never known.

Their souls danced together to the universal chord that connects all things. It was the most intimate experience they had ever shared. It was a dance that required no steps. This was the magic that weaves all things together, and the union Hawk had always deeply hungered for.

It was then that she appeared before him, smiling her beautiful smile. Her eyes shown with a light that came from within. She was young again, in her prime of youth, as was he.

She held her hand out and said, *Come, Hawk. I have been expecting you.* She said this without moving her lips, and her voice came from everywhere around him. He realized they were communicating without verbally speaking. They walked side-by-side looking forward. Two souls separate, yet moving as one.

There are others that have been expecting you.

As Hawk looked ahead, he noticed a beautiful fire. The flames danced hypnotically, turning colors he did not recognize. An overwhelming feeling of warmth and love emanated from the fire, drawing him closer. When he looked into the flames, the faces of all his dearest friends he'd had in his lifetime appeared. They changed from one face into the next. He recognized Jake, Eve, Sunkist, Posey, and Lorraine.

He watched in fascination as their faces merged as one, making the flames grow higher and higher, towering over their heads. They then dissipated into the heavens, becoming part of the universe, becoming a part of Hawk and Sophie's very soul. Everything around them became the color of a sunset right before it disappeared over the horizon. It was the exact light that Sophie loved to watch color the tops of the trees. It occurred to him that this light had signified both an end and a beginning, connecting their spirits. In this connection was the knowledge that they would always be together.

Sophie turned to Hawk, still holding his hand. She smiled as she looked into his eyes and asked the question that would never need an answer…

Ain't cha glad ya brought me along?

NOT THE END…

AUTHORS' NOTES

Sophie's Hawk: Spirit of the Raptor is a work of historical fiction.

. . .

THE THIEF

A soldiers lodge was a group of proven warriors who came together as law givers and decision-makers. More powerful than the chiefs or medicine men, their decisions and orders were never to be challenged or disobeyed. Their primary function was to lead the hunting parties, but they often took the lead in times of war.

The Thief was the head soldier of the soldiers lodge of Mankato's band of Mdewakanton Sioux. During the Sioux Conflict The Thief was one of the chiefs who led war parties at the battle at Fort Ridgely. He fought the battles at Red Wood Ferry, New Ulm, and Birch Coolie. He is not mentioned in the Dakota trial records and it is likely that he escaped with Little Crow to Dakota Territory after the battle at Wood Lake. Little more is known about him.

While the name "The Thief" is the name of an actual person involved in the Dakota Conflict, his part in this story is purely fictional.

. . .

PIERRE "PIG'S EYE" PARRANT

Pierre Parrant, or "Pig's Eye", was the first person of European descent to live within what is now the city limits of St. Paul. He was also the owner of the first business in St. Paul—a moonshine still. He was, by popular description, a man whose facial appearance was most displeasing. He had only one serviceable eye, the other having been lost in some unfortunate event during his experiences as a voyageur. The injured eye was the likeness of a pig's eye and from that he got the moniker, "Pig's Eye".

In around 1832, Parrant set up his distillery among the settlers around Fort Snelling and furnished whiskey to the soldiers at the fort as well as the nearby Indians and settlers. By 1835, the Indian agent at Fort Snelling, Major Lawrence Taliaferro, (pronounced 'Tolliver') had expanded the area of the military reserve to include the vicinity of Pig's Eye's still. He then ordered Parrant, along with many settlers, away from the fort in an effort to stop the not-quite-illegal whiskey trade.

Parrant moved his business to a place known as Fountain Cave where, much to the dismay of Major Taliaferro and the officials at the fort, he again set up his business. It wasn't long before others joined from the squatter camps and a small community developed. Money ran short for Parrant and he was forced to mortgage his claim to William Beaumette. The mortgage papers changed hands several times which ultimately led to Parrant's eviction. He then moved to what is now the area of downtown St. Paul, where Parrant immediately set up his saloon near Lambert's Landing and his business prospered. River men and settlers began to call the area "Pig's Eye".

Parrant became involved in another dispute over ownership of the land on which he ran his business and once again lost his claim. Angry at the loss, he set out for Lake Superior hoping to return to his homeland near Sault Ste. Marie. He apparently died en route, in approximately 1844.

. . .

BARLEY CORN AND SNANA

Barley Corn was the mother of Snana. Snana is remembered in history as the Sioux woman who saved the life of Mary Schwandt, one of the girls who had been captured by the Indians during the attacks on the agencies. Snana had lost a child due to illness a few days before the outbreak and, in her grief, asked for a captured white girl to replace the child she'd lost. Barley Corn bought the child from her captor for the price of one pony and gave her to Snana.

After the initial attacks on the Lower Sioux Agency, and the defeat of Captain Marsh at the Red Wood Ferry, the Lower Sioux went to the Sisseton and Winnebago Indians, who were friendly to the whites, and demanded they join them in their war. The Sissetons and Winnebagos refused. On September twenty-third Little Crow's army of 738 warriors went to do battle with Colonel Sibley's army of 1,619 men at Wood Lake and was defeated. On their way back to camp they once again went to the friendly Indians to try to force them to join the war. The Sissetons and Winnebagos knew Little Crow's forces would return, and, whether they won the battle or lost, they would try to take the captives and probably kill them all.

SOPHIE'S HAWK

To protect the children from the enemy and stray bullets in battle, the Indian women dug holes in the floor of their tepees to create a hiding place. They would put the child down into the hole, lay poles over the holes and blankets over the poles, then sat upon them until the danger had passed.

The Sissetons and Winnebagos repelled the Mdewakantons without bloodshed. The Mdewakantons left to return to their camp. A war party of the friendly Indians followed Little Crow's warriors back their camp, singing their war songs and firing their guns in the air as a show of force. They rode into the camp and demanded that Little Crow turn over the rest of his captives. Little Crow knew that if any more of the captives were killed it would destroy any chances of peace talks with Sibley so he ordered the release of the captives. When Henry Sibley came to take the prisoners that the friendlies had rescued from the Mdewakantons, Mary Schwandt was taken from Snana.

Snana and Mary Schwandt were reunited in the autumn of 1894.

. . .

CAMP RELEASE

After the defeat of Little Crow's warriors at the battle of Wood Lake, and the refusal of the Sissetons and Winnebagos to join their forces, the Mdewakantons escaped toward the plains of the Dakotas fearing that Sibley and his army would follow and destroy them. Sibley, in spite of his overwhelming forces, and for reasons known only to him, did not follow them. Instead, he went into camp near the village of the Sisseton and Winnebago Indians. While there, he sent word to all the Indians to come to him, surrender and turn over any and all prisoners they might have. Many Indians surrendered and released their prisoners, which prompted Sibley to name the camp "Camp Release".

In early October of 1862, there were 243 Indian camps at Camp Release. Sibley sent word that any Indian who surrendered would be treated as a prisoner of war and given the treatment due a soldier. He would only punish those Indians that had killed white civilians or were guilty of rape.

As word of Sibley's promise spread throughout the Indian community, more groups surrendered and the camp grew to over 2,200 people. A second camp was formed near the Yellow Medicine Agency. When Sibley concluded that all who were going to surrender had done so, he ordered his troops to surround the camps and disarm the Indians.

In an attempt to gather more hostiles, Sibley passed word to the Indians that the annuities were being distributed at the agency. When the families came to receive their payments, the men were sent through a back door where they were disarmed, chained and put under guard. The women were sent to the compound with the rest of the captured families. This tactic was criticized by many as a cheap trick, beneath the dignity of military men. This writer agrees.

Though he lacked the authority to do so, Sibley set up a military court and began trying the male prisoners for war crimes. The trials were conducted haphazardly and men were convicted of murder on even the slightest of evidence. Most of the Indians were tried, found guilty and sentenced to hang, and in many cases, all in the space of only a few minutes. By November, 303 Indians had been tried, found guilty and condemned to the gallows. They were then sent to a prison in Mankato to await execution. The rest of the Sioux were sent to prisons at Mankato and Fort Snelling to wait out the winter while the Minnesota government determined what should be done with them. Many of the Indians died of starvation and sickness while imprisoned.

Sibley formed civilian units and ordered them to search the countryside, especially the Big Woods area, for roving bands of hostile Sioux. Some were found and captured, or killed, but most escaped to parts unknown. Some never left Minnesota and their descendents still live here today.

The names of the condemned prisoners were sent to Washington for the approval of the president for immediate execution. President Lincoln demanded the transcripts of the trials be sent to him, then had them thoroughly studied by three trusted attorneys. Of the 303 condemned men listed, Lincoln found only 39 whom he considered to have had sufficient evidence brought against them to warrant execution. One of the 39 was given a reprieve because he was the brother of one of the Indians who had helped white people escape the war.

On December 26, 1862, thirty-eight Sioux were hanged en mass while a crowd of on onlookers cheered. It was, and still is, the largest mass execution in United States history.

. . .

THE THUNDER SPIRITS

Records left by early trappers and explorers tell of strange rumbling sounds emanating from the Black Hills of South Dakota. The sounds were like distant thunder and most assumed they were from unseen thunderstorms that frequent the hills. Thunder does travel for many miles through the hills and can be heard miles away from the storms, but the thunder was heard when there were no storms in the hills.

SOPHIE'S HAWK

Scientists have studied the reports of the thunder but have not found a conclusive explanation. The last reports of thunder sounds came in the later part of the nineteenth century. Prior to that time no geological studies had been done in the Black Hills. Geologists speculate that the sounds may have been caused by the spontaneous ignition of natural gasses that built up in the deep caves and in closed caverns deep underground, leaving no evidence at the surface. An educated guess at best, as there is no record of anyone actually having seen the explosions and therefore, no description exists.

The sounds have curiously stopped and the opportunity for further investigation is lost. The geology of Black Hills is alive and perhaps someday we will hear the "thunder spirits" talk again.

. . .

THE MÉTIS

The Métis (pronounced "may-TEE") were a community of mixed blood people of Canada—a mix of American natives and European immigrants. The Canadian government was reluctant to view them as Canadians where rights and privileges of Canadian citizens were concerned, and equally as reluctant to see them as Indians when it came to Indian rights and privileges. The Métis held more closely to the free roaming lifestyle of their Native American mothers than to the structured and prearranged society of their European fathers.

Expert horsemen and hunters, the Métis rode through the plains of Canada and the northern parts of America hunting buffalo for survival. They went where they could find buffalo and, as free people, national boundaries meant nothing to them. Although hard work was their way of life, agriculture was not one of their choices.

The Métis built the ox cart trade routes that contributed largely to the development of the Minnesota Territory. The trails started in Pembina, followed the Red River of the North southward and down the Minnesota Valley to Saint Paul. Several trails went across the state to Crow Wing City at the confluence of the Mississippi River and the Crow Wing River. The Red River Trails, as they were called, connected Pembina on the northwest corner of Minnesota with Saint Paul. Many of our present-day roads and highways still follow these trails. Today, U.S. Highway 10 follows one of these routes almost exactly.

From about 1820 to 1870 the Métis carried buffalo robes, buffalo tongue, furs, pemmican and other trade goods, as well as mail. When their cargo had been delivered, they loaded their carts with guns, gun powder, traps, blankets and goods not easily obtained in the remote parts of Minnesota, then headed back to Pembina.

The ox carts were made entirely of wood and rawhide using knives, axes, saws and draw knives. There were no metal parts used in the construction. The carts were pulled by a single ox, horse, or mule and in some accounts young buffalo were trained for the job. Each cart could carry up to 900 pounds of merchandise. Grease was not used on the axles and their squealing and groaning could be heard for miles. In places such as Old Crow Wing town near Brainerd and the plains of north-western Minnesota, the ruts cut by the wheels of their carts can still be seen today.

The Métis were a people unto themselves, independent and free roaming. In many accounts and diaries of early travelers and explorers, the Métis are mentioned showing up on the prairies in groups of hundreds on their way to the buffalo hunting grounds. Nowhere in my research did I find any instance where they were the least bit hostile to the Americans. In fact, in most cases they were perfectly willing to share what they had. They were an arrogant and proud people, and are to this day a credit to the populace of Minnesota.

. . .

THE HENRY REPEATING RIFLE

The rifle that would become the Henry Repeating Rifle, and later the famed "Winchester Lever Action Rifle", was first developed in 1855 by the Volcanic Repeating Arms Company of Norwich Connecticut.

In its original design, it fired a very unreliable round with too little power to be of interest to hunters or the military. Volcanic Arms went bankrupt and out of business. Oliver Winchester took control of the firm under the name New Haven Arms Company in New Haven, Connecticut. New Haven Arms Company saw potential in the new rifle and hired B. Tyler Henry, a machinist from Volcanic Arms, to develop a cartridge with more power and reliability. He came up with a round completely encased in a copper cartridge. It carried a .44 caliber conical bullet weighing 216 grains propelled by a charge of 25 grains of black powder. When discharged, the bullet left the muzzle at about 1400 feet per second. The rifle weighed 9.5 pounds.

The magazine beneath the barrel held fifteen shots, and with one round in the chamber, it could be fired sixteen times without reloading. Reloading was accomplished in fifteen seconds and the rifle was back in action. It was capable of extreme accuracy at two hundred yards in the hands of the common shooter. Thirty-two shots in the time it takes to load and shoot a muzzle loading musket once, makes brave men out of cowards.

The rifle was given the name Henry's Patent Repeating Rifle. New Haven Arms began to market their new product to hunters and sport shooters. Because the Henry was made available to sport shooters before it was presented to the military, there were dozens of them in the hands of settlers during the Sioux Conflict. In 1862, the soldiers of the Union Army realized the combat potential of the fast-shooting weapon. It could be fitted with a long barrel for use by common foot soldiers and a shorter barrel for cavalry.

Brigadier General James W. Ripley, Union Chief of Ordinance under Abraham Lincoln, was not receptive to new weapons. The general was particularly leery of repeaters, which he believed were expensive, wasteful of ammunition and too delicate for military service. Therefore, he decided not to purchase them for the Union Army. The Henry Rifle was used in the Civil War, most having been purchased by individuals out of their military pay. The soldier in the Union Army made thirteen dollars a month—a new Henry cost about forty-five dollars, depending on whose book you read. Many a soldier claimed it was well worth the price but the Confederate soldiers damned it and called it, "the gun you load on Sunday and shoot all week."

It could be argued that, had the rifle been issued to the Union soldiers early in the war, it would have saved countless dollars by bringing the war to an end much sooner and could have saved immeasurable cost in the lives of Union and Confederate soldiers. The Union Army didn't officially adopt a repeating rifle until the Krag Jorgenson bolt action rifle in 1892.

In the account of Cecelia Campbell Stay, a survivor of the attack on the Lower Sioux Agency, the presence of Henry Rifles is made known.

> *"Grandmother sat on the banking of the house bewailing the absence of her sons, father and Uncle Baptiste. Uncle Hippolite sat by Grandmother, a **sixteen shooter** by his side and a double-barreled shotgun across his knees; he said he would "defend with his life". Woe to the Indian that would have offered harm to us that day."*

Anderson, Gary Clayton, and Allen R. Woolworth. 1988. *Through Dakota Eyes: Narrative Accounts of the Minnesota Indian War of 1862.* The Minnesota Historical Society Press.

. . .

In the middle of the nineteenth century trade between the Hudson Bay Company in northern Canada and Saint Paul grew and the ox cart traffic increased along the Red River Trails. Immigrants began moving northward into the newly opened Red River Valley area in search of rich farming land. Wagon trains moved west through Minnesota to the gold fields of Montana, Idaho and the Fraser River in British Columbia. The trails they traveled closely followed the dividing line between the Chippewa and the Sioux territories. The Minnesota government soon realized the necessity to protect the travelers from possible attacks by the Indians, or from being caught in the middle of one of the frequent confrontations between the two tribes. The travelers would also need a place to stop, refresh their animals and re-stock their food stores—a roadside rest, as it were.

In 1858, construction began on a new fort at the head of navigation on the west side of the Red River of the North about 50 miles north of Lake Traverse. Shortly after commencement of the construction, a report from the war department warned that the sight was subject to springtime flooding and the project was abandoned.

In 1859, the Saint Paul Chamber of Commerce offered a $2,000.00 reward to the man who could put a boat on the Red River. Anson Northrup answered this challenge. He had purchased a small steamer to navigate the upper Mississippi from Little Falls to Grand Rapids. During the winter while the lakes and ponds were frozen over, he dismantled his boat and with 43 teams of horses and 60 men, carried it over land to the Red River. He named his boat 'The Anson Northrup' after himself.

With the new steamboat service on the Red River, the officials saw an even greater need for a fort and built it farther away from the river where flooding was not as likely to occur. By1860, the post was occupied by regular troops and named Fort Abercrombie after Lieutenant Colonel John J. Abercrombie who designed the fort. At the outbreak of the Civil War the troops were called away to fight in the South and small groups of volunteers manned the fort under the command of Captain John Vander Horck, a German immigrant and veteran of the Prussian wars.

In that year, treaty talks were planned with the Pembina and Red Lake bands of Chippewa Indians. Cattle and horses and other supplies were brought to the new fort for use during the treaty talks.

On August 23rd Vander Horck received word of the Sioux Uprising. The fort had no walls, so the commander put his troops to work stacking cordwood around the buildings and constructing breastworks between them. Nothing happened until the 30th of August when a band of Sioux appeared and drove off a large portion of the livestock. Forty of the animals were recovered the next day by a scouting party of soldiers. On September third, the Indians once again appeared. The size of the attacking force is different in each account you read, but most historians agree the count was probably around one hundred. The attacking Indians were driven off, thanks to the three twelve pounder cannon in the post. A second attack came at daybreak on the sixth of September, which was also thwarted by cannon fire and the guns of civilians determined to save their cattle. In the attacks, one civilian was killed and two wounded. The number of Indian dead, of course, could not be learned, but one report said, "Two bodies were found and *planted*". No further attacks followed, however a troop sent to Saint Paul encountered a band of Indians and two of the troops were shot dead.

Fort Abercrombie was abandoned in 1877. Today, Fort Abercrombie State Historic Site is free and open year round for visitors.

. . .

THE FLAT COUNTRY OF NORTH DAKOTA

The latest continental glaciers covered the northern parts of our country 10,000 to 70,000 years ago. As the glaciers pushed southward they plowed earth against their front. Geologists call these piles of pushed up earth 'terminal moraines'. The climate began to warm and the glaciers melted back, leaving the moraines where they stood. Water from the melting ice ponded between the front of the glacier and behind the moraines and a lake was formed. This was the largest lake in the world. Lake Aggasiz covered the northwestern corner of Minnesota and the eastern edge of North Dakota, nearly all of the province of Manitoba in Canada, and stretched to Hudson Bay. The lake continued to rise until, near what is now Brown's Valley, it began to spill over the earth dam formed by the moraines. For twelve hundred years, the waters of Lake Aggasiz flowed over the dam and down the valley of the Minnesota River, filling it from rim to rim with churning, rushing water.

In time, the ice melted back to Hudson Bay, opening drainage for Lake Aggasiz to the north. The lake drained and left its bottom dry and very flat— some of the flattest ground in the world. The soil left behind is the sediment of the lake bottom. It is fine grained, black mud that sticks to anything that touches it. Wagon wheels, the feet of the horses, and the shoes of travelers are quickly encased in this sticky mud.

Reports of travelers indicate that the grass on the Dakota Plains stood as high as a man. Now, of course, the ground has been plowed and turned into farmland and few scattered patches of the tall grass remain. Though extremely difficult to till, the soil in the Red River Valley is some of the richest farming land in the world.

. . .

STANDING BUFFALO
TATANKA NAJIN

Standing Buffalo was about twenty nine years old at the beginning of the Sioux Conflict. By all accounts he was handsome, intelligent and of good disposition. Born in 1833, Standing Buffalo grew up in a time when buffalo were becoming fewer on the plains and dependence on the white man was becoming more essential. In 1858, his father made him chief of the Sisseton band of Sioux. Standing Buffalo knew the Indians could no longer live on the diminishing numbers of buffalo on the plains, or the deer and elk of his home land, and now needed the help of the white man to feed themselves.

When the Mdewakantons attacked the agency at Red Wood, Standing Buffalo and his Sissetons were on the Dakota prairie hunting buffalo for the winter and knew nothing of the attack until they returned to their village. When the chief learned of the attacks on the agencies he told his people not to get involved. He wanted food and money for his people but he trusted that the government would provide for them if they maintained the peace. However, when some of his young braves saw the plunder the other Indians were bringing home, they wanted some of it. They told Standing Buffalo they were going hunting but instead they went to kill and steal.

Through the conflict, Standing Buffalo refused to get his people involved in the war. Little Crow and his warriors came to them and tried to force them to join them but the Sissetons resisted. After Little Crow's defeat at Wood Lake, Standing Buffalo led his people away from his land near Big Stone Lake and moved north into Dakota country and Devil's Lake. From there they went west. Because they happened to be at the wrong place at the wrong time they got involved in the battle of Big Mound with Sibley's army. And so, the Sissetons were then hunted as aggressively as the Mdewakantons were.

Standing Buffalo moved his village north heading toward Canada. In the summer of 1867, the village was stricken with smallpox. Standing Buffalo's mother, father, and many other close relatives died, including the children of his youngest wife who, in her grief, killed herself with the poison kept to kill coyotes.

At the age of thirty four, Standing Buffalo was grief stricken and alone. He wandered alone for eight years after that initial battle with Sibley. He had suffered hardship, famine, war, disease, and finally a Sioux warrior's death while still in the prime of his life. Standing Buffalo decided he was sick of life and decided to end it. He rode his horse into an Indian village and, to attract attention, killed four Indian women picking berries. He then threw down his weapons and allowed himself to be shot until he fell to the ground, mortally wounded.

Nothing remains of Standing Buffalo but stories and legends. His body was not properly buried and the exact location of his death and burial are unknown.

Diedrich, Mark. 1988. *The Odyssey of Chief Standing Buffalo.* Minneapolis: Coyote Books.

. . .

THE FANCY SHAWL DANCE

The Fancy Shawl Dance is not a dance of the historical period of this book but we thought it proper to include it because it is one of the most beautiful dances to be seen at modern day pow wows. It has its origins in recent history as the dance called the Blanket Dance. These dances were preformed by the men. But the women, not be held down, developed their own form of this dance and called it the Fancy Shawl, or Butterfly Dance.

The dancers are adorned in brightly colored shawls with long fringes on the edges, matching colored dresses, leggings, and beaded moccasins. The dance is reminiscent of a butterfly dancing on the wind. The dance is done in time with the changing rhythm of the drums. It is fast moving and very physical with steps that make the dancer appear as if her feet never touch the ground.

According to the legend of the Butterfly Dance, a butterfly lost her mate in a battle and in her grief she wrapped herself in her cocoon. She wandered around the world stepping on each and every stone until she found one beautiful enough to bring her out of her grief. She then emerged from her cocoon with beautifully colored wings. Now she flies around the world bringing happiness to the grief stricken.

The dance can be enjoyed at any of the pow wows staged year round in all of the states of the union and Iowa. Take time to visit a pow wow and we're sure you'll be delighted by the spectacle.

. . .

THE BATTLE AT MURFREESBORRO

The story of the battle at Murfreesboro, Tennessee, as told in this book, is true. Colonel Henry Lester did surrender his troops without a fight to Confederate General Nathan B. Forest. He did call two meetings of the officers in his command to secure the vote to surrender.

Sergeant Wambolt and his part in this story are fictional. During the fighting at Murfreesboro there were squads of soldiers who left Lester's command to go to the fighting, but to my knowledge no records exist to say who those men were.

· · ·

WABASHA

"White men go to war with their own brothers and kill more men than Wabasha can count all the days of his life. Great Spirit looks down and says, 'Good white man. He has my book; I love him, and will give him good place when he dies.' Indian has no Great Spirit book. He wild man. Kill one man— has scalp dance. Great Spirit very angry. Wabasha don't believe it." (Chief Wabasha.1863.)

· · ·

THE BIG WOODS

When I was a kid back in Ottertail County one of my favorite places to spend time was the woods south of town. I didn't know at that time that I was in the area called "the Big Woods". I didn't know that those woods covered more ground, and went farther than I had ever imagined. An old trapper once told me, "These here woods goes from Ioway clear up inta Canada." I was impressed, but still had no idea of the size, and I don't think he was any more aware than I was.

I once tried to impress my buddies with this bit of Minnesota trivia but, rather than being impressed, they responded with a dry, "So?" Then they resumed their discussion about Mickey Mantle and right-handed pitcher, Jim Bunning. What could possibly be more exciting than Mickey Mantle, batting left-handed, hitting his 200th homerun off a throw from a right-handed pitcher?

To this, I responded with a dry, "So?" In my humble opinion, watching the leaves decay on the floor of the Big Woods beats it, hands down.

Disappointed with my failure to distinguish myself as a well-informed member of adolescent society, I retreated into a world of reading and discovery. If that old trapper was still around today, I could try to impress him with what I have learned.

The Big Woods was an area of dense forest, prairie, and savanna, dotted with lakes and marsh, and laced with hundreds of miles of rivers and streams. It covered an area from Otter Tail County in west central Minnesota, down the middle of the state to the Iowa border. It was bounded, roughly, by the Minnesota River Valley on the west, and the Mississippi River on the east. In the central part of the state it merged with the boreal forests of northeastern Minnesota. The glacial lakes area, and the moraines left by the glaciers was host to the Big Woods. Look at a Minnesota road map and notice the string of lakes stretching from Detroit Lakes south-eastward to just west of the Twin Cities and southward to Le Sueur and Nicollet Counties. This is roughly the area covered by the original Big Woods.

The relatively flat plains to the east and west of the woods were subjected to natural prairie fires pushed on by dry, perpetual west winds. Native inhabitants set grassfires in the spring to burn off the cover of dead grass from the previous year and promote new growth and to bring the life-giving buffalo back from their wintering grounds. The fires killed off any trees that tried to grow there.

Conversely, the fires in the moraines were controlled or even prevented by the rivers, lakes and hills. Fire moves much more slowly downhill and does not spread as quickly as on the plains. Also, the winds that drove the fires on the plains were slowed in the woods. In the hills, young trees were allowed to take root, grow and multiply. A canopy of leaves shaded the ground and kept the carpet of fallen leaves moist, thus reducing the chances of fires starting or continuing. Also, sunlight was filtered out reducing growth of underbrush and leaving a park-like environment.

A survey done by the Minnesota Horticultural Society in 1878 lists over fifty varieties of trees and shrubs in the Big Woods. The Big Woods provided shelter and food for deer, bear, wolf, and elk—animals whose range would have otherwise been limited to the northern forests. Countless birds and insects that would have been driven out by the cold winters found shelter in the woods.

After the Civil War, pioneers began to move into Minnesota in search of farming land. The rich soil beneath the Big Woods drew farmers who cleared large portions of the land for fields. The majestic oak, elm, ash and basswood, were cut down to provide lumber and fuel, and millions of trees were cut for railroad ties. Scrub oaks, aspen, box elder and other less desirable timber took over the forest areas. Wetlands were filled in by settlers to provide even more farm land. On the prairies, settlers planted rows of fast growing trees and hedges to block the wind and to control the natural fires. The natural prairie grasses and plants were plowed under and the soil seeded with wheat, oats, barley and soybean—crops foreign to the Minnesota prairies and forests. The original Big Woods have now been reduced to a few small plots in southern Minnesota.

A drive down a country road through the Leaf Hills of Otter Tail County will give the viewer a taste of what the Big Woods might have been like two hundred years ago. In Minnesota there are still huge forests filled with wildlife and vegetation, but the grandeur of the original Big Woods is gone. Someday another glacier will cover this land, till the soil and allow Mother Nature to restore the Big Woods to its original majesty.

The Minnesota Department of Natural Resources is currently working to preserve what is left of the Big Woods and restore some of the prairies to their natural state. The process is slow and the work is hard, but the results are worth the effort.

That old trapper back home would be impressed with what I could tell him about the Big Woods. Now what the hail was his name? Aw hail, don't matter none enna ways.

He's dead now.

· · ·

For those who would like to find more information on this exciting and important chapter of Minnesota history, we would recommend reading:

A History of Minnesota, Volume II
William Watts Folwell
Minnesota Historical Society Press

Soldier, Settler, Sioux: Fort Ridgely and the Minnesota River Valley, 1853-1867
Paul N. Beck
Pine Hill Press

Little Crow: Spokesman for the Sioux
Gary Clayton Anderson
Minnesota Historical Society Press

Through Dakota Eyes: Narrative Accounts
of the Minnesota Indian War of 1862
Gary Clayton Anderson and Alan R. Woolworth
Minnesota Historical Society Press

. . .

We do hope you enjoyed this book and we encourage you to read on as the adventures of the *Pa Hin Sa* continue.

— ARVID LLOYD WILLIAMS
BONNIE SHALLBETTER

BIOGRAPHIES

ARVID LLOYD WILLIAMS

Arvid Lloyd Williams has teamed up with co-author Bonnie Shallbetter in the sequel to his successful debut novel, *Hawk's Valley: A Good Place to Die*. His extensive research into the history and geology of Minnesota has inspired this native historian to create a story that will educate and entertain the reader. Williams was born and raised in northern Minnesota. He is recently retired from the Wayzata School District and is an active contributing member of the Minnesota Historical Society.

BONNIE SHALLBETTER

Bonnie Shallbetter was born in Fairmont, Minnesota and was raised in Brooklyn Center. She is a graduate of the University of Minnesota where she received a Bachelor of Science degree in Outdoor Education. She has worked as a naturalist for the Three Rivers Park District and as an instructor for the Voyageur Outward Bound School. In her spare time, she enjoys traveling or taking in the Minnesota seasons and the vast array of outdoor activities that the state has to offer. She is married and has two sons.

the journey continues...

Hawk's adventures began in *Hawk's Valley*—the first book in this series. To order your autographed copy, please visit Hawk's website at *www.evergreenpublish.com/hawk* or use this order form.

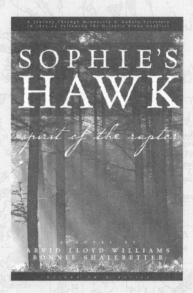

ORDER FORM

BOOK ONE
Hawk's Valley: A Good Place to Die

_____ x $15.95 = $ _____
QTY

BOOK TWO
Sophie's Hawk: Spirit of the Raptor

_____ x $15.95 = $ _____
QTY

Shipping ($4/title) = $ _____

Total = $ _____

NAME (PLEASE PRINT)

ADDRESS

CITY   STATE   ZIP

PHONE

EMAIL ADDRESS

SEND TO: Evergreen Publishing
              Attn: Order Center
              15539 Shadow Creek Road
              Minneapolis, MN 55311